PASSION'S SURRENDER

"They're just like everything in life," Price said with a hint of mystery, raising his hand slowly to offer Ellyn a lone rose.

"How so?" she wondered aloud.

"Whenever something is beautiful and worth having, there's pain, as well."

They stood close to each other, and when Ellyn looked up at him, their eyes met and held. She could feel the heat of his body and—through his gaze—the warmth of his soul.

"Are you like that, pretty lady?" His words were spoken softly.

Then he bent nearer, and their lips met, tenderly, carefully, as though he expected, at any moment, to feel the sudden sting of a hidden thorn.

But there was no sting—only the quiet beating of their hearts, and the whisper of petals on the wind as Ellyn surrendered to his now demanding embrace. . . .

FORBIDDEN FIRES

LOVE SPELL BOOKS NEW YORK CITY

For
Billy, David, Pat and Joan

LOVE SPELL®

April 1998

Published by

Dorchester Publishing Co., Inc.
276 Fifth Avenue
New York, NY 10001

ISBN 0-505-52258-6

The name "Love Spell" and its logo are trademarks of Dorchester Publishing Co., Inc.

Printed in the United States of America.

A very special note of thanks to two very special ladies: Mary Lou Mann of the Alton Area Historical Society, Alton, Illinois, and Elizabeth Taylor of Vicksburg Tourist Information Center, Vicksburg, Mississippi.

Prologue

As the War Between the States ends . . .

April, 1865
Vicksburg, Mississippi

The warmth of the late afternoon sun eased the aches of the newly freed Union soldiers as they trudged up the gangplank of the steamboat, *Sultana*. Although the memories of their ordeal at Andersonville Prison Camp were still sharp and painful, their mood was jubilant. The long delay of their parole was over. They were going home! Exultant at the prospect, they boarded the steamer, in seemingly unending numbers.

A tall, young Yankee officer stood at the rail of the boiler deck grimly watching the loading. The expression on his handsome, rugged features was one of stern disapproval. His lean, whipcord body was tense with frustrated anger. Capt. Price Richardson had witnessed many acts of imcompetence during his four years in the army but what was happening today was almost beyond belief. Price was enough of a riverman to know that it was foolhardy to challenge the Mississippi this way. Going upriver this time of year against the flood was hard enough on a steamboat, but on one that was seriously overloaded, it could be suicide. The river was a dangerous taskmaster in the best of times, but at flood stage the Mississippi could be a callous killer, destroying any and all who dared to defy her. Price ran a hand through his dark, unruly hair and glanced nervously about him. Few of the other soldiers seemed to notice the overcrowding. They had survived the hell of a Confederate prison and were free! Nothing could hurt them now! Their celebrating was joyous.

Irritation evident in the hard, unyielding line of his jaw, he turned to his friend, Lt. Jericho Cooper. "Look at the damn river! Don't they have any idea of what the hell they're doing?"

"Why? Do you think they're overdoing it?" Coop, as Jericho preferred to be called, remarked sarcastically.

Price grunted in disgust and turned away.

"For safety's safe, the least they could do is load some of these men on them," he said, indicating the two other boats that were also heading northward and were tied up nearby: the *Pauline Carroll* and the *Lady Gay*.

Coop smiled wryly in his usual way, as they watched column after column of men file aboard. "You have to remember that the Department of the Army is in charge of this."

Price refused to comment. It was a sore subject and one on which they agreed.

"How's your leg feeling?" Price asked as he noticed Coop leaning heavily on the railing.

"Hurts like hell," Coop answered, rubbing at his bandaged right thigh. "I'd still like to get my hands

8

on that crazy Reb guard."

"That makes two of us." Price looked at Coop seriously.

"I still can't believe that we could go through four years of war with barely a scratch and then, a week before we're paroled, I'm hit by a ricocheting bullet from some trigger-happy prison guard." Coop shook his head in disgust.

"Sit down for a while." Price suggested as Coop shifted uncomfortably. "From the looks of things, we won't be going anywhere soon."

"That's what I was afraid of. I just wish we'd get moving," Coop complained, lowering himself gingerly to the deck.

Price didn't reply as Coop leaned back against the rail and closed his eyes. Right now, his friend needed peace, quiet and competent medical care, and those things were definitely lacking on this boat that teemed with rejoicing troops. Price was sure that Coop's swollen limb was throbbing. There had been little the doctors could do in the poorly equipped prison hospital after Coop had been accidentally wounded. And the long journey from Andersonville to Camp Fisk to the Vicksburg riverfront had aggravated the already serious injury. Price focused once again on the wharf below and was startled by what was taking place.

The *Sultana*'s captain was blocking the gangplank and, although it was impossible to hear the conversation, Price reasoned that he must be refusing to take on any more passengers. As a seasoned riverboatman, the boat's captain knew the folly of disregarding the dangers of the flooding Mississippi. Despite his valid protest, the army officer in charge of the loading summarily overruled him and more soldiers were marched aboard.

As evening came, the *Sultana* was creaking and groaning under the onslaught of men forcing members of the steamer's crew to prop up the sagging decks. Price was trying to put his anxiety aside and sat on the deck with Coop as the last of the almost two thousand parolees found a space to rest. It was well past midnight when the dangerously overloaded packet was ready to begin what was to be her final trip north. From stem to stern, the *Sultana* was a solid mass of soldiers. The Union officials, in their eagerness to be rid of their charges, had put them all on this one ship, a ship with a legal passenger limit of only four hundred. Now, with her lights twinkling brightly and over twenty-three hundred passengers and crew aboard, the steamer wallowed out onto the swollen river.

For a full day and a half, the *Sultana* hugged the riverbank and managed to make steady progress northward. She stopped over briefly at Helena, Arkansas and again at Memphis before crossing the raging river to refuel.

As again the *Sultana* backed out into the torrent after loading her coal, Price was leaning restlessly against the railing staring off into the black velvet of the Mississippi River night. What had been a carefree trip for the others had turned into a nightmare for him. The first night out, Coop had taken ill and, despite the best efforts of those on board, his fever was still soaring. The river breeze had turned cold and damp, so Price had given Coop his blanket. Now he stood, his broad shoulders hunched against the penetrating dampness, his hands shoved deep into his pockets. Usually, he could sleep anywhere, at any time, but for some unknown reason, this night

Price couldn't rest. He was uneasy and anxious to be in Cairo, away from this listing steamer that had become his temporary home. Chilled to the bone, he finally laid down on the hard deck. Trying to ignore his discomfort, Price concentrated only on the rhythmic churning of the paddle wheels until his senses dulled and he finally fell asleep.

Price would never remember exactly what happened: all he could recall in the days and months to come was the shock of landing in the black, icy river water. As he sank into the river's depths, his reflexes took over for him and he struggled to the surface. Gagging on the rank water, he fought to get his bearings. The sight that greeted him, some two hundred feet away, was horrifying. The *Sultana* was in flames, her boilers blown. The pilothouse and smokestacks had been destroyed by the force of the blast and parts of the upper decks had collapsed.

The inferno eerily lit up the Mississippi and Price turned from the searing heat of the blaze to search for his sick friend. He saw only a jagged piece of wood near him and swam to meet it. Grasping it firmly, Price rested. Dazed, he clung limply to his float, and long minutes passed until finally the sounds of the steamer's death throes penetrated his mind. The agonizing screams and curses of the men still aboard were amplified ghoulishly across the water. Forcing himself into action, he tried to swim back toward the boat, but the current was against him and at length he gave up the struggle. As he helplessly listened to the echoing convulsive cries of the dying soldiers, despair overtook him. There was no sign of Coop though they had been lying next to one another. How was it possible that he had been thrown clear, but his friend had not?

As his momentary confusion cleared, the reality of

his situation hit him full force and he began to appreciate how fortunate he had been. The river near the *Sultana* was a mass of bodies all fighting to survive, and in the process they were killing each other. In their panic to escape the flames, hundreds of soldiers were leaping overboard, many of whom couldn't swim. The ones who could were fortunate if they weren't pulled under by their drowning comrades. On board, those who were trapped beneath the wreckage of the explosion were burned to death as the fire devoured all in its path. Desperately, with numb hands, Price hung onto his float and managed to pull it under his chest. The Mississippi carried him farther and farther from the fiery carcass of the *Sultana* and the graveyard that the river had become. He was motionless for some time, staring sightlessly into the red, fire-lit, shadowy darkness. What had happened to Coop? The thought assailed him along with the stench of burning human flesh. The prospect of Coop trapped on the drifting crematory tortured Price. As he grew colder, his thoughts grew jumbled and he began to shake uncontrollably. He wondered how much longer he could hold on. How much longer could he keep his head above water?

It took him by surprise when he collided with the bush. Later, he would be thankful that the current hadn't been stronger for the branch might have swept him from his support. Instinctively, he lifted leaden arms to grasp at the limb. Terrified when he felt his grip weaken, he gave one desperate lunge and threw an arm over the branch. As he hung there, the death-dealing river tugged forcefully at his body, trying to dislodge him from his haven. Price watched his board as it floated away, twisting aimlessly in the current until it disappeared from sight.

12

The *Sultana*, or what was left of her, had drifted around a bend in the river, and the blackness of the night enveloped Price. It was an empty, lonely darkness, one that spurred him into action. Reasoning that he was clinging to an overhanging bush and that the bank was only a few feet away, he loosened his grip. Inching his way along, he finally reached a thicker branch. Hugging it, he was stunned to discover his savior was no bush, but a tree and the top of one at that. He had been fooled by the river, tricked into believing that he was near safety when, in fact, he was probably a mile from the unseen shore. The Mississippi, now at its worst flood stage, was more than five miles wide. It had inundated the farmland on both sides and turned tall trees into bush. Knowing he would not be rescued this night, Price wedged himself there and wrapped his arms around the branch. He held on for his life, knowing one weak moment would throw him to the mercy of the black, deadly water.

His body came alive with pain as he clung there. But despite his agony, Price said a silent prayer of thanks that he'd been spared. A great weariness overcame him and he welcomed the release of unconsciousness.

Chapter One

The sound of the *Sultana*'s exploding boilers brought Ellyn Douglass bolt upright in bed. The slender young woman paused, waiting. Then, knowing she hadn't dreamed it, Ellyn threw off her blanket and climbed down from her high testor bed. Rushing to the window, she drew back the heavy drapes and looked out over the moonlit stillness of the Tennessee countryside. Puzzled by the dark, silent night that greeted her, she pulled on her long dressing gown and, hearing muted voices in the hallway, left her room.

"What was that, Grampa?" she asked, joining her grandfather and younger sister who'd also been roused by the thunderous blast.

"I thought the fighting was over," Charlotte, the younger of the two girls, said nervously.

"The war is over," Lawrence Douglass declared. "That must have been out on the river somewhere. Maybe a steamer—"

"A steamer?" Ellyn interrupted, moving down the hall. "Maybe we can see something from upstairs."

Lawrence and Charlotte quickly followed her up the curving staircase to the third floor and out into

15

the observation area called the Widow's Walk.

"Look!" Charlotte exclaimed as the sky glowed fiery red in the direction of the Mississippi.

"It was a boat! Must have blown her boilers," the aging patriarch of the Douglass clan remarked miserably, turning from the view. "Looks like they'll be needing me in town again."

"I'll come with you," Ellyn offered, knowing that as one of the few doctors in the area he would need all the help he could get.

"No," her grandfather told her, putting an affectionate arm around her shoulders. "If we're short-handed and I need you, I'll send word."

"You're sure?"

"I'm sure. There's no need to drag you out on a chilly night like this unless it's absolutely necessary."

"All right, but you know I just want to help you as much as I can," she replied, kissing his weathered cheek.

"You always do." He hugged her. "I'd best hurry. Lord only knows what condition the roads are in after all this rain."

He went back inside to dress, leaving Ellyn and Charlotte alone.

"It looks pretty bad," Ellyn said worriedly as she watched the glowing horizon.

"Well, there's nothing we can do about it," Charlotte said nonchalantly.

Ellyn paused, thinking. "When it's light, we can go down to the river and take a look around."

"By then it'll be too late anyway," Charlotte replied, balking at her sister's idea. "And, besides, what would Mother say? Why if she ever found out that we were down there like common white trash . . ."

"Who's going to tell her? We'll just go on down at sunup and she'll never have to find out."

16

"Not me," Charlotte retorted, swatting at a pesky mosquito in irritation. "I'm going back to bed and I suggest you do the same."

Ellyn watched as her sister re-entered the house. It never ceased to amaze her that they'd turned out so differently. They were both of average height—barely five-foot-four—and had the Douglass coloring—brown hair and hazel eyes—and there the similarity ended. Charlotte, fifteen, was four years younger than Ellyn and the essence of femininity. Slight of figure, she was graceful and dainty, never concerning herself with any issue more taxing than what gown to wear or what meals to serve. At nineteen, Ellyn's curves were as lush as her sister's were delicate. She was naturally beautiful in an unaffected way. Her mane of sun-lighted brunette hair had just enough curl to make it unruly, and on many a humid day Ellyn had longed to cut it short and be done with it. Determination and a goodly amount of will power showed in her slightly squared jaw and her flashing green-brown eyes reflected her emotions which, more often than not, were turbulent. To her mother's despair, from the time she could toddle, Ellyn had followed her father and older brother, Tommy, everywhere. She had always been fascinated by the workings of the plantation and had set out to learn all she could of management and crops. Such mannish pursuits had been actively discouraged by her mother, but her father had encouraged her and over the years, under his expert tutelage, she grew knowledgeable in all aspects of Riverwood's operation.

The betrothal of Ellyn and Rod Clarke, of the neighboring plantation Clarke's Landing, had been arranged many years before by their families. So, when the war broke out, it seemed most natural that the engagement be announced. She was certain that Rod disapproved of her active role in the running of Riverwood and that he felt he could change her once they married. She'd overheard Rod in conversation with her father one day before they'd gone to war. Rod had insisted that a woman's place was running the house and, to Ellyn's astonishment, her father had agreed. He had assured Rod that her involvement was a passing fancy—a whim of hers that he saw fit to indulge. Perhaps it was this, their condescending treatment of her and her desires, that had caused her to refuse a quick wedding to Rod.

She did not doubt that she cared for Rod, after all she'd known him all her life. And it was the fondest dream of both their families that they marry and unite the plantations. But Ellyn found the prospect of becoming Rod's docile wife unnerving. She was a creature of resource and intelligence who had been encouraged to develop those traits, not extinguish them beneath an exterior of domesticity.

Practically speaking, she was glad now that she'd taken the interest. After both her father and brother were killed in battle last year, all the responsibility for Riverwood had fallen to her. Her grandfather had been some help, but as a physician he was in constant demand and seldom home. Not that it was a home any longer. Since the deaths of Thomas Douglass and Tommy, Riverwood was more of a tomb.

Her mother, Constance, had been stricken by her double loss. The empty months of mourning had left her enraged and bitter and she directed all of that hatred toward men in blue. The Yankees were murderers, she declared, and she took every opportunity to voice her opinion, sometimes going on for hours about how they'd ruined her life.

Charlotte, who was easily browbeaten, always agreed with her mother, but Ellyn knew differently. Yankees felt pain the same as Southerners, the color of their uniforms made no difference. She'd learned that helping her grandfather in the Memphis hospital. Suffering equalized all men.

Wrapping her robe more tightly about her, Ellyn looked out toward the Mississippi. The steamer was farther south now, evidently drifting downstream with the current. Yes, she decided, with or without Charlotte, she would go down to the river at first light. After taking one last look at the glowing sky, Ellyn hurried inside, shivering from the damp coldness of the night air.

Dawn. At last the sky was lightening, turning from black velvet to deep blue. Dressed in her oldest cotton gown, her hair pulled back in a tight bun at the nape of her neck, Ellyn was ready, pacing her room. Had she been a man, she could have gone to the river during the night. Instead, she had to wait for daylight to make the excursion as respectable as possible. Frustrated at the long delay, she finally tiptoed from her bedroom as the eastern horizon took on a pink-and-orange-tinged hue. After cautiously moving past her mother's room, Ellyn hurried up to the third floor again. Perhaps now, in the light of day, she would be able to see something of what had happened.

Stepping out into the cool but humid morning air, she stared out over the still-shadowy pre-daybreak countryside. In the distance, she could make out the wide river—a deceptively peaceful looking body of water. Normally, the Mississippi was a good three miles from the house, but the flood this spring was so severe that the river had overflowed its banks to within a mile of the main buildings.

Of course, the practical Douglass who'd built the house in the late 1700s had had enough foresight and common sense to place the family home strategically on a small rise some distance from the river, but with convenient access to it by a backwater slough. Riverwood house was a study in practicality. From its original two rooms, it had grown with each generation. As the family and its fortunes had enlarged, the Douglasses built a new home nearby—a pillared, three-story structure, white and square and sturdy. The first house was converted to the kitchen and was connected to the new by a covered walkway. It had been a wonderful place to grow up and Ellyn loved it. She stood quietly for a moment savoring the serenity of this early morning hour.

As the bright golden sunlight broke free of the night's restraining grip, Ellyn was waiting with her grandfather's spyglass in hand. Focusing as best she could, she searched the muddy riverbank for signs of last night's disaster. A first surveillance revealed nothing unusual washed up on shore, so she scanned the river farther out, too. It was then that she saw it—something caught in a tree. The distance was considerable but judging from the force of the explosion last night, she knew it was from that boat.

Ellyn rushed downstairs and out the back entrance. Following the path, she went straight to the line of cabins that had once housed their slaves. Of all the slaves once owned by the Douglass family, only three remained: Franklin, Darnelle, his wife, and their teenage daughter, Glory. They felt working for room, board and whatever else Ellyn could afford to pay them was infinitely better than taking unknown chances up north. They worked side by side with Miss Ellyn, respecting her as their boss, not their owner.

"Miz Ellyn, what you doin' out here dis time o' day?" Franklin asked as she met him there.

"Franklin," she exclaimed excitedly. "I need your help. Is the skiff ready?"

He eyed her suspiciously, for he knew by her expression that they were about to do something outrageous. "Yes, ma'am."

"Good. We have to get it on the river right away."

"It's tied up at de dock," he answered, shaking his head in dismay. And then he hurried to follow her as she headed, with a single-mindedness of purpose, down the walk that led to Riverwood's dock.

"What we gonna do?" he questioned, finally, after she'd hiked up her skirts and climbed agilely into the small craft.

"Did you hear that explosion last night?"

He nodded, his eyes showing white with fear and he paused momentarily on the small wharf.

"Don't get scared on me! It was a steamer, not soldiers. Anyway, I was checking this morning and I saw something caught in a tree out there."

"What was it?"

"I'm not sure. It's too far away to tell."

He joined her then in the boat and pushed off, maneuvering skillfully toward the flooded grove of trees she'd indicated.

The morning sun was warm, promising an unseasonably hot day for late April. Franklin rowed expertly, his mind dwelling on Ellyn's motives. He knew without a doubt that Miz Constance wasn't aware of their actions. She sure didn't like the way Miz Ellyn carried on and often berated her for her willful independence. But Franklin, more than anyone else, realized that without Ellyn and her hard

21

work, they all would have starved by now. She alone had kept food on their table and the big house in passable repair by shrewd bartering and management. He was grateful for her leadership and always gave her his full cooperation.

"Just a little farther," she directed, pointing out the general area she'd seen from the house.

As Franklin paddled into the grove, they both spotted Price at the same time.

"Good God! It's a man!" Ellyn was shocked into silence by the sight of the lone figure stranded motionless in the treetop.

Franklin got them in close to the tree and threw a rope over a sturdy exposed limb. "Jes' sit still, Miz Ellyn, 'til Ah tie us up." Then, moving to the middle of the skiff, he directed, "Grab dat branch and hol' it steady whilst Ah pull him out."

Wedged in the crotch of the tree, the unconscious man held onto a branch with a deathlike grip. Franklin carefully pried him loose and pulled him awkwardly into the boat.

"He's still alive?" Ellyn asked as she knelt next to him in the wet bottom of the craft, unmindful of the filthy water soaking her gown.

"Yas'm, seems to be, though Ah don' know for how long. He's cut up pretty bad," he answered her.

Ellyn tore off a strip of petticoat and started to bandage his bloody head wound.

"Be still now," Franklin told her, as the boat rocked heavily. "Won't do him no good if you dump us in de river."

She was anxious to aid the injured man, but let her common sense rule and waited, taking the time to really look at him. He was tall and broad-shouldered, with thick, black hair that was matted with dried blood from the deep gash high on his forehead. His lean, chiseled features showed the ravages of the night just past; his coloring was pale beneath his full mustache and several days growth of dark beard. Much of his clothing had been ripped away by the force of the blast and his chest and arms had been burned in several places by the rain of scalding debris that had followed. She sat back on her heels, impatiently wanting to be back on dry land. Her eyes scanned the river but there was no sign of any other survivors. The man beside her groaned softly and Ellyn reached out a gentle hand to soothe his brow.

"Just a few more minutes, mister. Just hang on," she murmured encouragingly, not considering that he might not be able to hear her.

At long last, they reached the boat dock and after momentarily struggling with her soggy skirts, she jumped out and pulled the boat closer.

"I think we'll need old Mo, don't you?" Ellyn asked, knowing that they couldn't possibly carry him to the house without the help of their only mule.

"Ah'll get Mo and de dray. Where you want to take him? De main house?" Franklin asked as he secured the skiff.

"Of course," she replied, wondering at the question. "He's injured. I'll have to see—"

"Miz Ellyn," Franklin interrupted. "You bes' tak' a look at what's lef' of his uniform."

"A Yankee," she whispered, stunned as she finally recognized the tattered blue cloth. She paused only a moment. "No matter. He's hurt. Let's get him up to the main house as fast as we can."

Price was painfully quiet and still as they carried him to the conveyance a short while later. The mile-long trek along the path was accomplished in silence as Ellyn and Franklin both worried about Constance Douglass's reaction to a Yankee soldier at River-wood house.

Chapter Two

For Constance Royale Douglass the morning had begun as any other, with Darnelle serving her her usual cup of chicory coffee in bed. Constance had grimaced with distaste at the bitterness and had silently mourned the lack of the true beverage. How she hated this war! All it had done was destroy her gracious way of life. She had been raised to manage a plantation household and provide for the comforts of her husband. Yet now, her wealth and her husband were irretrievably lost to her. She rose quickly from the comfort of her canopied bed and moved to stand before her full-length mirror, thankful that, at least, she'd not lost her figure. She stared at the reflection there, objectively analyzing the woman's body that was barely concealed by the flowing gown she wore. A satisfied half-smile tilted her full, sensuous lips. Yes, she was still attractive. Her Creole blood was evident in her dark, widely spaced, flashing eyes and the thickness of her blue-black waist-length hair. Even now, her complexion was smooth and soft, with no telltale wrinkles to give away her true age of thirty-six. Running her hands seductively over her full breasts and hips, she grinned slyly, knowing that she could pass for much younger than her years. Why, just last month, hadn't the new doctor at the Memphis hospital mistaken her for Ellyn's sister? There were many times when, in fact, Constance wished she was. Ellyn had so much. Her youth, her beauty—yes, even though it irked her, she had to admit that her eldest daughter was attractive. And attractive in a way that men would burn with desire for her. Jealousy flared within her. Constance knew that experienced women like herself were attractive to men, but there was something about an innocent yet sensuous girl that could drive men wild. And Ellyn was definitely a sensuous innocent, although Constance knew her daughter was unaware of it. She snorted in disgust at Ellyn's behavior. Why, the way she'd treated Rod on his last leave had been ridiculous. Ellyn had allowed him no private movements with her at all, even though the family had given her ample opportunity. It had seemed as if she was uninterested in him as a man.

Rod Clarke. Constance sighed mellowly. If only she were ten years younger, she'd show him how a real woman could love. What a handsome devil he was! Rod was of average height, although his slimness made him seem taller. His hair was sun-streaked dark blond and his eyes were a glacial blue. Constance thought him very sexy, but until now had kept her fantasies in rein. When Thomas was alive there had been no time for thoughts of others, he'd been a most demanding lover. But Thomas would return to her bed no more and Constance knew that she couldn't possibly remain celibate for the rest of her life. Perhaps . . . perhaps her life wasn't over. A surge of desire burned through her body at the thought of being with a man. It had been so long! With determination, she stalked to the window and, throwing it open, breathed deeply of the sweet, cool morning air. Dwelling on such things only made her already miserable existence that much harder to bear.

Gazing out over Riverwood, Constance started in shock. Ellyn! In the skiff with Franklin! What was she doing? Seething with anger, she summoned Darnelle and with her help dressed quickly and hurried downstairs. Outraged by Ellyn's behavior, Constance knew she had had all she could stand from her. The girl was a hoyden.

Without pause, she swept into the dining room and demanded an explanation from a very apprehensive Charlotte. Confronted by her mother's fury, she was momentarily speechless and could only mumble incoherently about the explosion. Thinking that Charlotte was lying to protect Ellyn, Constance stormed out on the gallery to await her daughter's return.

Charlotte peeked out from behind the sitting room drapes, watching her mother, and shuddered, imagining what would transpire when Ellyn finally did return. Whenever Mother got in one of these moods, she knew it was best to stay out of her way. Letting the drape fall back in place, she hurried upstairs to her bedroom, determined to stay out of sight for the rest of the day.

"Miz Ellyn, look!"

It wasn't until she heeded Franklin's muttered warning that Ellyn saw her mother standing on the wide porch, her hands on her hips.

"Oh, no," she said, mainly to herself, but her companion nodded his agreement.

"Where have you been, Ellyn Douglass?" Constance demanded, her tone brooking no impertinence from the muddy, wet, bedraggled creature who stopped before her. "And what do you have on that dray?"

"A man," Ellyn answered, avoiding her mother's first question. "He was injured in the explosion last night. Charlotte did tell you, didn't she? We have to get him inside. I'm not sure how badly he's hurt."

When Ellyn moved to the man's side, Constance weakened. As mistress of Riverwood it was her duty to aid all in need. Lifting her skirts in a genteel manner, she descended the veranda steps. The concern that had been hers moments before was quickly replaced by revulsion as she saw the tatters of his blue uniform. A shriek of fury came from her as she realized that a Yankee lay before her.

"A filthy Yankee! Get him out of here!" she spat, backing away.

Ellyn looked up at her mother, stunned by her vicious reaction. "He's injured, Mother! Maybe dying! You can't refuse him aid."

"I can and I do! Get him away from me. Off your father's property," she demanded, pointing back toward the river. "Throw him back in to drown! It is what he deserves."

"Mother!" Ellyn was horrified by this side of her parent. "He is a man, first. A flesh and blood man. You can't condemn him to death just for the color of his uniform."

"I can't? Weren't your own father and brother murdered because of the color of their uniforms?" And with those last cutting words, she turned her back on Ellyn and moved to enter the house. At the door, she paused to glare at her speechless offspring. "If you care for that Yankee, I will no longer consider you my child." Constance entered the house, closing the door with a finality that under-scored her words.

"What we gonna do now, Miz Ellyn?" Franklin said worriedly, after a long silence. "Dis here soldier . . ."

"What?" she asked, focusing her attention once again on the man lying next to her. His coloring was lifeless and his breathing was strained and shallow. Ellyn knew that she had to help him. She could not let him die.

"Miz Ellyn?"

"Let's take him back to the cabin."

"Dem cabins ain't no good no more. Only one what's got a roof and dat's ours."

"Then . . . I know! We'll put him in the overseer's house."

Franklin seemed reluctant. "You sure? Miz Constance look lak' she mean bizness."

"This isn't the first time she's been angry with me." Ellyn shrugged, then quickly added, "Let's go before he gets any worse."

They led the mule around the big house and down the deserted path that led past the slave quarters. Pausing at Franklin's cabin to tell Glory to bring the necessary supplies, they continued on to the weather-beaten two-story overseer's house at the far end of the overgrown roadway. As it came into view, Ellyn was relieved to see that the roof was still intact. At least they would have basic shelter in case it rained again. The house somehow seemed to be watching their approach, its broken windows giving it a look of gaping surprise. Ellyn ran ahead of Franklin to check inside and make sure it was habitable. Hurrying up the few decrepit steps, she went to open the front door. Despite much tugging it stuck until, finally, with one huge jerk the top hinge of the offending portal gave way, and with a protesting groan it swung open. The sight that greeted her within was depressing and her shoulders slumped in recognition of the task to come. What once had been a suitable parlor was now a total wreck. The furniture that hadn't been stolen during the past few years was in shambles, destroyed by some malicious transient. The curtains were in shreds, blowing aimlessly at the open windows. Dust and cobwebs were everywhere. Ellyn searched the main floor futilely looking for some bedding and finally resorted to climbing the rickety, rotting staircase to the second story. At last in the largest bedroom, she found a dirty but serviceable mattress. Ellyn dragged it to the steps and pushed it down the stairs. Franklin and Glory came to her aid and moved the makeshift bed to a clear spot away from the drafty windows. Glory made the bed with patched but clean sheets while Ellyn and Franklin hurried to bring the injured soldier inside.

"You'd better help me undress him so he can be washed," Ellyn instructed the older man, after sending Glory off for more water.

Working silently beside her, Franklin noticed how she averted her eyes when he stripped and washed the lower half of the soldier's body. He quickly covered the man with a sheet as Ellyn moved away to get her few medical supplies.

"All de bleedin' done stopped but I think you'd bes' tak' a look at his arm," Franklin told her.

"His arm?"

" 'Pears to me as how it be broken." Franklin indicated the slight swelling of the soldier's left arm.

Ellyn, with all the expertise she'd learned from her grandfather, carefully explored his arm and found the break. She was attempting to set it when the pain reached through to Price's oblivious mind, and he rebelled against it. He twisted violently away from her probing hands.

"No," he mumbled. "I've got to find Coop."

"Franklin!" Ellyn called urgently and he came to help her, holding the arm immobile for her as she splinted and bound it. "Thanks," she breathed heavily, tucking a stray lock of her dark hair behind her ear.

The old man patted her shoulder. "You done jes' fine."

She smiled up at him. "I'd better have a look at these burns, too. Have Glory tear some more bandages for me, I'll be needing them."

As Franklin left in search of his daughter, Ellyn lowered the sheet to his waist and began applying the thick, white salve to the burns on his other arm. Her fingers were gentle as they tended his wounds and the soldier fought her no more. Her eyes followed her hands, skimming softly over his broad expanse of chest and firmly muscled shoulders. Had he not been seriously ill, Ellyn might have enjoyed the feel of his smooth, hard body beneath her ministering hands, but her concern was for his recovery and she took little notice of him as a virile creature. When she reached for the torn strips of cloth, she was startled to find him awake and watching her. She smiled at him broadly.

"Hello." Her tone was soft yet cheerful.

He spoke in a hushed, hoarse whisper, as he touched her gently on the cheek with his uninjured hand. "I thought I was dreaming. Who are you?"

"No, you're not dreaming and I'm Ellyn Douglass." Her pleasure at finding him awake caused her not to move away from his small caress.

It was a time for comforting and she sat quietly for

a moment while he struggled to straighten out his thoughts. After a moment, his arm dropped heavily back to the bed as if the effort to touch her had cost him much. He looked at her again and managed a lopsided, pain-denying grin.

"Well, Ellyn Douglass, I'm Price Richardson and from the feel of things I take it I'm not dead."

"Hardly," she laughed easily. "I'm sure you wouldn't feel so bad if you were."

"I would hope not." His smile faded and he gritted his teeth as he tried to shift positions on the uncomfortable mattress. "The boat . . . oh, God!"

He put his hand over his eyes and shuddered as his vicious memories assaulted him.

"Mr. Richardson?" Ellyn asked quietly, worriedly.

"I'm sorry," he said, refocusing on her, pulling his mind back from the fire and the black, cold river.

"If you could just lay quietly a few more minutes, I'll be through," Ellyn said, trying to distract his thoughts.

He turned his dark-eyed, pain-filled gaze to her and she grew unaccountably flustered as their eyes met. Ellyn sensed the private anguish held in that look and gave him a tender touch on his shoulder.

"I'll hurry."

Price closed his eyes and Ellyn felt greatly relieved. She dressed the burns and then expertly cleaned the deep scalp wound, wrapping it securely in a clean bandage. Although the wound was serious and no doubt painful, he held perfectly still while she treated him.

"Drink this." She offered him a cup of watered-down whiskey when she'd finished.

"Thanks," he murmured, appreciating the softness of her voice and manner.

She helped him, holding the cup to his lips as he drank thirstily. "Slow. Take it easy."

The simple act of drinking exhausted him and he lay back weakly. "I don't know how I got here, but . . ."

"Hush, now," she replied firmly, noticing how his jaw tightened in his effort to control the pain. "I'll give you more in a little while."

Price nodded slightly, wanting to know more of how he came to be here but feeling an overwhelming need for sleep. He rested and in a few minutes was asleep.

Ellyn remained at his side until he was quiet and then moved out onto the dilapidated porch where Glory waited.

"I have to clean up this room and I don't know how long he's going to sleep. Could you bring up a broom, mop and soap? I'll start as soon as you get back."

Glory hurried off toward the main house, while Ellyn and Franklin leaned wearily against the sagging porchrail.

"He gonna live?"

"I think so, although I'm going to have Grandfather examine him as soon as he returns from Memphis," she said as Franklin nodded his approval. "His name is Price Richardson."

They relaxed in companionable silence as the late-morning, golden sun shone down upon them. Ellyn swatted lazily at a noisy insect and let the tension flow from her. It was so peaceful.

"Miz Ellyn!" Glory's worried high-pitched voice broke the moment's solitude.

"What's the matter?" Ellyn responded, running from the porch.

"It's Miz Constance, She say dat I cain't have

33

anything dat's goin' to help no damn Yankee! Sh done snatched de broom right out o' my han'!" Glory related indignantly.

Ellyn sighed and put her arm around the young girl. "Don't worry. I'll take care of it. You did your best. Go on back with your pa while I go speak with my mother."

Glory went to join Franklin, as Ellyn straightened her shoulders and, head erect, walked toward the house preparing to do battle. Her mother was a formidable foe once her mind was set and Ellyn knew she had no easy task before her. Her only hope was her grandfather's support when he finally returned from town. Ellyn entered the house and went straight to the kitchen, gathering what she needed. Darnelle, torn by divided loyalties, absented herself while Ellyn worked. When she had enough food and cleaning supplies, she started outside.

"Just one minute." Her mother's imperious tone shattered her false calm and Ellyn faced her parent, setting her basket of necessities aside.

"Yes, Mother?"

"What do you have there?" Constance asked, stalking across the covered walkway.

"I have food and cleaning supplies."

"For what?" Her voice was acid.

"I've taken the Yankee to the overseer's house as you have refused him the comfort of our home."

"I told you my wishes about this matter." Constance's eyes were cold and deadly.

"I'm sorry, Mother. Grandfather taught me to respect all life and I cannot let this man suffer."

"Then kill him and put him out of his misery!" Constance hissed. "How can you choose to nurse a man who could possibly have shot your father or brother?"

Ellyn refused to be baited and turned to leave.

"Answer me, young woman!" Constance demanded, her face livid with anger.

"I have nothing to say to you. I'll be going now. Would you tell Grand—"

"I'll tell him nothing! This is the final straw! Since you have chosen to act like a trollop, you shall be treated like one. Get out of my house!"

Ellyn faced her mother squarely, her expression calm, her manner stiff as she exerted control over her raging temper. "Inform my grandfather, upon his return, that I need to see him immediately."

Her mother didn't reply, but turned her back and walked away from her. Ellyn shook with the force of her emotions, as fury at her mother's blind hatred overwhelmed her. She went out onto the gallery and sat down wearily on the steps. Her eyes were dull with worry as she stared unseeingly out at the overgrown cotton fields.

Would her father, had he lived, have reacted the same way as her mother? Somehow, Ellyn could not imagine that warm, gentle man refusing to help anyone in distress. No, her mother was a vengeful woman, full of hate, who would never be at peace again, for her way of life had been destroyed and there could be no going back, not now. Trying to rationalize her mother's actions did not alleviate the total disgust Ellyn felt for her. She got slowly to her feet and picked up the things she needed. Turning her back on Riverwood house, she moved off toward the end of the path and, unknowingly, her future.

Chapter Three

Price lay on the lumpy, musty mattress thinking it a most satisfactory bed. The tree he'd slept in the night before had offered little in the way of comfort. The house was quiet and seemingly deserted. He had no idea how long he'd been asleep. Staring up at the cracked, water-stained ceiling, he concentrated on his surroundings, pushing aside persistent thoughts of the past few months. It was still daylight. The shabby curtains moved wearily at the broken windows as a cooling breeze stirred them. He was surprised to find that the floor had been freshly scrubbed and the fireplace cleaned. Someone had been hard at work while he'd been resting.

Price wanted to sit up, to test his strength, but the pain that assailed him as he rolled to his good side discouraged any physical activity. He shuddered visibly, aching with the rawness of his wounds. Forced into idleness by the betrayal of his own body, he rested. Being incapacitated did not sit well with him. He was an active man, an outdoors man, who found the prospect of a lengthy, confined bedrest as abhorrent as the long weeks he'd spent in prison. At least then he'd been reasonably healthy. His mind slipped back to the day months before when he and Coop had been on that ill-fated patrol. There had been no warning, no clue that the Rebs were waiting. The ambush had been well-planned and successful. Taken completely by surprise, there had been no chance to escape. At first, they'd thought themselves lucky to be alive. But after having been sent to Andersonville where they subsisted on starvation rations, they'd wondered at their fate. Surely, after witnessing the violent deaths of so many of their comrades during the war, they wouldn't be left to die of dysentery or pneumonia at the prison camp? Just as their hopes for release were beginning to fade, news of the parole reached the camp. The men knew then that the war was nearing its end. Unencumbered joy had been theirs, despite Coop's accidental wounding, and the trip to Camp Fisk, though arduous, had been jubilant. But now, the horror of the past twenty-four hours haunted him. Robbing him of his peace of mind, it left him possessed with the fear that Coop had helplessly burned to death or drowned.

Price pulled his thoughts back from visions of the destroyed *Sultana,* determined to drive the horrible memories from his mind. His consciousness forced him into action. Physical pain was easier for him to deal with than emotional pain. Swinging his long legs to the floor, he slowly sat up. Breaking out in a cold sweat, he clenched his jaw against the agony that movement brought and waited as the crazily spinning room slowly righted itself. He must have groaned aloud for hurried footsteps sounded on the porch and Ellyn rushed in.

"Are you all right?" she asked in a worried voice then, noticing his state of undress, she blushed and looked away.

Hurriedly, Price pulled the blanket across his lap. "My apologies, ma'am. I was wondering where everyone had gone."

"I was just staying outside so you could rest," she answered lamely, wondering at her own breathlessness. "You've been asleep for over three hours."

"I knew it had been awhile. You got a lot of work done," he said conversationally, wrapping the cover more closely about himself and trying to put her at ease.

"Glory and Franklin helped me, I'd never have finished without them." Turning to him at last, her eyes were almost magnetically drawn to the powerful width of his shoulders and hair-roughened chest. Shaking herself mentally, she smiled as she remembered their efforts to scrub quietly lest they wake him. "Mr. Richardson?"

"Price, please," he returned.

"Price." Ellyn moved to a spindle-back chair and picked up a pair of worn work pants. "Franklin found these for you. Glory's trying to mend your uniform pants, but the shirt was a total loss."

"I can understand that," he replied, flexing his shoulders. He grimaced as his body rebelled against the motion.

"Will you need help?" she asked innocently.

"Yours?" He grinned in mocking amusement. "I think you'd better call Franklin to help with the pants."

"Yes, of course." The effect of his smile was devastating and she blushed again at his insinuation. As she hurried from the room, the sound of Price's soft laughter followed her.

With Franklin's help, Price donned the baggy pants and then lay down again, exhausted. His head throbbed as did his arm and he was glad for the dis-

38

traction when Ellyn returned with food and whiskey.

"Thank you, Ellyn." He paused and watched her movements around the room. "You don't mind if I call you by your Christian name, do you?"

"No, of course not," she answered, bringing a small table over next to his makeshift bed. "Do you think you can sit up for a while? The meal isn't much, but it'll be filling."

"It smells wonderful. Catfish?"

"Franklin caught it this afternoon," she said, nodding.

Price's spirits rose. He hadn't eaten catfish since their last leave—when Betsey, Coop's wife, had cooked it. Grimly, the specter of Coop assailed him.

"Has anyone else been rescued?"

"Not near here," she told him. "But when my grandfather gets back from Memphis, we'll find out more."

"Oh." His tone was remote and he started to eat.

"If there's someone you're concerned about, I can send word into town."

"Thank you." He seemed relieved. "His name is Jericho Cooper."

"I'll send a message right away." She left Price to his meal and went outdoors to find Franklin.

Price watched her go, admiring the sway of her hips beneath the mud-stained cotton gown. He sensed that Ellyn was a warm, passionate woman and for the first time in months he felt a stirring of desire. Too weak to humor himself, he finished his meal and lay back wondering about her.

Why had her grandfather left her alone, here in the country? Where was her family? Price was surprised that she was so concerned about him for, after all, this was Southern territory, and he seriously doubted that her kin had supported the Union.

Regardless, he was grateful for his rescue and would make sure that she was amply rewarded as soon as he got home.

His first impressions of Ellyn overshadowed his daydreaming as Price tried to picture her in a fashionable gown. He could only see her as she'd been when he'd first opened his eyes—her dark hair pulled back, just a few strands curling about her face. Her hazel eyes, large and round, were her dominant feature and Price instinctively knew that her very soul was reflected in those depths. Her cheekbones were high, her nose straight and her chin determined, yet feminine. She was attractive in spite of her serviceable, muddied dress. He was musing over these thoughts when he saw her through the open front door coming up the walk.

Ellyn walked toward the overseer's house, deep in thought. She pondered her reactions to this Yankee. Whenever his eyes were upon her, she felt like a schoolgirl. Possibly, she concluded, analyzing her feelings, it was just her lack of male companionship. Grandpa was seldom at home any length of time and there had been no word from Rod for almost eight months.

"Franklin is on his way. With any luck, we'll know something about your friend when he gets back tonight," she told him as she entered the house.

As Price smiled his gratitude at her, she continued, "Were you and Mr. Cooper close?"

"We were like brothers," he answered quietly, his expression solemn.

"Oh." Then trying to cheer him up, she teased, "Don't worry. I'm sure he's fine, probably better off than you are. Most likely, he didn't have to spend the night hanging in a tree."

Price saw the humor in her remark and, pushing

aside his gruesome worries, grinned. "Have you eaten?"

"I will later," she told him as she sat down in the chair near him. "I just wanted to check on you first. You're sure you feel all right? Would you like a glass of whiskey?" At his nod, she poured a good-sized portion into a glass. "Is this enough?"

"Fine. I don't want an extra headache in the morning. One is quite sufficient."

She helped him to a sitting position, bracing him comfortably against the wall with his pillow. As she moved to hand the drink to him, he grasped her wrist firmly and pulled her across him. Startled, crushed there against his chest, she lay quiescent as his mouth moved warmly over hers.

"Thank you," he said softly against her trembling lips.

She pushed away, trying to flee his touch, and accidentally spilled the drink.

"Oh! I'm sorry!" Ellyn exclaimed nervously, grabbing a rag and trying to soak up the whiskey that had splashed on his blanket.

"Ellyn." The timbre of his voice was deep and rich, the sound of her name was a caress.

She froze and slowly looked at him, her eyes wide in their uncertainty. Price reached out and slowly drew her closer until she sat next to him on the narrow mattress.

"I'm not," he told her just seconds before his mouth claimed hers again.

Ellyn knew she should be outraged. She knew she should pull away—she was engaged! But the touch of his lips on hers sent chills up and down her spine and she was breathless. Thoughts tumbled through her mind crazily and she broke off the kiss. Price smiled at her tenderly as she lay still in his embrace, her breathing ragged. Then, most innocently, she lifted her arms about his neck and kissed him, anxious to know if his second kiss could be as powerful as his first. His lips parted hers and, at the first surprising touch of his tongue, Ellyn felt a burning need to press herself to him, to feel his strength against her. The sound of Glory coming down the path jolted them back to reality. She pulled out of his arms and stood apart from him. Dazed by the reaction of her body, she didn't speak. A heat had flared deep within her, creating in its wake a demanding ache for completeness with this man. She had time to look at him for a moment before Glory entered and she found him watching her, his expression as puzzled and filled with yearning as hers.

"Miz Ellyn?" Glory spoke softly from the porch. Ellyn went quickly outside to Glory.

"My mama says it be all right if'n you want to come up to de big house now. Miz Constance takin' her nap."

"Thank you. I do need to get some things. Could you stay here with Mr. Richardson while I'm gone?"

"Yes, ma'am."

"Fine." They went inside to find Price reclining in seeming comfort against the wall. "Price, this is Glory. She's going to stay with you while I go up to the big house."

"Big house?"

"Riverwood, my family's home." She indicated the path.

"Ah, that explains it."

"Explains what?"

"What you're doing out here all alone in a broken-down house. I wondered."

"I'm not alone. It's just—" Before she could reply, he answered for her.

42

"They didn't want anything to do with a Yankee. Right?"

Although he smiled, Ellyn could find no humor in the situation. She was humiliated by her mother's lack of support and vowed silently not to let him learn of her viciousness. Price watched Ellyn's troubled expression and wrongly surmised that she, too, wanted him gone. He was certain that kissing her just now hadn't helped matters, either. Possibly, she'd heard of bloodthirsty Yankee marauders who roamed the countryside raping and pillaging and he was sure that she thought of him as a Yankee and not as a man. Chagrined, he spoke again.

"Don't worry. I do feel better and I promise to leave as soon as I'm strong enough." His tone was gentle.

The thought of leaving her bothered him. He'd met very few truly generous people in his twenty-nine years and she was one of them. Ellyn was a special person, he could sense it. He would tread lightly with her and maybe he could win her trust and friendship during the next few days. Perhaps he could convince her that Yankees were not really all that bad.

"I'll just rest while you're gone," he said, stretching out slowly.

"I'll be back before dark. Thanks, Glory," she said and left the house.

Lifting her skirts, she ran up the path, not stopping until she was near Riverwood house. Out of breath, she sat on the gallery steps. What had come over her? Maybe her mother was right, maybe she was a wanton. She put her hand to her lips and felt again the touch of his. There was something so special about this man—Price Richardson. She'd never responded this way to Rod's embrace; his kiss had left her unmoved. Ellyn had not known that it

43

could be any other way and so she'd been content. But now, this stranger who'd come out of the dark night had made a shambles of her orderly life. He had ignited a fiery desire within her that begged to be satisfied.

Ellyn got up wearily and went inside, carefully avoiding her mother's room. Entering her own bedroom, she got clean clothes and then returned to the kitchen to find Darnelle busy fixing the evening meal.

"Miz Ellyn, how you doin'?" Darnelle asked. "Glory says that the soldier gonna be all right."

"He should be fine in a few weeks," Ellyn told her as she sat down at the table. "I've got to have a bath and I don't dare try upstairs. Do you mind if I wash in the back room?"

"You go on. I've got plenty of hot water," she instructed.

Taking a full bucket, Ellyn went into the small room where the tub was stored. They made short order of filling it and after Darnelle brought her a towel and soap, she stripped off her filthy clothes and got in.

The deliciously hot water massaged the weariness from her as she relaxed back against the side of the small tub. Ellyn would have been surprised to know what a sensual picture she made, reclining there with her eyes closed and a satisfied half-smile on her lips. In rare moments like these when she allowed herself to be totally feminine, she was truly beautiful.

She was the essence of chaste womanhood and yet her body defied that. Her complexion was creamy and unblemished, her breasts were temptingly full, her hips slightly rounded. Hers was a body made for love, yet until today, no man had awakened her passionate nature. Price, with his searing, soul-touching kiss, had brought to life within her the flaming desire to know man. Ellyn's eyes flew open as that thought teasingly crossed her mind, bringing with it a remembrance of all the exquisite sensations his kiss had bestowed. She hurriedly started to bathe, dragging her concentration away from such notions.

Ellyn was completely unaware of the effect her attributes could have on the opposite sex. She had that quality about her that created within men the overwhelming desire to touch and possess her. But she had allowed herself no time during the past few years to indulge in any kind of romantic fantasy. Her sole purpose had been to keep Riverwood together, first for her father and brother, and then this past year for their own survival. Responsibility weighed heavily upon her and she often denied herself in order that her mother or sister might have a little more. Ellyn felt no resentment, she merely knew what had to be done and she did it as best she could.

Finishing her bath before the water cooled, Ellyn washed her hair and was relieved to be clean at last. The room seemed chilly as she stepped gracefully from the tub and she hastily dried herself, eager to be done with such things and back at the overseer's house with Price.

After donning a cotton daygown of soft blue with white trim, she sat in the kitchen, towel-drying her hair. It was quiet and peaceful as she worked her comb through the tangled mass and she dwelled on thoughts of the Northerner. Confusedly sighing, she plaited her long, glossy tresses and let the braid swing freely down her back.

"Is Mother still resting?" she asked Darnelle.

"Yes. I don't expect her to get up much before dinner."

"Good, I need a few things from upstairs and I

45

didn't want to run into her," Ellyn said as she crossed the walkway.

A few minutes later, she reappeared carrying a large blanket-wrapped bundle. On her walk back, she felt considerably lighter of spirit. Things were never as hopeless as they seemed, her grandfather had taught her that. Bittersweetly, she smiled to herself. What had happened with Price was a moment of let-down defenses that would not happen again. Even so, Ellyn had to admit that his kiss had been hauntingly wonderful and she doubted that she would forget it any too soon. She was so absorbed in her thoughts that she failed to notice the ominous black clouds that cast a premature darkness on the early evening; even the insects had quieted at their approach out of the southwest. Ellyn quickened her pace when she finally recognized the signs of a threatening storm. Briefly, Franklin crossed her mind and she hoped he would return before it began. Another torrential downpour could cause worse flooding and possibly isolate the entire area. Glory met her on the porch, anxious to get back home.

Price watched her as she quietly entered the dark house. He closed his eyes and listened to the pleasant rustle of her skirts as she moved about the room. At the sound of a striking match, he looked up to find the room filled with warm, flickering lamplight.

"Ellyn," he began and she started at the sound of his voice.

"Oh! You're awake!" She turned to face him.

Price smiled as his dark-eyed gaze swept over her. He warmed as he took in all of her—her shining, braided hair, the fairness of her complexion, the freshly washed feminine fragrance of her. Even in his imaginings he hadn't fancied her to be this beautiful.

"I'm aching too much to get any rest," he replied,

shifting uncomfortably.

"Would a glass of whiskey help?"

"Please. It's bound to do some good." He pushed up and levered himself against the wall as she poured a small glass of golden liquid and brought it to him.

"Thanks," he said.

"I brought back a few things I thought you could use," Ellyn told him as she brought the blanket-wrapped bundle to a table near his bed. "Would you like to shave?"

"It would be heaven," he commented dryly, running a hand over the bristly black growth.

"Fine. I've got everything right here. Maybe we can set up this table for you, unless you'd rather I did it?" Her question was naively put, thinking that it might be awkward for him.

"No, I'll do it," came his abrupt, gruff reply.

His curt tone bewildered Ellyn and she hurriedly turned from him, not wanting him to see the hurt in her eyes. She'd not expected an honest offer of help to be rejected so coldly. Their moment of incredible closeness had been just that—a moment. It was now gone forever. After all, hadn't he said that he'd be leaving as soon as possible?

"Oh, all right. I'll put these things right here, then," she said, pulling herself together, determined to follow his lead and be indifferent.

He downed his tumbler of whiskey in one swallow and swung around to sit shakily on the edge of the bed. Gritting his teeth, he rested, head in hand for a moment, until the pain receded. At last, he felt steady enough to hold the razor and he began, taking note when she went outside again.

Eyeing the sky warily, Ellyn noted the chilling shift in the wind and the heavy scent of rain in the air. It wouldn't be long now. Knowing that Franklin

47

couldn't possibly return before the storm broke, she hoped that he'd find adequate shelter in time.

A bolt of lightning erupted from the green-black clouds and the crack and rumble that accompanied it seemed to shake the very ground itself. There was a moment of dead silence then, before the rain came. Unleashed in its ferocity, the wind drove the rain almost parallel to the ground, forcing Ellyn to seek a safe haven indoors.

Price had just finished shaving and was wiping the remaining soap from his face when Ellyn entered, closing the doors as tightly as possible behind her.

"I hope the wind dies down, if not, it's going to get awfully damp in here," she remarked, turning to face him.

"I noticed," he nodded toward the blowing curtains as he set the towel aside. "I appreciate you bringing the razor. I almost feel like a new man."

"Well, you certainly look like one," she told him, taking in the firm, clean-shaven line of his jaw. Without the beard he seemed even more handsome to her. "Have you always worn a mustache?"

"For quite a few years now. Why? Don't you like it?" Amusement twinkled in his brown eyes.

"Yes, I do like it. It suits you somehow."

She seemed to be more comfortable in his presence now and Price was glad. The thought of nervous, stilted, one-sided conversations for the duration of his bedrest had depressed him. The temperature had dropped quickly with the advent of the storm and Ellyn shivered, regretting that she hadn't brought a shawl with her.

"You're cold?" he asked quickly. "Why don't we see if we can get a fire going?" Bracing his good arm against the wall he hauled himself to his feet and stood swaying momentarily.

"I can do it!" Ellyn insisted taking a step toward him.

"And I can at least help," Price returned. "If I stay in that bed too long, I may never be able to get out of it."

Ellyn had to agree with his logic, for inactivity and uselessness had done in just as many people as overwork. She set about bringing the wood over to the hearth and Price joined her there, kneeling beside the darkened fireplace. Within moments, he'd set the kindling ablaze and strategically added a few logs to it.

"That should do it," he said, wiping his good hand on his pants leg.

She stood behind him, enjoying the warmth of the newborn fire. Her gaze strayed to the man before her. She could not deny the attraction she felt for him as she stared down at his bare, broad shoulders. He turned to speak and Ellyn wrested her eyes from him and walked over to the blanket she'd brought back with her.

"I also brought these. I don't know which one will fit, but anything will help if it gets colder tonight." She held up two shirts.

Price got to his feet slowly and took the proffered clothing. After a quick glance, he handed one back.

"I'm sure that would be too small, but this one might do." He slipped his good arm into one sleeve, but could do no more. Automatically, Ellyn assisted him, smoothing the fabric across his back and trying to cover his injured limb.

"Just a second," she told him and, getting her small knife, she slit the sleeve so his splintered arm was partially covered. "That should do it. Are you comfortable?"

"Just fine, thanks." He went to the window as

another crack of lightning split the heavens. "When did you expect Franklin?"

"Not for at least another hour or two, but from the looks of things, I doubt if he'll make it back tonight at all."

"It's really pouring, he'd be wise to hole up somewhere till morning."

Ellyn nodded her agreement and then wondered what to do about sleeping arrangements. She had planned for Franklin to spend the night here with her. It had not occurred to her that she might find herself with Price overnight. That complicated things. Then, bravely, she decided it would only become difficult if her mother knew. She would just swear Glory and Darnelle to silence first thing in the morning. Then there'd be no way her mother could find out. Dismissing her worries, she cast a glance at Price who was painfully cradling his injured arm as he watched it rain.

"Why don't you sit down and I'll fix you another drink?"

He blinked, momentarily confused as though his thoughts had been miles away, and then went to sit on the bed. "Nasty night."

"Very," Ellyn handed him another whiskey.

"Well, I'm just thankful for a roof over my head. Last time it rained like this, Coop and I were stuck in a little four-by-four lean-to we'd built at the prison camp."

"Prison camp?" Ellyn was horrified. "You were in prison?"

Price smiled, almost cynically, at her astonishment. "And here, I thought you'd be glad about it."

"Never! Grandfather's told me what's been happening. Union and Confederate both. Where were you? It must have been terrible!" She was deeply distressed, remembering the stories her grandfather had related to her when trying to emphasize the horrors of war.

Price watched her, amazed that she'd known about such atrocities.

"I was at Andersonville," he stated matter-of-factly and Ellyn blanched. "So he told you about it?"

"Just a few of the basic facts."

"That's more than a lady should know," he cut her off, his tone condemning her grandfather. "Why were you even discussing it?"

"It was when I was helping him at the hospital in Memphis. One of the soldiers we were treating had escaped from there."

"Oh." Price reflected silently for a moment. "Lucky man. A lot of escapees didn't make it. Most of them were tracked down by the dogs."

Ellyn shivered at the thought and watched as Price finished off his drink. "More?"

"Please. Why don't you try a little? It should take off the chill."

She had shared a brandy on occasion with her father before the war and the thought of a small, relaxing drink seemed truly appealing. Ellyn refilled his glass with a good-sized portion and poured herself a small amount. She had been shocked by his announcement that he'd come from Andersonville prison. The name alone dredged up disquieting bits of conversation she'd overheard during her long hours in town. Overcrowding, starvation, disease.

"Were you there long?" The bold question slipped out.

Price looked at her, his expression stony. "Only three months. We were lucky."

"I can well imagine," she agreed. She sipped again

at her drink and was surprised to find the burning liquid almost gone. "Grandfather said it was horrendously overcrowded. What I don't understand is why they stopped the exchange."

"That's simple enough," Price replied, glad to be off the other subject. "The more Rebs they kept locked up, the fewer we had to fight."

Put so bluntly, Ellyn had to agree, but it did rankle her to hear her own fighting men described so callously.

"Now don't get upset because I spoke my mind. You seem to be a woman who says exactly what she means. Why sugar-coat anything? It would only have prolonged the killing if both sides were constantly paroling the other side's prisoners. Just be glad that it's over."

"I am," she replied softly, her ego soothed by the truth of his words. "Believe me, I am."

Ellyn stared into the flickering shadows of the room, picturing her brother and father—both tall, fair and handsome in their dashing gray uniforms. Both had been eager to be off to the fighting. A lone tear escaped before she could blink it back and Price saw it.

"Crying?" His voice was hoarse. "Please don't." He gently reached out to brush the tear away and Ellyn jerked from his unexpected touch.

He hadn't meant to upset her; she'd been the one to bring it up. He supposed her losses had been grievous and he was sorry to have reduced her to this state. Her sudden aversion to his touch was nerve-wracking. He wanted to hold her tenderly and tell her everything would turn out all right, but common sense told him that right now he would be rejected flat out.

"I'm fine," she told him, pouring herself another

52

small portion of whiskey, this time adding water. "I was just thinking of my father and brother. They're both dead now. They were killed last year."

"I'm sorry. Just because death has become a way of life does not make it any easier to accept."

"Yes, you're right." She started to sit on the hard-backed chair and then stopped. "Do you mind if I sit on the floor? This chair is quite uncomfortable."

"Be my guest." He gestured widely, glad that her depressed mood was gone as quickly as it had come.

Ellyn pulled the blanket she'd brought from the house with her and sat next to the bed, her back against it, the blanket cushioning her bottom.

"That's much better," she sighed, stretching her legs in front of her, yet keeping her skirts artfully arranged.

A smile played about his lips as he thought of how unaffected she was.

"Are you always this unconventional?" he teased.

"Suh?" she replied in a drawl.

"Nursing Yankees and sitting on the floor when it suits you?"

"Actually, I see myself as more practical than unconventional. I've always thought society's ways were a trifle binding to say the least." Thinking suddenly of corsets, she giggled, a light, musical sound that made his smile broaden.

"And what thought could possibly have amused you so?" he queried, wanting to understand this changeable creature seated by his side.

She glanced at him quickly from beneath lowered lashes, the look unknowingly seductive and Price had to restrain himself from caressing her cheek so close to his hand. Abruptly, her expression transformed to impish delight.

"I suppose I can trust you with my innermost,

53

secret thoughts. I was thinking of corsets."

"Corsets?" He threw his head back and laughed at her wit. "That's wonderful!" When he'd calmed a bit, he added. "I must admit I find your practical ways most refreshing."

"Good. I'd hate to have to change at this late date, although my mother, no doubt, would be thrilled," she added ruefully, sipping at her drink and feeling an inner warmth stealing over her.

"Oh, so she's more rigid in her social manner?"

"The best hostess in the county and the most beautiful."

"She must be," he told her and Ellyn looked at him sharply.

"Why do you say that?" she asked, her unguarded tone almost accusing.

"Well, her daughter is the loveliest woman I've ever met. Surely, she has to be beautiful, too," he told her simply, his expression gentle yet earnest.

Ellyn didn't respond, she was too busy thinking. Never before had she been told she was beautiful, except by her father, of course, and he was prejudiced. It made her tingle to think that this man found her attractive. She looked up at him after a long moment.

"You really mean it?"

Price was startled. He thought all women were aware of their own worth. Her candor delighted him.

"Yes," he answered quietly and was surprised when she smiled brightly.

"Thank you."

"You seem amazed. Surely you know how pretty you are?"

"Actually, no one has ever told me that before, except my father and he doesn't count."

"Didn't you have boyfriends before the war?"

"Just Rod."

"Rod?"

"Rod Clarke, my fiance," she sighed, deep in thought.

"And this Rod Clarke has never told you how attractive you are?" Price stiffened at the mention of the other man.

Ellyn suddenly realized that she didn't want to talk about Rod at all and got up quickly.

"Looks like you could use some more." She took his glass from him and fixed them both another drink, this time forgetting to water hers down. "You know you're right, this certainly did warm me up."

A vicious crack of thunder crashed overhead and Price sympathized openly with Franklin. "I hope Franklin found shelter. This is some bad storm." He wanted to find out more about this fiance of hers, for some unknown reason, but didn't know how to steer the conversation back to him.

He took the glass back from her and settled himself against the wall, "Talk to me," he requested. "About anything. It's been so long since I've had any female companionship that I'm finding this quite enjoyable."

Ellyn grinned and sat back down on the floor next to him after adding another log to the fire.

"I haven't really had anyone to talk to, either. Papa and Tommy left in '62, so when word came that they'd died last year it wasn't all that hard to accept." She paused to take a drink. "Rod left at the same time, but he joined a different regiment. I get letters, but not regularly. It's been quite awhile since his last one. Grandad is home, off and on, depending on how badly he's needed at the hospital in town. So I've been a little lonely."

"But surely your mother. . ."

"She hasn't been the same since Father died. And my sister, Charlotte, well, she's not interested in the same things I am."

"Oh." Price kept his expression unreadable. "So tell me about yourself. What you like and dislike—anything. It'll help keep my mind off my body."

"Still hurts, doesn't it?"

"Just a little," he said sardonically. "And although the whiskey helps, it doesn't deaden the pain. It merely makes me not care about it anymore."

She grinned at his observation. It was certainly the truth, for she hadn't worried at all about her unchaperoned state since before her last drink. Ellyn had to admit she felt wonderfully relaxed and quite at ease with this stranger. She started to yawn and put a hand to her mouth.

"They're numb!" she said, surprised.

"What's numb?" Price asked, totally confused.

"My lips! I can barely feel them!"

He laughed at her again. "I think, my dear, it might be advisable if you stop drinking for a while. As I recall from my early experiences with hard liquor, numb lips are the first sign of over-imbibing." He had to smother his laugh as she looked quite startled.

"I'm drunk?"

"No, not yet. Just relaxed."

"Well, that's true enough." She settled back against the bed again after draining the small amount left in her glass.

"So tell me about you."

"There's not that much to tell. I'm nineteen, one of three children—the oldest girl. My father and brother are dead. There's just my mother, my sister,

Charlotte, and Grandad left here at Riverwood. Franklin and his wife and daughter stayed on to work for room and board. That's all I could offer them.''

"You?"

"Mm-hmm," she answered positively, setting her glass on the floor. "Mother went to pieces when the news came about Papa and Tommy, so I took over. Grandad's gone so much."

"So you run everything?"

"As much as I can and that's just barely enough to keep food on the table." She sounded defeated.

"But that's quite an accomplishment, considering . . ."

Her anger at her circumstances flared and she snorted derisively—a very unladylike sound. "I was taught how to run this plantation! And all I've managed to accomplish in the past three years is to keep out of the poor house. Frankly, it seems almost like we became the poorhouse! We didn't even have to move!"

"Is money so important to you?" he asked, guardedly.

"I have found through bitter experience that *eating* is important to me," she answered bluntly. "We've been living on fish and what few vegetables we can grow. Our stock is gone, so are our horses. There's no way I can get a crop in the ground. And even if I had the money, there's no one to hire for field work," Ellyn concluded bitterly.

"I've been there, too," he told her confidingly. "Just keep your faith in yourself and your trust in God. Sometimes when things seem the worst, they're really on the upswing."

She didn't answer, as all the fight seemed to have gone out of her. Ellyn leaned her head wearily back against the mattress and made unexpected contact with his hard, muscled thigh. Price tensed but Ellyn didn't seem to notice.

"I've prayed a lot," she admitted, her eyes closed. "But I wonder if I'll ever be answered."

"The answers to your prayers are disguised sometimes and it's hard to recognize them." Price smiled as he remembered Adele Cooper coming to his rescue all those years ago when, as a young boy, he'd been alone and desperate.

He paused as thunder again rumbled deeply overhead. The flickering golden warmth of the fire, along with the rage of the storm outside had lent a protected coziness to the room. Price was pleased that Ellyn had not pulled away from him. He looked down at the dark head resting upon his leg. She was turned from him slightly and he couldn't see her face.

"Ellyn?"

She faced him, her eyes luminous in the semi-darkness. Lost in Ellyn's gentle beauty, he could only stare at her, savoring the long, quiet moment. He remembered how sweet she'd tasted when he'd kissed her earlier and now unbidden imaginings of how she'd feel pressed to his body bombarded him, leaving him trembling with desire. Price almost surrendered to the urge to pull her to him but the innocent look in her eyes stopped him. Angry with himself for forgetting his earlier plan to win her trust, he abruptly tried to think of something halfway intelligent to say.

"Could I have another drink?" he asked brusquely.

Had Price known the direction of Ellyn's thoughts, he wouldn't have been so irritated with himself. Little did he suspect that her whole being was wishing to be swept into his arms and carried away to live happily ever after. He seemed to her to be the most sensitive, caring man she'd ever met, yet in being so he'd lost none of his masculine appeal. For the first time in her life, she wanted to be held and cherished and protected. And for the first time ever, she wanted to forget the responsibility of Riverwood and lean on someone else . . . this man. A man she hadn't even known twenty-four hours ago.

"Oh," she answered, surprised by the sudden hardness in his expression and tone. "Sure."

Getting up, she refilled both their glasses. A sudden crack of lightning momentarily invaded the secluded safety of their haven and a deafening roar of thunder soon followed. Leaving the drinks on the small table, Ellyn hurried to look outside as the wind howled unnervingly around the small house. She was forced away from the window, though, as the wind shifted and rain came pouring in.

"Getting worse?"

"If that's possible, yes," she told him, coming back to the bed with the glasses. "There'll be a lot of trees down after this, and the river . . ." Ellyn glanced over her shoulder once again at the curtains flapping noisily.

"Know any good ghost stories?" he teased and she giggled.

"Yes, as a matter of fact, I do, but tonight I don't want to be scared."

"What do you want tonight?" Price asked. His voice was low and seductive as he took the proffered drink.

Ellyn almost stammered at his question and searched her whiskey-befuddled mind for a quick, witty reply.

"Um . . ." She took a drink to give herself more

time to think. "I want to know your life story. I've just spent the last hour boring you with mine. Now it's your turn."

"To bore you?"

"No," she said with a laugh. "To tell me your innermost thoughts!"

"Oh," he said, drawing out the word, grinning at her as she once more took her seat on the floor next to him. This time, however, she turned facing him and rested her arm on the mattress close to his hip.

"Go on. I'm all ears," she encouraged him, smiling happily.

"Hardly," he muttered to himself, his eyes lingering on the fullness of her breasts.

"What?"

"Nothing," he replied, scowling.

"If you don't want to . . . I mean it's all right," she said, wondering at his volatile moods.

"No, no. What would you like to know?" He smiled, after sensing her wariness.

"Everthing." Her eyes sparkled. "Your deepest, darkest secrets."

"I get the idea!" He laughed and in a friendly gesture took her hand.

The contact was electric as a sudden thrill shot through her. Ellyn looked down at the lean, long-fingered hand holding hers and was amazed that such an innocent touch could cause her breath to catch in her throat. She raised her eyes to his and, as their gazes met, time suspended. An attraction they could not deny magnetically drew them together. In a single fluid motion Ellyn rose to her knees and met him halfway in a searing, heart-stirring kiss. It was everything Ellyn remembered and more. She shivered as he parted her lips, deepening the kiss. She couldn't suppress the small, muffled moan of desire that escaped from her as he tenderly cupped her face with his uninjured hand, seeming to bond them together. Slowly then and quite gently, he withdrew from her just far enough to look at her intently. Trying to control the willfulness of his aroused body, he smiled at her.

"I believe you were interested in my fascinating childhood?"

"I'm interested in everything about you," she told him guilelessly as they moved apart and Ellyn was secretly delighted when once again he took her hand.

"And I, you," he responded and they both relaxed as honesty eased any doubts they might have had about each other.

"Well, you know all there is to know about me," she said, sipping at her drink.

"I do?" Price asked, wondering at the unmentioned fiancé.

"Everything important," she looked up at him trustingly, her engagement to Rod Clarke the farthest thing from her mind. For the first time in years, she was having fun and tonight her bemused mind refused to drag forth its overworked conscience.

"All right, then, I'll tell you everything you could possibly need to know." He watched in awe as she finished her whiskey. He hadn't even touched his. "I was born and raised in Alton, Illinois. I'm an only child and my parents both died when I was twelve. The Coopers took me in and Adele Cooper raised me as her own."

"No wonder you were so worried about Mr. Cooper. I hope Franklin can find something out."

"Me, too," he sighed and squeezed her hand reassuringly. "He's got a wife and baby waiting at home for him."

"How awful for her! Did she know you were in prison?"

"I'm not sure. There was no mail, no news." He paused. "I only hope they didn't tell her that we were dead."

"What happened?"

"We were out on patrol and some Rebs ambushed us. We were lucky to get out of that alive, a lot of my men were killed," he spoke quietly.

"So, what did you do in Alton?" she asked, changing the subject. "Where is that, anyway?"

"North of St. Louis, it's a busy port, there's a lot of river traffic. The Missouri River comes in a little downstream from us, so we get the benefit of both businesswise. That's why Coop and I started our own transshipping company?"

"Coop?"

"Jericho Cooper—Coop's his nickname."

"Oh," she said and Price paused, gently lacing their fingers together in a more intimate gesture.

"Ellyn?" She looked up at him questioningly. "Thanks."

"For what?"

"For keeping this light. There's been so much ugliness in my life these last few years, I'm just thankful that I'm heading home in one piece."

"So am I."

"It's all because of you," he told her seriously.

Ellyn smiled and then, too tipsy to ignore her true feelings any longer, she asked him straight out, "Are you married?"

He threw back his head and laughed loudly. "No, pretty lady, I'm not married. I'd never found a woman worth marrying before."

More than a little affected by the whiskey, Ellyn looked up at him with open admiration. And Price, never one to refuse an invitation, pulled her up next to him. Careful of his injuries, Ellyn came to him, unaware of the conflict going on within him. Price barely succeeded in controlling his desire, and almost convinced himself that he could hold her close and not do more until he felt her weight beside him and her hard-tipped breasts pushing against his chest. He wanted her. God knows she was everything he needed—beauty, warmth, softness. His honorable intentions nearly escaped him as he turned toward her. But he cared for this woman, she was everything he'd ever dreamed of and thought he'd never find. Rational thought seemed lost for a moment. He was here and she was willing . . . . To deny himself now seemed the ultimate in self-sacrifice. Yet, as he met her heavy-lidded, innocent-passionate gaze, Price knew he could not take her, not without her full consent. His eyes swept over her flushed features as they lay facing each other, Ellyn with her head resting on her arm.

"Comfortable?" he asked.

"Mm-hmm," she murmured, watching him closely. "And you? Your arm?"

"It's fine," he said, shifting so his injured forearm was free. "Ellyn?"

"I love the way you say my name," she said softly.

And Price knew than that this was going to be more difficult than he had thought.

"Ellyn?"

"Price, please kiss me." Her eyes closed and she moved even closer, abandoning herself into his care.

With a muttered curse, he drew her nearer still and kissed her with a ferocity that surprised them both. It was a flaming, devouring kiss that, as she returned it full measure, destroyed his good intentions and freed the passionate man within.

"You feel so good to me," he told her as their lips met again and again, exploring, testing, tempting.

Ellyn didn't answer, but wrapped her arms around him, holding him to her. She felt no shame as his hands caressed her breast, teasing her already hardened nipples. Sensing the now-familiar ache growing within her, she thrust her hips instinctively against him. Her body telling her that she needed his hardness to satisfy her, to complete her.

"Oh, Price," she breathed against his mouth as his hand freed the tiny buttons at the bodice of her dress.

She arched her back, offering herself in the age old movement as his lips explored the sweet flesh that his fingers exposed. Brushing aside the bothersome fabric, his mouth sought and found the tender, pink peak of her breast. Ellyn stiffened in surprise at the intimate touch of his lips, but gave in willingly as rapturous waves of pleasure overtook her. She held his head to her, savoring the unceasing pulses of desire that flowed through her.

Price kissed her once more, a passion-drugged kiss that left them both breathless. Ellyn lay against him, enjoying the feel of his thighs pressed tightly to hers, leaving no doubt of his arousal. She could never remember feeling so wonderful, so wanted. Eyes closed, she sighed as he pressed tender, soft kisses on her throat. His control was nearly gone and he could hardly bear to keep a tight rein on his raging urge to take her . . . and quickly.

"Ellyn," he whispered hoarsely. "Ellyn, I want you."

When there was no response, he pulled back, looking down at her. Nestled tightly against him, Ellyn was sound asleep. It took Price a long, painful moment to realize exactly what had happened.

He gently touched her cheek. "Ellyn?"

She stirred but didn't awaken. And Price, making an earnest effort not to take advantage of her, moved slightly away. Lying back, he rested his arm across his forehead and waited for his body to cool down. He glanced at her and felt heat flush through him at the sight of her bared bosom, her nipples still hard from his enjoyment of them. With gritted teeth, he reached out and touched her again, and then against all of his basic instincts, he buttoned her dress once more.

Sighing, he shifted his hips away from the honeyed pressure of hers. He started to lay back again, but hesitated. After a moment's thought, he leaned over her and kissed her sweetly on the lips.

"Sleep well, pretty lady," he said and stretched out, trying to rest.

Grinning wryly to himself, he had to admit that twenty-four hours ago he would never have dreamed he'd be spending the night, albeit innocently, in bed with a beautiful woman . . . a very tired, beautiful woman. He closed his eyes against the sight of her next to him and sought sleep in vain.

It was three a.m. The lightning and high winds had ceased. Now there was just the steady drumming of the rain as it pounded into the already saturated earth. Usually, that monotonous sound would lull Constance straight to sleep, but not tonight. She was up, pacing her room in a frenzy of barely contained rage. This long night was almost over and Franklin had not returned. She knew for a fact that Ellyn was spending the night alone with the Yankee. Fury ravaged her indignant soul. How could she allow Rod to be cuckolded this way? She respected him too much to allow him to marry her daughter. A daughter who'd stayed unchaperoned with a Union soldier, doing God-knows-what all night long! Perhaps Rod could marry Charlotte instead. The thought gave her pause. Although she was sure that Charlotte was pure and untouched, the girl was basically an uninspiring chit, and for that reason Constance discarded the idea.

No, Rod deserved the best and Constance knew, now, that there was only one solution to her dilemma. If she wanted to combine Riverwood and Clarke's Landing as planned, she would have to marry Rod herself. Her face lit with an expression that was pure predatory female and even her eyes seemed to take on a determined, feverish glow.

It seemed that it had been weeks since she'd been able to picture Thomas in her mind. Vaguely, she remembered his massive body and gentle ways, but his face was always a blur to her. This had caused her much grief in the beginning, but now all she felt was relief. If she was to concentrate on a way to win Rod's affections, she didn't want any lingering thoughts of a long-dead spouse haunting her.

Constance paused by the window and peered out toward the overseer's house. She could see nothing. The night was black. There was no flicker of lights from the direction of the cabin. Rain suddenly pelted against the glass and startled her. Leaving the drapes pulled aside, she climbed back into her solitary bed, wishing that Rod was there waiting for her. She didn't stop to think it odd that she could see Rod clearly in her mind's eye. She only knew that she wanted him and that, if at all possible, she was going to have him. Her body tingled in anticipation as her thoughts raced through fantasy after fantasy of how he would make love. An actual physical ache for possession overtook her as her active imagination

66

rovided her with all the intimate details of his
aresses: how his mouth would feel sucking at her
breast, his hands lifting her hips to fit her to him
most intimately. Constance could almost feel him
part her legs and come into her. She groaned aloud
and tossed on the bed. She was hot and alive with
useless passion. Frustrated, forcing the image of Rod
away, she got up again, vowing to herself that it
would not be long before she possessed him.

Chapter Four

It was just past dawn. Crystalline raindrops be-jewelled the grass and trees as the first rays of sunshine illuminated them, giving them a sparkling life of their own. Watery sunbeams filtered through the tattered curtains, forming a kaleidoscope of light patterns on the rough-hewn cabin floor with each puff of crisp morning breeze. Outside, the birds chorused a cheery melody, eager for the warm spring morning to begin after the tempest of the night just past. It was going to be a glorious day.

Indoors, in the far corner of the cabin, the man and woman slept on, oblivious to the brightness of the new day. At long length, Ellyn stirred and awoke. Surprised to find herself pressed closely to Price's warmth, she moved quickly away. As remem-brance of their passionate lovemaking came to her, her hand flew to the bodice of her dress and she frowned in confusion to find it buttoned up securely. Had she dreamed it all? His touch? His kiss? She rubbed her breast gently, noticing the slight tender-ness of the nipple. No, she hadn't been dreaming. It had all been real, too real.

With her head pounding fiercely from the afterfects of the liquor, Ellyn found coherent thought ext to impossible. She climbed off the bed, slowly, silently, making certain that she didn't disturb him. She didn't need a "morning after" confrontation right now. She needed peace and quiet and time to sort out her jumbled feelings.

Ellyn watched Price as he slept on peacefully. She had enjoyed his company so much that she'd given no thought at all to the repercussions of spending the entire night with him, alone. She'd been only concerned with how wonderfully warm and safe she'd felt. But in morning's hard light, Ellyn was worried. She forced herself to try to think logically. After all, nothing had happened. She was still a virgin. At least that was reassuring. And who was to know that she had spent the night in his arms? No one, unless they chose to tell.

Even so, by all dictates of society's rules, Ellyn had compromised herself. She'd spent the night unchaperoned with a man. The only easy way out of this awkward situation, she decided, was to make sure that Constance never found out. While her conscience was clear—nothing *really* happened, she insisted to herself again and again—it was very important to keep this from her mother, for she would surely be outraged.

Her mind made up about what to do, Ellyn nervously smoothed her dress and hair. Then, pausing, she felt herself almost compelled to look at Price again. A man she'd just slept with. A man she'd known only twenty-four hours.

As she stood there, her mind traced his features, memorizing the strong, unyielding line of his jaw, already darkened with an overnight growth of beard, the curve of his black brows, his straight nose and his full mouth. She noted dark circles beneath his eyes and wondered if he'd passed the night in pain. He looked very tired even as he rested. She watched the slow, even rise and fall of his chest and was glad that he had no fever. An infection was always dangerous and she wasn't sure just how soon her grandfather would return. Relieved that he wasn't ill, she drew a deep breath.

Ellyn was jerked from her musings by the sound of Glory mounting the porch steps. Startled into action, she met the girl at the door.

"Glory! I have to talk to you!" she whispered, nervously looking over her shoulder to see if Price was stirring. When she was certain that he was still asleep, she took Glory's hand and pulled her to the far side of the porch. "Glory, you've got to help me with something very important."

"Yes, ma'am, anything."

"You've got to promise not to let my mother know that I was here unchaperoned last night. All right?"

"Yes, ma'am, but . . ."

"Hopefully, she'll never find out," Ellyn interrupted, glancing quickly toward the open doorway. "Will you stay here with him? I've got to talk to your mother for a minute. Has she gone up to the big house yet?"

"Yes, ma'am, she went up 'bout an hour ago, but . . ."

"Thanks, I'll be back as soon as I can."

Before Glory could tell her that her mother already knew, Ellyn was off at a run, leaving the worried young girl behind shaking her head in dismay.

The first blast of sunlight that greeted Ellyn on the sun-dappled path reminded her that she had quite a headache. Poetic justice, she thought, recounting her liquor consumption. Trying to ignore the discomfort, she concentrated as best she could on what she was about to ask of Darnelle. The hurried pace she'd set for herself made her stomach queasy and halfway to the big house she was forced to slow down and breathe deeply of the sweet morning air. Somehow, Ellyn fought down her nausea. But she was so intent on convincing herself she wasn't sick that she made a tactical error. She failed to note that things were not the same as usual this morning at Riverwood House.

There was no smoke coming from the kitchen chimney. Her mother's bedroom drapes were wide open, an unusual occurrence for this time of day. Constance had a habit of sleeping late and had Ellyn noticed the parted curtains, she would have been prepared for what happened next. As it was, she entered the kitchen intent on her own private thoughts and came face to face with her very angry mother. Shocked into speechlessness, her head throbbing painfully, Ellyn waited in stunned silence for Constance to speak.

"How can you calmly enter your father's home sullied as you are?" Constance asked scathingly as Ellyn reddened at her mother's implications. Before she could respond, Constance continued, "At least you have the grace to show that you're embarrassed. You've acted in a common manner before, but never in my wildest imaginings did I think you would do something like this. My God, Ellyn Douglass, an all-night tryst with a Yankee!"

Constance came toward her and stopped abruptly, sniffing suspiciously. "Liquor? Have you been drinking, too?" she shrieked, outraged.

Ellyn winced visibly at the last accusation, confirming her guilt to her mother. She knew the evidence against her was overwhelming, but she also

71

knew that though she had spent the night with Price, her maidenhead was still intact.

"Mother," she said as calmly as possible. "Nothing happened."

"Of course you deny it! What could you possibly have to gain by admitting such an indiscretion?" Constance stormed about the room. "And what about Rod, off fighting valiantly for the cause? He expects to gain a virginal bride when he returns home," she sneered. "Where is your pride? Your sense of duty and honor?"

Irritated though she was, Ellyn knew that on the point of duty and honor, her mother was right. She had compromised herself and, were these normal times, there undoubtedly would have been a duel or a very quick, quiet wedding. But then, these were not normal times.

"I am very aware of my engagement to Rod and I have done nothing I'm ashamed of." The truth, Ellyn told herself.

Constance swelled with indignation. "You have nursed the enemy."

"The war has been over for weeks now!"

"It will never be over in the South! They may have defeated us militarily, but they will never conquer us!"

Ellyn listened half-heartedly to the tirade that she had heard so many times before, but she was caught off-guard when Constance suddenly turned her diatribe to Rod.

"How can you expect Rod, a man of honor, to want you after what has happened with this Yankee?" Constance asked hatefully.

"And just what have I done? Nursed an injured man when no one else would do it? I'd certainly want someone to help Rod if he had been hurt or captured." Ellyn's long-controlled temper flared; she didn't like being convicted for something she hadn't done.

"But," her mother retorted, "as a gentleman, he will find your conduct unforgivable."

"And who's going to tell him? You would tell him your vicious story—"

"My true story!" Constance insisted.

"And destroy the chance to unite Riverwood and Clarke's Landing?" Ellyn continued as though her mother hadn't interrupted.

"He deserves to know the truth," Constance said slyly, recalling her fantasies of Rod.

"You sound as though you love him yourself, Mother!" she challenged recklessly. "Do you?"

The words had barely left Ellyn's lips when Constance slapped her, the action one of complete frustration. She had put up with her daughter's childish bungling of situations before but she would not allow her to interfere in her plans involving Rod. She could not afford to let Ellyn follow through on that train of thought. Here and now, she had to prove to her that she had no interest in him other than as her future son-in-law.

"Your thoughts are as crude as your actions! Get your things and move into the overseer's house permanently. I want you out of here now!"

Though Ellyn had, in fact, unwittingly spoken the truth, her mother's carefully orchestrated response convinced her otherwise. Her expression inscrutable, Ellyn drew herself up to her full height and, ignoring her mother, turned to Darnelle, who had witnessed the entire scene.

"Darnelle, please tell my grandfather where I am when he returns." She eyed her mother coldly. "If you'll excuse me."

After Ellyn left the kitchen and disappeared inside the main house, Constance spoke.

"Since I had such a horrible night, I am going to my room to rest. Please see that I am not disturbed." She exited regally, a self-satisfied smile on her lips.

Her mind spinning, Constance entered her bedroom, closing the door behind her. It was almost *too* perfect. Things couldn't have gone any better. Ellyn was *so* predictable, she thought drolly. Moving to her bed, she kicked off her low-heeled slippers and lay down. Constance knew beyond a doubt that Ellyn was still a virgin, but that didn't really matter, not anymore. Ellyn was the only obstacle between Constance and her desire and as such she had to be removed. Constance grinned evilly. She would see to it personally that, upon his return home, Rod was made aware of her behavior. Truly, Ellyn had forfeited the right to his devotion by her indiscretions. And, now that she was banished from the big house, who knew how many nights she would be spending alone with the Yankee? And what trouble she could get herself into? Stretching lazily, Constance relaxed, her once-troubled mind now set on a definite plan of action.

At the far end of the hall in her own bedroom, Ellyn stood staring out the window at the budding Tennessee farmland. Below in the overgrown gardens the dogwood and magnolia were in full bloom, their pink and white blossoms sweetly scenting the air, and she breathed deeply of their fragrance. Her enjoyment was short-lived, however, as she felt once again the sting of her mother's hand. She touched her cheek gingerly. They had argued many times but never before had her mother lost control. Ellyn felt contrite and knew that she had been impudent in her

74

accusations. While they did disagree on most things, Constance was her parent and as such deserving of at least Ellyn's respect. Sighing heavily, she knew the only logical thing to do was to beat a tactical retreat and await her grandfather's return. Maybe he would be able to straighten everything out. He'd always helped her before and Ellyn hoped this time would be no exception.

Price entered her thoughts gently, the sensation almost like a warm embrace. She smiled tenderly as she remembered their hours together. But her mother had placed a seed of doubt in her mind. Could she trust Price or would he take advantage of her situation? So far, she had managed to retain her virtue, but could she keep it if he tried to make love to her again? She knew that she had responded to him wildly, passionately. Yet, how much had been her true feelings and how much had been the liquor? For Ellyn knew without a doubt that she had had far too much to drink last night. Only time would tell, but she was more than a little afraid at what the answer might be. She wondered, too, what he would say when he saw her again. Would he think her a woman of loose morals or would he understand what had really happened between them?

She turned from the window and began packing the few remaining items she needed in a small carpetbag. In the past few days, the dismal life she'd been leading had disappeared. In its place had come a chaotic existence that challenged everything she'd ever been taught about genteel living. But who was left to care if you obeyed the rules or not? Ellyn was confused. Her grandfather had told her that survival was all that mattered. He'd told her to trust in her own judgment and do what she thought was right. She had followed her instincts and yet now she was disowned by her own mother and forced from her family home. Reviewing her actions of the past thirty-six hours, Ellyn knew, given the choice, that she would do the same things again. No longer questioning herself, she squared her shoulders in an unconscious gesture of determination, picked up her bag, and left the house.

In the years before the war, the trip from Memphis to Riverwood was a long but pleasant one. The roadway had been well-maintained and had been bordered by fertile, thriving fields, magnificent plantation houses and the Mississippi River—sometimes distant, sometimes close, but always eye-catching in its splendor. There was nothing splendid about it this morning though, as it edged ever closer to what little was left of Riverwood Road. Dangerous was a better description, destructive. Franklin eyed the muddy, ugly waters warily as he plodded home on the back of ol' Mo. Another heavy rain like they'd had the night before and there'd be no travel in or out of Riverwood.

He dismissed the idea as something beyond his control and glanced up the hill to his right. All that was left of Clarke's Landing stood at the top of that rise. Where once the white, three-story frame house had been stood only a crumbling brick foundation. The spacious country home had burned the year before and now nature was reclaiming her own. With no one left to tend them, the manicured lawns that had surrounded Clarke's Landing had disappeared, overtaken by an eager attack of uncontrolled weeds. Amid the wild growth an occasional splash of color indicated the remaining presence of one of Mrs. Clarke's carefully chosen flowering plants. Her garden had been the most prized in all the county, but now it, too, lay ruined, strangled by the overgrowth of brush.

Franklin knew that the fate of the Clarkes was similar to that of many Southern families. The menfolk had gone off to war, leaving the women and children behind. Some managed to hold things together, like Miz Ellyn, but old Mrs. Clarke, her husband many years dead, had been alone and had abandoned her home in favor of living with relatives in town. He'd heard that she'd died last year, about the same time that the house had burned. Shaking his head in sympathy, Franklin knew Rod Clarke had his work cut out for him when he returned.

Prodding the mule around a fallen tree, a victim of the fury of last night's storm, Franklin and ol' Mo began the final stretch toward home. Sensing Riverwood and rest at last, the beast picked up his pace, jarring his rider to the bone with his uneven gait. Franklin tightened his grip and thought miserably of what he'd seen in town.

He'd gone to the riverfront first and, after meeting some of the roustabouts he'd known before the war, soon had all the gruesome facts. The *Sultana* had been grossly overloaded with Union soldiers and her boilers let loose north of town. Once Memphis had known of the disaster she'd done all she could, but rescue operations had been hampered by the darkness. Rumor had it that barely a third of the passengers had survived, but there was no real way of finding out for no accurate boarding lists had been made.

A line of unadorned pine coffins seemed to stretch endlessly on the Memphis wharf, but that bleak reminder had seemed sterile compared to what Franklin had seen next. While he questioned men on the riverfront about Jericho Cooper, a small boat had tied up and begun to unload more victims of the explosion. Bloated and disfigured, the bodies had been found floating in the river south of Memphis. The sight was a horror that would stay with him the rest of his life.

Having no success in finding Jericho Cooper or any information about him, Franklin had gone to the hospitals, beginning with the one where Mr. Lawrence worked. The old physician had been working ceaselessly since arriving in town early the day before and had been glad for the chance to take a short break to visit with Franklin. After telling Mr. Lawrence of Miz Ellyn's rescue of the soldier, an act of which he heartily approved, they had gone over the hospital roles together, but had found no listing for Jericho Cooper. Mr. Lawrence had encouraged Franklin to check the other hospitals, but not to be too discouraged if there was no trace of him. The injured survivors had been leaving town as soon as possible on other boats and most of the dead and injured had had no identification on them, having lost all during the tragedy, including their clothes. Mr. Lawrence had given Franklin money for food in case his search took longer than expected and had returned to his ward to help the burned and mutilated men who had been pulled from the jaws of death.

Franklin saw the front gates of Riverwood and ol' Mo picked up his pace even more. No, this had not been a fun trip for him. His quest had been in vain for there had been no Jericho Cooper in any of the hospitals or among the identifiable dead. He hoped Miz Ellyn wouldn't be too disappointed in him or in the fact that he'd been forced by the storm to spend the night in Memphis with Mr. Lawrence. Franklin saw Ellyn as she was coming down the gallery steps and his call caught her attention. She waved and, dropping her bag, ran to greet him.

"Franklin!" Her voice was breathless. "I am so glad you're back!"

"Ah's sorry Ah couldn't get back las' night, but de storm. . ."

"Oh, I know," she agreed. "It was a bad one and you were wise to wait it out in town. How was your ride? The road?"

"It's mud, all mud. One mo' bad rain lak' dat one, Miz Ellyn, and dere won't be no gettin' in or out of Riverwood."

"I was afraid of that. The river's really that high?"

"Yes, ma'am."

They were silent for a moment as Ellyn looked anxiously up at the now-blue sky.

"Did you manage to see Grandfather?"

"Sho' did. Ah spent de night wid him at de hospital."

"Good. How is he? Is he coming home soon?"

"He wasn't sure, Miz Ellyn, de hospital is so crowded. He didn't know jes' how soon he'd be back."

Ellyn felt greatly disappointed at that news. Now she would have to continue to deal with her situation on her own and just pray that he would return quickly.

"What about Mr. Cooper?" she asked after a moment's pause. "Did you find him?"

"No, ma'am. Ah done checked de riverfront and all de hospitals. Mr. Lawrence, he say dat too many soldiers died with no identification. He tol' me dat de healthy ones done gone on upriver and de res' too sick to know who dey is."

"It must be terrible in town," she said with a shudder.

"All de hospitals full and de riverfront . . ." he stopped, remembering the scene there.

"What was happening down there?"

"Dat's where dey was linin' up de coffins. Seem lak' dere was hundreds of 'em," he answered, skirting the real reason for the horror he felt.

Ellyn knew that it was a good thing she'd gotten Price out of the tree or he too might be occupying one of those caskets. As they neared the house, she picked up her case and turned to him.

"I'm sure you're tired and hungry. Darnelle was in the kitchen last time I saw her, so why don't you get something to eat and rest awhile? I'll just go on back and relieve Glory. She's been staying with Mr. Richardson while I was up here."

"How's he feelin'?"

"Last night he seemed better. He was still asleep when I left him this morning."

"Good. Mr. Lawrence, he done tol' me to tell you dat you done jes' fine gettin' him out of de river."

The unexpected vote of confidence buoyed her flagging spirits and she smiled brightly.

"I'll see you later, Franklin. And, Franklin?" she said as he started up the steps after tying up the mule.

"Yes, ma'am?"

"Thanks."

Franklin shook his head in wonder as she moved off quickly. Turning, he hurried inside to find his wife.

Ellyn's steps were almost lighthearted as she walked down the path and she even took a moment to pick a few sprays of wild roses, thinking their brilliance and sweet scent would help brighten the otherwise dreary cabin. Knowing that she had her grandfather's approval for her rescue effort helped to cheer her and she hoped she would have his moral support, too. She would ignore her mother's accusations for the time being. And if Constance did tell Rod when he returned, well, she would worry about that then. There was nothing more she could do now.

Dismissing all worrisome thoughts, Ellyn instead concentrated on her plans for the day, making mental lists of all she had to do. Happily, she noted that her headache was gone and she found that singularly amazing considering the morning she'd just passed. She was thankful that she would face Price for the first time this morning with a clear head.

From his seat in an old rocker on the cabin's porch, Price watched her approach. She seemed carefree and he wondered at her quixotic smile. Ellyn wore the same dress as the night before and her long, dark hair was still tied back in the single, heavy braid, but Price sensed a change in her. Perhaps it was the way she was walking, as if she hadn't a worry, or maybe it was the wildflowers she clutched so dearly in her hand. He didn't know exactly why but for some reason he was seeing a different woman today and, if it were possible, he liked this one even more.

"Good morning, pretty lady," he called, and he smiled when she looked up. She appeared startled by his greeting. Her reaction reminded him of a doe in the forest—first wary at an unexpected noise and then relaxing as she sensed no danger.

"Good morning, sir. I fear you are too kind with

your compliments," she told him as she climbed the porch steps.

"As you come to know me, Ellyn, you'll learn that I am not loose with compliments. I say only what I really think, always," he spoke in a gentle serious tone, emphasizing the last word.

Ellyn was touched by the warm feeling of intimacy between them, as if they'd shared much more than just a bed last night. She glanced at him quickly, wanting to read his expression, but whatever he was really feeling was masked by an amused look. His dark eyes twinkled and his chiseled lips quirked in a teasing half-smile. It was as though he'd known her thoughts and was determined to keep her off balance. Price had in fact accomplished this and Ellyn knew she had to keep the conversation more impersonal or she'd be lost. She wasn't quite sure how to take him. She had tried to anticipate how he would react but she had never expected this casual, confiding manner from him. Ellyn had thought it a good possibility that he might have lost all respect for her. But here he was, devilishly handsome even in his ill-fitting clothes, treating her as a friend. That sudden thought made her feel even more happy and she smiled.

"Thank you for the compliment, then," she said, pleased.

He grinned at the sudden easing of her manner. "You're welcome. Are the flowers for me? I've never had a woman bring me flowers before. I always thought it was the man who brought the gifts when you're courting." He almost laughed aloud at her stunned expression, but managed to smother it behind a very phony cough.

"Yes . . . er, uh, no. I mean they're for the house. I thought it could use a little brightening up." Ellyn was staring at him, trying to figure him out and wondering at the same time if his bad cough was a sign that he was getting sick. "Are you feeling all right? Your head and arm?"

"I'm just fine. I felt so good that I had to come outside. Glory helped me drag this old chair out and here I am. I'm not one for staying indoors on a sunny day."

"Good," she replied, taking in how easily he ws sitting up and the healthy gleam in his eyes. "Where's Glory?"

"She went to work in the garden about half an hour ago." When Ellyn looked a little irritated, he added, "Now don't be angry with her. I talked her into it. She told me that you'd instructed her to stay with me, but I was feeling so much stronger that I didn't see the need for someone to hover over me. Shall we put those in water?" he asked, coming to his feet.

Before she could reply, Price took the flowers from her and ushered her inside. While she set her bag down, he rummaged with his free hand through the cupboard and found a small jar.

"I've found a priceless vase, can you get the water?" he asked over his shoulder as he worked awkwardly to get the stems in the container. "Ouch!"

"What's wrong?" Ellyn said worriedly, hurrying to his side with the water pitcher. "Are you hurt?"

"Worse than that, I'm bleeding!" He held up his thorn-pricked finger. "I've already lost the use of one hand, I can't afford to injure my other!"

"I think you'll be amazed at how fast you recover from this wound." She grinned up at him.

Ellyn handed him a small handkerchief and he wiped off the blood.

"It's just like everything in life," he said mysteriously.

"What is?"

"Roses. Anytime anything is beautiful and worth having, there's pain involved."

They stood close to each other and as Ellyn looked up at him, their eyes met and held. She could feel the heat of his body and, through his gaze, the heat of his soul.

"Are you like that, pretty lady?" His words were spoken softly.

He bent nearer and their lips met, tenderly, softly, as though he expected, at any moment, to feel the sudden sting of a hidden thorn. He had worried that she would be angry with him when she returned. He was greatly relieved that she was not. And though Price wanted to take her in his arms and make passionate love to her, to finish what had been started last night, he broke off the kiss, satisfied with his small victory. She had accepted his embrace freely and that was step one. For Price Richardson had decided that for the first time in his life, he had found a woman worth marrying and he intended to have her. He'd spent all morning going over the time they'd been together, and he knew that she was one special woman. Ellyn was brave, intelligent, easy to look upon and just independent enough to keep life interesting. Price wasn't sure how attached she was to this Rod character, but he was going to find out. She was a prize worth winning and when Price decided he wanted something, he did his level best to get it. All was fair in love and war and as a captain in the cavalry, he'd had plenty of battlefield experience. In Ellyn's case a full frontal assault would never work, he would have to win her subtly by planning his strategy and waiting for the moment when her defenses were down.

"Good morning. I was disappointed to find you'd gone when I woke up," he told her, his tone warm with remembered desire.

She had been standing, her head still tilted as though receiving his kiss, mesmerized by his touch and voice, when his insinuating words washed over her like cold water. Ellyn wasn't sure how to react. It was certainly unchivalrous of him to refer to their night together in those terms.

"Sir," she said icily, as all of her mother's hateful words came to surface and broke the spell he'd cast over her. "What happened here last night was an accident. I was . . . um, I overimbibed and you took advantage of my condition!"

She knew even as she spoke that it was all a lie. Well, she had been more than a little tipsy. That part was the truth. She just hoped that she would make him angry enough to leave her alone. The one small kiss they'd just shared had proven to her that it had not been the liquor that had made her want him. She was afraid—afraid of him and of herself, because she did want him so badly. Ellyn watched him from beneath lowered lashes, waiting to see his expression change from tenderness to irritation, but to her surprise, he laughed. And Ellyn, shocked by his mirth, stalked to her bag and pretended interest in unpacking it.

"Oh, Ellyn, you are wonderful." He sighed, coming up behind her and pulling her back against him. He held her there easily, his good arm encircling her beneath her breasts.

"Please let me go," she stated sternly, trying not to lean wearily against the firm comfort of his chest.

"So, you ran into trouble up at the big house?" he

asked, thinking—the thorn.

"Yes—no—" She glared over her shoulder at him, wondering how he could know so much.

"Ellyn," he said softly, turning her to him. "The truth?"

She tried to avoid his probing gaze, looking everywhere but at him.

"Ellyn," Price repeated, his tone brooking no denial. "Tell me."

She sighed and the fight went out of her. A small voice in the back of her mind teased her unmercifully with the knowledge that she had met her match. She had fallen hopelessly in love with a man who was not her fiance, yet who could make her wild with desire for him with just a touch. He was everything that Rod was not—easygoing and gentle, with an inborn kindness that she'd only known before in her father. And yet, she knew that she had to deny her passion for him.

Ellyn bravely met his eyes. "What would you like to know? That my own mother has judged and condemned me for spending the night with you? That she accused me of every kind of lurid behavior? Well, she has."

"Does it matter so much? Her opinion? I know I didn't take you and so do you," he said softly, tenderly caressing her cheek. "Is it important?"

Ellyn looked miserable. "She said that she was going to tell Rod."

Price stiffened. "Ah, the elusive fiance. I wondered when I'd be hearing about him."

"But it's important."

"Why? Do you love him?" Price virtually demanded, repeating himself when she didn't answer immediately. "Ellyn, I asked you if you loved him!"

"Well, of course I do! After all, we're to be

married," she said quickly, hating each deceiving word.

"So you spent all those hours in my arms imagining that I was Rod?" he pressed, merciless in his quest to know her true feelings.

"No! That's not true!" she denied vehemently and was caught in his trap. This was happening too fast!

"I thought not," Price stated matter-of-factly, pleased to know that at least she reponded to him physically.

Ellyn glared up at him. She wondered if he was being smug, but decided not. He had no reason to be. But he was wrong in thinking that her life was simple, that she could do as she pleased. It wasn't that easy. Nothing was ever black and white—there were always those complex shades of gray that influenced every decision.

"Tell me about Rod," price insisted.

"Why?"

"Because I want to know." His tone softened. "I need to know."

At his blatant honesty, she relented. "He owns Clarke's Landing."

"Clarke's Landing?"

"The plantation next to ours."

"Oh."

"The plan has been to unite Riverwood and Clarke's Landing so we'd be the biggest plantation in the state."

"Whose plan?" Price had found the weakness he'd been looking for.

"My father's, of course. And Rod's."

"Hasn't the war changed all that?" he asked logically. "I mean, you don't even have the money to keep Riverwood running. How could you possibly hope to take on Clarke's Landing, too?"

"Well, with Rod's help . . ."

"Rod must be a very rich, miracle worker then," Price concluded.

Ellyn was faced with a future the truth about which she'd avoided, until now. Things were not ever going to be the same. She had managed to make it so far by concentrating on her day-to-day tasks and hoping for Rod's return. Unlike her mother, Ellyn didn't react to this with hate. She just felt very tired and very sad.

"Ellyn," Price was saying, claiming her attention once more. "If he invested everything he had in Confederate bonds, well, they're not worth the paper they're printed on."

"Why are you doing this?" she asked him tearfully, feeling as though she'd been defeated.

"Because I care about you. I need to know what it is you want. Do you want to keep on working yourself every day until you drop? And for what? So you can be torn apart by an ungrateful mother who has no idea what true gentility really is?"

"Stop! Just stop!" she cried furiously, wiping away her tears.

"Stop what? Telling you the truth? It's time you faced it. Rod may not get back, ever."

And the painful possibility that she'd dreaded for the past twelve months was finally out in the open.

"Ellyn, do you love him?" Price asked her again quickly, diverting her from the depressing realization she'd just faced.

He knew that if she answered his question as a woman in love, then he would stop. If she truly loved the man that her family had chosen for her, he would respect and honor her feelings and commitment. But everything he'd managed to learn from earlier that morning indicated differently. He waited with agonizing patience.

"Do you?" he coached, her hesitation telling him everything he wanted to know.

"We are engaged. I care for him deeply," she replied, turning from him and moving away, aware that Price now knew the truth.

Price had his answer. The nervousness he'd felt at pushing her this way drained from him, leaving him exhausted, but pleased. He watched her for a moment while she toyed with the roses, then he walked to the bed. Fiance be damned, he was going to win her.

"I fear I've been up too long. I'd better rest for a while," he spoke to her back as he lay down.

Ellyn nodded and went out onto the porch. She needed time to think, to get her life straightened out, away from his influence. She found Glory and instructed her to bring Price his lunch. Then Ellyn set to work catching up on all she'd not had time for yesterday. The peace and happiness she'd felt earlier was gone, destroyed by Price's disturbing questions.

It was near sunset when Ellyn finally started back to the overseer's house . . . and Price. Despite the firm resolutions she had made to herself that afternoon, Ellyn couldn't suppress the excitement she felt at the thought of seeing him again. The hours since she'd left him had passed quickly. She'd worked alongside Glory in the garden putting in the sweet potatoes that would feed them in the fall. They'd been happy to see the small quantity of corn they'd planted was already up and they both hoped the pumpkin and watermelon vines would soon make a healthy appearance. At least, Ellyn thought, they'd have some food this summer. When she'd stopped at the big house for a minute, Darnelle had insisted she bathe and change. So, carefully avoiding Constance, Ellyn had been allowed the luxury of a quick bath. Clean and relaxed, she'd been sent on her way with enough food for their dinner. Now with her arms laden with food, she was determined to have a long discussion with Price.

She had decided, during her long hours toiling with Glory, that she must not become involved with him. Ellyn was sure that the only reason he cared for her was because she had saved him from the river. And although it was admirable of him to think he could help, all he'd succeeded in doing was to complicate her life. No, she didn't want anything from him. But she would take his friendship, if it was offered, and then only if it was given freely with no sense of obligation.

She didn't deny that she liked Price and found him very attractive, but Ellyn had convinced herself that she couldn't possibly love him. After all, you just didn't fall in love *that* fast. No, it was an infatuation brought on by loneliness and once he was gone, she'd be fine. The longing she felt for him would disappear. Out of sight, out of mind. Determined that she had thought it through correctly, she went to see him again and wondered why her heart was pounding so.

When she came within sight of the small house and he wasn't waiting for her on the porch, she felt disappointed. But her disappointment turned to anger. Why should she care if he was there or not? She stomped up the steps and went in, surprised to find Price deep in conversation with Franklin. At her sudden appearance, the discussion stopped and silence fell upon them.

"Good evening," he offered.

"Good evening," she returned nervously. "I've got your supper here."

"Wonderful, I am hungry." He moved toward her. "Franklin was just telling me about how things were in Memphis."

Ellyn paled, turning to face him. "I'm sorry, I had every intention of telling you his news this morning, but . . ."

"This morning was just a little hectic, don't you think?" He smiled at her tenderly.

"Yes. Yes, it was that."

"Ah be goin' now, Miz Ellyn, Mr. Price."

"Fine, Franklin."

"Thank you, Franklin, for all your help," Price told him as he left.

"Yes, suh."

Ellyn busily set out the food on the table near the bed while Price watched Franklin disappear up the path.

"Ready?" she asked, and he came to sit on the bed.

"How was your day?" he inquired conversationally.

"Fine." Her answer was noncommittal. "Price, we have to talk."

"I know. Things are not as I would like them to be between us."

"That's what I mean. There is no *us*," she insisted, and he merely quirked an eyebrow at her. Ellyn looked nervously away from him. "You expect too much of me."

"And you expect too much of me," he retorted. "You almost make love to me, you sleep in my arms all night and yet you expect me to pretend it never happened?" Price stood up and stalked away from her. "I can't act that well, in fact, I'm not

91

even a very good liar. You won't play any games with me!"

"I am not playing any games with you. I just want to be left alone."

The words had barely escaped her when Price hauled her to her feet and pulled her into his arms. His mouth covered hers before she could protest and he kissed her violently, punishing her for refusing to acknowledge what lay between them. But Price knew that pain would not win her, so he softened his kiss. He pressed sensuously against her, wanting to feel her surrender. And surrender she did at the first lessening of force in his embrace. Looping her arms willingly around his neck, she clung to him, craving his touch, needing it. But abruptly he let her go.

"Can you deny what you feel? Can't you sense it between us?"

"Yes, oh, yes," she sighed, almost collapsing against him.

Price gently pushed her back into her chair.

"Now, my dear, what did you want to talk about?" Humor glinted in his eyes as he watched her compose herself.

"What do you want from me?"

"Only what you're prepared to give."

"But . . ."

"Sleep on it, Ellyn. Maybe in the morning things will seem less confusing."

They finished eating in silence.

"Franklin prepared a bed for you upstairs."

"Oh, good." She was relieved.

"I thought you'd be pleased," he teased.

She ignored his taunt. "Why don't you lay down and I'll change your bandages."

While he shed his shirt, he thought, a trifle wickedly, that if she knew how much he wanted to feel her hands on him, she wouldn't be quite so willing to check his wounds. Price smiled benignly at her and stretched out on the bed.

"You're awfully agreeable," she told him as she got her medical supplies.

"For you, anything."

Ellyn suppressed a smile and felt the tension between them lesson. Kneeling beside him, she carefully unwrapped the bandages that covered his burns.

"What do you think, doc?" he asked as she examined him.

"They look much better today. Darnelle's salve does work wonders."

"It doesn't feel too bad, either," Price told her, looking at his arm.

"We'd better keep it covered for at least one more day, though," she said as she reapplied the salve and wrapped the wound in a clean, soft dressing.

When she innocently leaned across him to check his splint, Price couldn't pass up the opportunity to hug her to him.

"Price!" she gasped in surprise, pinned to his naked chest. "Let me go!"

"Pretty lady, do you have any idea how good it feels to have your hands on my body?"

Ellyn blushed. "Stop, I still have to take a look at that cut on your forehead." She pushed ineffectually against his chest. "Price!"

"I'll make a deal with you—an exchange. A kiss for your freedom."

"You'll really let me go?"

"Yes, I'll really let you go," he repeated teasingly. Then he added in more serious tones, "Just make sure it's a good one."

She gave him a condescending look, joining him in

his playfulness. "As if any of my kisses wouldn't be good. All right, it's a deal, but you'll have to loosen up a bit."

Wiggling slightly free, she bent toward his mouth, just grazing his chest with the bodice of her dress. Their lips met and parted, tasting of each other deeply as Price sought to bend her will to his. Panting, Ellyn broke off the kiss and rested on his shoulder, not wanting to move away from him.

"I have such a desire to hold you again as I did last night—with your bare breasts crushed against me." He groaned. "You'd better get on with your doctoring or I'm going to find some other activities to keep us busy."

Ellyn moved quickly from his side and tended his head wound as Price congratulated himself on his self-control.

"It's healing quite nicely," she told him. "If you're careful we can leave the bandage off."

"That suits me fine. I did feel a bit like an Egyptian mummy," he said and Ellyn laughed. "Don't laugh. I saw one once and this is what they really looked like. Well, almost."

"Where did you see it?"

"In an exposition at the St. Louis Museum before the war. You'd have liked it."

"I would have," Ellyn agreed enthusiastically. "Did you travel a lot then?"

"Only on business. I had to make regular trips to St. Louis and St. Charles, but other than that I didn't feel the need to. I had everything I wanted right at home, so why bother?"

"That's true. And now, since you enlisted, you've probably seen more than you ever wanted to, to begin with."

"Nobody really wanted to go, we knew it

94

wouldn't be fun. But I never expected it to last this long. I don't think anyone did."

"You're right, my father said it'd only last a month, two at the most . . . ." Her voice trailed off and the silence that followed hung heavily for long minutes until the sound of footsteps brought them both back to reality.

"Darnelle, I am so glad to see you," Ellyn told her as the older woman entered, her arms full of blankets.

"Franklin done tol' me that he made up some beds upstairs and Ah come to stay wid you."

"Thank you," Ellyn said appreciatively.

"Well, after dis mornin', Ah knew Ah couldn't leave you all alone ag'in tonight," she said confidingly. "You Mr. Richardson? Ah'm Darnelle, Franklin's wife."

"Pleased to meet you and thanks for all you've done to help Ellyn," Price said earnestly.

Darnelle flushed at his praise. "She knows Ah do whatever Ah can to help. She done helped us enough."

"I think I'm ready to go up, if you are."

"Yes, ma'am. Ah'm tuckered out tonight," Darnelle said, picking up a lamp and starting up the rickety staircase.

"I'll be right there."

"Fine."

When she'd disappeared at the top of the stairs, Ellyn turned to Price. "Shall I leave a lamp burning?"

"No, but do put it here by the bed, just in case."

"All right." She knelt to place the lamp on the floor by him and started to get up, when he grasped her hand.

"Price," she whispered, looking nervously at the steps.

"Just one more thing."

"What?"

"Open your hand," he said and she did. He turned her palm up and placed a warm, intimate kiss there. Then he closed her hand. "Save it for later—when you're thinking of me."

Her breath was short and her heart pounded crazily as she looked into the smoldering depths of his dark eyes.

"Good night, Ellyn."

"Good night, Price," she said and hurried toward the stairs.

"Oh, and Ellyn?"

"Yes?"

"Sweet dreams. I'll see you in the morning."

"Good night," she said hastily and she fled upstairs, her emotions in a turmoil.

Price, on the contrary, chuckled to himself and blew out the light, ready for his first good night's sleep in what seemed like ages.

Chapter Five

It was morning at last and the new day hadn't come a moment too soon as far as Ellyn was concerned. She had tossed and turned all night trying to deal with the yearnings of her heart. What little sleep she'd managed had been fitful and she felt even more tired now than she had at bedtime. The wandering, disjointed thoughts of her exhausted mind lingered briefly on her carefree childhood. How she longed for those simple days when her biggest concern had been how to sneak away from her mother in order to spend more time outdoors. There had always been someone to protect and guide her then and to make all of the major decisions. It had all been so easy for her—too easy, for it was one of those pronouncements that had resulted in the confusion of her life today. Her parents had determined that she should marry Rod and she, in all naivete, had agreed without thought.

Ellyn rolled over, sighing. She cast a quick glance at Darnelle, who she thought was asleep on the other pallet next to hers, and was surprised to find Darnelle watching her with knowing eyes.

"You sho' kept me 'wake all night wid your rollin'

around,'' she told her, trying not to smile.

"Oh, I'm sorry," Ellyn began.

"Chile, doan' you worry none. Mr. Richardson is one fine lookin' man."

"Darnelle!" Ellyn was scandalized to hear her own thoughts spoken aloud.

"Honey, Ah knows 'xactly what you feelin'," Darnelle spoke boldly, openly, realizing that Ellyn had very little experience with men and love and that there was no one to guide her, for certainly she could not go to Constance.

Ellyn blushed. "Am I that obvious?"

"No."

"Good," she sighed, relieved. "I don't know how to handle this. I've never felt this way before."

"Miz Ellyn, why you hafta do anything? Jes' let nature take its course."

"But, Darnelle, you know I'm engaged to Rod."

"Yes, ma'am, but he aint' here. He could be dead. Mr. Richardson is mighty alive and he cares about you."

"How do you know?"

"Ah kin tell by how he looks at you. Why, dat man's eyes are all over you all de time."

"Oh." Ellyn stopped, marveling at Darnelle's observation. "Really?" A warm, loving smile curved her lips.

"Yes, ma'am. He wants you in de worst way. And 'pears to me he's the kind of man what gets what he wants," Darnelle finished sagely.

"But Rod . . ."

"You ain't married to him yet, chile," Darnelle spoke common sense.

"I know, but . . ."

"Miz Ellyn, would you be happy married to Mr. Rod now that you done met Mr. Richardson?"

Ellyn sighed, she knew the answer to that question all too well. "Thank you, Darnelle."

"You jes' do what makes you happy, all right?"

Ellyn smiled brightly up at her. "I guess we better get up."

"Ah know Ah better, you mama doan' know Ah spent de night here. Why doan' you try to sleep jes' a little mo'. Ah knows you needs it."

Ellyn felt more relaxed now than she had all night and she lay back, wishing for once that she really was a lady of leisure.

"I think I will, for another hour or so," Ellyn said contentedly.

"Good. When you is ready for breakfast you let me know."

"Thanks, Darnelle . . . for everything."

"You sho' is welcome. Ah jes' like you to be happy, Miz Ellyn. Ain't been no happiness 'round here for ages," she responded as she started quietly down the creaky stairs.

Ellyn heard Darnelle's footsteps as she left the house and, feeling oddly comforted, pulled a blanket over her shoulder and turned on her side, thinking of how she'd just rest another hour.

Price heard someone coming downstairs and feigned sleep. He was so intent on the dream he'd just had of Ellyn that he wasn't quite ready to talk to anyone yet. He watched Darnelle leave the cabin through slitted eyes, glad to be alone again. But quickly the thought came, Where was Ellyn? Had she gone before he'd awakened? He lay still, but heard no further movement upstairs. Damn! he thought to himself. He'd wanted to see her sometime this morning, if for no other reason than to tease her about spending another night together. Price rested, reviewing his sensuous dream of the night just past. God, he wanted her so badly. The determination to win her gripped him anew and he knew somehow he would have her for his own.

Long minutes passed. Outside the birds chirped noisily, eagerly greeting another fresh spring day. Price rose, no longer content to lay abed. He got cleaned up and was about to go outside when he heard something upstairs. Stopping in midstride he waited, his own breathing harsh in his ears. When no further sounds came, he decided to investigate, hoping against hope that Ellyn was still up there, asleep.

Price mounted the rickety steps, taking care not to make any noise. The second-floor hall was dirty and unkempt and he felt a pang of guilt that the women had been forced to spend the night under these conditions. But all such thoughts flew from his mind when he entered the bedroom. This sight of Ellyn actually there, asleep on the pallet was more erotic than the dream he'd had of her. She lay on her side clad only in her chemise, a blanket twisted about her hips. Her breasts were barely contained by the garment that had been made for her before she had matured. Her hair was unbound and it fell silkily about her. He swallowed nervously, trying valiantly to refrain from touching her, but the temptation was too great. He shed his shirt and stretched out beside her, being sure not to disturb her. Price wanted to savor this moment for as long as possible. He gazed upon her, feasting his eyes on her flawless features, particularly her slightly parted lips. The desire to kiss her awake was almost overpowering, but he held back, not knowing how she would react. Reaching out, he toyed with the top button of her chemise and was a most surprised and delighted man when it unbuttoned, seemingly of its own will. With that little bit of freedom, her breasts came close to spilling forth. Price was eager to expose them, for her nipples were still hidden from him, but he waited, enjoying instead the sense of power at having her body unresisting and open to his inspection.

Ellyn lay sound asleep, unaware of the man at her side. The long sleepless hours of the night before, when she'd clutched his "saved" kiss in her hand, had taken their toll. She did not awaken.

Price fingered the second button on her bodice. He could feel the heat of her and all the maleness in him demanded he caress the smooth, white flesh. Denying his instincts, he worked at that next restriction until it, too, gave way and the fullness of her bosom was exposed. As her breasts lay temptingly uncovered, the tightness of her chemise beneath them seemed to press them upward and his breath caught in his throat at the sight of their beauty. He wanted to kiss their pink peaks to hardness, to caress them with his mouth and tongue, but he paused watching to see if she was waking.

Ellyn stirred but only to roll onto her back, flinging an arm up over her head. She murmured something and was soon deep in her dreams of Price again.

Price delighted in having the freedom to explore her, if only with his eyes. He had dreamed of the time when he could take her as his own. He had already done it in his mind and now it was just a matter of actually having her. Price knew his will to resist the unconsciously made offering of her breasts was fading. He could no longer control the urge to touch her, to delve into every mystery of her now-passive body. His body surged to life with the need to penetrate her, to feel her tight, virginal wetness hold him within, making them one. But he knew that what would happen this morning must happen slowly, naturally, if it was to be savored to the fullest. Ellyn was not just a body to be used and discarded. She was an unaroused, inexperienced virgin and he would take care so that when the moment came she would want it, too.

Gently, he touched her breast and watched with pleasure as the nipple hardened against his fingers. Unable to stop, not even wanting to at this point, Price leaned over her and kissed the peak, drawing it into his mouth and sucking it to erection.

Ellyn felt the moist, hot drawing at her breast and knew she was dreaming of Price again. She had been haunted by the feel of his mouth on her since the night he'd first touched her there. It was an exquisite agony that coursed through her almost nude body and pulsed to life between her thighs. Not awake, she instinctively tightened her legs and was glad that the blanket was there giving her added pressure to ease that aching desire. She murmured his name, relishing the suckling at first one nipple then the other. To Ellyn, this was her most wonderful dream ever and she arched her back sensuously, moving her hips at the same time.

Price drew back quickly, lest he forgot himself and bury himself within her depths. He paused, breathing heavily, and watched Ellyn's unsuspecting reaction.

Her head thrown back in sleep-dimmed ecstasy, she whispered his name and wondered why the marvelous sensations had ceased. Eyes closed, she ran her hands over her bosom and touched herself between her legs. The ache went on, growing stronger by the minute and somehow at that point, she came fully awake, realizing that what she was feeling was no fantasy.

"Oh, Price," she breathed, seeing him beside her. "Please, oh, please."

And the victor was the vanquished as he gave himself up to the longing he'd held in check all this time. He kissed her, moving atop her, fitting himself to her as intimately as possible. Instinctively she thrust her hips to his, encouraging his possession and Price responded, matching her movements. Breaking off the kiss, he shed his pants and then finished unbuttoning her chemise, pushing it easily from her. Finally, she was naked beneath him and he delighted in the feel of her silken thighs pressed to his. He caressed her breasts and then gently explored the essence of her femininity.

Ellyn was lost in the wonder of Price's embrace. Surrendering herself to his ardent touch, she knew she would not resist anything he chose to do to her. It was too late. She needed the satisfaction only he could give her—body and soul.

Kissing her deeply, he positioned himself and entered her as slowly as was possible for him. Ellyn tried to escape his tender assault only momentarily and then she was swept up by the intensity of the emotion that life's greatest commitment afforded. His carefully checked movements, though torture for him, were heavenly for Ellyn. Arms clasping him to her, she looked up at him in awe of the sensations he inspired. The slight discomfort she'd felt when he'd first entered her had passed and now she only felt a drugging sense of ecstasy. Ellyn pulled his head down to hers and kissed him aggressively, giving free reign to the passionate woman within her.

Price was overcome by her response to him. He thrust eagerly into her and she matched his rhythm with abandon. They gained their mutual release in a crescendo of passion that left Ellyn marveling at the wonders of her own body and Price more firmly convinced than ever that she was his.

It was the noisy morning sounds of the chattering birds that brought them both back to awareness. Price lifted himself above her and kissed her sweetly. Ellyn responded, but guardedly. Her whole being was in a furor of confusion, stunned by what had just happened. It had been so wonderful, she thought, and so wrong, her conscious added. She shivered involuntarily.

"Cold?" Price asked softly, dipping his head to kiss her throat. He was pleased when he felt her nipples harden against his chest. "Does this feel good?"

Ellyn couldn't speak. She was torn between the growing desire to have him again and the puritanical need to break away from his embrace and chastise herself unmercifully. Price had taken the gift of her innocence and yet had made no pledge of love. She felt the icy chill of fear grip her, but it was swept away by the fires he ignited when his lips caressed the tops of her breasts. Holding his head to her, she was lost in a maelstrom of emotion, so powerful that it left her breathless and pliant beneath him. She molded herself to him, giving herself up to his knowing hands and mouth. Her orgasm was so sudden and intense that she cried out in surprise at the rapture of it. Transported, she lay languorously beneath him as he took his own delayed pleasure in her body, releasing his life-giving seed deep within her womb. Price collapsed on top of her, his heart beating thunderously against hers.

"Ellyn, I . . ." he began after a long moment of silence. But he stopped, moving slightly away from her at the sound of voices on the path.

"Oh, my God!" Ellyn whispered and tore herself away from his still-protective embrace. "Hurry! Oh, hurry!"

She struggled into her chemise and pulled on her dress, hastily buttoning it, ignoring the soreness and blood between her thighs. Looking up, she found him already dressed, watching her with a warm smile curving his handsome lips.

"It's not funny, you fool!" she challenged hotly.

"You're beautiful, Ellyn. I . . ." He took her in his arms and kissed her passionately.

"That sounded like Glory and Charlotte. They'll be here in a minute," she said, pushing away from him. "I'll meet them on the porch and tell them you're sleeping."

"Ah, you are so resourceful." He grinned. "Do you think they'll suspect?"

"No! Not if you can stop looking so healthy for a few minutes! Act like you're sick!" she ordered and hurried downstairs and outside.

Price chuckled and followed at a more leisurely pace, climbing into bed and practicing a few small groans.

Ellyn managed to look serene as she walked up the path to meet Glory and Charlotte.

"Good morning, Glory, Charlotte. What are you doing coming down here?"

"I thought it was time that I saw this Yankee of yours."

"He's no Yankee of mine! He's a very sick man."

"That's not what Darnelle said. She said he seemed right nice last night and I want to meet him."

"Well, he's still asleep and I was just on my way back up to the big house to see about breakfast."

"Can't I just take a peek at him?" Charlotte begged.

"No! Let him sleep. He needs his rest," Ellyn demanded. Then to sidetrack her, she added, "Come back down this afternoon, when you're supposed to be napping. He'll be awake by then. All right?"

"Oh, all right," Charlotte replied, a little irritated. "You know Mother sure is mad at you this time."

"Believe me, I know."

And as Charlotte prattled on about their mother's anger, Ellyn's mind drifted to thoughts of Price and his embrace. Ellyn had never known that anything could be so fulfilling. He had made love to her with a gentle tenderness that had left her enthralled. Her body was alive this morning, suddenly aware of its own sensuality. There was no way that, now, she could refuse to admit her desire for him. She wanted Price and Price only. She had offered him no resistance nor had she wanted to. Careful to ignore the possibility that he might have been using her—a possibility that subconsciously threatened her—Ellyn instead concentrated on the pleasure they had shared and how she couldn't wait to see him again. As for Rod, Darnelle had been right. Now that she had been with Price, there was no way she could accept him as a husband and lover. When he returned—if he returned—she would break off the engagement and follow the dictates of her heart. Dragging herself back to the present, she realized that Charlotte had asked her a question.

"What did you say? My mind was on something else."

"I asked you how soon he could leave. The sooner we get rid of him the better. You know Mother will be just impossible as long as he's around."

"I know." Ellyn was startled by the knowledge. "I imagine he should be healthy enough to leave in about a week."

"Thank heaven. We don't need any Yankees around here. Why, what if Rod came back and found him here?" Charlotte shivered.

"Don't worry, Charlotte. Rod won't be back for months and Mr. Richardson will be gone by then."

"Good."

They fell silent as they neared Riverwood House. Ellyn and Glory went in to see Darnelle. Charlotte went on up to her room, deciding that it was safer to ler her mother think she'd slept late.

Darnelle was in the kitchen busily preparing breakfast when they entered.

"Did you get back to sleep?"

"Yes and I do feel so much better," Ellyn answered, avoiding Darnelle's gaze.

"Good. You was kinda pale but you got some color in your cheeks," Darnelle told her, her womanly intuition telling her that something had happened between Ellyn and Price. "Glory, you take dis food to Mr. Richardson. If he's still restin', jes' leave it."

"Yes, ma'am." Glory took the food from her mother and headed back toward the overseer's house.

Darnelle knew Ellyn well enough to know when not to force conversation, so she went about her chores, trying to ignore the young woman sitting at the table. After a few minutes, Ellyn got up without speaking and left. Darnelle smiled to herself as she watched her start working in the garden.

Ellyn avoided the overseer's house all morning. She busied herself with tasks near the big house and forced all daydreaming from her mind. But try as she might, he was always haunting her. He was in her thoughts with every move she made, from the soreness she felt when she walked to the tenderness of her breasts. Finally in exasperation, Ellyn sought out Darnelle again, hoping for some light conversation.

"Would you like to take you' bath now?" Darnelle offered when she took note of Ellyn's appearance.

"That sounds wonderful," she said thankfully.

After filling the tub, Darnelle left the room to get her some fresh clothes. Grateful to be alone when she stripped, Ellyn practically tore the dress and chemise from her body and sank down in the tub. She scrubbed herself vigorously, wanting no trace of Price visible when Darnelle returned. But Darnelle was wise and she left Ellyn alone with her thoughts for long, private minutes before bringing her the clean garments.

"All done?"

"Yes. That was just what I needed," Ellyn told her as she climbed out of the bath and dried off.

Darnelle left her to dress and went back to her cooking. Ellyn pulled on the chemise and dress and, combing her hair, went out into the kitchen. Sitting at the table, she worked the long strands until they were tangle-free and then braided it. She ate the lunch that was set before her and was about to go back to work when Darnelle stopped her.

"Glory's busy helpin' Franklin, so you' gonna hafta take this on down to Mr. Richardson." She handed Ellyn a lunch bucket.

Knowing she couldn't refuse without raising her suspicions even further, Ellyn started back to see Price, more than a little concerned about the reception she'd get.

Price had pulled the old rocker into the sunshine and was sitting there on the porch with his shirt off, enjoying the mild heat of the day.

"Don't you think you should put on your shirt?" she asked shrewishly.

"Why?" He grinned. "It feels great sitting like this in the sun. You ought to try it sometime."

Ellyn blushed and stomped past him. "I've brought your lunch."

"I noticed. And you also took a bath and changed," he said, following her inside. "You smell wonderful."

When she'd put the food down, she turned to make a hasty retreat but he blocked her path.

"Don't be so skittish. I'm not about to harm you," he told her soothingly, taking her in his arms. She was tense at first, but finally relaxed and leaned against him. "That was some close call, wasn't it?" he teased, his eyes twinkling. Tilting her face up to his, he gave her a chaste kiss. "I don't usually make love and run."

"What do you *usually* do?" she asked sarcastically. He grinned at her.

"Are you jealous, pretty lady?"

"No," she replied, trying to sound indifferent. "Just curious."

"Oh well, I don't think I'll tell you."

She gave him an unconcerned look and walked away from him. "Oh? Why not?"

"Because I'd much rather show you."

She gasped and looked at him in surprise but he was only smiling good-naturedly at her.

"Ellyn, I . . ." he began.

"Ellyn?" Charlotte's voice called interrupting him.

Ellyn jumped guiltily at the sound of her sister's voice.

"That's my sister, Charlotte. She's anxious to meet you. I managed to distract her this morning. I told her you were sick and asleep."

"Oh, so that's who it was."

Ellyn didn't have time to answer, for Charlotte was already up the steps and coming in the door. She halted, her eyes widening at the sight of the bare-chested man standing next to Ellyn.

"Ellyn!" Charlotte was shocked.

"Come on in, Charlotte," Ellyn said coolly, as she took Price's arm and began to unwrap the bandages. "I'm just checking Mr. Richardson's burns."

"But he's—" Charlotte swallowed hard—"practically naked."

Price grinned ruefully at Ellyn.

"I can hardly examine his injuries if he keeps his shirt on," Ellyn told her sister, keeping her eyes on Price's arm.

Charlotte came into the room slowly, offended by her sister's familiarity with this strange man. She thought that it was no wonder their mother had been so furious, if this was the way Ellyn behaved. Unmarried ladies did not do this sort of thing! Charlotte felt very proper now and put on her most ladylike manner.

Ellyn, meanwhile, was carefully checking Price's burns.

"Can we leave the bandages off?" he asked, fully aware of Charlotte's disapproval.

"If you take care."

"Good," he told her, examining the still-sore redness of his arm.

After putting away her medical supplies, Ellyn handed Price his shirt and turned to Charlotte.

110

Charlotte was looking about the room, taking in the broken windows and furniture with a look of distaste on her delicate features.

"Charlotte, this is Price Richardson. Price, this is my sister, Charlotte Douglass."

"A pleasure, Miss Douglass."

"How do you do?" she replied, greatly relieved that he had put his shirt back on.

Now that he was not so offensively undressed, Charlotte took the time to observe him. He was the first Yankee she'd ever seen up close. She found him to be somehow too masculine—why, just his size intimidated her. He would be attractive to some women, she supposed, but he didn't appeal to her. She dismissed him as insignificant, wondering why Ellyn would be stupid enough to endanger her reputation over such a man. Rod certainly was more handsome and much more refined.

"I'm glad to see that you are doing so well. It's been no small concern to us," she told him, moving daintily about the room.

Price took pleasure in reading her double entendres, but let them pass for fear of causing more trouble for Ellyn.

"Thank you for your concern," he replied gallantly, waiting for the question he was sure was coming next.

"Since you are up and moving, will you be leaving us soon?"

"I'm not sure how soon he'll be able to leave," Ellyn interrupted. "I want Grandfather to take a look at his arm before we even think about his traveling into town."

"Oh well, Grandfather should be back anytime now," Charlotte said emphatically before taking a last glance about the room. "Well, just take care.

111

I've got to get back now. Nice meeting you, sir," she told him cordially and then left quickly.

"Your sister must take after your mother."

"How did you ever guess?"

"She was just too nice."

"I know."

"Has she ever met a Yankee before?"

"I doubt it. Mother keeps a very tight rein on Charlotte."

"What about you?"

"I think she gave up on me years ago." Ellyn laughed.

"Thank God," he agreed, laughing. "But I don't intend to ever give up on you," he added huskily, remembering.

"Price, please stop," she insisted, moving warily away.

"Stop what?" His dark eyes glittered wickedly as he followed her.

"I can't think when you're constantly touching me!" she said in exasperation.

"I don't want you to think, only to feel," he whispered as he bent to kiss her, but Ellyn was too fast for him and she escaped him again.

"This morning . . . well, this morning . . ."

"Was wonderful," he finished for her. "Admit it."

"Well, yes it was, but . . ."

"No buts, I enjoyed it and I hope you did, too."

"Yes, but . . ."

"Ellyn!"

"Price! I am trying to have a serious conversation with you!"

"About what?" he feigned innocence and finally managed to catch her and pull her to him. Holding

112

her tightly, he pressed her close to his hard male form.

Ellyn was surprised by her instant reaction to him. Her heart was pounding and her breathing was labored. Her breasts swelled, their peaks hardening when they came in contact with the solid heat of his chest. Excitement flushed through her as she remembered the intimacy of his most ardent embrace. Tilting her head to look up at him, Ellyn was stunned by the fierce look on his features. Frightened by the unknown emotion she saw there, she tried to pull free, but he held her captive. His mouth claimed her in a ravishing kiss that seared her very soul.

"I need to have you, Ellyn. I have to make you mine again!" he told her fervently before capturing her lips in another heart-stirring kiss.

Her body craved this man without thought and though Ellyn knew it was dangerous—good heavens, it was broad daylight and anybody might come in—she gave in to the new reckless longings that he aroused.

"Oh, yes, Price, please. I want to be yours, only yours," she whispered as they moved to the bed.

As he unbuttoned her dress and helped her to shed her garments, Price gloried in the symmetry of her—her full breasts, small waist and the curve of her hips and thighs. Ellyn wanted to cover herself, but he held her still.

"You are so gorgeous. Everything about you is perfect," he murmured. "Did I hurt you this morning?"

"No."

Glad that he hadn't, he kissed her tenderly, guiding her down on the bed. He left her for a moment to remove his own clothes and then joined her there. As his hands and mouth caressed her, the lovers were lost in a blaze of fiery passion. Clinging to each other, he entered her. They moved rapturously together, committing to memory all the details of these joy-filled moments when they were one. They reached the height of desire together, straining toward each other, wanting the closeness that only this most sensual of embraces could give to go on forever.

Price eased his weight from her and Ellyn suddenly felt very vulnerable and alone. When they were joined, she knew they belonged together, it seemed so right. But now, as the coolness of the air chilled her sweat-damp body, she felt forsaken, deserted. Before she could stop them, the words were out.

"Don't leave me!" she whispered, sounding for a moment like a small child.

Price looked at her in surprise and then gathered her to him.

"I couldn't leave you," he told her sincerely. "You're in my blood and I can't get enough of you."

Relieved by his reassuring embrace, she moved even closer.

"It does seem so right—being with you."

"It is right," he said fiercely. "I want you more than I've ever wanted anything in my life."

Ellyn smiled up at him, "Good, for I feel the same way about you."

Price searched her face for the true meaning of her words. Did he dare hope that she loved him? That she was ready to forsake her childish dreams and be his? He knew the attraction between them was over-powering, but he was no callow youth lusting after her. He was a man and yet, he could barely keep his hands off her when she was near. And it seemed that she felt the same way about him, but was it love or just newly awakened desire on her part? He had to know, for he could not tell Ellyn of his feelings until he was sure of hers. Care for her as he did, he would not play the fool and propose to another man's fiancee.

"I'm glad," he told her, bending down to kiss her. "Then you're ready to break off with Rod?"

She was jolted by his train of thought. "But I can't, he . . ."

Her quick refusal tore him apart. How could she use him this way? In an almost violent gesture, he pushed her from him and left the bed. Pulling on his pants, he glanced over at her. She looked so stunned, so innocent. How could she make love to him and yet still plan to marry Rod? Price was so angry, he just wanted to get away from her.

"Price, I . . ."

"Shut up, Ellyn. Just shut up." He started to leave the room and then turned back to face her. She lay naked before him, her eyes pleading with him, but he ignored it. "Get dressed. Someone may show up. It wouldn't do to let anyone know about us. After all, you are the one who told me that there is no us."

Then he was gone. Ellyn was so surprised by what had happened that she felt cheapened. Sobbing, she pulled a blanket up over her. Price hadn't let her finish. He hadn't let her explain that she couldn't do anything until Rod returned home. She owed him that much at least. Price had to understand that she couldn't just walk away. A cold, hard fact quickly stopped Ellyn's crying. Why, Price hadn't offered her anything! He hadn't declared himself! He'd only wanted her. Did he think . . . no, the possibility that he only wanted her for his mistress degraded Ellyn and she shunned that idea. Carefully, more logically, she went over their conversation and then realized how her refusal to leave Rod had sounded. It had led him to believe that she still intended to marry another man, even after she'd been with him. Finally, Ellyn understood his barely contained rage. She got up and dressed, knowing that she had to straighten out the misunderstanding. But she also knew it would be foolhardy to attempt it now. It was best to let him calm down a bit before she explained. Confident that she could handle the uncomfortable situation, she left the house.

As gray, dingy clouds crowded the early afternoon sun from its place of prominence, the aged, mud-spattered carriage came to a bumpy halt at River-wood's main entrance. The sway-backed sorrel nag that had pulled the conveyance was a little livelier than ol' Mo, but not much, and it stood at the hitch, its head drooping with exhaustion, glad to be back home. Lawrence Douglass climbed stiffly down, looking much older than his sixty-two years. His clothing was rumpled and stained with gore, his eyes were bloodshot and his usually steady hands were shaking with fatigue. He had been without sleep since he'd left home, two and a half days before, and he was as close as he'd ever been to collapse. The only thing that kept him going was instinct. He was even too weary now to feel the rage that had engulfed him in town. The carnage he'd witnessed in Memphis had infuriated him, and yet there had been little he could do except treat the survivors. It had been the ultimate in stupidity to overload a steamer that way. Shaking his head at his memories of the injured, Lawrence tied the horse to the post. Then grumbling to himself, he slowly mounted the stairs to the gallery. Once in the cool, welcoming shade of the porch he paused to stretch the aching muscles of his back. It had been a long couple of days, but at last he was back to the peace and tranquility of his beloved home.

The semidarkness of the entry hall made the whole house seem gloomy and he wondered at the unnatural quiet that greeted him.

"Ellyn? Charlotte?" When no one answered, he went out back to the kitchen, hoping to find Darnelle. "Do you have anything to eat?"

Darnelle looked up happily as Mr. Lawrence entered the kitchen. "Yes, suh. You come on in here an' Ah'll fix somethin' right away."

Lawrence allowed himself to be ushered into the room and seated. Within minutes she had a plate of hot stew before him and he relaxed as he savored each bite.

"You sho' look plum worn out, Mr. Lawrence," she said, bringing him a second helping.

"I am, Darnelle, I am. I didn't get any sleep in town. There was too much to do."

"Well, you finish eatin' and Ah'll go turn back your bed."

"Thank you. I'll be needing a bath, too."

"Yes, suh," Darnelle responded as she left the room.

By the time Lawrence made his way to his room, Darnelle had aired it, changed his sheets and prepared a hot bath for him.

"Thank you, Darnelle. This is just what I needed. Oh, by the way, where is Ellyn?"

"I ain't seen her since dis mornin'," she answered truthfully, wanting to steer clear of trouble.

"Did she really rescue a Yankee?"

117

"Yes, suh, and he's a right nice man, too," she stated.

"Good. Well, after I get a little rest, I'll go meet Ellyn's Yankee. Where is he?"

"He be stayin' out at de overseer's cabin," Darnelle said.

"Oh, really?" Lawrence was a little confused by this but was too tired to worry about it for long. "You send Ellyn up here to wake me at suppertime. I'd like to talk to her."

"Yes, suh."

"Where are Constance and Charlotte?"

"They both be restin' right now."

When Darnelle had gone, he shed his filthy clothes and stepped into the hip bath. The heat of the water eased the aches and pains of his body, but did little to soothe the emotional stress he felt. The useless rage he'd known in town surged forth again. All those young men, their bodies burned and broken, their futures changed forever by that one act of supreme idiocy—the criminal overloading of that steamer. Lawrence shuddered violently as the revulsion he had for all senseless death rushed over him. Greatly agitated, he got ready for bed and lay across it, trying to force the gruesome memories from his mind. Eventually, the exhaustion he felt overwhelmed his anger and he slept.

It was almost dusk when Darnelle knocked at the bedroom door.

"Dinner's ready downstairs, Mr. Lawrence."

"Thank you, Darnelle. I'll be right there," he called groggily as he got up and splashed cold water on his face.

It took him longer than usual but finally he was dressed and on his way down to dinner. Lawrence was looking forward to finding out more about

118

Ellyn's resourceful rescue of the soldier. That girl was always doing something worthwhile, he mused proudly, and he was glad that she'd taken the time to listen to what he'd told her these past years.

He entered the dining room and reflected sadly on the changes there. At the height of the Douglasses' wealth, the dining-room had been the most elegant room in the house. At one time a grandiose, gold-trimmed oval mirror had hung above the imported black marble mantel. Now, the fireplace was still the same, but the mirror was missing, traded long ago for much-needed foodstuffs. All that remained to show that it had been there was a forlorn, dirt-framed bare spot on the wall. Both the magnificent white frieze of individual, delicately molded magnolia blossoms and the apricot-colored walls were stained and dingy from years of neglect. The once sumptuous velvet drapes, which were of the same apricot shade as the room, now hung listlessly at the windows in desperate need of a good cleaning. The fine cherrywood furniture no longer sparkled, for the myriad of hands that had polished it were long since gone. Even the expensive carpet was threadbare. Lawrence wondered why Constance insisted that they dine in here. Surely she found the shabbiness as depressing as he did. Lawrence was surprised to find only Constance and Charlotte awaiting him, he had expected the entire family.

"Good evening, Grandfather," Charlotte offered a bit nervously.

"Evenin', Constance, Charlotte," he returned, wondering at Charlotte's nervous manner and taking his seat. "Where's Ellyn?"

"I haven't seen her since this afternoon," Charlotte told him honestly.

"Where is this young man she rescued? Are his

119

injuries so serious that he can't join us?''

Constance blanched. "Surely, Lawrence, you' can't expect me to invite a filthy Yankee to share my evening meal.''

Lawrence had been casually spreading his napkin on his lap when he froze at her words. "What are you saying, woman?''

Constance was indignant at his tone. "I am saying that no Yankee shall ever be invited to my table again! They are not welcome here!''

"You mean you denied an injured man the sanctuary of Riverwood House?''

"Naturally. The man is little better than an animal. Ellyn should have left him in the river to die.''

"And just where is Ellyn?''

"She will not be joining us this evening,'' Constance said regally and Charlotte paled at the look on her grandfather's face.

"And why not?''

"I'm sure she can explain that to you better than I,'' Constance said primly.

Lawrence came to his feet and stalked out to the staircase. "Ellyn! Come down here right now!''

Silence greeted him and he strode back into the dining room. "Where is she?''

Constance noted the anger in his voice and, drawing on years of training for just such stressful times, she told him easily, "Ellyn is not here, Lawrence.''

"What do you mean she's not here?'' he demanded. "What is going on around here? I'm gone for two days and chaos sets in. Where is she?''

When neither woman responded, he continued, "Since you two ladies refuse to answer my questions, I will find someone who will.''

Lawrence quit the room and headed out of the house. Franklin met him at the back door.

"Franklin, what the hell is going on around here?"

"Ah'll show you," Franklin said, much relieved by Lawrence's concern.

"What has happened while I was away?" he asked as they walked in the dark down the path.

"Miz Ellyn, she tell you 'bout all that. She doan' go up to de big house much no mo', not since Miz Constance threw her out."

"What!" Lawrence was totally shocked.

"Miz Constance, she tell Miz Ellyn to get outta her house and Miz Ellyn go. But I bin worryin' and worryin' 'bout dis."

Lawrence could not imagine why Constance would do something so crazy.

"Where is she?"

"Dey's stayin' in de overseer's house," Franklin informed him.

"They? Oh, you mean she's with the soldier?"

"Yes, suh."

"Is he that bad that she must stay with him?"

"Miz Ellyn will 'splain it all to you."

"Ellyn?" Lawrence called as he started up the porchsteps and Franklin went on back home.

"Grandfather!" he heard her exclaim and the door flew open as she rushed outside. "Oh, I am so glad that you are here!"

The day had been a difficult one and Ellyn was relieved that he was back. She and Price had avoided each other all afternoon. They had just come face to face for the first time since he'd stormed out, only minutes ago when she'd brought him his dinner. Her attempts to draw him into conversation had failed miserably. Price had been curt, cold and distant to

121

her and she knew then that it would take more than simple talk to right things between them. She was going to have to show him how deeply she loved him, whether he loved her or not. She could not allow him to go on harboring bad thoughts about her. She had been about to embark on a plan of action when she'd heard her grandfather's call. Glad that he was home at last, she ran to him and was enfolded in a warm, loving hug.

"Now, young lady," he said, releasing her, "what are you doing out here?"

"First come inside and meet Mr. Richardson," she told him. "Then I'll explain everything that's happened."

Taking his hand, she led him inside. Price, who had been sitting on the bed, stood up and came forward.

"Price Richardson, sir."

"Nice to meet you, Mr. Richardson. I'm Lawrence Douglass."

"My pleasure, sir," Price said, offering his hand which was quickly clasped in a strong, warm grip.

Lawrence liked this man on sight and his first impressions were seldom wrong. He prided himself on being an excellent judge of character.

"You're feeling better? You've been getting along all right, Mr. Richardson?"

"Please, call me Price. And yes, I'm doing very well, thanks to your granddaughter."

Price looked at Ellyn, standing close to her grandfather's side, and was genuinely surprised when she met his gaze honestly and unflinchingly.

"She is one capable girl," Lawrence said proudly.

"Grandfather, would you check his arm for me? I set it with Franklin's help, but I'd like to make sure that it's right," Ellyn asked, trying to avoid an awkward scene.

"Be glad to, honey. Price, why don't you finish eating and then I'll take a look at that arm," Lawrence instructed.

Price went back to his half-finished meal while Lawrence and Ellyn went outside.

"What happened? Why are you staying here, of all places?" he asked, looking around in disgust at the run-down condition of the small house.

"Mother wouldn't let me bring him inside the big house," Ellyn said, shrugging, trying not to have any further run-ins with her mother.

"What?"

"She refused to let me nurse him there. It was quite a rude awakening for me."

"I can well imagine," Lawrence said thoughtfully. "As much as she prides herself on her graciousness and dignity, it's hard to believe that she could turn away an injured man."

"I know," Ellyn said solemnly.

"So you brought him straight here?"

"There was nowhere else."

Lawrence was silent for a long minute. "Tell me about it."

"The morning after you left, I went back upstairs to see if I could spot anything and I caught sight of him."

"Franklin told me that he was hanging in a tree-top?" Lawrence asked incredulously.

"Yes, somehow he'd pulled himself up in the branches." Ellyn smiled. "We went out in the skiff and got him down. He looked worse than he really was. He had a bad cut on his head, some burns and the broken arm. He's much better today, but I'd like you to give him a good examination."

"Let's see if he's finished with his meal and I'll take a look at your handiwork. We can talk some more when I'm finished," Lawrence told her, still wondering why Constance had refused to allow Ellyn in the house. He would get to the bottom of that later.

"Good. I've missed you and I do need some advice."

Price had just finished eating when they entered, and Ellyn hurried to move the table out of their way.

"If you'll just lie down for me, Price, I'll take a look at you."

"Fine," he replied and stretched out on the bed. Price extended his splinted arm and Lawrence carefully scrutinized Ellyn's work.

"Excellent job, Ellyn," he complimented her. "Nice and tight."

"It was a clean, simple break," she told him. "Did you take a look at the cut on his head?"

Lawrence checked it. "It's healing nicely. There will be a scar, but it'll be hidden by your hair."

"I'm glad to hear that," Price joked.

When he'd completed his examination, he pulled up a chair.

"You were a very lucky man," Lawrence said seriously.

"I know. Thanks to Ellyn," Price told him, sitting up on the bed.

"I've been in Memphis all this time working at the hospital with the men who'd been rescued."

"Were there many?"

"All the hospitals were full, but from what I understand only one-third of those on board were saved."

"God," Price agonized.

"Would you like some whiskey? I certainly could

124

use some," he asked and Ellyn moved to get the bottle and two glasses.

"Yes, thank you."

Ellyn served them their drinks and went out on the porch to leave the two men alone in their discussion of the tragedy. The moon was full, round and bright, blanketing the surrounding fields and woods in silver light. She sighed, comforted by the stillness of the night and the deep, indistinct murmur of the men's voices. It was a peaceful pause in her otherwise troubled day. Sitting down in Price's old rocker, she leaned her head back and closed her eyes. Almost half an hour later, Price and Lawrence found her there, sound asleep.

"She must be tired," Lawrence concluded.

"I'm sure she is. She told me she didn't sleep well last night."

"Ellyn?"

At the sound of her grandfather's voice so close, she awoke with a start.

"I must have fallen asleep," she said quite unnecessarily.

"Obviously." Both men smiled at her and she was aware of a subtle change in Price's previously cold attitude.

Yawning, she stood up. "Oh, excuse me. It's just been such a long, tiring day."

"I think we all feel that way," Lawrence said. "Well, Ellyn, it's time we said good-night to Price and got back home."

"But Mother . . ." Ellyn hesitated.

"Let me handle your mother. Price has explained everything to me."

"He did?" Ellyn questioned. She searched Price's face but found his expression to be one of indifference.

125

"Yes, he did. I'm proud of you. Your mother overreacted, as is her wont of late."

"Yes," Ellyn agreed faintly. Her mother may have overreacted at the beginning, but she was right now.

"Well, let's go." Lawrence hustled Ellyn off of the porch. "Price, we'll see you in the morning."

"Fine, sir. Thank you."

"Goodnight."

"Goodnight, sir, Ellyn."

"Goodnight, Price," Ellyn called, wondering what in the world he'd told her grandfather.

When they were well away from the cabin, Lawrence spoke, "Why didn't you tell Price that your mother had thrown you out?"

Ellyn sighed. "I thought it was too embarrassing. She had so little faith in me . . . and he'd been feeling really bad. I saw no need. Especially since Darnelle stayed there with us last night."

Lawrence understood Ellyn's pride perfectly. "You're not to worry about a thing. We'll just make sure that you're never alone with him again. That way Constance will have no reason to make accusations. I'll stand by you."

"Thank you, Grandpa," she whispered, feeling like a young child, as he took her hand and squeezed it.

"Now, have you eaten yet, young lady?"

"No, I haven't. I hadn't even thought of it until now."

"Good. I haven't either. We'll dine together."

Fondly, they smiled at each other as they reached Riverwood House and went inside.

Price paced the floor of the overseer's House. He felt ill at ease, confined. It went against his nature to lie, and yet lie he did to preserve Ellyn's precious reputation. The impulse to tell Lawrence Douglass the truth had been overpowering—to declare himself Ellyn's lover and ask for an immediate wedding. But Price had hidden that from the older man and instead had told him what he'd wanted to hear. Fairy tales! He'd said that Ellyn had spent the first night at the house unchaperoned because he'd been in such bad pain. That, he now correctly assumed, was the reason why her mother had thrown her out of her home. He wondered why Ellyn hadn't told him. If he'd known what she had suffered because of that first night . . . no, he decided, he could not have refrained from loving her, no matter what. It had all been too perfect until this afternoon. Until she'd refused to break away from the plans her family had made for her. If she'd been the woman he thought her to be, there would have been no difficulty in the choice.

Tense with frustration, he went out onto the porch and sat in the rocker. Pride holding him together, he decided to leave this place as quickly as possible. It would only be torture to see her continually and never have her again. He knew what she was really like now. The discovery had hurt him, but he would manage. At least the hours he'd spent dwelling on Ellyn had distracted him from depressing thoughts of Coop. Price knew he had to get home to Betsey. She would need him.

Ellyn lay in her own bed enjoying its softness. It was restful to be back in her own room. Everything was still the same—except her. She knew she was a woman now. No longer could she deny the sexual side of herself which for years she'd buried under long hours of hard work. Now, she understood her body and had enjoyed it to its fullest, thanks to the man she loved. Her heart thudded as she thought of those long moments in his arms. Price was a wonderful lover and after tonight she knew that he was still her friend. He had protected her. He had defended her. She would make certain that he knew her true feelings as soon as she could arrange to be alone with him. For not only did she want his friendship and his love, Ellyn wanted his respect. Curling on her side, she hugged the pillow to her and drifted off to sleep, unaware of the confrontation taking place between her mother and grandfather.

Constance had been waiting to catch her father-in-law alone. When she'd heard Ellyn go into her room, she'd started downstairs with a vengeance.

Cornering Lawrence in the library, she demanded. "How dare you bring her back into my home?"

Lawrence pierced her with a cold stare. "This is also my home and Ellyn's."

"I had forbidden her to come back. She spent the night unchaperoned with a Yankee! How can you ignore that?"

"If you had allowed her to nurse the man here, the situation would never have developed," he told Constance accusingly.

Constance cursed Lawrence under her breath for being such a meddling old man. "I could not allow any Yankees in Thomas's house! They killed him!"

Lawrence knew that she was trying to blackmail him emotionally and so easily ignored her arguments.

"Constance, we've killed as many, if not more, Yankees."

"Good," she answered, her voice full of hate.

Lawrence was losing patience with his daughter-in-law. He knew that it had been difficult for her this past year, but it was time for her to pick up the pieces of her life and go on.

"As the only man left in this family, I am now the head of this household and as such my orders will be obeyed. Ellyn will stay here. She will not, however, be alone with the Yankee again. He has assured me that she is untouched."

"And you believe *him?*"

"Do you know differently, or are you judging Ellyn by yourself?" he asked wickedly.

Constance went pale. "What are you implying?"

"Why, nothing," he said in knowing innocence, hiding the fact that years before his son had confided that his bride had not been a virgin when she came to him.

"There is no point to this conversation."

"You're right about that, Constance," he told her. "Good night, and remember, I want Ellyn treated as she deserves."

Constance left the room in a huff, determined to prove herself right. She could not let her carefully thought out plan fall apart because of Lawrence. Hadn't he wanted the plantations to merge, too? She thought about the possibility of telling him her new idea for uniting Clarke's Landing and Riverwood, but decided against it. He cared too much for her foolish daughter. In Lawrence's eyes, Ellyn could do no wrong. Determined to make things work out the way she wanted them to, Constance went on to bed. She was confident that she would think of something by morning.

*   *   *

129

"Your mother and I had a long discussion last night after you went to bed," Lawrence told Ellyn as they walked along the path the next morning.

Ellyn, who was carrying Price's breakfast, looked up quickly at her grandfather. "Oh?"

"She's still quite upset about everything."

"I know. I sometimes wonder if she will ever be herself again," Ellyn remarked sadly.

"I think you're right. She wants things as they were, and if they can't be exactly the same, then she's determined to pretend they are."

Ellyn nodded her understanding. "What do you think I should do? Stay away from her? I know how she feels about me, what she thinks of me. I mean, I know she was always liked Charlotte best, because Charlotte did everything so perfectly."

"That's not true," Lawrence told her. "She did show favoritism to Charlotte but it was because she was so easily controlled. Charlotte worships your mother and would do anything to please her. Whereas you couldn't wait to chase after Tommy and your father. Somehow, Constance didn't know how to deal with you."

"She still doesn't and I've given up trying to get along with her."

"You can't do that. She is your mother. You must remember that."

Ellyn looked slightly defeated. She'd thought she was past the stage where she had to please anybody but herself.

"What do you think I should do? She's not realistic at all."

"It's too painful for her to be realistic, Ellyn. She has lost everything she held dear. Right now, she's fighting to keep some semblance of order in her life," Lawrence spoke sympathetically.

"You sound like you feel sorry for her."

"All wounds are not of the body," he remarked sagely. "You're a survivor, Ellyn. Your mother . . ."

Ellyn pondered that. She supposed it had been a shock for her mother to see a Yankee at the door of Riverwood House, and by defying her, Ellyn had only made matters worse.

"You're right, as always." She smiled at her mentor as they came near the overseer's house.

If they'd only known how very wrong they were in their assessment of Constance, they wouldn't have dropped the matter so easily. In her own way, Constance was a survivor, too. Her own childhood had been marred by unhappiness. Her father was a Louisiana planter and though he was land-rich, he was always in debt. He had been a bitter man, who'd hated his wife for bearing him three "useless" daughters. The placée he'd kept in New Orleans had given him two fine sons, but he could claim neither one. When Constance was ten, her mother died and Constance suspected it was more from heartbreak than anything else. From this point on, she and her sisters, Annabelle and Michelle, had been ignored by their father who spent all his time in New Orleans. He arranged marriages for both of the older girls and soon Constance was left with just the servants on the big plantation. Innocent and eager for affection, she was easily seduced by the young, handsome overseer. Thinking herself madly in love, she had been mortified to learn of her coming marriage to a stranger from upriver (the wedding have been arranged to help settle her father's gambling debts). Torn from the arms of her regretful lover, who had refused to

131

run away with her, having valued his job more than her love, she'd learned the hard way that women were so much chattel. She had gone to her marriage bed and pleased her new husband so much that he'd cared little about her lack of innocence. She was a hot-blooded woman who'd been smart enough to figure out that the way to control a man was by using her body. And use it she did in any and every way she could to keep Thomas Douglass entranced with her. Though she did not love him, she knew what to do to keep him happy. And if he was satisfied then he would have no reason to keep a mistress. So during their eighteen years of marriage, she had indirectly made every decision regarding their life together. When she had presented him with a son, he'd been so overjoyed that he hadn't been able to do enough to please her. And even the subsequent birth of two daughters had not diminished Thomas's desire for her.

Constance had been aware of her father-in-law's thoughts as he'd watched his son be manipulated, but she paid the old man little mind. Thomas wanted her. He craved her. He cherished her and gave her everything she wanted. Obviously, Lawrence had little influence on her husband and so Constance had not been concerned.

She had not paid much attention to her daughters over the years except to reprimand them and she reflected her own father's opinion in her dealings with them. They were only there to make the most advantageous marriages they could. Marriages that would improve their parents' lot in life. Charlotte had been easy to train, but her elder—Ellyn—had been an incurable tomboy. And Thomas, entertained by her antics, had let her have full rein.

Now, here she was burdened with a daughter

whose reputation was, in her opinion, damaged beyond repair. A simple solution, Constance realized, would be to marry Ellyn off to the Yankee, but she quickly dismissed the thought. As much as she was disgusted by her child's behavior, she could not tolerate a Yankee for a son-in-law. No, Ellyn's punishment was decided as far as Constance was concerned. She would remain unmarried. An old maid, the thought made Constance smile. If Ellyn was so intent on doing good works, then she could dedicate her whole life to it!

Smiling at her momentous decision, Constance rang for Darnelle and propped herself up in bed. It only remained for her to find a way to keep Lawrence away from the house when Rod returned. Until he did, there was really very little for her to do, so she would just relax and anticipate her reunion with him.

Price was up and dressed when Ellyn and Lawrence arrived. He looked healthy, except for his arm, and Ellyn wished that she was alone with him, so she could tell him everything she wanted to say. Instead, she had to go about her work nonchalantly, ignoring her longing to be in his arms.

For his part, Price appeared indifferent to her presence. He conversed easily with Lawrence, virtually ignoring her except for a perfunctory "Thank you" when she set out his breakfast. Ellyn knew that somehow she had to arrange to see him privately. She wasn't sure how, but she would do it.

"Price," her grandfather was saying, "I've decided that it's best for Ellyn not to be with you alone. From now on there will be someone else with her when she comes out here. Her mother is quite upset by what has occurred. Why, if this had happened five years ago, you two would be married by now!"

The thought had been spoken teasingly, but both Ellyn and Price stiffened. Lawrence, however, didn't notice.

"Even though I'm a Yankee?" Price returned, covering his tenseness.

"Five years ago, it wouldn't have mattered, but now . . ." He paused. "Well, it's best that we get you healthy and on your way back home."

"If my presence here is causing your family problems, I'll leave. After all that Ellyn's done for me—" he cast her a cruel glance which Lawrence missed—"I couldn't stay on if I thought I was making things difficult for her."

"No, no," Lawrence said. "Everything is under control now. We'll just make sure there are no more incidents to upset Mrs. Douglass."

"I understand perfectly," Price responded and for the first time, he was beginning to grasp the pressures being exerted on Ellyn by her family.

He had never been exposed to this before. His experiences with relatives had been far from pleasant. Certainly the early years of his childhood had been happy, but Price remembered little of what life had been like before he was eleven. He only sensed a feeling of warmth about those times when he did indeed have a family. But both of his parents were killed in a tragic accident and his only other relative had been his widowed Aunt Rachel Kent who immediately set her eyes upon his inheritance. She'd taken over his life, dominating him, using up all his money on herself and her son, Alex. Alex was three years older than Price. He was a mean, vicious boy and he'd taken great pleasure in brutalizing Price.

Finally, after more than a year, Price had run away from home. Warm memories of loving parents had been replaced by the fear that Rachel and Alex might come after him. He need not have worried; they were glad for the most part that he'd gone.

Adele Cooper had found Price a few months later on the wharf. He'd been barely surviving on handouts and what few odd jobs he could do until she took him into her home and raised him as her own son, with Jericho.

No, he reasoned, he'd never had family pressure as Ellyn did. But then again he was a man. He suddenly became aware of Lawrence speaking to him and he forced his thoughts to the present.

"We'd better get to work. You get plenty of rest today and I'll send Franklin out with your noon meal," he was saying.

"Yes, sir," Price replied, watching silently as they left.

After they'd disappeared up the path, a heavy silence descended, interrupted only by the occasional noise of the birds. The emptiness of the day stretched before Price and for the first time he realized how long and tiring it would be without Ellyn's company. Trying to ignore his desire to be with her, he dredged up the memory of her refusing to break off with Rod. But even that took on new meaning now, for he'd come to understand the subtle force a family could use. The only force Price had ever dealt with in his life had been brute and he'd always been able to face it squarely. But coercion was another matter, he could see now that Ellyn had had little choice in her refusal. When he'd asked her to end her engagement, he'd offered her no alternative, no sanctuary. He'd, in effect, asked her to forsake her family for the unknown and Ellyn hadn't been able to do it. She didn't know him well enough to understand that his motives were honorable. The whole ugly scene from yesterday took on new meaning for Price and he shook his head sadly. No wonder she'd been able to meet his gaze with such forthrightness last night. She was a victim, trying for a little happiness while it was offered to her. The need to be with her overtook him once more and he wondered how he could ever get her alone again. He had to let her know his feelings, even if they could do no more about them. Anything was better than to leave her thinking that he despised her.

Ellyn sat miserably at the dining room table. The day had been long and tiring and very boring. She'd been unable to think of anything clearly, all her concentration was focused on Price and the problem of how to be with him. All Grandfather could talk about was how soon he could leave and Ellyn was desperate. She couldn't let him go home until she'd told him of her feelings. She was aware of the trivial conversation that drifted around her, but she gave it little attention. Constance had appeared indifferent to her presence this evening and so Ellyn had made no effort to be cordial. Now, all she wanted was to escape to the solitude of her room to figure out her dilemma. Finally, they were all finished and she managed to say a hurried goodnight before disappearing upstairs.

With the door closed and locked safely behind her, Ellyn climbed up on her bed and rested. As she could see it, her only hope was to sneak out after everyone was asleep. Since no one suspected her of caring for Price, she doubted that it would be difficult. The hard part, she knew would be staying awake until everyone else went to bed. Her eyes grew heavy with fatigue as she lay there and though her spirit was willing . . . She awoke with a start and jumped up nervously. Disoriented for a minute, she could only stand in the middle of the room staring about her. Slowly, it all came back to her. Was it time? She moved quietly to the window and gazed out. The moon was bright and full again, pouring eerie, magical light upon all the creatures of the night. Ellyn shivered. What price would she pay if she were caught? The thought stopped her and she debated with herself. Which was more important? Her reputation or her love? There was no real choice. She had to go to him.

Listening carefully at her door, Ellyn heard nothing but the usual sounds of the night. She made her way outside, taking great care. There was no going back now, Ellyn thought, as she raced silently down the path past Franklin and Darnelle's cabin. If Price still wanted her, then they would work it out together. Even being his mistress was better than staying here under her mother's condemning eyes. She had decided she would take him on any terms. Allowing herself no possible thought of rejection, she hurried on.

Her steps slowed as the overseer's house came into sight. It looked cold and uninviting. All was dark. The curtains flapped noisily back and forth through the broken windows and the front door hung open tilting crazily on its broken hinge. It looked to be the proverbial haunted house, luminated as it was by the moon's glow, which here didn't seem magical at all. If anything it was a pale, unearthly light that cast ghostlike shadows everywhere in its revealing of the night. A stiff breeze came up suddenly and the rustling of the trees sent a chill down her spine. Ellyn almost turned back, unnerved by the scene before her, but her need for Price drove her on and she entered the house, soundlessly.

The room was in deep shadow, except for an occasional brightening when the curtains fluttered open. She could barely make out Price as he lay on the bed. Crossing the room silently, she stood for a time, watching him and wondering why this man above all others could set her aflame.

Price opened his eyes. He sensed something was different, almost as if . . . He turned and his breath caught in his throat. Ellyn stood near the bed, looking down at him.

"You came," he whispered.

"I had to. I—" Before she could tell him all that was in her heart, he grabbed her by the wrist and pulled her down next to him.

"I know, it's irresistible—this thing between us," he told her as he ravished her with kisses. Price didn't want to think that in the morning she would turn from him again. He didn't want to worry that she couldn't marry him and be his for the rest of their lives. He only knew that he'd been offered a chance to have her again and in desperation, he would take her. These few stolen hours would last a lifetime, if necessary. He would show her tenderness and kindness and hope that when he was gone, she would be all right. He knew that he could not force her to love him, but they could share their mutual desire for however long they had.

At the touch of his lips on hers, Ellyn was thrilled. He still wanted her! She ignored the nagging voice in the back of her mind that told her a man would be a fool to turn down any woman who offered herself so brazenly. She wanted him and he felt the same way. If he didn't want to take her with him, then at least she would have these hours with him to remember.

Putting aside all thought, Ellyn gave herself up to the sensuality of her body and for the first time aggressively sought his touch. She brushed aside his hand and quickly unbuttoned her bodice. Then, positioning herself above him, she offered him her breasts. He feasted upon them, sucking and biting until she was moving against him, eager for the moment of their union. Ellyn was unable to deny the heat within her and she pulled her skirts up and pressed her bare limbs to his. The hardness of him burned against her thigh and she reached down to guide him inside her, but he pushed her hand aside.

"Not yet. I'm not done with you yet," he spoke to the softness of her breast, unwilling to stop his burning kisses.

They rolled over as Price continued his ravaging caresses, his hand finding her moistness and teasing her driving hips to new heights of excitement. When she climaxed, her whole being pulsed in unexpected waves of tormented pleasure and she lay rigid, as they radiated from the center of her. Before she could move, Price slid deep within her and sought his own satisfaction. His desire had been as great as hers and he reached his summit quickly. Sated, he rested with her. And in each other's arms, they fell asleep, each anxious to tell the other his thoughts.

It was the not-too-distant rumble of thunder that awoke Ellyn and, realizing that a storm was imminent, she jumped from the bed.

"What's wrong?" Price came awake.

"There's a storm," she told him nervously, pushing her breasts back inside the bodice and straightening her skirts.

"Come here," he beckoned.

"I must go."

"Ellyn," he coaxed and she knelt by the bed.

Price pushed aside the unbuttoned dress and pulled down the strap on her chemise to expose the creamy smoothness of her. The nipples were erect in anticipation of his touch and a low moan escaped her as his lips caressed the hard, pink peaks. She clutched his head to her, encouraging the searing wetness of his mouth.

It took a blinding flash of lightning and a nerve-shattering crash of thunder to tear them apart.

"I have to go," she told him, smoothing her clothes.

"I know," he said resignedly.

"I have to talk to you," she said, pausing at the door. "Somehow. Tomorrow."

And she was gone, leaving Price alone to cope with the storm without and the storm within.

Chapter Six

As far as the eye could see, the threatening gray-green clouds churned ominously overhead. Turbulent, raw winds buffeted the creaking overseer's house. Lightning erupted, streaking untamed across the leaden sky, illuminating the dull morning in harsh, brilliant relief. The deep growl of thunder soon followed echoing across the water-soaked fields and forests. The cloudburst, when it finally let loose, pelted the country-side with hail and torrents of driving rain.

Ellyn stared resentfully out the parlor window at the heavy downpour. It was already well past noon and there had been no letup in the rain since it had begun in earnest late the night before.

Last night, she sighed. Those hours with Price had been so enchanted that she now doubted their reality. She'd awakened this morning eager to see him and tell him of her love, but Mother Nature had conspired against her. It was not to be, not yet. Irritated at being denied the chance to clear up the misunderstanding, Ellyn paced the house, looking for something to occupy her time. Giving up the fruitless search, she followed her mother's and sister's examples and went to her room to nap.

The drumming of the rain on the roof, at any other time, would have had the power to lull Price to sleep, but today it only served to set his nerves on edge. Stretched out full length on his bed, his good arm folded beneath his head, he waited. For what, he wasn't quite sure. The rain to stop? Ellyn to appear? Either option would have satisfied him, but as it was he had to suffer his own company in the small, decrepit, uncomfortable house. His mood was black. With nothing to distract him, his mind had wandered all day. At first, crystal visions of Ellyn's embrace had besieged him and when he'd finally gotten them under control, memories of the *Sultana* and his last worrisome hours with Coop had followed. Now, as he lay there, he was frustrated by his lack of control over his own situation.

His emotions were at war. On one hand, his passion for Ellyn held him spellbound. To leave her behind would take the utmost in self-denial. He wanted her as he had never wanted any woman. Could he go home without her? Grimly, he realized that the choice was not his to make. He could not force her to care for him, even though he was sure that she felt the same physical desire he did. Having never been aroused before, it was only natural for her to want to experiment. Price didn't like the idea that he was just a means to an end for her, but at this point he would take anything that she could give, without question or judgment. He loved her that much. But he also loved Betsey and the possibility that she might think both Coop and he were dead harassed him. He almost had his full strength back now and he knew he had to leave. He had to return

142

to Alton and get his life back in order. Price was certain that Betsy needed him and he had to be there for her.

His choice was made for him as he finally thought it through logically. He had to go home. As soon as he could he'd book passage north. There was no sense in playing with fire and Ellyn was definitely fire. What if she became pregnant? The idea pleased him, she'd have to marry him then—Rod or no Rod.

Angry at the weather which held him immobile, he stood up and stalked about the room, pausing before the wilting wildflowers. He reached out and touched a hidden thorn gently, so as not to cut himself. Handled easily, the pain was minimal. It was only when you tried to grasp the prize firmly that you were hurt. Price was more convinced than ever that the way to win Ellyn was by gentle loving. And so, he planned that for whatever time they managed together before he had to depart, he'd give her all of his love tenderly. He would not rush her. Ellyn had to make the decision by herself.

When Price heard the footsteps on the porch, he jumped, turning quickly from the flowers.

"Afternoon, Mr. Richardson," Franklin greeted him, shedding the soaked jacket he wore.

"Franklin, it's good to see you," he told him enthusiastically.

"Ah thought you might be needin' some company long 'bout now." Franklin grinned.

"You're right about that. I'm almost stir crazy. I'm not used to so much solitude." He shrugged. "How's Ellyn today?"

"Jes' fine, but it's been a borin' day for everybody. Ah went fishin' though and had some good luck."

"Do you think I could join you sometime?"

"Yesh, suh. Ah'd lak' dat."

"Tomorrow then? Or are you going again tonight?"

"Yes, suh, Ah is, but you cain't. Mr. Lawrence, he done invited you up to the big house for supper."

"Are you serious?" Price asked in disbelief.

"Yes, suh. Dat's why Ah'm here. To invite you and to tell you dat if you wants a bath, Darnelle will fix one for you."

"That sounds great. When you go back up—"

"Ah'll jes' tak' you wid me. Then you can tak' your time gettin' cleaned up."

Price smiled for the first time that day. He didn't relish meeting Ellyn's mother but he also didn't want to spend the evening here alone. When the pounding rain finally slacked off, they hurried up the path to Riverwood House. Franklin left him in the kitchen where Darnelle fixed him a hot bath. He soaked for a long time, enjoying the idea of finally getting really clean. Darnelle also provided him with a change of clothing and he dressed quickly, anxious to feel normal again. When he had some difficulty with the shirt, she came to his aid, helping him with the sleeve as Ellyn had. Price used the comb and razor Darnelle offered him and, observing himself in the small hand mirror, he decided that he didn't look too badly after all. The black pants and white shirt he'd been given to wear fit him reasonably well and while he'd relaxed in the bath, his boots had been whisked away and polished. Now, feeling human once more, he presented himself to Darnelle who was still preparing dinner in the kitchen.

"You sho' is one fine lookin' man," she told him as she took in his wide-shouldered, slim-hipped figure. Mr. Thomas's things fit him perfectly.

"Why thank you." He grinned. "I have to admit,

144

I do feel a lot better.''

"You sho' look better, too.'' Darnelle returned his smile. "Mr. Lawrence brought de clothes down for you. Dey belonged to Miz Ellyn's daddy.''

"Oh.'' Price paused.

"You bes' get on over to de house. Dey's waitin' in de parlor.''

"Fine,'' he said, starting out of the room. "Darnelle?''

"Yes, suh?''

"Thanks.''

"You welcome, Mr. Richardson.''

Constance glared at her father-in-law. "You've *what*?''

"I have invited Mr. Richardson to join us for dinner,'' Lawrence stated firmly.

"How dare you! You know how I feel about Yankee trash!''

"I told you earlier today that I am now head of this household and as such I have asked him to come.''

"But—''

"Your opinions on the matter are not important. He will be leaving us soon and until then, I intend for you to extend him every courtesy. You would do well to heed my words.''

"Well, I never!''

"I know that, Constance, but things are going to be different around here now.''

"Not if I can help it!'' she hissed. "I will not eat at the same table with that man! Let him eat in that shack where he belongs.''

Trying to force Lawrence's hand, Constance drew the battle line.

"I'm sorry you feel that way," Lawrence replied with seeming uninterest.

"Lawrence!" Constance gasped.

"Grandfather!" Even Charlotte was shocked.

Ellyn could only stare at her grandfather and wonder at his game.

Constance drew herself up. "If you'll excuse me then. I have no wish to entertain a man who could be my husband's murderer! Lest you forget how your son and grandson died, Lawrence Douglass! Goodnight. Charlotte?" Constance asked imperiously.

"Charlotte will be dining with us." Lawrence stood his ground.

Regally, Constance lifted her skirts and left the room. As she hurried into the wide hallway, she came face to face with Price. Price had been there by the doorway throughout most of the argument, but he had not wanted to interrupt a private discussion. He knew his first meeting with Constance Douglass was going to be a tense one but he'd never imagined it would be this bad.

"Madam," he said, giving her a small bow.

Constance stared at him in mute surprise. Her eyes took in everything about him. Womanly instinct told her that although he was an attractive, sensual man, he would be quite a formidable foe. She almost acknowledged his greeting until she recognized the clothes he had on. She paled at the sight of Thomas's things on the Yankee. Knowing it was useless to voice her outrage, she turned from him coldly and disappeared up the stairs.

Price watched her ascent. He knew now where Ellyn got her figure. Her mother was still a very beautiful woman. But besides her looks, in those seconds that their eyes met, he recognized a steely determination in her. She was no one's fool and

Price knew he would do best to avoid her whenover possible. She was filled with hate and that hate was ready to explode. She'd been pushed into a corner now and that would make her even more dangerous. When he heard the conversation begin again, he entered the parlor.

"Good evening ladies, Lawrence," he greeted them.

All eyes turned to him, wondering if he'd witnessed the scene just played out.

"Good evening, Price. Come in. Would you care for a bourbon?"

"Yes, please," he told Lawrence. Then he said to Ellyn, "Will your mother be joining us?"

"No, I'm afraid she's not feeling well tonight," she answered quickly.

"That's too bad, I was looking forward to meeting her," he told Ellyn, his eyes twinkling.

"Here you are."

"Thanks," Price said, taking the proffered drink from his host. "I appreciate the dinner invitation. I was getting stir crazy out there by myself."

"I can imagine," Lawrence sympathized. "We've had quite a quiet day ourselves. Not that I mind, but I know Ellyn likes to keep busy." He looked at his granddaughter fondly.

Charlotte, meanwhile, sat in a wing chair taking mental notes on the whole conversation. She knew that her mother would want to know every detail as soon as possible.

Ellyn paid little attention to anything but Price. Her senses were full of him. The sight of his tall, lean body moving easily about her home and the mellow sound of his deep, rich voice combined to send chills up and down her spine. How she longed to be in his arms, telling him of her love. Instead, she had to

147

play out this silly charade and hope that later they could find a forbidden moment together.

Darnelle called them to eat and dinner progressed smoothly. Controversial subjects were avoided and the meal passed pleasantly enough.

"How soon do you think I can leave? I must be getting back, as there was no word about my friend."

"If it hadn't rained so hard today, I'd say you could go tomorrow or the day after. As it is, I'll have to check Riverwood Road before we decide. If it's as bad as I think it is you may be stuck here until the river drops again."

"How long will that take? Two, maybe three days?"

"It could be as long as a week. I've never seen this much rain all at once before. But don't worry, I'll ride out in the morning and see how high the water is."

"Good. Now that I'm feeling better, I'm anxious to head home. I've got to find out what happened to Coop."

"I understand completely," Lawrence agreed.

Ellyn sat silently, panic riddling her. He wanted to leave, even after last night! Now she knew they had to talk and soon. Somehow, this night, they would be together. Her mind racing, she conceived and discarded plan after plan of how to be alone with him. Nothing seemed plausible except her going to him at the overseer's house. Making up her mind, risky or not, she would do it again. Ellyn raised her eyes to look at him and found him staring at her, his expression enigmatic. Giving him a small smile, she turned her attention to what her grandfather was saying.

It was near eleven when Ellyn followed Charlotte's

148

example and excused herself. With disappointment, she noticed no change in Price's demeanor. He was courteous and friendly, but in a most distant manner, not showing any reluctance at her leaving. She didn't know what she'd expected from him but it hadn't been total aloofness.

When she reached her bedroom, she left the door ajar so she would know when Price left to go back to the overseer's house. Ellyn waited impatiently for the two men to call it an evening. Finally, she heard them emerge into the hall below and bid each other goodnight. She watched from her window then, as Price left the house and started back down the path. With all her heart, Ellyn willed him to stop and look back at her and she was overjoyed when, indeed, he did. The night was so dark that she could only make out the whiteness of his shirt in the shadowed gloom, but she could tell when he waved and she returned the greeting happily. Then after a long pause, he turned and walked on until he was completely out of sight.

Ellyn managed to contain herself for about another hour. She saw Darnelle leave the kitchen and go home and she heard her grandfather retire to his room down the hall. At long last, when she felt certain that everyone was abed, she started for the door. A moment of total unreasoning fear assailed her as she saw the knob on her door turn. The portal opened seemingly of its own accord and before she could move or cry out Price loomed before her. He closed it quickly behind him and locked it. The sound of the latch seemed a hundred times louder than it actually was and they both froze, expecting at any moment to be discovered. Silence engulfed them again and Price smiled at her.

"I had to come," he spoke softly, reaching out to

touch her cheek. "You looked so beautiful in the window. I couldn't stay away."

"I was just about to come to you," she told him, leaning into the caress of his hand.

"You were?"

"We have to talk. It couldn't wait any longer."

"I know. There's so much I want to say to you, but first . . ." He kissed her sweetly, without passion.

Ellyn clung to him for a long minute, enjoying his strength and the comfort of his embrace. He'd come to her! He did care! She pulled away and took his hand, leading him to her bed. He sat down and started to pull her on his lap, but she resisted.

"If I get that close to you, I won't be able to keep my mind on what I've got to say," she said, holding up a hand to ward him off. "You sit right there and I'll sit here."

She pulled up the small chair that went with her vanity and seated herself facing him. At last they were face to face and Ellyn couldn't speak. The words she'd longed to tell him stuck in her throat. The simple "I love you" would not come out. So she searched helplessly for something to say.

"Yesterday . . . our fight . . ." Before she could continue, he began.

"I'm sorry, Ellyn. I had absolutely no right to say what I did to you and I'm sorry."

"But . . ."

"No buts," he said seriously. "I had no right to ask you to break your engagement. If you—"

Feeling the conversation slipping away from her purpose, she interrupted, "I'm glad you're sorry for getting angry, because you had nothing to be angry about. If you'd let me finish what I was about to say, we could have avoided a very unpleasant scene."

"What?"

"I was going to tell you that I couldn't break off with Rod until he gets back. I just can't go away without telling him the reasons myself. If you can wait until . . ."

"Oh darling." His voice was hoarse as he pulled her to him. "Pretty lady, I can wait forever for you."

He kissed her deeply and they rolled back upon the bed together, totally lost in the splendor of the spell of love. Ellyn thought at first that she'd imagined the soft tap at her door and so did nothing to interrupt their embrace. It was only when it came again that she moved away from Price's ardent caresses.

"Ellyn? Are you still up?"

"Yes, Grandpa, just a minute," she answered him softly.

Price got up quickly and, at Ellyn's pantomimed instructions, hid himself under the bed. Shaking nervously from being almost discovered, Ellyn pulled a long dressing gown on over her dress and, after making sure that there was no sign of Price's presence, she opened her door to admit her grandfather.

"I'm glad you're still awake. I thought it might be good if we could talk for a while."

"Of course, sit down. I haven't been able to sleep at all." Ellyn sat on the bed while Lawrence sat on the chair. Price held his breath as the bed sagged heavily under Ellyn's weight.

"Because of Price?"

"What?"

"You care for him, don't you?" He put her on the spot.

Ellyn hesitated, not sure how to answer him. Certainly, she couldn't tell him the truth, not yet.

"I think he's a fine man," she answered.

Lawrence wasn't completely satisfied with her answer, but let it pass. He'd sensed something in Ellyn tonight that he'd never noticed before. For the first time, she had seemed a full-grown woman to him. He didn't know why, he just knew that she was no longer a willful child. Now, she was a fine young lady with a mind of her own and he wondered fleetingly if the Yankee had caused the metamorphosis or if he'd just never thought of her as an adult before.

"Yes, that he is, but I'll be glad when he's gone."

"Why?"

"There's no telling when Rod will show up."

"Shouldn't you be saying 'if'?" she asked pointedly.

"There's no point in thinking the worst. He'll be back."

"Well, it will be a relief when he does get here."

"Yes, the sooner the better, but I think it could be very dangerous if Price was still here. Lord only knows what shape Rod will be in and I'd hate to have a confrontation between them."

"But why would there be?" Ellyn asked, not comprehending what he was leading up to.

"Ellyn, I can only protect you from your mother for so long. If she somehow manages to speak to Rod of the time you spent with Price, why, he'll certainly think the worst."

"He wouldn't trust me?" She was outraged.

"It's a matter of honor."

"This is ridiculous," she told him, finally beginning to understand.

"I've felt that way about the whole war, Ellyn," he replied solemnly. "I just don't want anyone to get hurt. So the faster Price leaves, the better for all of us."

152

She nodded miserably, afraid for Price.

"Well, I'm going on to bed now. Tomorrow I'll tell your mother that he'll be gone by the end of the week, weather and travel permitting. That should soothe some of her ruffled feathers," Lawrence said as he stood and moved to the door. "Good night, darlin'."

"Night, Grampa."

The door shut behind him and Ellyn was fearful of locking it right away, lest he hear. She sat down wearily on the bed. Price inched silently out from underneath and came to her, taking her in his arms. Ellyn leaned against his shoulder, her spirit almost exhausted.

"Don't worry," he whispered. "I love you. We'll work it out."

At the sound of the words she'd longed for, tears filled her eyes, "I love you, too."

He kissed her brow and pressed her head to his chest. She rested on his heart, gaining strength of purpose from its steady beat.

"We'll be fine," he murmured to her, smoothing her hair.

"I know that now," she said, moving from the intimate safety of his arms to lock the bedroom door again.

She sat beside him on the bed and he kissed her, softly.

"I thought of you all day," she said when their lips parted, her breath coming hard and fast. She slipped the dressing down off and moved closer to him.

"And I you," he responded, pressing fevered kisses on her throat.

His hand rested lightly on her breast and a thrill of excitement surged through him as he felt the nipple harden against his palm. Agilely, he unbuttoned her dress and chemise and parted them. Ellyn lay back on the bed and Price followed her down. She shivered as he freed her bosom and the cool night air touched her aroused heated flesh. The ecstasy of waiting for his next caress forced her to remain still, as the pulsing coil of desire drew tighter and tighter in the pit of her belly. But Price refrained from exploring her silken skin. Instead, he slowly undressed her, sliding the gown and underthings from her sensuously, so that each inch of her body was exposed to him in an age-old offering. Naked before him, she reached up to clasp him to her, but he avoided her, catching both her hands in his. He held them captive over her head as he nuzzled at her breast. Eager to hold him, yet restrained by his gentle force, Ellyn arched herself to him, encouraging him. Anxious to feel the heat of him deep within her, she rubbed her hips excitedly against his. Though Ellyn grew almost frenzied in her attempts to make him lose control and take her, Price resisted the temptation. He continued his caresses, merciless in his stimulation of her, forcing her body to respond even more wildly by his refusal to enter her. He loved the feel of her nude body trembling beneath him. He only wished that they were totally alone so he could say all that he wanted to to complete her arousal. She tried to free her arms, but he wouldn't release her.

Turning pleading, passion-drugged eyes to him, she begged, "Please."

"Please what?" he growled, moving suggestively against her.

"I want you."

His mouth covered hers in a burning, breathtaking kiss and he released her hands, wanting to feel them on his body. Not ending the kiss, she unbuttoned his shirt and shivered as her breasts came in contact with his hair-roughened chest. Price felt his control slipping as she boldly caressed the hardness of him and he tore himself away from her long enough to shed his clothes. When he rejoined her on the bed, Ellyn was ready for him, opening herself for his entry. He came to her then, surging within her, losing himself in the tight, velvety sweetness of her. Wrapping her legs about his waist, she gloried in his possession. They reached the peak of satisfaction together and descended the heights in each other's arms. The glow of their passionate union remained with them as they held each other, murmuring soft endearments and touching one another in gentle wonder.

How much time passed, they had no idea. They spent the hours of darkness absorbed in learning all they could about each other, both mentally and physically. As they lay exhausted from another heated mating, Price knew he had to ask the question that had been tormenting him all night.

"Ellyn, will you come with me when I leave?" He rolled on his side so he was facing her and waited for the answer he knew was coming.

She turned toward him and caressed the hard line of his jaw. Desire flared deep within her once more as he pressed a kiss into the palm of her hand. She'd never known that his mouth on her hand could be so erotic and she trembled.

"Price, you know I want to more than anything. Being with you means everything. I can never go back to being who I was a week ago. You've made me into a woman—your woman." Her eyes held his in serious intent. "But . . ."

"Ah, pretty lady, the thorn again." He gave her a

heart-tugging grin.

Ellyn felt tears come to her eyes at the sound of his voice. "I have to wait. To break off honestly with Rod."

A deep sigh shuddered from Price as he heard the response he was expecting.

"Then marry me now, before I leave. So we can be sure of each other," he told her fiercely.

"Do you doubt me, after the hours we've just spent?" she asked seductively, her hands reaching out to stroke him.

"I love you, Ellyn. I've never said that to another woman. I don't want to risk losing you," he explained, amazed at what the touch of her hands could do to him.

"I feel the same way about you," she told him fervently. "Nothing can come between us. I promise you."

She kissed him deeply, suddenly needing to be safe within his arms.

"As soon as Rod gets back, I'll tell him and then I'll come to you."

"It could be months before he returns," Price complained, not wanting to be separated from her.

"Then stay here. We could find some way."

"No," he paused. "Ellyn, I heard everything that was said in the parlor this evening. I know how your mother feels. And I understand it. It wouldn't work."

Ellyn knew he was right. There was no real way for him to stay once the river went down.

"My love," she raised tear-filled eyes to him. "We have at least a few more nights together."

"And then a lifetime." He kissed her, sealing their love. "I'll send you money for your passage and I'll write."

"That's not enough. *That* will never be enough!" she cried brokenly on his shoulder.

"It will have to be, unless you'll come with me now."

"I can't, you know I can't. Not yet."

"I know," he told her soothingly and held her tightly to him.

As the birds began their morning serenade, they lay quietly together, savoring what little time they had left. The sky was lightening when Price finally spoke.

"I must go. I don't want to complicate things any worse than they already are," he said, moving from her to begin dressing.

At the thought that they might not manage to be alone again, Ellyn rose and went to him. He had started to tuck his shirt into is pants when she embraced him from behind, pulling the shirt free.

"Don't leave me yet," she whispered wantonly, her hands searching and finding him.

"Ellyn! Do you want to get caught?" he asked, trying to put her from him, but she was not to be denied.

"If we're quiet, no one will ever know," she told him, slipping a hand within the waistband of the trousers and grasping him firmly. Ellyn smiled to herself as she heard the sharp intake of his breath.

He turned and embraced her.

"You know I want you," he said gruffly. "But I don't want to pass Darnelle on my way back to the overseer's house."

Pressing a quick kiss on her parted lips, he held her gently away from him, "Tonight . . . somehow."

She nodded mutely as he again tucked his shirt in and headed for the door.

"Oh, Price," she whispered, miserably.

He came to her and kissed her passionately and was gone before she could speak. Ellyn stared for a long moment at the closed door and then lay down, mentally and physically exhausted.

Constance stood at her bedroom window waiting for the sun to come up. She'd slept fitfully all night, worried about how to handle Lawrence. He'd had the upper hand last night and she was bound and determined that that would never happen to her again. The incessant chirping of the miserable birds irritated her and she started to move away from the window when she saw someone come out of the house. Quickly moving behind her drape, she hid, wanting to watch, unobserved.

It was the Yankee! He'd spent the night in her home! Anger and disgust raced through her. It was bad enough that she was expected to be cordial to him, but to have him sleeping under her own roof was almost more than she could bear. Her eyes followed him as he moved off down the path and Constance wondered why he was returning to the overseer's house if Lawrence had invited him to sleep here? Sensing something unusual going on, she left her room and went down the hall to Ellyn's. She opened the door and looked in.

Constance was shocked by the sight of her daughter, stark naked, asleep on the bed. Had the Yankee spent the night here? There was no sign that he had, but Constance's curiosity had been aroused and she would not give up until she knew exactly what was happening.

She quietly closed the door and went back to her own room to think. If Ellyn and the Yankee were lovers then all the better for her plan. She knew she would find out, but when she did, she was not about to tell anyone. At least, not until the Yankee was gone. For otherwise, Lawrence might condone their marriage. If there was one thing Constance was sure of, it was the fact that Ellyn would pay for humiliating her.

Constance smiled as she went back to bed. Things were working out better than she'd thought. When the sun finally rose, it found her sleeping soundly, unaware of the brightness of the new day.

Darnelle shook her head solemnly as she saw Price on his way back to the overseer's house. She was glad that Franklin was already gone and that Glory was still asleep. In fact, she wished she hadn't seen him at all for it made things far too complicated for her. Not that she had any doubts about where he'd been. She'd known at a glance, last night, how Price and Ellyn felt about each other. It was written all over them and she wondered why no one else suspected. Torn between the desire to help them and the need to stay uninvolved, she went on about her chores, hoping that she didn't have to make that decision any time soon. Still, the thought that Rod might return nagged her and she worried that Ellyn might be in for some real trouble.

When the old woman saw the Reb ride into her yard, she hurried out to greet him.

"Evenin', ma'am," the officer greeted her, tipping his hat.

"Evenin'," she said, a little cautiously. Rumor had it that the war had been over for weeks, but she still knew a stab of fear every time she saw a man in uniform.

"I was wondering if I could impose upon you for some water. It's been a long and dusty ride today." His tone was friendly and his manner confident.

Mattie Hardin looked him up and down real good before she assented. He was a true gentleman, she could tell. First, by the way he sat his horse with an easy fluid grace and second, by the fact that he'd taken the time to ask her permission to use the well. The Yankees took—they never asked—and the Crackers, damn them, just stole what she wouldn't give.

"Please, help yourself, suh," she told him.

"Thank you, ma'am. You are a ministering angel." He flashed her a smile and in that instant she was charmed.

The man climbed down and led his horse to the trough before pulling up a bucket of cool, well water for himself. When he'd finished drinking, he turned to her again.

"My apologies, ma'am. I'm Colonel Roderick Clarke, late of Johnston's army."

"Colonel, it's nice to see a friendly face. I'm Mattie Hardin," she said, impressed by his cavalier ways. "Would you join me inside, I do have a small meal I can offer you."

"I'd be honored, as long as you're sure. I wouldn't want to impose upon you."

"Nonsense. I'd be grateful for your company, Colonel."

Rod brushed as much dirt as he could from his worn uniform and followed the little old lady into her cabin. At her direction, he seated himself at the small table in the center of the room and she brought him a plate of stew. After she'd joined him and they said grace, he ate voraciously. Mattie watched in amusement as the food disappeared.

"How long has it been since you had a hot home-cooked meal, Colonel?"

"Too long, Miss Hardin, too long."

"It's Mrs. Hardin, really, but call me Mattie, everybody does," she told him as she began her own meal. When he'd finished what she'd given him, she rose. "I'll get you more."

"Thank you, it's delicious. Will there be enough for your husband?"

"Don't worry about Jacob. He was killed at the battle of Kennesaw Mountain. So was my son," she said, refilling his dish.

"My sympathies. Then you're here unprotected."

"Yes, but I'm not afraid. Everybody in these parts knows me and they check on me regular enough."

"Good. I would take care if I were you. There are still bands of guerrillas roaming the countryside."

"So the war is over? It's true?"

"Yes. Lee surrendered earlier this month and General Johnston just last week."

Mattie looked grieved and somehow relieved at the same time. "I suppose I'm glad, but it makes the loss of Jacob and little Jake all that much harder to justify. They died for nothing."

Rod Clarke stiffened and looked at her for a long minute. "We can never say that our men died for nothing! No, our cause was real and worth the struggle. Why if I thought that all the men I saw killed in action died for no reason . . . we were just outgunned. No supplies, no food, no medicine. If we could have ended it in the first two years when we had enough strength to bargain. But the longer it dragged on, the more our lack of industry hurt us."

"What will you do now?" she asked, hoping to

change the topic.

"Go home. It's the only thing left for me to do. My men had talked about fighting on—raiding in small groups. But there's no victory or honor in that." Rod looked at Mattie.

"You don't sound happy about going home. Don't you have a wife and children?" she wondered.

"I have a fiancée, but I haven't heard from her for almost a year."

"She must be a very beautiful lady to have caught a good-looking young buck like you!" Mattie teased, hoping to cheer him.

Rod's expression came to life as he thought of Ellyn. "She is beautiful."

"I thought so," she remarked. "Tell me about her."

"I've known her all my life. She's much younger than I am, but a marriage between us seemed the perfect answer to all our dreams."

"What dreams?"

"We own neighboring plantations and we wanted to unite them so we'd be bigger and better."

"Where are you from?"

"Tennessee, a little north of Memphis. Have you ever been there?"

"No. Jacob and I never left this county. Spent all my life right near here. Seemed no reason to leave."

"I can surely understand your desire to stay near your home. The last news I got from Ellyn—my fiancée—was that my mother had passed on and our house had burned."

"How terrible!"

"It was all a blow. Mother was all the family I had left."

"Well, I'm sure your little gal—Ellyn, did you say?" At his affirmative nod, Mattie continued,

"I'm sure she's waitin' for you. Probably wonderin' where you are right now."

"I hope so. Lord knows I've spent nearly all my time worrying about her and the Landing."

"She's just fine, I've no doubt, and she's mighty lucky to have you comin' home to her."

Rod smiled at her, enjoying a woman's chatter after all the long months of being with men. "Ellyn's a strong-willed girl."

"Then you've no worry. She's probably taking care of whatever needs doin' until you get home."

He nodded silently, somehow knowing that Ellyn would always manage to work things out.

"Would you like to get cleaned up?"

Rod looked startled for a moment and then said, "It would be a delight."

"You rest, while I fix you some hot water. A bath will at least make you feel a little better."

"I'm sure it will make me feel a *lot* better." He grinned. "Especially if you've got some strong soap."

Mattie smiled as she put the water on the stove. "I fought lice often enough to know how to deal with them. Don't worry about a thing."

She liked this Confederate colonel and was determined to make him as comfortable as possible. Even though she had been married and widowed, she could still appreciate a handsome man and he was one. She could hardly believe the change in his appearance when he emerged from the small tub, washed and shaved. His manner was pure Southern aristocracy. His normally dark blond hair was sunbleached. His face—now clean shaven—was classic in its perfection and his piercing blue eyes seemed an even more dominant feature with the wild growth of beard gone. His figure was fit but on the thin side

163

and Mattie wished she had enough good food to really fix him a decent meal. She'd given him some of Jacob's old clothes to wear while she washed his uniform and was pleased to see that they were only a little too large.

"Will you spend the night? There's plenty of room here."

"Thank you. I'd like that, but first I must see to my horse. He's just about all I've got right now."

"There's still a small outbuilding you can use for a stable if you've a mind. It's right around back."

Rod disappeared outside to see to his steed and Mattie went about preparing her son's bed for him.

It was just about dark when he returned. And, as was her custom, Mattie read her Bible. Rod listened but could not accept all that was being read to him, not anymore. There had come a time during the past years that he'd had to question God's existence and the answer he'd received hadn't been a happy one. Surely a loving, living God would not punish his people so! But the war had gone on, as had the killing—and Rod had grown colder and more merciless with each useless death that he'd witnessed. He felt now that religion was a hoax—a sop for the weak masses—and that the strong of society, the survivors, would eventually rule. Not because of any extra grace of God's, but because they knew how to fight harder to get what they wanted—and they didn't worry about stupid rules. And so Rod Clarke had become a cynic, expecting the worst from fate and, of late, he had seldom been disappointed.

When Mattie finally put the the Bible away, she noticed the hard look on his face.

"Have you lost your faith?"

He glanced at her quickly. "I don't know that I ever had it to lose."

"It's all I have now to give me peace. Without it I don't think I could keep on."

Rod was tempted to tell her that she was wasting her time. That there was no heaven and that hell was here on Earth, right now, but he remembered his mother and how she always drew comfort from prayer.

"I've seen too much pain and death, Mattie."

"We all have, son. We all have." There was a long pregnant pause. "Well, I'm off to bed. You get a good night's sleep."

"I appreciate your generosity."

"It gives me pleasure to help you, Colonel. Good night, now." She made her way to her small bedroom. "God bless you."

"Good night, Mattie."

As Rod lay back to rest on the bed of Mattie's dead son, he let his mind wander to the days ahead and his reunion with the Douglasses. He wondered how Tommy was. They'd been good friends since childhood and Rod hoped that he was well. He had mixed feeling about seeing Ellyn again. They'd not parted on the best of terms, for he'd wanted a fast marriage and she'd refused. Her refusal had been just one of many things that had irritated him about her. She was far too headstrong and independent and Rod hoped that the years apart had mellowed her into a more pliable woman. The one thing he did not need at this point in his life was an opinionated shrew. He truly wished that, upon his return, Ellyn could be more like her mother.

Constance Douglass in his opinion was the perfect woman. Lovely to look upon, full of figure, Rod had found her to be his ideal female many years ago, but had kept the fantasy hidden while he waited for her daughter to grow up. The war had forced his hand early and he'd proposed before he'd intended to, but he was confident that the results would be the same. Ellyn would have grown up to be an improved—if at all possible—version of her mother.

With visions of Ellyn and Constance floating through his mind, he finally managed to relax and sleep came as he thought of Ellyn's greeting when he arrived home.

Ellyn had passed a boring day of ordinary drudgery. Her grandfather had brought her the news that Riverwood Road was underwater and that it would be at least two more days before it would be passable. She felt great relief in knowing that Price wouldn't be leaving yet. But still the knowledge that he was near and yet unattainable drove her to distraction.

It made matters even worse when her mother announced that she was joining them for dinner tonight, Yankee or no Yankee. It was her house and she refused to be driven from it by some bluebelly. Lawrence had even been surprised by this statement and had told Ellyn so. It was such an about-face from her declaration of the night past that they were both confused.

Lawrence had also been confused by Constance's sudden interest in the Yankee. She'd even asked if he'd spent the night in her house and when he'd told her no, she'd seemed inordinately pleased. Maybe that was why she'd finally relented and agreed to join them. She thought that she could tolerate two more days if it were only at the dinner hour.

Price's day had been a little more eventful than Ellyn's and Lawrence's. He went fishing with Franklin early that morning and then slept all afternoon to make up for his wild, sleepless night. He hadn't seen anyone else all day, for Franklin had brought the message down from the big house that the road was flooded and there'd be no way out for the next few days. Pleased at being isolated with Ellyn, and yet wishing that they were here alone, he spent most of his waking hours trying to keep his mind from straying to remembrances of her in his arms. He felt great relief when sundown came and it was time to go to the house for the evening meal.

Darnelle once again prepared him a bath and he made himself as presentable as possible before joining the family in the parlor. He was surprised to find Constance already present when he reached the sitting room.

"Good evening," he said boldly as he entered.

Lawrence came to hand him a drink and directed him to Constance.

"Price, I'd like to present to you my daughter-in-law, Constance Douglass. Constance, this is Price Richardson, the man Ellyn rescued."

"How fortunate that you could join us for dinner, Mr. Richardson," she said silkily, extending her hand.

Price bowed over it, replying, "My pleasure. I always enjoy the company of beautiful women."

Charlotte, who was seated nearby, giggled and Ellyn blushed. Only Constance remained unimpressed.

"How kind you are, sir. Shall we go in?" she asked, taking his arm.

Price watched her expression warily and noted, with some satisfaction, that there was a look of malicious intent in her gaze. He made a mental note to keep his own reactions neutral and indifferent just in case she suspected that he cared for Ellyn.

After they were all seated at the table, Constance played her role as hostess to the hilt.

"So tell me about yourself, Mr. Richardson. All I can rightly remember is that you are a Yankee whom Ellyn pulled from the river. Surely there is more to you than that." Her tone was cordial, but the question was pointed and snide.

"I fear I am a most boring topic. Why don't you tell me all about yourself and life here at Riverwood. It seems to be such a beautiful, peaceful place," he said, not at all adverse to playing verbal games with her.

"Riverwood is my life. My late husband and I created it. I will not let it suffer, not for any reason."

"You must love your home very much," he observed.

"I do!" she began heatedly, but Lawrence interrupted.

"We all love Riverwood."

"I can understand that. I'm very fond of Alton. It's one of the most scenic towns on the Mississippi. High bluffs, the river—it's quite lovely."

"And you'll be glad to be going back?"

"Of course. I've been away over a year now."

"And you have family?"

"No blood relations. Just Coop's family."

"Coop?" Constance asked in pretended interest.

"He's my friend who was lost in the explosion."

"How terrible for you. Are you sure that he's not alive?"

"Franklin checked in town for me. There was no word, anywhere."

"Perhaps when you return home, you'll find that he's preceded you."

"The thought has occurred to me, but I doubt that

it's a real possibility. Lawrence has told me how few men actually were rescued."

A small smile was quickly suppressed. "What was the attitude in town, Lawrence?"

"Generally very helpful. There were a few—" Then he realized what she wanted to hear and he stopped.

"A few who what?" Charlotte spoke up, surprising everyone.

"There were some who were glad, even rejoicing over it," Lawrence responded coldly and he watched as Price's expression hardened.

"Oh, really?" Constance felt secretly delighted, but made an attempt to hide it.

"Yes, really. In fact, there was a rumor going around that a spy had planted a bomb in the coal," he explained. "But there was no proof of that."

Price felt sick as he watched Constance eagerly gleaning each word that Lawrence offered. She was a cruel woman, despite all of her manners and he knew then that it would be useless for him to try to deal with her. The safest thing for Ellyn and him, both, was to stay as far away from her as possible.

Constance was covertly observing Price's and Ellyn's every move. She was determined to discover if anything was going on between them. The conversation was flowing just as she'd wanted it to and she was pleased to note the Yankee's discomfort. The bastard! she thought to herself, how dare he sit at her table so calmly, almost as though he belonged. As if reading her thoughts, Price suddenly excused himself and left the room. His departure irritated Constance. She glanced quickly to Ellyn who seemed quite mystified by his actions and Constance's suspicions waned. Perhaps he'd just come up to the kitchen with Darnelle for an early breakfast. Or maybe he had been helping Franklin. There were several possibilities but none satisfied her. No, she would keep a very close watch on them both tonight and see what developed. If nothing, then all she'd lost would be one night's sleep. Constance turned her attention back to what Lawrence was saying.

"It is really unnecessary for you to gloat, Constance," Lawrence criticized.

"Excuse me?"

"Your entire attitude is far too smug, considering the circumstances."

"And what are my circumstances."

"Contrary to what you'd like to believe, you are an impoverished war widow," he told her bluntly.

Constance felt herself flush in indignation. "Sir, I may indeed be a widow, but I am far from impoverished. I own this magnificent home and thousands of acres of fertile cotton-growing soil! Thomas has also left me quite secure. We have Confederate war bonds."

"That aren't worth the paper they're printed on. And you're going to have to come up with the money to pay the taxes on this magnificent plantation very shortly. You'd have lost Riverwood long ago if it hadn't been for Ellyn."

Constance rose, looking at Lawrence and Ellyn in disgust. "Yes, I must remember that I owe all my good fortune to you two. Now, if you'll excuse me, it has been a long tiring day."

After she'd gone, Charlotte was surprised and disappointed to find the subject dropped. All day long, her mother had prodded her for every detail that she could recall from the previous evening. She'd been very upset, too, when all Charlotte could tell her was that Ellyn sat quietly listening to the men talk and that she, herself, had grown bored with it all

170

and had gone on to bed. Now, tonight, she was ready to learn everything she could and there was nothing to concern herself with.

"Ellyn, as you can see, we must help him leave here as soon as possible."

"I know. Living with hate is hard to deal with. Especially when you've been through so much already."

"I think the road will be clear enough by late tomorrow and the following morning I'll take him into town. I'm confident that he'll have no trouble booking passage out of Memphis."

"May I ride along?" she questioned hesitantly, but Charlotte zeroed in on Ellyn's request.

"I don't see why not. It will do you good to get away from Riverwood for the day. Why don't we plan on it?"

Ellyn seemed to sigh in relief and Charlotte wondered at her eagerness to be near the Yankee. The rest of the evening passed uneventfully and soon Ellyn was in her room waiting for the household to settle down for the night.

She didn't have to wait too long before all the lights were extinguished and she heard her grandfather retire. When she was certain that it was safe, she crept from her room, unaware that her mother was watching the path.

The night was cool and misty with river fog. Cold clammy tentacles seemed to touch her as she hurried toward her lover. Ellyn felt a spine-tingling chill go down her back and she shivered, wrapping her arms tightly around herself. Reaching the overseer's house, she rushed inside the poorly lighted cabin, wanting to feel the warmth and security of Price's embrace. She stopped suddenly as she found him sitting on the bed, braced negligently against the wall, his long legs stretched out before him on the mattress, his expression one of pure disgust. He lifted the almost-empty whiskey bottle in a silent toast to her.

"Why are you here?" he demanded, his words cutting, demeaning.

"I wanted to be with you," her voice quivered.

"Why?" he asked sharply.

"I . . ." Then realizing that the bottle of whiskey had been half full that afternoon, she replied, "You're drunk!"

"An astute observation, my love. But you didn't answer my question. Why did you want to be with me?"

"Because I love you," she stated firmly and she watched helplessly as he took the last swig from the bottle.

Dropping it carelessly on the floor, Price rose in one agile motion and stood before her. He looked down at her, his features harsh in the semidarkness of the room. His hand snaked out to twist painfully in her hair, which had fallen free of its confines during her race to be away from the big house.

Pulling her tightly to him, he snarled, "You don't love *me*. You love what I can make you feel."

His mouth ground down on hers, forcing her lips open, raping her mouth. Ellyn struggled against his hateful force, afraid of this stranger he'd become. He jerked her back to him as she tried to get away and tears came to her eyes.

"Do you want me now?" he asked nastily, kissing her neck and feeling her nipples harden involuntarily against his chest.

"No!" she shrieked, lashing out at him.

The contact of her hand with his face seemed to freeze them both and they stared at each other,

172

unable to move. Ellyn suddenly collapsed against his shoulder, throwing her arms around him, sobbing uncontrollably.

"Don't do this to me. I love you. I love you."

He stood still for a moment longer, slowly realizing what he'd almost done. Then his arms encircled her and he softly kissed her hair.

"I'm sorry, I'm sorry," he groaned and she raised her lips to his, wanting the warmth that only his truest loving could give. "I love you, Ellyn," he whispered before he met her in that tender exchange.

They blended together, touching yet not undressing. Needing the sweet consolation of each other's love, they lay upon the bed together, gently caressing until the fire that existed between them flared to life once again. There was no time to remove all their clothes as passion swept them away. His mouth pressed hot, damp kisses on her breasts through the material of her gown and Ellyn moaned at the new sensation. She helped him push her skirts aside, and then reached out to free him from his pants. Holding the hot, pulsing length of him, she stroked him, telling him of her love and her need for him. Price shuddered, groaning at the arousing touch of her fingers on him. He wanted her now. Moving over her, he entered her and thrust deeply within. Ellyn responded, lifting and arching her hips to bring him the most pleasure she could.

"I love you," she whispered. "I love you."

Ellyn clasped him closely to her as she felt the white-hot explosion of pulsing desire within her and Price, knowing he'd satisfied her, climaxed quickly wanting to share the moment of total union with her. They rested, unaware of Constance at the window.

Constance backed away from the window of the cabin, astonished. Though she'd suspected that

173

they might care for each other, until now it had seemed a remote possibility that they had done anything about it. "Like mother, like daughter" flashed through her mind and she frowned.

Turning away, she hurried home, her mind in a turmoil. What to do? How to play this to her advantage? Breathless from rushing back, Constance collapsed across her bed, her thoughts finally in order. She was not going to tell anyone about what she'd seen. The knowledge that they were lovers would be her ace in the hole. She would only use it if her situation became desperate.

Constance felt confident now that nothing could come between her and Rod. There was no way he'd marry Ellyn once he found out about her bedding a Yankee. Reliving for a moment what she'd observed, she felt disgusted. How could a decent Southern woman give herself willingly to Yankee trash? She shuddered in revulsion. She'd always thought Ellyn was a fool, but now she knew it to be a fact. Satisfied with the way things were going, Constance undressed and climbed beneath the covers, knowing she would sleep well this night.

It was very late. The lovers lay entwined on the small bed, too tired to move. They were at peace—alone, secluded, in love. It was a time of bliss, a time of no cares or worries and they were savoring each second to the fullest.

"You're so beautiful," he murmured, propping himself up on his good elbow to look down at her.

She smiled dreamily. "You make me feel that way—beautiful, desirable and very sexy." Her fingers toyed with the buttons on his shirt.

He bent and kissed her. "How long did we sleep?"

"I don't know. I hope not too long. We've only got one day left and I don't want to waste a minute of it."

"Me either," he agreed, reaching out to unbutton her dress. "Don't you think it's time we undressed?"

She laughed delightedly. "I think it's way past time!"

Getting up, she quickly took off her things and then helped him with his.

"This could become habit-forming," she told him as she pulled the shirt from his broad shoulders.

Unfastening his pants, Ellyn slid them from his hips and was pleased to see that Price was aroused. She was slowly beginning to realize the power she had over him. Emboldened, Ellyn brazenly caressed him, growing excited as she for the first time became the aggressor.

Price had to force himself to remain still under her wandering hands. He fought for control as Ellyn's exploring touch set him aflame and he had to grit his teeth against the urge to take her right then.

As she teased him, trying unsuccessfully to break his iron-willed self-control, Ellyn grew even more daring. Leaning over him, she kissed Price, rubbing her breasts against him. Her mouth left his and trailed hot kissed over his neck and chest. Price held his breath as her lips innocently moved lower.

"Oh God, Ellyn," he groaned, feeling the heat of her breath upon him.

Pleased to learn that this was how to weaken his restraint, she continued her exploration. A tremor of excitement shook him at the first touch of her lips on his throbbing manhood. Her mouth roamed over him, bringing him to new raging heights of desire.

Suddenly, rational thought was lost to him and he took control, pulling her upward and onto him.

Ellyn was as eager as he was for their coupling and at his guidance, straddled him and slowly impaled herself upon his hardness. Burning with the need to possess him completely, she held him deep within her as they moved together rhythmically. Too excited to deny himself any longer, Price shuddered as the throes of the ultimate ecstasy claimed him. Sated, he rested, holding her against him until the thunderous pounding of their hearts slowed.

They didn't speak as they enjoyed the peace-filled moments still joined as one. Sleep came easily as the exhausted lovers clung to each other, fearful of losing what little time they had left together.

The morning star glowed brightly in the blackness of the pre-dawn sky as Franklin left the comfort of his cabin. He was on his way to the overseer's house, for Price had told him that he wanted to go fishing again this morning.

Franklin was still half asleep and it took him a minute to make out the two figures embracing passionately on the porch. Shocked, he paused at the edge of the trees so he wouldn't interrupt. When Ellyn tore herself from Price's arms and rushed off toward the main house, Franklin stepped back into the woods so he could go unnoticed. He was deeply disturbed by the knowledge that the two were lovers. Ellyn was very special to him and he didn't want her to be hurt. And though Price was a very nice man, he was still a Yankee—a fact that Ellyn must have forgotten, Franklin concluded. Confused about what to do, he decided to talk to Darnelle first and he set out for home once again.

"Darnelle?" he called quietly as he entered the cabin afraid he might wake Glory.

"What's wrong?" came her anxious whisper from their bed.

"There's goin' to be bad trouble," he answered coming to sit by her.

"Why?"

"Ah jes' saw Miz Ellyn leavin' the overseer's house."

Darnelle was quiet, thinking of how crazy Ellyn was to take such a chance. "Ah know."

"You know?"

"Dey been together fo' a few days now. Ah was hopin' dat no one but we would see."

"Ah jes' saw plenty."

"Well, you jes' keep your mouth shut!" she ordered. "Them two's gonna be all right, if everybody leaves 'em alone."

"But Ah got to tell Mr. Lawrence!"

"Why? It'll jes' get Ellyn in a lot of trouble. You know how dem folks is."

Franklin considered this for a time before agreeing.

"Tell you what, you go on and get de boat ready and Ah'll go talk to Mr. Price."

"What you gonna say?"

"Ah ain't sure yet, but Ah'll think of somethin'."

"You tell him to meet me. Ah'll be waitin'."

Darnelle rose and dressed, following Franklin from the cabin. She watched her husband as he disappeared in the direction of the boat and then started up the noisy porch steps.

At the sound of footsteps on the porch, Price quickly opened the door wondering why Ellyn had returned.

"Ellyn? You're back?" he asked before seeing who it was. When he saw Darnelle, he was worried about what he'd just said and his expression reflected

177

his concern. "Darnelle!"

"Mornin', Mr. Price."

"I thought you were Ellyn," he muttered, trying to cover his mistake.

"Ah know and so does Franklin, now."

"You know?" he was stunned.

"Since the first," she told him.

"How? Did Ellyn tell you?"

"No, suh. She's a lady!" Darnelle quickly defended Ellyn. "Ah could jes' tell by lookin' at you. But Franklin, he jes' saw you dis mornin'."

"He did?"

"He was comin' down to take you fishin' and he saw Miz Ellyn leavin'."

"I'd better talk with him," Price said and they walked inside.

"Don't you worry 'bout Franklin. He ain't gonna tell nobody. Ah done tol' him to keep quiet."

"Thank you."

"Ain't no need to thank me. I don't want Miz Ellyn hurt," she said looking him straight in the eye.

Price nodded his understanding. "I love her, too."

"What you gonna do? You supposed to be leavin' here tomorrow mornin'," Darnelle demanded.

"I've already asked her to marry me, but she wants to talk to her fiance first."

"Oh, Mr. Rod."

"Yes."

Darnelle nodded sagely. "Ah'm glad."

Price looked surprised. "You're probably the only one around here who will be when the news gets out."

"Ah love her and Ah want what makes her happy."

"I'll do everything I can," he promised seriously.

"Franklin's waitin' at de boat for you. You bes' hurry." Reassured by his words she left him.

Price sat down heavily on the bed, worrying about the conversation he'd just had. If Franklin and Darnelle both knew, then maybe . . . no, if anyone in her family knew they'd have said something by now. A little relieved, he finished dressing and went to meet Franklin.

Ellyn leaned back in the tub of hot, scented water, her head aching, her muscles stiff and sore. The day had been long and tiring and, having had little sleep the previous night, Ellyn was exhausted. The hot water that Darnelle had brought up for her was relaxing but it did little to ease the pounding in her head. She finally gave up trying to rest in the bath and got out.

It seemed to her, and not unreasonably so, that Darnelle had been inventing heavy jobs for them to do today. They had started working right after breakfast and hadn't quit, except for a short lunch, until near sunset. Now, here Ellyn was, trying to get moving so she could be ready in time for dinner. Her last with Price.

As she dressed, Ellyn took extra care, wanting to look her best for him tonight. Brushing her dark hair until it shone, she twisted it into a becoming top-knot, allowing just a few strands to curl freely about her face and neck. Pinching her cheeks for added color, Ellyn left the upstairs dressing room and went downstairs.

Everyone was already there when Ellyn entered the parlor.

"Good evenin, darlin'," Lawrence greeted her as she came through the door and joined him.

179

"Good evening," she returned, her eyes lingering on Price's tall figure as he stood next to her grandfather.

"Ellyn," he greeted, stifling a tender smile. How he wanted to take her in his arms!

"So glad you could join us," Constance remarked sarcastically. "We've all been waiting for you."

"Sorry I'm so late, but after the hard day Darnelle and I put in, I wanted to freshen up."

Ignoring her statement, her mother continued, "The meal has already been announced."

Moving ahead of them, Constance led the way into the dining room and waited for Lawrence to seat her. Observing Price and Ellyn closely, Constance was irritated by their feigned indifference to each other. What cool actors they were. Perhaps if she'd not witnessed the scene of the night before she could have believed their ploy, but Constance knew the truth. Resenting their deception, she deliberately set out to make the evening miserable for them. The meal was nearly finished when she finally had the opportunity to begin.

"I understand that you'll be leaving us in the morning." She directed the statement to Price.

"Yes, ma'am, if the road is passable."

"When will you know?" she asked Lawrence.

"I'll check it first thing in the morning," Lawrence replied. "It's a good distance into Memphis and I want to get an early start, don't you Ellyn?"

"What does she have to do with this?" Constance demanded.

"She'll be riding with us."

"Why?"

"I'd like to see Mr. Richardson off, Mother," Ellyn answered, not liking the direction of the conversation.

"Whatever for?" Her tone was cold and condescending as she looked at her daughter.

"Constance, I thought it would be a good idea for Ellyn to get away for the day, nothing more," he said trying to de-emphasize Price's role in the trip.

But Constance knew better and felt Lawrence was a fool to give Ellyn her way with this Northerner. He might not know what was going on, but she sure did.

"If the road's been underwater, the mud will be so bad that the carriage won't be able to get through."

"We should be all right," Lawrence insisted.

"I think it's very foolish of you to risk our one and only conveyance on a trip that you needn't make at all!" she responded angrily. "There's no real reason to take the carriage. Why, if Ellyn stays here, you two can ride the horse and mule and it should take you only half the time."

Lawrence finally had to agree with her, knowing that it would be a slow, messy trip by carriage.

"Your mother does have a point," he said to Ellyn. "And I'm sure you wouldn't want us to get stuck halfway there."

"I was looking forward to it," she said defensively, resenting the fact that she was subtly being forced to remain at home.

"I'm sorry dear, but it would be easier if we were to ride in," Lawrence stated. "How's that suit you, Price? I'll plan on just the two of us. Ellyn can say goodbye to you here."

"Sounds fine," Price agreed.

"Good. It's all settled then." Lawrence was pleased that Price was going along with his plans. "We'll leave as soon as I get back from checking the river. It'll probably be around eight."

Constance sat back watching the exchange with

181

little real interest. For Ellyn's part, Constance had seen what she had been looking for—her quickly subdued anger and resentment at not being allowed to accompany Price to town. Had Constance not been watching for it, she would have missed it, but she'd been ready and had not been disappointed.

Richardson, on the other hand, seemed cold and uninvolved and Constance wondered if, in fact, he really didn't care. It occurred to her that maybe he was just using Ellyn for his own purposes and, therefore, had no trouble hiding his feelings, for he had none to conceal. If that was true, then Constance was all the more determined to make Ellyn pay for her stupidity. Somehow, she would make sure that Ellyn and Price were not alone together before he left Riverwood. A devious idea suddenly came to her and she was amazed at the simplicity of it.

With a calculated casualness, Constance excused herself from the table for a moment and went out to the kitchen to speak with Darnelle. Before returning to the dining room, she went upstairs and got three of the sleeping potions that Lawrence kept in his bag. She reached the bottom of the stairs just as Darnelle was coming in the back door.

"Here's you wine, Miz Constance." Darnelle handed her the bottle, which had already been opened.

"Thank you, Darnelle."

"That sho' was a good hiding place, why Ah didn't even know there was any wine lef'."

"I hid it years ago when the Yankees first came through and I thought it would be suitable to drink it tonight. After all, the Yankee is leaving tomorrow."

"Yes, ma'am," Darnelle said and went back to the kitchen.

Pausing for a moment in the hall, Constance

poured the potions into the already potent wine. If this didn't put Ellyn to sleep for the night, nothing would.

"I have a surprise," Constance announced, coming in to join them again.

"Oh?" Lawrence asked, wondering at Constance's behavior.

"Wine?" Ellyn and Charlotte asked in unison. "Where did you find it, Mother? We haven't had any in years!"

"I know. I've had the bottle hidden away waiting for a celebration and I thought that it might be just the thing for tonight."

Price watched her through heavy-lidded eyes. This was not in character for Constance at all. He knew without a doubt that she was up to something.

Constance handed the bottle to Lawrence who did the honors.

"This is a very unexpected pleasure, my dear," he told her as he handed her a glass. "I haven't had a good glass of wine since '62."

"None of us has." She took a small sip of the red liquid, smiling confidently when she found that the wine had disguised the bitter taste of the medicine.

She watched with concealed enjoyment as Ellyn finished her glass and had another. The Yankee, however, drank from his sparingly. As he felt Constance observing him, Price looked up and their gazes met and clashed.

"I am honored by this offering, Mrs. Douglass," he said politely, his eyes daring hers.

"My pleasure, Mr. Richardson." She returned his regard unafraid. "Tonight is a celebration of sorts. After all, you will be gone after tomorrow and things can get back to normal around here."

Ellyn gasped at her mother's bluntness. "Mother, really!"

"Ellyn," Price interrupted sternly. "It's not a problem. In some instances honesty is much easier to deal with. This happens to be one of those occasions."

"I'm glad we understand each other." Constance raised her glass in a mock toast.

"To your health, madam," he replied, draining his drink. "Now, if you all will excuse me, I'm going to retire early this evening as I have a big day tomorrow. Ladies, Lawrence."

Ellyn watched as he left the room, and she suddenly felt alone. More than a little tired, she was glad the evening was drawing to a close. She hoped everyone would fall asleep quickly tonight so she could go to Price that much sooner. Their last night together! The thought scared her. It had to be perfect. She had to give him wonderful memories to take with him. Memories that would bind him to her, even across the long miles.

Ellyn was relieved when Charlotte excused herself and she soon followed suit, leaving her mother and grandfather behind.

"I don't understand your change of attitude, but I'm not complaining," Lawrence told Constance after the girls had left the room. "I'm glad that you treated him with respect this evening."

"I realized how foolish I'd been behaving," she answered, gritting her teeth over the lie. "I thought the wine would make a pleasant diversion."

"It was a treat and I thank you for sharing it."

She noted his yawn. "You must be exhausted, too."

"I am more tired than I thought," he apologized. "I believe I'll follow the girls' example. Good night, Constance."

"Good night, Lawrence."

* * *

Ellyn deliberately sat on her uncomfortable vanity chair in hopes that it would keep her awake. The events of the last few days seemed to have taken their toll and all she could think of was sleep. Not even her desire to be with Price could overcome the dreaded drowsiness she now felt. Getting up groggily, she stood at the open window breathing deeply of the fresh night air, thinking that it would clear her head. Ellyn yawned wearily and noting that the light in the parlor was still on, she decided to stretch out on her bed while she waited. The softness of the mattress was inviting and Ellyn closed her eyes to enjoy its comfort to the fullest, certain that she would rest only a few minutes and then go to Price. She didn't want to keep him waiting.

A little later, when Constance retired, she was happy to find Ellyn, Charlotte and Lawrence all sound asleep in their rooms. Well satisfied with her plan, she went on to bed, pleased at how the night had turned out.

Price paced the cabin floor fighting down the urge to sleep. Where was Ellyn? He'd been waiting for what seemed like hours and still she had not come.

He couldn't decide whether to be angry or worried. Was she deliberately staying away or was she trapped by circumstances beyond her control in the house? Shaking off the lethargy that threatened to hold him, he left the house and went quietly up the path to Riverwood House. Staying hidden in the trees, Price watched the house for some time. When he could see no one around, he carefully made his way inside and up the carpeted stairs to Ellyn's room.

Hesitating only briefly, he tried her door and was

relieved to find it unlocked. Quickly, silently, he entered, shutting and locking it behind him. The room was dark; only fragile moonlight provided him a glimpse of her fully dressed sleeping figure on the bed. Eagerly, he went to her, wanting to awaken her with his passionate kisses. The bed sank under his weight and Price had expected her to stir at the disturbance, but Ellyn didn't move.

"Ellyn," he murmured, leaning over her and kissing her cheek tenderly.

When she only murmured sleepily, he grew concerned. Rolling her over on her back, he shook her gently.

"Wake up," he said anxiously, for he knew Ellyn to be a light sleeper.

Price was worried. He felt her forehead, but she was cool—no sign of illness. Throwing all caution aside, he lit the lamp on the small bedside table. When he noticed her pallor and the shallowness of her breathing, his first thought was that she'd taken a drug similiar to what was used for pain in the hospitals. Certainly, she was too soundly asleep to be aware of him or anything else. But why would she take something to put herself to sleep? Ellyn had wanted this night as much as he had. Surely she wouldn't have taken a sleeping potion deliberately . . . The wine! Constance! The pieces of this evening's puzzle fell into place. She knew about them. Somehow, she had found out.

Disgust and anger gripped him. The memory of her mocking toast came back to him and he grimaced. She was one vicious woman and he would have to be even more careful in the future when it came to dealing with her.

Realizing that the night was a total loss, he made Ellyn as comfortable as possible despite her sleepy protests before he headed back to his solitary bed. Kissing her, he left her room. He closed the door to her room, softly, anxious to be gone from here. He almost made it to the stairs, when Constance's door opened and she stepped into the hall.

"I've been waiting for you. I knew you'd come to check on her."

Price froze at the sound of her voice.

"She wasn't very lively this evening, was she?" Constance said, her voice seductive. "Not like last night."

Price turned to face her, his jaw tense as he tried to control his anger.

"Yes, I came to see if she was all right."

"I thought you might since you didn't drink much of my potent wine at dinner," she said.

In the dim hallway light, with her long, dark hair loose about her, Constance looked much younger than her age. Price, against his will, was attracted to her beauty. Her figure was full and lush and she wore a sheer gown to emphasize it. She hadn't fastened the concealing wrapper she had on, but had let it hang open to give him a better view of her body. Constance knew that men could be controlled easily as long as their minds were busy planning a seduction, so she moved closer to him in the hall.

"I'm glad now that I didn't."

"I'm sure you are." She reached easily into the pocket of her dressing gown.

"If you'll excuse me," Price began, wanting to get away from her. She had surprised him once and he wouldn't let it happen again.

"I think not," she stated firmly, pointing a small derringer at him.

Price's eyes widened at the sight of the gun bearing down on him. This woman was crazy!

"You know, I should shoot you for what you've done," she said calmly.

"What have I done?"

"Mr. Richardson, or shall I call you Price? No, we'd better keep this formal under the circumstances." She was talking mostly to herself. "Mr. Richardson, I just happened to have seen you leaving the house the night before last. So I decided to find out what was going on."

"And what is going on?" he asked, playing for time, wondering what to do.

"I followed Ellyn last night." She paused for emphasis. "As one of the participants in the main event, I'm sure you remember what happened next, unless you'd like me to refresh your memory?"

"Hardly," he replied.

"I thought not." She smiled tightly. "Shall we go downstairs and discuss this?"

"Madam, you're calling the shots, so to speak." He indicated the weapon in her hand. "I am at your disposal."

"Then precede me, sir, but know that I will not hesitate to use this."

"I will not underestimate you again," he told her as he led the way down to the main floor.

"Ah, at last an intelligent man. I've searched all my life to find one and now that I have . . . it's a shame that you're a Yankee."

Price didn't reply as his mind was racing, trying to figure a way out of the situation. He knew she hated him, but obviously, not enough to kill him. She could have shot him right away when he'd been defenseless. Price instinctively knew that Constance was a dead shot so her hesitance to use the weapon gave him hope.

"Go on into the parlor," she directed coldly, the

gun aimed at his back.

Moving easily into the dark room, he lit a lamp at her instruction. Then sitting on the sofa, he waited as she sat at the opposite end, a reasonable distance between them. His eyes took in all of her, as she posed seductively there. His first flare of lust for her had died, replaced by dangerous amusement. She was beautiful to look at but quite deadly and he had no intention of falling into that trap.

Gun held loosely in her practiced grip, Constance smiled at him. "I intend for you to stay away from my daughter."

Deciding to play the cynic, he replied nonchalantly, "That's an odd statement coming from you, after all, you're the one who threw us together."

"A mere miscalculation on my part. I thought you were dying."

"Sorry to disappoint you."

"I've gotten over that disappointment, but I want you away from here first thing in the morning." Her eyes were cold as she observed him.

"I believe that was plan," he stated, shrugging indifferently.

Constance was amazed at his attitude. He really didn't care for Ellyn. He had just been using her. She smiled, life did seem to repeat itself.

"Fine, then we're in agreement. I want you to—" At the sound in the hall, Constance reacted without thought, pocketing the gun, pulling down her gown and throwing herself onto Price's lap.

Ellyn had awakened disturbed as the voices in the hall outside her door seemed to pound in her head. They'd stopped at long last and she rested. A few minutes later she awoke with a start, realizing that she had to get to Price. Barely able to keep her eyes

189

open, she'd pulled herself out of bed and had gone out into the hall. Her steps had seemed to drag as she started downstairs, drawn by the sound of people talking and a light on in the parlor. Who was up at this hour? Their tones·were hushed and indistinct and Ellyn moved toward them as if in a dream. She bumped into the small table in the hall just as she staggered into the lamp-lit parlor.

Her eyes widened in shock at the scene on the sofa. Her mother! Price! They were saying something to each other and hadn't noticed her yet. Ellyn was horrified at the sight of her mother's scantily clad body pressed tightly to Price. Her wrapper and gown had slipped from her shoulder and Price's hand intimately cupped her full breast. Their movements seemed slow and restrained as they turned in unison to see her.

"Price . . ." She could only whisper as she swayed at the door.

Feeling nauseated, Ellyn rushed from the room and disappeared outside into the blackness of the night.

"Ellyn!" Price's strangled call came too late as he stood, dumping Constance unceremoniously on the floor.

He ran after her but she was gone. Furious at what had happened, he turned to Constance who stood smugly in the parlor doorway.

"I couldn't have managed that little tableau any better even if I'd planned it," she declared happily. "Who would have dreamed that she would wake up after all that wine?"

Price's fists clenched as he fought down the urge to throttle her. The night should have been a beautiful one for them and now it was a total disaster. He turned from Constance's cruel joy and left the house

190

in search of Ellyn.

"Good night, Price," Constance called as he walked away and her sarcastic laughter followed him, echoing through the night.

Dawn. The sky was vivid blue with no trace of clouds. The grass was damp with dew and the trees rustled easily as a soft breeze blew in off the river. Birds were singing and fussing as they welcomed the new day in their usual happy manner.

Ellyn sat, cold and miserable, in the stable. She'd heard Price's call last night as he'd searched for her, but she hadn't responded. Ellyn hadn't known what to do and there had been no one to go to, to talk. So she'd hidden there in a cramped, dark corner and, somehow, she'd managed to fall asleep. Her grand-father had awakened her when he'd saddled up Mo earlier, but Ellyn hadn't revealed herself. Instead, she'd been extra careful not to, so as to avoid all the questions she knew would be coming. She knew it was time to go back to the house, but fear gripped her. In that one instant, all her dreams had been shattered forever. The man she loved and her mother! How was it possible? After all that they'd been to each other? She was heartsick.

Dragging herself to her feet, she walked outdoors into the sunshine. With the warmth of the sun, a little of her spirit returned. If she could get through these next few hours, Ellyn knew she could get through anything. In a conscious gesture of unyield-ing determination, she squared her shoulders and headed toward the big house.

Sitting in the decrepit rocker on the porch of the

overseer's house, Price was exhausted. He'd spent the entire night looking unsuccessfully for Ellyn. For the first time in his adult life, he felt defeated . . . lost. He had to straighten things out with Ellyn before he left. He refused to be manipulated by Constance. She would not dictate his life to him! But as the sun rose and the heat of the day greeted him, he began to doubt seriously that he would get the opportunity to talk with her. His only hope was to leave a note for her with Darnelle explaining everything. As far as he was concerned, nothing had changed, he still wanted to marry her as soon as possible. Price got up and started on his way to the main house to find Darnelle.

Constance had enjoyed herself tremendously last night and she lounged in bed this morning feeling quite pleased with the way things were going. She was certain that her quickly acted-out charade had fooled Ellyn, for the silly girl still had not returned to the house. Constance could hardly believe Ellyn was that stupid, but . . . she wouldn't argue with success. She had set out to destroy Ellyn's feelings for Richardson and she'd succeeded. If the Yankee didn't care about Ellyn then her troubles were over for now. But if he did, her only problem was to get him away from Riverwood before he cornered Ellyn alone. Richardson was no fool and she knew that she'd have to move carefully from here on out. She rang for Darnelle to help her dress.

"Good morning, Mr. Price," Darnelle greeted him cheerfully. Then noticing his grim expression, she asked, "What's the matter?"

"It's Ellyn. Have you seen her?" he asked as he entered the kitchen.

192

"No, suh. Ah ain't seen her since supper. What happened?"

"There's been a misunderstanding between us and I wanted to straighten it out before I have to leave."

"Bad?"

"I'm afraid so and I don't have much time. I expect Lawrence to get back at any time now from checking the road."

"He should be," Darnelle agreed. "If you want, you can leave a note with me and Ah'll give it to her."

"I may have to if I don't find her in time. Do you have pen and paper?"

"Ah'll get 'em for you." Darnelle went in the back room for a minute and reappeared with the writing instruments.

"Thanks."

The bell rang from Constance's room and Darnelle hurried off, leaving Price alone with his thoughts.

Ellyn entered the house quietly and crept upstairs. She took extra care to go unnoticed as she passed her mother's room, for she could hear her talking with Darnelle. But Constance caught sight of her and called out.

"Ellyn! Good morning! Have you been out for a walk?"

Ellyn's newly restored determination almost failed her and she blinked back the tears that threatened to fall. Before facing her mother, she took a deep breath and then went into the bedroom.

"Yes, I was up early this morning."

"I know, I heard you. Did you really enjoy getting up at that hour?"

"No. It's dangerous to wander around at that time of night."

"Why? What happened?" Constance taunted.

193

"There were some vicious animals out last night."

"You weren't hurt were you?"

"No, I wasn't hurt." She paused as she noticed Darnelle watching her with great interest. "Well, I'll be in my room for a while. Did Grandfather get back yet?"

"No, but he should be back at any time," Constance told her as Ellyn moved to leave. "I'll call you when they're ready to go."

Ellyn didn't reply but went on to her bedroom.

When Darnelle finally got back to the kitchen, she found Price waiting.

"Miz Ellyn's back."

Looking pleased and surprised, he stood and started out the door.

"You bes' not go lookin' for trouble. Miz Constance is awake. There's somethin' strange goin' on with them."

"I know," he said, stopping at the door. "Darnelle, would you tell her that I've got to see her?"

"Ah'll try. You jes' wait here." But as she started across the walkway, Lawrence returned.

"Darnelle, have you seen Price?" he called to her.

"Yes, suh," she replied, distracted from her original purpose. Returning to the kitchen, she found Price. "Mr. Lawrence is back and he wants to see you."

Price looked up angrily. "I've got to see her! Could you take this note to her and tell her I'll stall down here as long as I can."

"Yes, suh." Darnelle hurried off, the folded paper in hand, as Price went out to greet Lawrence.

Darnelle stopped only long enough to read the missive before continuing upstairs. Shocked by what she'd read, she knew that she had to give Ellyn the letter, but as she rushed down the hall, Constance stopped her.

"I'll take that note," she demanded, holding out her hand.

"But it's for Miz Ellyn," Darnelle protested.

"Give it to me. She doesn't need to hear any more of his lies."

"But . . ."

"Now!"

Against her better judgment, Darnelle handed Constance the letter.

"Thank you. Now, you may go. I'll handle this from here."

Darnelle went back downstairs, worrying about what was taking place. Miz Constance was determined to keep Ellyn away from Price so she wouldn't discover the truth. And what an ugly truth it was. Shaking her head, she went outdoors to locate Price.

He was watching for her and came to meet her.

"Is she coming down? Did she read the letter?"

"Ah didn't get to give it to her. Miz Constance was watchin' us and she took de letter."

"Damn!" Price was furious. "Do you know if she'll be down at all?"

"When Ah was with Miz Constance earlier, she told Miz Ellyn that she'd call her when it was time to come down and tell you goodbye."

"Good. Can you help me be alone with her? I've got to talk with her if only for a few minutes," he asked in desperation.

"Ah'll see what Ah can do," she agreed. "But Ah can't promise nothin'. Miz Constance will be with her."

"I know," he stated flatly and looked up to see Lawrence and Franklin coming toward him leading

Mo and the Douglasses' only horse.

As he started to follow Darnelle up the gallery steps and into the house, Constance, Charlotte and Ellyn emerged. Constance looked at him in almost open amusement. She knew now that he did love Ellyn. Why else would he be so frustrated and angry. And that note! How she'd loved destroying it, after she'd read it, of course. Ellyn had not wanted to face Price, but Constance had insisted. If the tie was to be completely severed, Constance knew Ellyn would have to see him this one last time.

Price eyed Constance warily, noting the wicked, self-satisfied gleam in her eyes. Boldly, he mounted the steps and faced them.

Miss Douglass, it's been a pleasure meeting you," he said to Charlotte and then turned to Constance. "Mrs. Douglass, you are beyond compare. It's been memorable."

"I'm sure I feel the same about you."

"Ellyn, if I may have a word with you?" He extended his hand, but she did not take it.

"I don't think that's wise," Constance put in.

"And your thoughts on the matter are unimportant," he said, standing before Ellyn. "Ellyn?"

She looked up at him for an instant and their eyes clashed. Locked in mental combat, they stood silently.

"Ellyn," he murmured and kissed her cheek, whispering, "Trust me, I love you. Darnelle will explain everything." Then louder, he added, "Thank you for all you've done for me."

Constance was greatly agitated when he stepped away from Ellyn. She hadn't heard anything except the thank you, but she knew he was up to something.

"Well, Mr. Richardson, please don't let us hold you up. I'm sure you're anxious to get home."

"It will be a comfort to be wanted," he responded, taking a long, hard look at Ellyn. "Ladies, thanks again. Goodbye."

He left them standing there on the gallery and mounted the horse. With a final wave, Lawrence and Price started down the drive to begin their long journey back to town.

Ellyn watched bravely as he rode away. Gone, just like her dreams. All ruined. There were no tears left, she'd cried them all out last night. She felt only a great emptiness within her breast. It had taken all her courage to look him in the eye and she'd been amazed at the pain she'd seen in Price's face. What had he meant, "Trust me"? And "Darnelle will explain"? Explain what? That he had been making love to both her mother and herself? She didn't want to hear any excuses. He had used her and she felt cheapened by the whole sordid affair.

Turning back into the house, she went up to her room and locked the door. What she needed most of all now was sleep. Once she was rested, things would seem better. They always did.

Chapter Seven

The chirping of the sparrows and the raucous call of an early-rising jay broke through the last vestiges of the night's heavy silence. The chilly zephyr that stirred the sheer bedroom curtains promised a cool day ahead, an unusual occurrence for this late in June. Streaks of orange and pink decorated the rapidly brightening sky, making this dawn seem almost festive. It was a new day, a new beginning.

In the master bedroom of the Montague house, Mary Anne came awake suddenly. Startled to find the man slumbering soundly beside her, she lay still, her slender figure tense for a long moment until remembrance of the night just past came to her. She smiled then, quite pleased with herself. She did what she had set out to do. It had been more complex than she had expected, but she had done it.

Turning her head, she looked at the man lying next to her. Her pride in her accomplishment dimmed as she took in his plain, ordinary features, his nondescript light brown hair and his flabby body. No, to Mary Anne, there was nothing even remotely attractive about Alex Kent except his money. And there was plenty of that attribute, now. Now that

Price Richardson had been listed by the army as missing, presumed dead.

Lifting her hand, she stared at the huge diamond engagement ring Alex had given her when he'd proposed last night. Overcome by both guilt and sadness, she sighed. Desperation could force a person to do things she normally wouldn't do. Turning on her side, away from him, she watched the sky change colors and wondered about what might have been.

Four years ago, her parents had died and she'd finally been free of their restraining influence. She'd been young and carefree and rich—and she'd had Price. He had set her world aflame with his dark good looks and his sensuous charm. Although she had not been a virgin, he'd made her feel as one, as he'd taught her all the secrets of love she'd never known. It had been a wondrous time in her life, a time of self-discovery and excitement.

That she had loved him went without saying. That he'd been wealthy had been unimportant, then. Mary Anne knew now that her actions then had been foolish, but at that point in time she had been eager for new experiences. When Alex had come calling, she'd gone with him, flattered by his attentions, for he had belonged to the fast, rich crowd that she'd never been a part of. Mary Anne had arranged to see him only when she was certain that Price was not coming by. And she'd carried off the deception quite successfully until that one fateful night when Price had stopped in intending to surprise her and had found her in a passionate embrace with his hated cousin, Alex. Even though it had been four years ago, she still remembered vividly the terrible moment when Alex had laughingly greeted him and Price had left in a rage. She had tried to explain to Price later, but he had refused to see her in private and had severed their relationship completely.

Losing the one man she'd really cared about had almost destroyed her emotionally, but slowly Mary Anne came to realize that her life had to continue. And so, she had hidden her deep love for Price behind a facade of gaiety and wild living, always believing secretly that one day he would come back to her. But when Price had gone off to war without even saying goodbye, she had been heartbroken. None of her friends had ever been aware of her anguish, for she had disguised it most successfully by her pseudo-carefree lifestyle.

No one knew that she lived in constant hope of Price's return to her. But during the past six months, it had become more of a prayer than a hope, for Mary Anne had gotten herself into deep financial trouble and she was now in dire straights. The only solution that occurred to her was to find a wealthy husband.

The end of the war had come fortuitously and she had listened anxiously to all the gossip, wanting to find out the moment Price returned. It had been a horrible day for her when she'd gotten the news from his aunt Rachel Kent that he was presumed dead. Mary Anne had hidden herself away for days, crying out her sorrow and mourning what she had fantasized might have been. Finally conquering her grief, she knew what she had to do.

The richest available man was Alex Kent. Destined to inherit all of Price's holdings and already well-to-do in his own right, he was the perfect choice. Her goal set, Mary Anne had done everything in her power to induce him to propose marriage. And, at long last, this past night during their candlelight dinner, he had finally done it.

Mary Anne looked at the ring again, its large stone

seeming cold and lifeless in the clear morning light. Yes, she thought, it reminded her of what her married life to Alex would be like. Barren.

Glancing at Alex, she was glad to see that he was still asleep. She was exhausted from a long night of his lovemaking and was not ready yet for more. She needed time to think, to prepare herself for her future.

Sighing, she supposed drearily that they would have to marry soon. Her money situation was desperate and there was little point in postponing the inevitable. Plus, rumors would surely be flying now that he'd spent the entire night here.

She shivered at the caress of the cool breeze and pulled the sheet up over her bare shoulder, closing her eyes against the ever-brightening new day. Maybe a short nap would improve her outlook, for after all, the decision was made and now she would have to live with it. She'd been through it all so many times that she knew that there was no other way. Slowly, the conviction that she had done the right thing returned and Mary Anne fell asleep, her worries about money finally put to rest.

Alex Kent stirred and came awake slowly, his senses full of the beautiful woman sleeping with him. He rolled over carefully, so as not to awaken her for he wanted a few minutes to savor the sweetness of this time.

He knew that his mother would be quite proud of him for he'd found the solution to their dilemma. Ever since their money had begun to run out, Rachel had been searching for new ways to improve their financial outlook. Now, Alex had the answer: a rich wife.

It was a bonus for him that Mary Anne was attractive, for at this point in time, in order to maintain his luxurious lifestyle, he would have married just about anyone, as long as she was well-off. Now, he considered himself quite fortunate for Mary Anne was exactly the type of woman that he would have picked even if he hadn't needed her money. She was slim, almost to the point of boyishness, and petite, barely topping five feet. Her hair was black and lustrous, her complexion fashionably pale and flawless. Her eyes were tip-tilted and amber in color, accented by gently curving dark brows. Her nose was small and straight, her mouth sensuous and expressive.

Alex let his mind roam over the night they'd just spent together, recalling her acceptance of his proposal and the passionate lovemaking that had followed. What a wanton she could be! She satisfied him more than any woman he'd ever known and he couldn't wait to have her again.

Reaching out, rousing her from a deep sleep, he pulled her back against him, pressing his erection against her buttocks.

"Good morning, my future bride," he murmured throatily in her ear, before pressing hot kisses down her neck and shoulders.

Taken by surprise by his ardor, Mary Anne twisted toward him and pushed at his chest, trying ineffectually to break away.

"Alex! Stop!" She struggled momentarily.

"Oh, no. Not now," he laughed, kissing her.

Common sense told her to give in gracefully to his passion, for after all, he was her fiance. So brushing aside the cobwebs of her dreams of Price, she surrendered to Alex's demands.

Mary Anne responded with unrestrained enthusiasm, as the woman she had become during these past years took over. She was a creature of pleasure, seeking and taking whatever sensual thrills she could find.

Alex, for all that he was not handsome, was enough of a man to satisfy her. He assaulted her senses, teasing her to the heights of passion, bringing her close to completion time and again before finally providing the release she was begging for. Mary Anne stiffened as waves of pleasure surged through her body. Clutching frantically at Alex's shoulders, she urged him to join with her. To fill the aching void within her.

Alex was pleased that he'd managed to arouse Mary Anne, in spite of her initial reluctance. He entered her then and relished the hot wetness of her as he moved deep inside her body. Beyond control, he gained his own satisfaction quickly and rolled away from her, breathing heavily.

"I think we'll do well together." He smiled at her confidently.

Feeling weak and sore, Mary Anne managed a lazy smile.

"Yes, we will," she agreed, thankful that at least she wouldn't be sexually frustrated in her married life.

Alex reached out and touched her breast, mentally praising her trim, almost boyish figure. Then reluctantly, he withdrew his hand.

"As much as I'd like to spend the day here in bed with you, I must get going."

"What do you have to do today?" she asked, not really caring.

"Mother and I are finalizing our plans to take over Price's holdings at Alton Transshipping. Today, I believe, we're scheduled to see an attorney so we can determine exactly where we stand."

"Oh." She had been uninterested until she'd heard him mention Price. Suddenly, it was drilled home to her again with a vengeance, he wouldn't be coming back . . . ever. Somewhere on some bloody battlefield, he'd died and his body had never been recovered. Her eyes burned with unshed tears. Faking a yawn, Mary Anne rubbed at them sleepily, hoping to hide the emotion reflected there.

"You go back to sleep," Alex told her, getting up and beginning to dress. "I'll see myself out."

"That sounds good," she agreed huskily, pulling the sheet over her.

"I don't know if I'll be able to get away tonight or not."

"I'll be right here, waiting to hear from you."

"Fine." Alex pulled on his jacket and leaned over the bed to kiss her once more. "I'll see you later."

Mary Anne stared at her ring for a long time after he'd gone. Finally, when she could stand it no longer, she cried, burying her face in the pillow to muffle her sobs. She would marry Alex, for it didn't really matter at all anymore what she did. Price was gone, gone for good.

Chapter Eight

As the Westlake side-wheeler, the *Louisiana Lady*, churned her way northward toward St. Louis, Capt. Price Richardson stood at the rail of the Texas deck watching with little real interest the monotonous passing of the green Missouri country-side. Though he looked fit and healthy in the new uniform the Union officials had given him in Memphis, the past three days aboard the boat had taken their toll. His dark eyes seemed haunted and his manner was nervous as he waited impatiently for the voyage to be over. Nightly he'd been bombarded by fiendish memories of those final fateful hours on the *Sultana*. Unable to sleep in the close confines of his cabin, he had restlessly prowled the decks, each unexpected sound convincing him that an explosion was imminent. Having spent the better part of his life working on steamers, he knew that this boat was safe. Less than a year old, she was the flagship of the Westlake Line out of St. Louis. Graceful, fast and luxurious, everything about her bespoke of elegance, from her crystal and brass chandeliers to her hand-painted china. Had Price been interested in his own creature comforts, he would have enjoyed the

Louisiana Lady's impressive appointments. As it was, his only desire was to get home. So he continued his vigil, waiting even more anxiously now as they neared St. Louis hoping to dock later this afternoon.

Memphis, Tennessee to Cairo, Illinois. Cairo to Cape Girardeau, Missouri. Cape to Sainte Genevieve, Missouri. Sainte Gen to St. Louis. All those beautiful historic names meant nothing to him as the hours dragged by, each day seeming an eternity to him. Torn in three directions by his concern for Betsey, his fear of losing Ellyn and the nagging possibility of an explosion, Price was for all practical purposes immobilized. He had eaten little and socialized even less, being in no mood for idle pleasantries. Shortly, he would have to face Betsey and tell her that Coop was dead. He wished that there was a way to avoid the confrontation, but he knew that it was important for her to hear everything from him. Betsey, in addition to being a wonderful wife to Coop, was his own good friend and he owed it to her.

Price wondered if she had received his telegram. He'd sent word from Memphis that he was on his way back and would probably arrive in Alton either late today or early tomorrow. This boat went only as far north as St. Louis, so he would have to arrange transport to Alton from there.

The *Louisiana Lady* was skimming past Jefferson Barracks on a direct run for the St. Louis riverfront when Price looked up and saw the boat's captain, Jim Westlake, approaching.

"Captain Richardson," Captain Westlake spoke cheerfully. "I'm sorry I haven't had the opportunity to speak with you before. Have you been enjoying the trip?"

"You have a most impressive boat," Price replied, extending his hand to the other man. "She's relatively new, isn't she?"

"She was just commissioned last fall. She's a dream, all right," Jim Westlake said with pride. "Can I buy you a drink?"

Price hesitated, wondering how far they were from St. Louis.

"Don't worry," Jim told him, noticing his concern. "We've got a good half an hour before I have to get back to work."

"Then I gladly accept." Price smiled and relaxed a little.

"Are you from St. Louis?"

"No, Alton. And it's been a long time since I've been home."

"You should be able to get a boat out this afternoon."

"Good."

"Were you injured in battle?" the captain asked, indicating his arm.

"No." Price said abruptly, frowning, and he was glad for the respite from the conversation as they entered the grand salon.

Jim Westlake spoke casually with his passengers as they walked the length of the steamer and went into the bar. After getting their drinks, he directed Price to a table in the far corner. Settling in easily, he looked over at Price, taking note of his anxious state.

"Were you on the *Sultana?*"

Price was completely surprised by the question and his expression darkened. "How could you tell?"

"Just a hunch. I remember that you came aboard at Memphis and with the new uniform and all." He stopped when he noticed Price's discomfort. "That explosion's been the talk of the river for the past week or so.''

"I can well imagine," Price said with as little emotion as was possible for him. Raising his tumbler with a shaking hand, he drained his bourbon.

"That bad?" Westlake signalled for another round as he finished his scotch.

"Worse."

"Then I'll bet you've had a hell of a time these past few days," Jim empathized.

Price grinned, acknowledging the humor of his situation. "You're right about that."

"I thought so. I was the same way for months after the first *Louisiana Lady*'s boilers let go back in '61. That was one day I'll never be able to forget." Jim took the bottles that the bartender brought to the table. "Thanks, Ollie," he told the old man who then returned to his duties at the bar.

"It was a nightmare. I'm lucky to be alive."

Westlake nodded in sympathetic understanding and they were silent for a long minute as he refilled their glasses.

"So what did you do before the war?"

"I'm part owner of Alton Transshipping."

"Alton Transshipping? I know your boats. You run a very profitable business."

"Very and I'll be glad to get back to it."

"I just wonder how we'll be able to hold out against the railroads."

"I've thought about that, too." Price drank deeply of the potent liquor, relaxing as he felt its heat take the edge off his tension. He massaged his neck in a tired effort. "My business will be relatively stable until they put a bridge in. Yours . . ."

"I know. With the war over I'm afraid they'll be taking all of our passenger business." Jim was interrupted by the loud whistle from above and he rose. "It's about that time. Would you like to join me in the pilot's house?"

"Thanks, I would."

The two men left the bar and made their way to the pilothouse. The view of the bustling St. Louis levee was a magnificent vista of white, glistening steamers, nestled close to each other at their moorings. Though the riverfront wasn't as crowded with merchandise as it had been in the pre-war years, it was still the hub of activity for the city.

Home. Familiar places, familiar people. Price searched the crowd below in hopes of seeing someone he knew, but there was no one he recognized. That would come in just a few hours, in Alton.

After thanking Westlake and bidding him goodbye, Price got his things from his cabin and left the boat, eager to find transport to Alton. By four that afternoon, he was on his way. Now Alton was only a matter of hours away, not days.

The Bluff City, as Alton was so aptly nicknamed, was the North's equivalent of Vicksburg. Situated on scenic palisades overlooking the Mississippi, it was a busy port and industrial center. The war had enhanced Alton's prominence on the river for it had become a major supply point for the Union troops.

Price was thrilled as his hometown came into view. There had been times during the past few years when he'd thought he wouldn't live to see it again. His heart swelled with emotion as he wished that Coop was with him now. Gathering his few things, he waited eagerly for the packet to tie up at a wharf boat.

It was after six p.m. when they finally docked at the foot of Piasa Street. Price was one of the first passengers down the gangplank. There were a few people waiting, but Betsey was not among them. A little disheartened, but still glad for the reprieve, Price headed for Coop's house on Henry Street. He almost stopped by his company office, but then realized that he was just looking for a reason to delay the inevitable. He had to tell Betsey that Coop was dead.

The thought occurred to him that she might have good news about Coop, but he ignored the musing as wishful thinking. Everything he'd seen and heard in Memphis had convinced him that there was no hope of finding Coop alive. Deep in thought, he trudged up the steep hill, not noticing the carriage coming toward him. It was only when the horse stopped nearby that Price glanced up.

"Price!" two voices greeted him joyously.

Stunned by the sound of the one voice he had never thought to her again, Price could only stare up at the buggy where Coop and Betsey sat smiling.

"Coop?" His tone was incredulous. "You're alive?"

Betsey jumped down and threw herself into Price's arms. "Of course, silly. He got home three days ago!"

Overcome by Coop's unexpected presence, Price kissed Betsey in good-natured excitement and hugged her tightly.

"What a wonderful homecoming. You don't know what I've gone through thinking you'd . . ."

"I know. I know," Coop told him. "We'll talk later."

"We have to," Price agreed, smiling up at his friend. Then kissing Betsey once more he asked, "Now, where is my godson? That's one young man I'm anxious to meet."

"He's at the house with his nurse, just waiting to meet his Unca Pry. Come on," she insisted, tugging on his good arm. "I've planned a big welcome-home feast!"

Price allowed himself to be pulled along. After helping Betsey back into the carriage, he climbed in, tossing his small bag of belongings behind the seat. It was then that Price noticed Coop's cane.

"Your leg? How is it?"

"Amazingly enough, it's much improved. A doctor in the Memphis hospital fixed me up. I've still got a lot of soreness, but it should be all right eventually."

"Good." Price was relieved.

They rode back to the Cooper house in peaceful, relief-filled silence. They were all together again.

"Everything looks the same," he remarked as they came to a halt in front of the stately two-story brick home on Henry Street.

"It is, except for our star boarder," Betsey teased.

"Well, let's go meet him." Price got out and turned to swing Betsey down. After Coop handed the reins to the stableboy, he climbed slowly from the carriage, favoring his injured limb.

"I'm moving slowly, but at least I'm moving." He grinned at Price when he caught him watching. "Thank God I've still got two."

The men went into the study for a drink while Betsey left to organize the food and to bring Jason down to meet his godfather. Staring at each other across the room, Price and Coop could hardly believe their good fortune. Grinning in light-hearted happiness, they embraced.

"I'm glad you're all right," Price told him earnestly when they had refilled their glasses and settled into the two facing wing chairs.

"You wouldn't have believed how excited I was when we got your telegram. After watching what went on that night, well, I really thought you were dead."

"I know. I felt the same way. I was blown off the boat by the explosion and by the time I got myself oriented, I couldn't find you anywhere. I tried to swim back to the boat to see if you were trapped but I was downstream. God, it was terrible." He groaned, momentarily reliving the horror of that death-filled night. Running a hand nervously through his thick, dark hair, he rose and stalked to the window. "You'd have laughed at how jumpy I was all the way home."

"No, I wouldn't. I was the same way!" Coop laughed, trying to calm his friend. "We have both been working on boats all our lives but I've never been as scared as I was on my second attempt to leave Memphis. If there had been any other way to get back—a train or walking, even! But I figured if I walked, Jason would probably be ten or eleven before I got home."

Price chuckled. "Today it's funny, but yesterday, I thought I'd never get here. And then the worry about telling Betsey—I figured that was going to be the hardest thing I would ever have to do in my life."

Coop nodded his understanding. "How did you get out of the river?"

"I managed to catch on to a tree, but I didn't get picked up until the next morning."

"Who rescued you? One of the steamers? From what I understand, they were combing the river for survivors the whole following day."

"No. In fact, I didn't see any of those boats. An old man and a girl from a plantation on the Tennessee side came out and got me in a skiff. I

212

don't remember too much about it."

"You were lucky," Coop said.

Price was quiet then as thoughts of Ellyn flooded him. He could almost feel the warmth of her in his arms and smell her sweet scent.

"Ellyn set my arm for me."

"Ellyn?" Coop asked, wondering at the softening of Price's expression. "How old is this 'girl'?"

Price laughed in genuine amusement. "I know what you're thinking and you're right. If I could have persuaded her to come with me, we would have been married right away."

"Why didn't she? I've never known you to have any trouble getting what you wanted from women."

"She had obligations."

"She wasn't married already, was she?" Coop asked sharply.

"No. Just engaged and she wouldn't break it off until she could tell him face to face." Price came to sit down opposite Coop again. "Ellyn told me she'd come north as soon as she could. But he's in the army and she didn't know when he'd return."

"That could take a while, maybe months!"

"I know, but she's worth the wait." He paused, remembering. "Now, tell me, who rescued you?"

"Nobody quite so romantic, thank goodness! Betsey would have shot me!"

They laughed.

"I ended up in the water, too, and when I couldn't find you I grabbed onto a board and floated downstream. There were three other men with me and they kept me awake."

"Who pulled you out?"

"Some soldiers at Fort Pickens," Coop told him.

"That far? That's three miles south of town!"

"Yeah, we floated right on past Memphis and

213

nobody even saw us or heard us. It was quite a swim."

"Then what? Did you get passage north from there?"

"No, the soldiers took us to a hospital in town. It was two full days before I got transport home." He paused. "That was some homecoming. I hadn't had time to send word ahead, so I took Betsey completely by surprise."

"I'll bet you did!" Price was interrupted as Betsey came in carrying a chubby, blond toddler in her arms.

"It was the best surprise I've ever had!" She smiled tenderly at her husband.

Price looked up at the cherubic face of his godson. "So, this is Jason Jericho Cooper? He's beautiful, Betsey."

"I know." She smiled, her face alight with maternal pride. "He must get his looks from me. I doubt if Coop was ever this cute."

Both men laughed as Betsey put Jason on Price's lap. Jason eyed this strange man warily, not quite certain that he trusted him. His bottom lip quivered nervously until his mother sat on the floor at Price's feet. Satisfied that he hadn't been deserted, he turned his full attention to the mustachioed, dark-haired man who was holding him. Reaching out, Jason poked playfully at Price's mustache, fascinated by it. Feeling quite foolish, Price couldn't stop himself from smiling at the child.

"Hi, little guy," he said, sounding, he thought, ridiculous.

"Don't worry, Price, you'll get used to him. I talk to him all the time. It's great right now, he can't argue with me yet."

Price grinned at Betsey, whose wholesome

214

loveliness had been transformed to pure beauty by her undisguised love. "How did he take to his father?"

"They were friends at first sight and it's only gotten better."

"It's really something, Price—my own son." Coop looked fondly at his child sitting calmly on his closest friend's lap.

When the maid announced dinner, Betsey took Jason back upstairs to his nurse, before joining the men to eat. It was a wonderful finish to a nerve-wracking day, as they relaxed comfortably savoring the delicious home-cooked meal and then taking their after-dinner brandies in the study.

Betsey sat a little away from Price and Coop wanting to just enjoy watching them. How lonely she'd been without them! Jericho—her husband, her lover, her life. Price—her dear friend and confidant.

She half-listened to their easy banter. Price's return had been just what Coop had needed to cheer him up. Though he'd been overjoyed at coming home, the trauma he'd been through had taken its toll on him. His first night back, he and Betsey had stayed up until dawn, talking. He had told her everything ending with what he'd thought had been Price's death. When they'd received Price's telegram the following day they had been ecstatic. Now they were reunited and life could go on much as it had before the war.

"How soon do you think Ellyn will get here?" Betsey asked anxiously, for they had discussed his situation at length during the meal.

"I hope it won't be more than another month. It all depends on where Rod Clarke was when the fighting ended. If he's in Virginia, it's going to be a while before he gets home."

"That's too bad. I'm looking forward to meeting her. She must be very special. There will be a lot of disappointed ladies when the news finally gets out that you're getting married!" Betsey teased, her blue eyes twinkling. "Oh, I forgot to tell you, Mary Anne Montague asked about you just last week."

"Mary Anne?" Price's voice was cold.

"She wanted to know if it was true that you were dead."

"I wonder why the interest. There's no chance in hell that she'd be in my will."

"Maybe she still cares for you?" Betsey suggested.

"No, Betsey. That ended years ago by her own choice. No, there must be another reason."

Betsey was silent, remembering how much Price had cared for Mary Anne before the war. But Mary Anne had been wild and when he'd found her in a compromising position with his cousin Alex . . . well, that had been that. He'd left her and had never looked back, despite all her pleadings that she could explain. Since then he'd had women, but had taken none of them seriously. He'd devoted himself mainly to the business and had been glad of it. Betsey hoped that Ellyn was as wonderful as Price said she was for he deserved some happiness in his life.

"Betsey," Coop was saying. "Didn't you tell me that Mary Anne had been seeing Alex again? Maybe he put her up to it?"

"That sounds like Alex," Price said disgustedly.

"And Tim tells me that Rachel has been to the office making inquiries. I think she really hopes that you're dead."

"No doubt." He smiled cynically. "Why, if Rachel was sure that I was dead, she'd be in line at the bank before I could be lowered in the ground."

"She does want your money." Coop grinned.

216

"The point is, she's already had it once and wasted it, now she wants to try again."

"We'll just make sure she doesn't get the opportunity," Coop told him.

"Right," Price agreed, finishing off his drink. "Well, I don't know about you, but I'm exhausted. Shall we call it a night?"

"Fine. I'll tell you, I haven't been this relaxed in days. I just might sleep tonight."

"When was the last time you got any rest?"

"A very long four days ago."

They climbed the stairs together, Price slowing his pace to stay with Coop.

"Goodnight, Price. I'll see you in the morning and we'll start taking care of business," Coop said, entering the master bedroom where Betsey awaited him.

"All right. Goodnight, Coop," Price called softly as he continued down the hall to the guest bedroom.

After undressing, Price stretched out on the soft double bed at peace with himself. He felt his life would be perfect just as soon as Ellyn became his wife. Coop's mention of Mary Anne had stirred memories that had years ago lost their power to hurt. His short involvement with her had taught him much about life and numerous times since, he'd been grateful for the lesson. Especially now, for if he'd married sooner, he would never have fallen in love with Ellyn.

Ellyn. How he missed her and they'd only been apart for three days. Had it only been four nights ago that he'd kissed her as she slept? Sighing in remorse over that final wasted night at Riverwood, he fell into an exhausted, dreamless sleep.

At the same time, some three hundred miles away, Ellyn lay tossing in her bed. Price had dominated her thoughts all day. No matter how often she'd forced herself to think of his deceit with her mother, the memories came back of his final words to her. Trust me . . . Darnelle will explain everything. But Constance had sent Darnelle into town that same day and they hadn't had a chance to talk yet. With a sob, she threw off the bedclothes and moved to stand at her bedroom window. Where was he now? Did he miss her? Think of her? Everything had been so wonderful between them . . . until that last night. Tears fell unbidden. How could he have done that to her? Staring miserably in the direction of the overseer's house, she almost wished that she'd never met him, for the pain of having to give him up was devastating. Drawing a ragged breath, she lay down again hoping to gain release from her torment through sleep.

Constance sat in the parlor alone, enjoying the solitude. Things were at last back to normal. Lawrence was constantly traveling to Memphis to take care of whatever it was he did there; Ellyn and Glory were keeping the house running and Franklin was keeping food on the table. Constance had sent Darnelle into Memphis on a fictitious mercy mission to a friend's house just to keep her away from Ellyn for a few days.

Constance had had a long talk with Lawrence about the Yankee and they had both agreed that his leaving had been for the best. Lawrence had come to realize that Ellyn had been attracted to Richardson and he admitted that removing the temptation had been the best solution. He'd also agreed to give Constance any of Ellyn's correspondence that came from Price. Together they would prevent any contact

218

between the two. Completely convinced that she'd won, Constance went up to bed eagerly awaiting Rod Clarke's return.

Price slept soundly for the first time since leaving Memphis. The familiarity of his surroundings plus the knowledge that Coop was alive and well helped him get the rest he so desperately needed. He woke at dawn completely refreshed and lay in bed listening to the sounds of the house as it slowly came to life. Getting up, he dressed and after finding a pen and paper in the desk, he sat down to write to Ellyn. His letter was cheerful and confident, though in the back of his mind, he feared that Ellyn's trust in him had been destroyed by Constance's one incriminating embrace. His only hope was Darnelle and if Ellyn didn't believe her . . . Ignoring that defeatist thought, he wrote positively. He explained everything to her as he wrote, telling her that he could hardly wait to be with her again. After finishing, he went downstairs to meet Coop and have breakfast.

It was near noon when Coop and Price arrived at the bank. They'd spent the better part of the morning arranging Price's discharge from the army. Assured that it would be completed as soon as possible, he was given an indefinite leave. Glad to know that his military career was about to come to an end, they headed for the bank to check on the state of their finances.

Mr. Lowrey, the bank's president, looked up as the two men entered his office.

"Mr. Cooper! Mr. Richardson! How wonderful to see you both! I'd heard you were both dead!"

Coop grinned, indicating his leg. "Well, the Rebs tried real hard but we were too ornery for them."

Coming around his desk, Mr. Lowrey shook hands with both men. "What can I do for you?"

"We'd like to go over both our personal and business accounts, if you have the time," Coop said.

"No problem. You two just sit down and make yourselves comfortable and I'll have the file clerk bring in your books so we can go over everything."

As Mr. Lowrey hurried from his office, Price and Coop seated themselves in the two chairs that faced his desk. He returned quickly.

"He'll be here in a moment with all the information we need."

"Good. We're anxious to know our status as far as the business is concerned."

"Are you thinking of expanding your operations?"

"The thought had crossed my mind," Coop said. "But first, we have to see how our cash flow is."

"Understandable, of course. And with the war over now, I just don't know how river transportation is going to hold its own in direct competition with the railroads." He paused. "When did you get back?"

"I arrived yesterday," Price explained. "But Coop beat me back by a good four days."

"I thought perhaps that you'd returned together."

"It started off that way, but we were separated at Memphis," Coop said easily, not wanting to get into a long explanation about the *Sultana*.

"Well, the important thing is that you are back." Then, unable to contain his curiosity any longer, Mr. Lowrey asked, "Were you injured in battle?"

Coop grimaced. "We were in Andersonville prison camp and I was shot by a damn fool guard."

"And I had an accident in Memphis," Price added wryly.

220

"But you'll both be all right, won't you?"

"Should be in no time."

"Good. Oh, here's Charles with your accounts now."

A harried-looking young man spread the ledgers before them. They went over the office books first. Then, satisfied with those figures, they examined Coop's and Price's accounts. As Mr. Lowrey began to explain the figures in Price's ledger, he smiled up at Price.

"I'll bet your Aunt Rachel was happy to see you, after last week."

"My aunt? Actually, Mr. Lowrey, I haven't spoken with my aunt yet. We're not on the best of terms."

"Oh, dear." The bespectacled older man paled. "I'm afraid this is very awkward then."

"What is?" Price wondered, giving the banker a curious glance.

"Well, just last week she came in to see me about your money. She had the telegram from the army informing her that you were presumed dead." Lowrey swallowed nervously.

"So?"

"I assumed, since she was your only living relative."

"Yes?" Price was clearly agitated.

"I assumed it would be acceptable to advance her monies from your funds, since the government had sent her the notification."

Price's eyes grew cold. "You what?"

"I advanced her money against your estate."

"How much?" he demanded icily.

Mr. Lowrey took off his wire-rimmed glasses and polished them in a nervous gesture. "I let her have a thousand dollars."

"A thousand dollars!" Price was furious.

"She pleaded hardship," Lowrey was quick to explain as Price rose and paced angrily about the room.

"Hardship?" His voice was cutting. "I don't think she knows the meaning of the word!"

Price looked quickly at Coop, who was trying to hide a smile.

"And just what do you think is so funny?"

"You've got to give the woman credit. She's always trying to better herself."

"At my expense. She's a damn vulture!"

"Is that one advance all she got?" Coop asked Mr. Lowrey, who was bewildered by the interplay between them.

"Yes. Only one withdrawal over these past four years. And that was with my approval, last week."

Coop moved to look more closely at the figures of Price's account.

"Price, come here and take a look at this."

Price grudgingly came to stand by the desk. Glancing quickly over the figures, he smiled.

Mr. Lowrey spoke unsurely, "I'll make restitution to you for my error in judgment, but it may . . ."

"No need, Mr. Lowrey," Price said at once, totally relaxed.

"Not bad?" Coop grinned.

"I suppose I can spare it." Price turned to the bank president. "I want you to make sure that no one ever has access to my funds except myself and Mr. Cooper. No matter what. Especially Rachel or Alex Kent."

"Fine." Lowrey made the necessary notations, breathing easier now that he didn't have to make up the money given to Rachel Kent.

"Is there anything else I can do for you?"

"I do need a bank draft."

"All right. How much and who should we make it out to?"

"Three hundred dollars and make it out to a Miss Ellyn Douglass."

When Mr. Lowrey left them alone in the office, Coop spoke, "Why the draft?"

"Once Ellyn breaks off her engagement, I don't think her family's going to be very supportive," he explained. "I want to make sure she's got enough money to get here."

"We can drop it off at the post office on our way back."

"Good. The sooner I get this to her, the better."

As soon as Mr. Lowrey brought them the draft they left the bank, totally satisfied by their findings. They were the rich co-owners of a flourishing business.

Climbing into the carriage, Coop smiled. "How does it feel to be rich?"

"I don't know yet," Price returned. "But remind me to thank Tim Radcliffe the next time I see him. He did a helluva job managing ATC for us while we were gone."

"That's for sure. But you aren't exactly exuberant for a man who's just found out he's wealthy. What's wrong?"

"It's Rachel."

"What about her?"

"I want her out of Richardson House," he said with determination.

Coop was surprised and showed it. "Why now? After all this time?"

"I spent a lot of time in Andersonville, trying to decide what was important to me. I know now. Richardson House and Ellyn. I have to have them both."

"How are you going to get her out? She's lived there for years—ever since your parents died."

"Money. If they're really as hard up as Lowrey says, well, I think she'll jump at my offer."

"Well, friend, I wish you luck. She's one vicious, conniving woman, so be careful."

"Don't worry. I'm going to make them an offer they can't refuse."

Though the morning had been beautiful and the weather superb, Ellyn had taken no notice. She sat in the decrepit rocker, staring dully out at the landscape. She was confused, her mind cluttered with everything Darnelle had just told her. She had thought coming out here to the overseer's house would help straighten it all out, but it had only made things worse. Memories of Price were everywhere—his tenderness, his ardor, his love.

Ellyn frowned. Price had loved her . . . or at least he'd been capable of a good imitation. Could things have changed so quickly between them? According to Darnelle, they hadn't. This morning, Darnelle had finally gotten the opportunity to tell her Price's version of what had happened that last night. But why had her mother given her the impression that she and Price were lovers? Why would she lie? Suddenly, all of the pieces seemed to fall into place, as Ellyn once again realized just how much Constance hated Yankees and the lengths she would go to tear the two of them apart. Constance had staged that whole scene just to ruin Ellyn's relationship with Price and she had succeeded. Ellyn had let Price leave, not knowing how deeply she loved him.

Now, she hoped everything that Darnelle had told her was the truth. That Price felt the same way he always had and that he still wanted them to be married as soon as possible. Relieved by her understanding, Ellyn rested back in the old, creaky chair. It was just like he'd said—there was always pain involved anytime something was worth having.

Ellyn's only concern now was Rod. She knew it was going to be awkward and painful to end their relationship, but she could do it as long as she knew Price was waiting for her. Leaving the old house, she made her way home, planning to write to Price that very evening. He'd only been gone a few days, but to Ellyn it seemed a lifetime.

Chapter Nine

The Richardson estate was a magnificent three-story brick home located on fashionable State Street high on a bluff overlooking the Mississippi. In all seasons, the view the house afforded was breathtaking. When the river flooded in the springtime, it became a raging muddy torrent filled to bursting with not only her own debris but with that of the Illinois River which joined with her just a few miles to the north. In the summer, the Mississippi appeared deceptively sluggish, as if enjoying a calm vacation after such a strenuous spring. Fall brought a bright burst of dying color to her tree-shrouded banks and made her seem a life line to the warmer states to the south. Barren and icy during the frigid winter months, the river threatened all who sailed upon her with the sharp chunks of ice that were making their way haphazardly downstream in pursuit of their own destruction. And Price had witnessed it all during those happy years of his early childhood.

Sitting alone in his carriage before his family home, Price studied the mansion with eager eyes, admiring its stately splendor. From a distance, the long years of neglect were not obvious, but, as he left the carriage and approached, he could tell that it was in need of major repairs.

With a heavy hand, he let the tarnished brass knocker fall and waited impatiently for someone to come. Alex finally opened the door.

"You're alive!" He gaped, astonished by the sight of his cousin.

"How perceptive of you," Price remarked derisively, brushing past Alex and entering the house. "I need to see Rachel right away."

"Mother isn't up yet. Whatever you have to say, you can say to me." Alex moved, trying to block Price's way.

"Go get her," he commanded, his tone quiet and deadly. "I'll be in the sitting room."

Price walked away, leaving Alex standing, dumbfounded, by the open front door. As Price entered the parlor, he heard Alex close the portal and hurry upstairs.

He turned his attention to his surroundings and was shocked by the condition of the room. The expensive furnishings that had graced it were gone, no doubt sold for ready cash. Furious, he moved from room to room only to find that the house had been stripped of all valuables. Too angry to remain in the empty rooms, he stalked into the hallway, anxious for this confrontation to be over.

Rachel, however, took her time about coming down and at least half an hour passed before she appeared at the top of the stairs with Alex by her side.

Short on stature, long on nerve, Rachel Kent stood momentarily on the landing looking down at him, her lips curled in disgust as she stared. Of all the rotten luck! Why did he have to show up now? Just when things were going so well.

Price looked up at his mother's older sister. How was it possible that two women reared in the same household could turn out so differently? Rachel was an embittered woman. She had hated her younger, more attractive sister from the moment she'd been born and that vicious emotion had colored her entire life.

Things had always come easily to fair Anna who was as gentle as she was beautiful. Anna attracted people and put them at ease with her joy of living. Rachel, on the other hand, had to force herself to make conversation and then it was always awkward and stilted. She believed herself to be less than attractive and so she reflected that attitude. And while it was true that Rachel had married first, it had been a poor match and her husband, Ebenezer Kent, had died leaving her penniless. By that time, Anna had married William Richardson, a very successful businessman. With their parents dead, Rachel had been forced to come to Anna and William for help. They had been quite generous with her, setting her up in a comfortable small cottage and helping her to find employment to supplement what little income she had.

To Rachel, this type of help had been a slap in the face. Why hadn't they taken her in? She was a close blood relative—how could they leave her to starve on her small wages?

What Rachel was too dense to realize was that Anna was aware of her feelings and wanted nothing to do with her. It was mostly at William's insistence that Anna had agreed to do as much as they did and so, Rachel's hostility grew while Anna did her best to avoid her graceless older sister.

The only mistake that Anna and William made during their happy life together was not drawing up a will and providing a guardian for their much-adored son. Had they made such a provision, Price would have been spared the horror that had been forced upon him. But as it was, they had both died in the same tragic accident and Rachel had descended like the vulture she was to pick at the remains. Their son be damned; let him beg for a while. And that had been how Price had ended up—begging for food on the Alton levee.

As he looked at her now, he felt nothing but contempt. She was a greedy bitch, who had not improved with age. Fat and dumpy, she looked much older than her fifty-two years. Her gray-streaked, mousy brown hair was pulled back in a plain, severe style that emphasized her heavy-jowled countenance. Her shifty, dark eyes were deep-set and beady, giving full disclosure to her real personality. Price kept his face carefully blank, but tensed physically in remembrance of her cruelties.

"So it really is you," she said flatly, descending to stand before him.

"The Rebs did their best, but I was too tough for them." Price grinned evilly. "It must have been my upbringing that helped me to survive in prison camp."

Rachel didn't react, she just stared at him dispassionately. "What do you want?"

"Ever to the point," Price commented derisively. "I'd suggest we sit down, but the rooms are all so bare."

"Money has been tight since the war began," Rachel said through gritted teeth.

"But was it really necessary to sell the furniture?" he countered coldly. "It couldn't have brought in that much. If things were really so bad, however did you keep up appearances?"

Rachel eyed him suspiciously and Alex stiffened as he realized that Price was now a force to be reckoned with.

"In all honesty, Aunt Rachel," he said, emphasizing the word aunt, "I want this to be a brief but fruitful discussion for all involved. I'm here to make you an offer."

"An offer? For what?"

" 'For what' is correct, for everything you say you own is in truth mine—purchased with my money." He waited for his words to sink in. "You see, I was at the bank yesterday checking on my account and Mr. Lowrey told me how he'd advanced you money from my funds, because you thought I'd been killed. He said you pleaded hardship? It must have been a very touching story and I'm sure that when you made your appeal there wasn't a dry eye in the place."

Rachel and Alex were both silent, growing ever more apprehensive of their dangerous adversary.

"Well, I have the solution to all your problems."

"You have?" Alex asked, amazed by Price's remarks.

"You have something I want and I, most certainly, have something you need."

"And just what is that?"

"I'll give you seventy-five hundred dollars to use as you see fit, as soon as you move out of this house?"

"What?" Rachel shrieked. "You want me to leave my home?"

"Rephrase that." Price smiled cynically. "I want you to leave *my* home."

Alex and Rachel exchanged worried glances. "And if we refuse?"

"Oh, I doubt you'll refuse," he replied, bored

with the conversation. "For then I'd have to have you evicted with no money and you wouldn't want that, now would you?" Price folded his arms across his chest and waited for their reactions.

Momentarily stunned, Rachel glared at him.

"How soon?"

Price looked at her, his expression one of indifference. "Day after tomorrow. That should give you enough time to find suitable lodgings. But make no mistake, this will be the last money you ever get out of me."

"Just like that, after all these years, you want us out. Why?" Rachel finally had gathered her wits.

Price didn't answer right away. "Let's just say that the Richardson family's heritage is here and I'd like to keep it that way. Now, if you'll excuse me, I must be going. What's still here stays here. Don't remove any more of my property. Do you understand me, Rachel?"

She turned from him and started upstairs in a huff with Alex following her.

"By the way, I'm staying with the Coopers, so if you need to contact me you can find me there," Price called to her as he let himself out.

Mission accomplished, he hoped that this was the last time he would ever have to deal with Rachel.

Leaning leisurely against the doorjamb, Alex watched Rachel as she stormed about her bedroom in a fury.

"So he wants it back, does he? He can have it!" she shrieked. Then, looking at her son, she demanded, "How can you be so calm?"

"What's to be upset about? I think he's being very generous with us. Seventy-five hundred dollars is a

231

lot of money, Mother," Alex told her, glad to be leaving this monstrosity of a house. "I hate this place anyway. I never have understood your attachment to it."

"You wouldn't," she said sarcastically. "Why couldn't he be dead?"

Alex looked slightly bored. "There's really no point in dwelling on that."

"You won't think so once this seventy-five-hundred dollars is gone. We have to think of something else. They're not going to get away with this again!"

"They?"

She looked at him, her eyes wild. "You wouldn't understand. Just trust me, have I ever given you the wrong advice?"

"No."

"Good. Now listen, we'll move out of here real quietlike, but keep your ears and eyes open. I want to know everything there is to know about Price and I want to know it right away."

"Why? What are we going to do?"

"If necessary, we're going to arrange an accident for him, but not until the money runs out. Until then, we'll be real nice. Why, who would ever suspect that I wanted my beloved nephew dead?"

Alex smiled at her cunning. "Sometimes, Mother, you amaze me."

"Just do what I tell you and we'll be all right. It may take awhile, but . . ."

Price sat with Coop, Betsey and Jason in the parlor that night after dinner.

"How did it go?" Coop asked, anxious to know about Price's visit.

"Surprisingly enough, it went quite well," Price said as he relaxed on the sofa. "You should have seen how eager Alex was when I offered them the money."

"And Rachel?"

"I'm not sure, she's harder to read than he is," Price told him.

"Yes," Coop agreed. "Rachel's in a class all her own."

Betsey laughed. "My but you two are gracious tonight. Is it my presence or have you finally become gentlemen?"

Price looked at her fondly as she sat on the floor playing with Jason. "For your sake—and Jason's, of course—I thought it would be best to discuss this civilly."

"Well, I'm glad we have some good influence on you," she teased.

"Always," Coop told her, pulling her up onto his lap and giving her a quick kiss. Jason, angry at having his play interrupted, toddled to his father's knee and fussed loudly at them. Laughing, Betsey picked up her son and they sat together comfortably.

Price felt a pang of loneliness as he watched them. They were so happy and so complete in each other. He hoped that some day very soon he and Ellyn would have that same closeness and love. The thought of Ellyn and Memphis also brought to mind the article he'd seen in the paper that day.

"According to the *Telegraph* this afternoon, they've started an inquiry into the *Sultana's* explosion," Price informed them.

"It's about time. I wonder who ordered it?"

"The secretary of war, from what I understand. It'll be interesting to see if anything is ever done about it."

233

"You think they'll go public with the findings?"

Price snorted in disbelief. "With all the uproar over Lincoln's assassination? I doubt it. Compared to the death of the president, fifteen hundred men dying is nothing."

Coop was silent, remembering the terror of that night.

"It's over now, Coop," Betsey reminded him gently.

"Yes, it is." He kissed her cheek. "Shall we go on up to bed? Looks like Jason's already asleep."

Jason was indeed asleep on his mother's breast, curled tightly against her, his thumb in his mouth. Smiling at the sweetness of the innocent, they all retired for the night.

Mary Anne was relaxing in her bedroom having just taken a warm, scented bath when her maid knocked on the door.

"Yes, Belle, what is it?" she called languidly from her bed.

"Mr. Kent is here to see you," the maid told her, entering the room.

Mary Anne hesitated a moment, considering the hour and then got up.

"Tell him I'll be right down," she said, pulling a satin wrapper on over her nakedness.

Pausing only briefly to run a brush through her freshly washed hair, she hurried downstairs. She hadn't heard from him since he'd left her bed yesterday morning and she wondered how his meeting had gone with the lawyer.

"Alex, I'm so glad you've come." She went to him and kissed him lightly. Then noticing how tired he looked, she added, "Come sit down while I get you a drink."

"I could use one. It's been a very rough day."

"Oh? How did your meeting go yesterday?"

"It was very successful and Mother and I knew exactly what we had to do. But this morning . . ."

At the sound of the frustrated anger in his voice, she looked up at him from where she was pouring his bourbon. "What happened this morning?"

Taking the glass she brought to him, he answered, his tone flat. "Price got back."

"What!" Mary Anne froze. His words pierced her soul. "He's supposed to be dead!"

"That's what we all believed." Alex downed his drink in one swallow. "We made all those plans—for nothing. All that money wasted on lawyers' fees—for nothing."

Shaking his head at the irony of the whole situation, he got up and poured himself another bourbon.

Mary Anne stood, unmoving. Price was alive! Her heart was singing, but she carefully kept her feelings hidden. How unfair that as soon as she agreed to marry Alex, her one true love should return. Sighing, she sat down on the sofa and waited for Alex to join her.

"How did you find out?" she asked, trying not to sound too interested."

"He came by the house this morning, demanding that we move. Seems that after all this time, he's decided that he wants it back," Alex explained.

"Price wants Richardson House back?" She was surprised, for years ago he had mentioned all the bad memories that it held for him.

Alex nodded, coming to sit by her.

"How's your mother taking all of this?"

"Not too well, I'm afraid. She was certainly

counting on Price's money."

"You're not having financial difficulties, are you?" She nervously awaited his answer.

"No, but as far as Mother's concerned, there's no such thing as enough money."

Nodding in agreement, Mary Anne urged him on. "What else did you find out?"

"He injured his arm somehow, he's got it in a sling." Alex's mouth twisted bitterly. "Too bad he didn't break more than his arm!"

"How did he do it?"

"Nobody seems to know. And frankly, I could care less." He paused, setting his glass aside. "He's given us a day to get out, so Mother and I spent all day today looking for something suitable."

"Did you find anything you liked?"

"Mother bought the old Lord house on Belle Street. It should suit her needs just fine." Alex finished off his second drink.

"Is Price staying with Coop and Betsey?" she inquired conversationally. But all the while Mary Anne was trying to figure out when she could get away to see him.

"That's what he said," Alex answered, turning his attention to her scantily clad figure for the first time. "Do you know, you are enough to stir a man's blood, even when he's got the worries of the world bearing down on him."

Untying the sash, he parted her silken cover.

"You are so lovely," he murmured before pressing her close to him and kissing her deeply.

"Do you want to stay the night?" Mary Anne asked. Her tone was seductive but she was praying with all her might that he would refuse, for she needed time to think. Time to decide what to do. She had to see Price again. She had to!

"No, I can't tonight. But maybe I'd better close the door."

Moving away from her, he shut the sliding parlor doors and strode back to her, taking off his jacket and shirt and tossing them casually on a chair. Pulling her to her feet, he slipped the dressing gown from her. Mary Anne went into his arms, hoping she could encourage him to hurry, but Alex had other ideas. He wanted to lose himself in her lovemaking.

Taking her with him, they stretched out on the sofa and Alex delighted in the way she lay seductively against him. Alex ached with the need to possess her, to feel that he was in command of at least some portion of his life.

Mary Anne was always eager to please him and tonight seemed no different as her hands caressed him boldly.

"Slow down, or I won't be able to wait for you," he told her huskily as she unfastened his pants and reached inside to hold his erection.

"That's all right, I just want to make you happy," she lied, trying to urge him on with her brazen touch.

Eager to be alone with her thoughts of Price, Mary Anne used every ploy she knew to excite him and she breathed a sigh of relief when he finally thrust deeply into her.

"You feel so good to me," she groaned, twisting and arching beneath him. She was proud of her sexual prowess for it helped her to control Alex without his being aware of it.

When at last he climaxed and lay heavily atop her, Mary Anne smiled to herself.

Alex shifted his weight from her and stood up, fastening his pants. Picking up her silken robe, he helped her put it on. As he sat down, Mary Anne brought him his shirt and jacket and he finished dressing.

"I really have to get going," he told her apologetically.

"I understand, you must have a lot to do, and I imagine Rachel needs you, too."

Alex nodded, rising. "If we get settled in tomorrow, I'll be by later in the day."

"Good. I'll be anxious to hear how it goes."

Pulling her up to him, he kissed her once more. "Come, walk me to the door."

Mary Anne had to contain herself. She could hardly wait until he was gone.

Pressing her close to his side, they made their way out of the parlor and down the hall.

"I'll be in touch," he said as he left and Mary Anne stood obediently at the door, watching until he'd ridden off.

As soon as he was out of sight, she shut and locked the door. Rushing back upstairs, she threw herself across her bed, hard put to contain the joy she felt. He was alive! He was alive!

It didn't matter to her that they hadn't been lovers for over four years. Somehow, some way, Mary Anne was determined that she would have Price again.

A sudden thought that he might not want to marry her was quickly dismissed. Even being Price's mistress was preferable to being Alex's wife. Especially since Alex was not inheriting Price's money.

Mary Anne wasn't a fool, though, and she had no intention of breaking off her engagement to Alex until she was sure of Price. A bird in the hand . . .

She lay awake most of the night nourishing her fantasies of Price and how they would be together.

Morning couldn't come quickly enough for Mary Anne. She awoke from what little sleep she'd had, convinced that she would soon be with Price. Rising early, she planned her day. She would go to visit Coop and Price on the pretense of welcoming them home and see what happened. If Price gave an indication that he cared·for her, she would break off with Alex right away. Paying extra attention to her toilette, Mary Anne chose her most attractive daygown and dressed carefully. Sure that she was at her best, she left for Coop's house, eager for the coming reunion.

Mary Anne was more than a little nervous as she waited at the Cooper's front door.

"Good morning, Miss Montague," the maid greeted her, responding to her knock. "Do come in. The family's in the parlor."

"Thank you, Rosalie," Mary Anne said as she swept gracefully indoors and gave her parasol over to the maid's safekeeping. "You don't have to show me in, I know my way."

Betsey had heard Mary Anne's entrance and went to meet her as she came down the hall.

"Mary Anne, it's so nice to see you again. Do come in and join us. You know Coop and Price are back?"

"I just found out last night and I knew I had to come and welcome them home," Mary Anne responded, sounding a little breathless.

Entering the parlor ahead of Betsey, Mary Anne's face lit up at the sight of Price. Both men rose as she came into the room.

"Mary Anne, so good of you to stop by," Coop greeted her, casting a quick sideways glance at Price.

"Coop, you look wonderful. Price . . ."

"Mary Anne," Price began, but before he could finish she came to him and kissed him warmly on the mouth.

"I am so relieved that you are home at last. Why I've done nothing but worry since they told me you were presumed dead." She stepped back to look at him. "Your arm! My goodness, I had no idea you were injured. Are you in much pain?"

It was all Coop and Betsey could do to keep straight faces.

"I'm fine, Mary Anne," he said. When she looked about to protest, he added, "Really."

"Well, if you are sure . . ."

"Mary Anne, would you like a cup of tea or coffee?" Betsey interrupted.

"Tea would be delightful, Betsey, thanks," she replied, seating herself next to Price on the sofa, as Betsey left to get her drink.

Jason, who'd been eating a chocolate cookie and playing contentedly by himself, noticed the new lady in the room and toddled over to her, babbling happily. Mary Anne watched the child's approach distastefully. She'd been so careful with her morning toilette that the thought of this grubby little boy pawing at her with his cookie-covered hands almost made her want to run from the room. Stoically, she sat still as Jason grabbed hold of her skirt and hung on.

"He certainly has grown, Coop," she remarked conversationally, trying to ignore the chocolate he was smearing all over her best dress. "Why I haven't seen him in months. He's really getting around now, isn't he?"

"He's getting faster every day. It won't be too long before he'll be able to outdistance me," Coop said good-naturedly.

"I heard about your leg. How are you doing?"

"I'll be just fine in time."

"Good."

"Here's your tea." Betsey came into the room. "Oh, Jason! Look what he's done to your skirt."

Betsey was horrified to see two big chocolate smudges on the skirt of Mary Anne's dress and snatched Jason away.

"Come with me," Betsey instructed after handing Jason over to Coop.

Leading the way, she took Mary Anne down the hall to the kitchen. Coop and Price grinned in amusement.

"Somehow, I can't see Mary Anne surrounded by a bunch of children," Price quipped.

"Me, either," Coop agreed. "Did you notice her ring?"

"What ring?"

"It must be an engagement ring, judging by the size of it. Do you think Alex finally proposed?"

Price looked up sharply. "Betsey did say that they'd been seeing each other, didn't she?" His expression was thoughtful.

Jason caught their attention then, and they played with him until the women returned a few minutes later.

"All taken care of," Betsey said brightly, as she took her son and handed him over to the maid. "I think this young man needs a bath."

"Yes, ma'am," Rosalie replied and took Jason upstairs.

"Now, we can visit in peace." Betsey sank down on her favorite chair.

Mary Anne resumed her place beside Price, irritated at not having had a chance to be alone with him.

"Mary Anne, I noticed your ring. Have you become engaged?" Coop inquired with great interest.

"As a matter of fact, Price and I will be family shortly," she said, laying a warm hand on his arm. "Alex proposed."

"How wonderful!" Betsey exclaimed, encouraging Mary Anne to tell her all the details.

"When's the big day?" Betsey was asking.

"We haven't set the date, but I hope it won't be too far off."

"I'm sure you'll be very happy together," Price offered. And after taking her hand to admire the ring, he couldn't help but wonder what Alex had sold from the estate in order to purchase it. "It's lovely."

"Indeed," Coop added. "Our heartiest congratulations. Let us know as soon as you set the date."

"Oh, I will, thank you." Mary Anne rose. "Well, I must be going. I just wanted to stop by and welcome you home. It's so good to see that you're both doing well and I'm sure we will be seeing each other more frequently now that life is finally getting back to normal."

"I'm sure," Betsey agreed and showed Mary Anne to the door.

When the women were out of earshot, Coop spoke. "You know, Mary Anne was eyeing you quite hungrily the whole time. Do you think she still cares about you?"

"There's nothing between us. There hasn't been for years."

"I know that and you know that, but Betsey seemed to sense that she did. I'll bet if you gave her the least encouragement, she'd drop Alex like a hot potato."

"Possibly, but you don't have to worry about that. I have no intention of getting involved with her again. Once was more than enough."

"Oh?"

"It's all past history." Price ended the discussion, not wanting to dredge up the intimate details of his affair with Mary Anne.

"What's all past history?" Betsey asked, coming in on the end of their conversation.

"Price's relationship with Mary Anne," Coop supplied.

"He may think so, but I'll just bet she's still crazy about you," Betsey said knowingly.

Price looked exasperated. "It's been over since before the war!"

"Maybe for you it has been, but for Mary Anne I'd almost bet money that it's not."

"Well, it'll have to be, because I have no interest in her at all."

"Then stay far away from her. She's learned a lot in the past few years."

"She knew a lot before I left!" Price laughed. "Don't worry, Betsey. Ellyn's the only woman I want or need."

"All right. But I still don't trust Mary Anne, especially now that she's teamed up with Alex."

"Believe me, I'm going to keep close track of Rachel and Alex. Besides, I think Alex proposed to Mary Anne basically to get her money."

"Really?"

"Yeah, according to Mr. Lowrey at the bank they were getting desperate since they hadn't been able to get control of my half of the company."

"That sounds like Alex," Betsey agreed. "The easiest way to get money is to marry it. But, you know, according to local gossip . . ."

"Betsey, I had no idea you paid any attention to all that!" Coop teased.

She glared at him even as she smiled. "You'd be

surprised how much you can learn. Of course, you have to take everything with a grain of salt."

"Yes, so?"

"According to my sources, who will remain nameless, Mary Anne is broke."

"What!" Coop and Price were both astonished.

Betsey nodded. "It seems she's been living so wildly since your relationship ended that she's just about gone through her whole inheritance. Rumor has it that she's in the market for a rich husband."

"And she thinks Alex is rich?"

"Obviously."

Coop and Price started laughing. "They were meant for each other! I hope they both don't find out until after the wedding."

Coop smiled widely. "Think how upset Rachel will be when she thinks she's getting a wealthy daughter-in-law and all she ends up with is more bills!"

"You two are terrible, but it is funny. Wouldn't it be easier if Alex just went to work?"

"I'm sure it would, but Alex has never worked in his life and I doubt that he'll start now!"

"Well, it's certainly going to be interesting to see how this turns out." Coop chuckled. "Let us know what you hear, Betsey. I'm sure the rumor mill will have a field day with her engagement to Alex."

"And Price's return," Betsey added, her eyes twinkling mischievously.

Mary Anne traveled the short distance to her home reflecting on her feelings for Price. After all these years, she still found him irresistibly attractive. But the kiss she'd given him had brought no answering response. Mary Anne let herself remember how it had been for them so long ago and she wondered if it would be possible to attract him again. Recalling only the good parts of their time together, Mary Anne decided to make the attempt to win Price. And as for Alex—well, she'd keep him dangling on the side for now. She wasn't sure enough of Price to risk breaking off with Alex yet. Humming to herself, delighted with the idea, Mary Anne entered her home, ready to begin her seduction of Price.

Chapter Ten

The month of May and much of June passed in a haze of warm sunny days. Life at Riverwood continued much as before, but what had once been routine work for Ellyn was now drudgery. She felt terrible and she looked it. Price had been gone for over seven weeks and she hadn't heard a word from him. Nothing. Her appetite disappeared and she had to force herself to eat, almost gagging on every bite.

What had gone wrong? Was he all right? Tormented and worried, Ellyn had hardly noticed that her time of the month had come and gone with no results. She tried to keep busy working in the garden and helping Darnelle, but that kind of work didn't occupy her mind. Left free to wander, her thoughts inevitably came to Price and their wonderful days together. But why hadn't he written? He'd promised, and in light of Darnelle's explanation, Ellyn couldn't understand the lack of communication. And then there was Constance, always smirking at her whenever she asked about the mail, always reminding her that Price hadn't answered any of the letters she'd written.

Depressed and lonely, Ellyn put aside her garden

tools and followed the path on back to the overseer's house. She didn't hesitate on the porch but went straight inside to its cool, shaded safety. Somehow, every day she managed to spend a little time here, keeping her love alive. He did love her, she knew it! And every time she entered the cabin she remembered his devotion. Tired beyond belief, she lay down on the bed that Price had slept in and stared up at the ceiling. Rod was due home any time—and still she had had no message from Price. Only now did it dawn on her that she'd not had her monthly flow since before she'd rescued him. Pregnant? Her eyes widened in disbelief. Oh, no! She got up quickly and paced nervously back and forth. Pausing, Ellyn gently rested a hand on her stomach. Could she really be having Price's child? As she thought on it, she knew without a doubt that she was. Her weight loss, her lack of appetite . . . and she was tired all the time. Yes, it all added up. But what was she to do? Having had no word from him in all this time, she couldn't help but doubt.

Constance met Lawrence on the gallery as he returned from town.

"How was your trip?" she inquired politely.

"It was fair. There's a little of the fever going around," he told her. Then taking a letter from his vest pocket, he handed it to her. "Here's another one."

"My, he certainly does write a lot, doesn't he?" Constance was amazed, for this was the twelfth letter they'd received from him since he'd left.

Lawrence just grunted and went on inside. He knew that Ellyn and the Yankee should be kept apart, but he wondered if this was the way to do it.

He'd been watching Ellyn for the past few weeks and she seemed listless and unhappy. Her color was pale and there were dark circles beneath her eyes, indicating that she was not sleeping well. Shaking his head in consternation, he went to his room to get cleaned up.

Constance, Price's letter in hand, retired to the privacy of the sitting room to read it. She opened it in delight hoping that he'd sent more money; that first bank draft had come in very handy. When she found no money, she read it quickly. Bored by Price's declarations and questions, Constance crumpled the note and went out to the kitchen where she tossed it into the fire. Darnelle watched her with no little interest and as soon as Constance left the room, she salvaged what was left of the paper. Recognizing who it was from, it took her only a minute to realize what had been going on the past few weeks. Folding the note, she put it in her pocket for safekeeping.

Constance had been gone from the room for only minutes when Darnelle heard her call.

"Lawrence, Charlotte, hurry! Oh, Look!"

Darnelle ran from the kitchen, thinking that something terrible was happening, but to her surprise Constance was off the porch hurrying down the drive toward a lone, gray-clad rider. Rod was back! Forgetting everything else, Darnelle ran back through the house and down the path toward the garden looking for Ellyn.

"Miz Ellyn!" she called excitedly as she neared the overseer's house. When Ellyn hadn't been in the garden, Darnelle had decided to look in the next most obvious place.

Ellyn heard Darnelle's call and came out on the porch to greet her. At the sight of her, Darnelle

248

suddenly realized how frail she had become.

"What's wrong?" Ellyn worried, noting the look of concern on her face.

"It's Mr. Rod. He's back!"

"Rod!" The name escaped her in a terrified whisper. The moment she'd dreaded had finally come. Ellyn paused and looked back into the cabin, as if searching for strength. Then squaring her shoulders, she wiped her hands nervously on her skirt and started back up the path with Darnelle.

Constance had left the kitchen totally pleased with herself. She had effectively eliminated all correspondence between Ellyn and Price. Smiling in amusement at her own duplicity, she strolled along the side gallery. A movement on the front drive caught her attention and she called ecstatically for Lawrence and Charlotte. Ignoring Darnelle, who had responded to her frantic call, she rushed from the porch, running as fast as her full skirts would allow, toward the Confederate cavalryman riding up to the house.

Rod Clarke had left Mattie Hardin's house well over a month ago and had been on the road ever since. The going had been slow and dangerous but after four years of hard-driven fighting, Rod could handle anything. Finally, late yesterday, after long hours in the saddle, he'd arrived at the Landing. Vine-covered ruins were all that was left of his once-stately home. Knowing that the house had burned and actually seeing it had been two different things. The deserted acres taunted him with memories of a finer time when life had been young and full of promise. The reminders of his youth and innocence pushed him closer than he'd ever been to his breaking point. His home and family gone, the war lost, his dreams taken from him, Rod stood amidst the wreckage an embittered, disillusioned man. Exhausted beyond words, he'd spent the night camped in the ruins and rested there until he felt emotionally strong enough to face the Douglasses.

Now, as he rode slowly up the drive to the Douglass home, he could not suppress the resentment he felt at the fact that Riverwood was intact while the Landing had been destroyed. Trying to dismiss the feelings as unworthy of him, he spurred his weary stallion on, hoping to find his friends back home and safe. Looking up, he saw the woman running toward him and, assuming it was Ellyn, he reined in, dismounted and opened his arms. Without pause, Constance rushed into his embrace.

"You're back! At last!" she breathed and kissed him squarely on the mouth.

It took him a moment to realize that this was not Ellyn in his arms and when he finally did, he held the woman back away from him to look at her. Dark eyes bright with unshed tears gazed up at him in open adoration, her lips moist and parted as if begging for another kiss.

"Constance!" He was surprised.

"Oh, Rod, we've waited so long. But there was no word. We were so afraid that you'd been killed, like . . ."

"Not Tommy?" His voice was thick with agony.

Constance nodded. "And Thomas, too. Over a year ago."

"Oh, Constance, I'm so sorry."

Taking advantage of the situation, she wept forced tears on his shoulder, relishing the feel of a strong male body against her. Slowly, she allowed herself to gain control and then took his arm as if she needed his support.

"I'm being so silly. But seeing you again and having you home . . . you will consider Riverwood your home, won't you?" she spoke gently.

"I'd be honored," he told her, enjoying the feeling that he was protecting her.

"Good." She smiled up at him and Rod felt his breath catch in his throat.

Damn, but she was a beautiful woman. If anything, she seemed more lovely to him now than she had before he'd gone to war. She was better than he'd remembered—her hair softer, her eyes more kind, her voice more gentle, her body . . . Jerking his mind away from those thoughts, he berated himself. She was a widow, for God's sake! How unchivalrous of him to think of her that way. But glancing at her again, he had to admit that she was the sexiest widow he'd ever met.

Arm in arm, they started back toward the house where Lawrence and Charlotte had gathered to meet him.

"Rod! So good to see you!"

"Lawrence, it's wonderful to be back!" They embraced and he kissed Charlotte who beamed under his attentions.

Going indoors, they settled in the parlor and Lawrence quickly poured them a double bourbon.

"To your return," he toasted him and they drained their glasses.

Gasping for breath, they laughed in light-hearted relief.

"Where's Ellyn?" Lawrence boomed at Constance.

"I haven't seen her since early this morning. I

think Darnelle went to find her."

"So Darnelle stayed with you?" Rod asked.

"Franklin and Glory, too," Lawrence added. "We pay them what we can, but the way things are now, it's not much."

"I understand." Rod's tone was somber. "I'm sure everyone's in the same condition."

There was a sad silence for a moment as they all thought of the days when life had been easy.

"Here's Ellyn, now," Charlotte said as she heard Darnelle and Ellyn enter through the back of the house.

Rod glanced up, expecting to see a younger version of Constance. To his disappointment, she didn't resemble her mother in the slightest. Painfully thin and pale, she looked almost sickly and Rod worried that she'd been ill.

"Ellyn," he greeted her, and taking her hands in his. "How good to see you."

He bent to kiss her, but somehow Ellyn turned her head and all he was rewarded with was her cheek.

"It's good to see you, too, Rod," she said softly and moved away from him slightly.

A frown creased his handsome brow as he noticed her skittishness. So she hadn't changed at all. If anything she seemed worse than when he'd left. He hoped that her cool reception was just shyness and not a true reflection of her feelings for him, for he wanted them to be married as soon as possible. He'd been without a woman for a long time and the thought of a warm and willing wife pleased him greatly.

"Let's leave Rod and Ellyn alone for a few minutes," Constance suggested, deviously. "I'm sure they have much to say to each other."

Constance stopped at Rod's side as she left the

252

room. "It's wonderful to have you back!" she told him, kissing him lightly and, in a concealed movement, pressing her ample breasts to his arm.

Surrounded by a cloud of Constance's sensuous perfume, it took all of Rod's self-control not to kiss her back passionately.

"It's wonderful being back," he answered, their eyes meeting in a challenge as old as time.

As the others followed Constance from the room, Rod turned all of his newly awakened desire to his fiancee. He had to admit that Ellyn's present appearance was almost enough to discourage the most ardent of suitors, for compared to Constance's flamboyant, buxom beauty, Ellyn seemed a lifeless rag doll. But long-enforced celibacy could help a man overlook certain flaws in a woman, so he concentrated on drawing her out and hopefully into his arms.

"Are you feeling all right? You seem a little pale."

"No, I'm fine, really," she spoke almost too hastily and hurriedly sat down on the sofa.

Rod moved easily to join her there, slipping an arm around her shoulders.

"I've missed you," he whispered. He pressed a warm kiss on her neck and she jumped agitatedly.

"Rod . . . don't," Ellyn protested, hating the feel of his hot, wet mouth on her skin, longing for another man and another time.

"All right," he agreed, chagrined. "I promise to restrain myself for now, but I want us to be married as soon as possible."

"Rod, I . . ."

"No discussion. We'll be married as soon as I can arrange it," he declared, expecting no further disagreement from her.

Just then Constance, Charlotte and Lawrence returned.

"I've had Darnelle prepare the guest room for you. You'll also want to bathe, won't you?" Constance asked.

"Yes, please." Rod rose. "I'll just bring in my saddlebags and get settled in. I appreciate your hospitality more than I can ever say. Someday I'll repay you for your kindness."

"Nonsense, Rod," Lawrence huffed, "you're family."

He and Rod shook hands and Rod disappeared outside to retrieve his few belongings.

Constance took the opportunity to observe Ellyn, who was still sitting there, pale and unattractive. Her eyes sparkled as she thought of Rod comparing the two of them. Constance had no doubt who the winner would be. Drawing a deep breath, she straightened her shoulders and went to show him to his room.

The heat of the water relaxed Rod completely and he sighed, enjoyed the peace of the moment. It had been easier than he thought it would be . . . coming back. Not that Ellyn had made him feel welcome. If anything, she had appeared to be quite upset by his return. Not once had she seemed actually glad to see him. Now Constance was another story. She'd been warm and attentive from the first and Rod wondered idly if his engagement to Ellyn wasn't a bad mistake. It seemed to him that a lifetime tied to a frigid, skinny woman was too high a price to pay just to join the two plantations. Dismissing the thought, he decided that Ellyn was just timid and that she would come around in time.

Closing his eyes, he pictured his good friend Tommy as he'd been on the day they'd all signed up.

They'd both been so excited then and anxious to beat the damn Yankees! His mouth tightened in pain and humiliation. Losing gracefully was not one of his character traits. He would hate them and all they stood for as long as he lived and breathed. With these troubled thoughts, he got out of the bath and shaved. Then, after dressing, he started downstairs, hoping that once he was in the gentler company of the women, he would have a little peace of mind again.

Ellyn went to her room to freshen up. Frightened by the situation she found herself in, she didn't know where to turn. Had she heard from Price during these last long weeks, she would have known exactly what to do, but, as it was, she felt abandoned at the climactic moment of her young life. Stretching out across the bed, she gave into her frustrated fears and cried. Great heartbreaking sobs tore through her thin body as she wept for herself and her child. When, at long last, she quieted; Ellyn sat up and tried to pull herself together.

There was no chance of marrying Rod—not when she was pregnant with another man's child. No, she definitely had to end her engagement and the sooner, the better. No longer in doubt about what course to take, Ellyn rose and got ready for dinner.

The evening meal was a celebration as Darnelle produced the best of everything to welcome Rod home. He was impressed by the meal and thanked them profusely for their kindness. Seated at Constance's side near the head of the table with Ellyn directly across from him, he was afforded an easy view of both women. And, as Constance had hoped, he found Ellyn wanting in every way when compared to her mother. Where Constance was warm and genuinely interested, Ellyn paid little attention. Constance was gay and easy to laugh; Ellyn seldom smiled and never joined in the lighthearted conversation. Constance had dressed seductively, her gown exposing most of her ample cleavage. Ellyn, on the other hand, had worn a plain gown that was high-necked and long-sleeved. Rod longed to strip it from her just to get a look at her.

Determined not to encourage Rod, Ellyn managed to make herself as unattractive as possible. She was actually relieved to have her mother dominating the talk at the table. Though she truly liked Rod, she felt no desire for him and the thought of marrying him, after knowing Price, was unbearable. Ellyn realized that Constance had posed a question and she had missed it.

"I'm sorry, Mother. What did you say?"

"I was just telling Rod that there was a lot of excitement around here just awhile back, why, with the boat explosion and all. Ellyn was quite a little heroine; she rescued a Yankee from right out of the river!"

"She what!" Rod exclaimed, dropping his fork with a clatter.

"Why the *Sultana*—you heard about that didn't you?"

"No," he answered curtly.

"Well, this steamer was transporting Yankees home and it blew up right out there in the river. Ellyn saw this man caught up in a tree and she and Franklin rescued him."

Rod's expression grew thunderous and he asked pointedly in disbelief, "You rescued a Yankee?"

"Yes, I . . ."

"She did and she nursed him back to health," Charlotte interrupted, happy to be the one to finish the tale.

"This is true? You took care of a Yankee?" Rod questioned again, furious with her.

"I just said yes," she retorted, unafraid, her eyes glittering dangerously.

"She couldn't just leave him out there to die," Lawrence stated, coming to her defense. "It was very brave of her, risking herself like that."

"It was stupid of her. Why, no self-respecting Southern lady would ever dream of doing such a crazy thing," he said in condemnation, glaring at her.

"I did what any Christian would do," she remarked, giving as good as she got.

Rod's anger grew. How dare she respond to him in such a manner.

"No wife of mine will ever . . ."

"Then maybe I shouldn't be a wife of yours!" she replied, rising. "Suh, you may consider our engagement officially over. Grandfather, if you'll excuse me."

Barely holding herself in check, she stalked from the dining room, leaving a furious ex-fiance, a perplexed grandfather, an amazed sister, and an amused and happy mother behind.

"Rod, perhaps you'd like to join me in the study for a drink?" Lawrence offered.

"Yes, suh, I would." His voice was stilted as he rose and followed Lawrence from the room.

"Mother, what do you suppose came over Ellyn? Why would she do something so stupid?"

"I don't know, Charlotte. Personally, I think Rod is a fine man and any woman would be proud to have him for a husband."

Charlotte paused thoughtfully. "Do you think he'd be interested in me?"

"Heavens, no! He's far too old for you!" Constance was shocked by the thought of more competition. "We'll find you a suitable young man very soon, for I truly feel that Rod Clarke is far too experienced for someone as young and innocent as you are, my dear."

"Oh, all right." Charlotte was crestfallen. "Whatever you say, Mother." The thought of defying her mother never occurred to her.

They finished their meal in peaceful solitude, biding their time until they could join the men.

"You mustn't be so upset with Ellyn," Lawrence was saying. "You knew before you left that she was a headstrong girl."

"I knew, but I always believed that she would settle down and take the idea of being a wife seriously."

"Oh, she takes it seriously, all right." Lawrence chuckled. "But I'm afraid you are just far too different to ever be really happy together. Ellyn's a good girl, but she's also very determined."

"Determined to ruin her life."

"Do you think you can stop her or change her?"

"I don't even want to try—not if she has such little regard for the things her father and Tommy died for. Nursing a Yankee!" He spat out the last phrase in hate-filled disgust.

"Then leave her be," Lawrence stated firmly.

"With pleasure," Rod sneered, taking a deep drink.

Constance and Charlotte knocked lightly at the

door and came in to visit with them. In short order, Constance had distracted his irate thoughts and had him engaged in relaxing conversation. It was late before they all decided to call it a night. At the foot of the stairs, Rod paused and took Charlotte's hand, kissing it gallantly.

"Thank you for a pleasant evening, Charlotte."

"Thank you." She blushed, thrilled at his touch. When he released her, she seemed to float on upstairs, oblivious to everything.

Lawrence followed, leaving Rod alone with Constance.

"Constance, this evening ended wonderfully. It was almost like a night from before the war. I kept expecting Thomas . . ."

Constance quickly put her fingers to his lips. "Please. Don't mention Thomas. He's part of the past and it's gone. Now is what counts."

The portent of her words sank in slowly and his eyes met hers in understanding. He kissed the soft finger tips pressed to his lips.

"Until tomorrow."

"Yes, tomorrow," and Constance went on up to her solitary bed for what she hoped was the last time.

More than a little upset by everything that had happened to him this day, Rod went outside onto the gallery and stood in the darkness, thinking. He was truly relieved that he hadn't married Ellyn before the war for she had turned out to be nothing like her mother. Constance was everything he'd remembered and more. She had excited him tonight just by her few chosen words. She was his ideal woman—the woman he'd measured all other women by and found them lacking. And Constance was now unattached. It seemed almost a dream come true.

Breathing deeply of the sweet, moisture-laden

night air, he turned and went inside, anxious for the first time in years for the start of a new day.

Ellyn lay in her bed, unable to sleep. The insomnia had worried her at first, but now she was used to the long, almost endless hours from midnight till dawn. Hours when her mind, body and soul yearned for Price and his tender embrace. How she needed him near her, supporting and helping her! Why had she ever let him go? Tears threatened to spill from her eyes and she blinked them away.

Breaking off with Rod had happened so easily that she didn't for a moment regret it. She was only sorry that Price wasn't here so she could be with him right away. Not sure what she should do next, she shut her eyes and tried to get a little rest. Maybe things would seem more clear in the morning.

Price stood with the group of men, only half-listening to their business conversation. Smothering a yawn, he took another drink. It had been an extremely boring evening and he regretted coming. Excusing himself from the group, he left the study and went back to the ballroom. The dancers seemed to float by as he waited by the doors, looking for a familiar face. Betsey and Coop were among the dancers and, when she saw Price, Betsey directed her husband over to him.

"Where have you been?" she asked breathlessly as they left the dance floor and came to stand with him.

"Talking business," he replied, hard-pressed to keep the boredom from his voice.

"I've been waiting for you," she flirted.

"You have?" His brows raised in question, his

eyes twinkling.

"So have I," Coop said gruffly, but with good humor. "My leg is killing me. You get out there and dance with her for a while."

"My pleasure. Mrs. Cooper, may I?" Price teased, offering his arm.

"I'd be delighted," she countered as he led her out on the dance floor. "How's your arm feeling?" Betsey asked as they whirled away into the crowd.

"It's a little stiff, but not bad. The doctor said it would be another week or so before it was normal."

Betsey nodded and let her eyes sweep around the room. "Bored?"

"Am I that obvious?"

"Only to me."

He smiled. "It's just that these parties seem like such a waste of time." Shrugging, he dropped the thought.

"You'll feel differently about it when Ellyn finally gets here," she responded. "For now, you'll just have to put up with all the ambitious mamas and their eligible daughters. Besides, who knows what kind of new business contacts you can make."

"I miss her, Betsey," he said quietly, catching her completely off-guard with his confession.

"Price, you've never said a word in all these weeks. Why didn't you tell me sooner?"

"I kept thinking that I'd hear from her any day, but she hasn't even written one letter."

Betsey looked up at his proud face and noticed for the first time the sadness in his eyes. She knew how much that confession had cost him.

"Do you think you should go get her?"

"I don't know. Things were so confused when I left."

"Oh, no!" Betsey whispered, wanting to change

261

the subject. She would talk to him about Ellyn later in private.

"What?"

"Guess who just got here?"

"I have no idea."

"Alex and Mary Anne and she's already spotted you!"

Price grinned. "It looks like you just won a dancing partner for the rest of the night."

Betsey laughed, glad to have taken his mind off Ellyn. But, deep inside, Betsey was angry with this unknown woman for hurting her friend. He'd been home for almost two months and hadn't heard a word from her. Betsey knew that he wrote regularly and Coop had told her that he'd even sent money for her passage to Alton. But still she hadn't written or acknowledged his generosity. If that was love, Betsey didn't want any part of it. Price was her friend and she didn't like to see him this way.

"How's the house coming?"

"Not bad. I've managed to buy back most of what they sold off and the workmen have been painting for a week now."

"Then you're making good progress?"

"It should be finished in the next couple of weeks. Maybe when it's finished, I'll take a week off and go to Memphis."

"That's a good idea. You have to know one way or the other."

The waltz came to an end and he led her back to Coop on the side of the dance floor.

"Well, you certainly were lighter on your feet than I was."

Price grinned at his friend. "Right now, you're not very hard to beat."

"That's for sure!" Coop laughed, then muttered,

"Look out."

"For what?" Price asked.

"Why, Betsey and Jericho and Price. How good to see you," Mary Anne greeted them as she and Alex arrived.

"Good evening, Mary Anne, Alex," Coop answered, standing and shaking hands with Alex.

"Mary Anne, Alex," Price said indifferently, as his gaze swept over Mary Anne, taking in every detail of her appearance.

Ever alert to Price's moods, Mary Anne smiled softly at him. Alex did not miss her ploy and tightened his grip on her waist. Enjoying his possessiveness, she looked up at Alex lovingly.

"Will you dance with me, Alex?"

"Of course, my dear." He led her onto the floor as a quadrille was forming.

As Price watched them join the dancers, he murmured in a stage whisper to Betsey and Coop, "Frankly, I think they're perfect for each other!"

Coop laughed. "I think you're right!"

Betsey elbowed him in the ribs. "Be nice, you two!" she threatened mockingly.

Making their way to the refreshments, they each enjoyed a glass of the spiked punch.

"Well, I think I'm going to call it a night," Price told them as the quadrille came to an end.

"Fine, I'll see you in the morning at the office."

Price kissed Betsey lightly. "Thanks for the dance, gorgeous."

"It's a good thing I'm a married lady or you'd be in for a lot of trouble!" she teased, smiling at him.

"That's why I'm still single, Betsey. No one can compare to you." With a wink, he was gone.

Price had just made his excuses and was walking down the hall when he heard someone call his name.

Looking around, he saw Mary Anne coming toward him.

"Leaving so soon?"

"It's been a long day."

"Will you dance one dance with me before you go?"

"Well, I . . ."

"Please." She pouted prettily. "We are almost family, you know."

Caught in an awkward position, he had to give in. "All right."

Triumphantly, Mary Anne took his arm and they re-entered the ballroom. A waltz had just begun and Mary Anne was transported as he took her in his arms. Gliding smoothly together round the floor, she marvelled at how perfectly they moved to the music.

"We always did dance well together," she said, hoping he'd respond.

"You're an excellent partner," he replied as non-committally as possible.

"It's not the only thing that we did well together," she hinted suggestively.

Price glanced at her sharply, noting the excitement in her eyes. She was a beautiful woman and he had desired her, until he'd found out that she wasn't capable of fidelity. Why, even now, he knew that if he wanted her, he could take her. But he had no wish to entangle himself with her again. He would wait for Ellyn. She was the only woman he wanted. Arching an eyebrow at Mary Anne, he spoke, "Oh, really?"

Blushing at his deliberate snub, Mary Anne answered him heatedly, "You know what I mean."

"Yes, I do," he said seriously. "And I also know that your fiancé is standing in the doorway watching us. When is the wedding, anyway?"

"We haven't set a date yet. And I won't, if you don't want me to," she told him blatantly.

"Me? What have I got to do with you and Alex?" he asked, feigning innocence.

Mary Anne ran her hand sensuously over his back and neck and leaned closer to him. "Everything," she whispered.

Admiring the way his perfectly tailored dress clothes fit his lean body, Mary Anne felt a surge of sexual heat run through her. She wanted him badly. Just being this close to him excited her.

"We could be good together again. I know it."

Her voice was full of desire and Price was thoroughly disgusted.

"I agreed to a dance, not an oral seduction," he said coldly. At her gasp, he continued, "I believe the music's ending. Thank you for the waltz."

He bowed shortly to her and left her standing alone on the ballroom floor.

This time Price made it outside without interruption. Climbing into his carriage, he headed home. Entering the house a short time later, he realized how truly miserable he was without Ellyn. All night at the ball women had been coming on to him, hoping to arouse his interest. He supposed that he'd been a little rough on Mary Anne, but she had been the last of a long line of aggressive, mate-seeking women and he'd had enough for one night.

He moved slowly down the dark, lonely hall of his home and a great weariness overtook him. He was tired. Tired of being alone. He longed for Ellyn's gentle presence—her warmth, her love. Lighting a lamp, he made his way to the liquor cabinet in the study and poured himself a generous portion of bourbon. Price drained the glass without even tasting it and then refilled it. Taking the bottle with him, he sat down on the sofa. Leaning back, he closed his eyes, waiting for the whiskey to take effect. For a moment he forgot his solitude as more thoughts of Ellyn crept sweetly into his mind. Relaxing completely then, he let his guard down, admitting to himself that he couldn't wait much longer for her. If he did not hear from her by the time the repairs were completed on the house, he would go after her and bring her back.

Glad that the waiting was almost over and that he finally had something to look forward to, he finished off his drink and went up to the bed, feeling content for the first time in weeks.

Ellyn dozed off just before dawn and managed to sleep for a few hours before the morning sounds of the house woke her. She lay totally quiet, still exhausted after yet another restless night. From outside her window, voices drifted up to her and she listened as Franklin brought Rod's horse to him. Rod rode off after telling him that he would be inspecting the Landing and his fields for the better part of the day.

Knowing that it was getting late, Ellyn forced herself to get out of bed. Feeling unusually weak and dizzy, she had only taken a few steps before she became desperately nauseous. Darnelle heard a strange noise as she passed by Ellyn's room and she hesitated only a second before entering unheralded.

"Let me help you, Miz Ellyn," Darnelle offered, bringing her the chamber pot and getting a cool, damp rag from the washstand.

Ellyn felt too miserable to answer as she wretched uncontrollably.

"This been goin' on long?" Darnelle asked,

already knowing the answer.

"Over a week now," Ellyn managed, her stomach quieting.

"You know why?" Darnelle pressed.

Ellyn nodded dumbly and climbed back into bed. "I know. I know."

Darnelle looked at her as she sat so helplessly on the bed.

"Don't worry, Ah'll help you."

"Help her do what?" Constance interrupted, walking into the bedroom unannounced. Taking a quick look around, she wrinkled her nose in distaste. "What may I ask is going on in here?"

Ellyn and Darnelle were shocked by Constance's entrance and they both just stared at her in dumb confusion.

"Ellyn, you aren't . . . you're not . . . oh, my God, you are! You're pregnant!" Constance exclaimed in astonishment as she put two and two together. Too upset to even think about it, she backed out of the room, slamming the door behind her.

Darnelle looked at Ellyn, who was pale and shaking, "You jes' rest while Ah clean dis up and den Ah'll bring you up a cup of hot, sweet tea."

"Thanks," Ellyn said softly and she lay back on her pillows, too weak to move.

Constance rushed downstairs, horrified by what she'd just discovered. It was bad enough that Ellyn had made love to that Yankee, but to go and get pregnant by him. Constance was outraged.

"Franklin, where is Mr. Clarke?"

"He lef' for de day, Miz Constance."

"Did he say where he was going?"

"Yes, ma'am. He said he'd be at de Landing."

"Thank you. Saddle the horse and bring him around for me."

Franklin was surprised by her request but did as he was instructed.

"Yes, ma'am. Right away."

He brought the horse up to the house and helped her to mount. Then, as he watched from the gallery steps, Constance rode off in search of Rod.

By the time Darnelle returned with the hot tea for Ellyn, she had already fallen asleep, her eyes swollen from crying. Darnelle was tempted to leave the part of Price's letter that she had salvaged there for Ellyn, but she was afraid someone else would find it. Putting it safely in her pocket, Darnelle waited anxiously for Ellyn to awaken, so she could tell her everything she'd found out.

Constance whipped the old horse viciously as she galloped toward Clarke's Landing. She was furious, and the nag was forced to endure the brunt of her anger. Finally, nearing the remains of the neighboring plantation, she slowed the old beast to a walk.

She was finished with the life she had been forced to lead. No longer would she force herself to play the grieving widow. Constance knew what she wanted and knew how to get it. She was tired of waiting. She would delay no longer!

As she turned onto the main drive, she spotted Rod's unsaddled horse tethered near the front of the house's ruins. Reining in, Constance dismounted. After tying her mount nearby, she went in search of him.

Rod had spent the better part of the morning clearing brush from his family's graveyard. He was to begin his new life today and he would start by honoring his parents' memory. Though he missed them, Rod was glad that they hadn't lived to see the collapse of their world. He knew without a doubt that the old gracious way of living was gone.

The failure that the war had been had frustrated him. Rod had had little control over those fateful events and yet he still felt in some remote way responsible. Now, however, the real test was before him. He had to re-establish Clarke's Landing. If he failed, he would fail as a man. From now on, Rod was on his own.

He had shed his shirt long hours before and now stood, sweat glistening on his tanned back and chest, in the noonday sun. Wiping his forehead with his forearm, he proudly surveyed the freshly cleared gravesites. It was a small task, but an important one to him, and Rod felt a positive sense of accomplishment at having finished it. He knew the rest of the distasteful jobs in his life wouldn't be dispatched so easily, but each little victory helped.

Rod walked over to his saddle blanket, spread out under a tree in the garden, got his canteen and took a long drink of the cool water. Thirst quenched, he poured the rest of it over his neck. He shivered at the almost sensual feel of the liquid running down his body. He knew he was being too sensitive, but Constance's suggestiveness the night before had haunted him all morning long. If it hadn't been for the hard work here, he probably would have been out of control by now. Grateful for the tiring, distracting tasks, Rod turned back toward the graves and was startled to find Constance standing there, staring at him.

Constance had caught sight of him as he had walked from the gravesides to his shaded blanket. Just looking at his bare, lean torso had heated her blood and she stood, mesmerized by the animalistic beauty of his powerful male form. Though Rod was not a big man, he was muscular and hardened from the years at war. Her gaze touched him everywhere, admiring the strength of his sun-bronzed shoulders and arms, his trim waist and the snug fit of his trousers. Constance found the flesh and blood Rod even more attractive than her fantasies and it took all of her will power not to rush to him.

It was as though she willed it when he looked up and their eyes met. Lifting her skirts, she started through the weeds and brush toward him as gracefully as was possible.

"Constance, is something wrong?" he asked worriedly.

"No. I just needed to get away." She joined him near his blanket.

Constance could feel the heat emanating from his body and she longed to have the freedom to run her hands over the firm ridges of his torso.

Rod fought the urge to take her in his arms. Memories of her seductive promise of the night before flooded him and he hardened instinctively. Not wanting Constance to see the flagrant proof of his desire for her, Rod turned away and busied himself with putting up the canteen. This was not the time or place to make his feelings for her known, for Constance was a lady and as such she commanded his respect. With an effort, he brought his obstinate body under control and turned back to her.

"I'm glad you came," he said, casually. The truth of his words hidden by the offhand manner in which he'd spoken them. "I was just getting ready to take a break."

"You've been working in the cemetery?"

"All morning. It seemed like the best place to start."

"I see," Constance replied politely, but she was appalled by the thought of him doing such menial labor.

Rod caught the undercurrent of her real thoughts and smiled. "It is hard to accept, isn't it?"

"I'm afraid I . . ."

"You can't disguise your thoughts from me, Constance," he said half angrily. "I wasn't raised for this type of existence and neither were you."

Constance was astounded that he could read her so easily.

"Let's not pretend with each other. The old days are gone. Forever."

"I've been afraid to admit that to myself, although I know it's the truth. There doesn't seem to be any way out of all this!" She gestured at the untamed countryside. "Life used to have a purpose. Everything was so orderly."

"We'll have to start over if we want to make it a reality again," he told her seriously. Then, after a long pause, "Will you work with me?"

Constance, who had been staring at the crumbling foundation of Clarke House, turned quickly to Rod. Their eyes met and their gazes locked. Hers questioning; his challenging. If she was half the woman he thought her to be, Rod knew she wouldn't refuse.

"What about Ellyn?" She broached the sore subject.

"That's over." Then, more boldly, "It would never have worked."

"Why?" Constance pushed.

Rod looked irritated for a moment and then answered. "Because, next to you, she fades into oblivion."

Constance drew a deep, satisfying breath. He was aware of her as a woman! She tingled with excitement and threw caution to the wind as she reached out to lay a hand on the heated skin of his chest. The contact was electric and her eyes darkened with desire. It had been so long and she needed him desperately, as only an experienced, passionate woman could. Her body hungered for the touch of his. Constance wanted his weight upon her, his strength within her. Her knees went weak as she imagined Rod's lovemaking.

"Rod . . ." His name was a breathless whisper as she moved against him. "Please . . . I want you."

Her words freed him from all restraint and he pulled her fiercely to him. Groaning at the feel of her in his arms, he kissed her, their mouths opening in invitation, their tongues meeting in passion's play.

Constance arched against him, feverish in her desperation. This was Rod and he was hers! She guided his hand to the buttons at the bodice of her gown.

"Constance!" His voice was strangled as he broke off the kiss.

As he released the buttons, Rod pushed the material aside and bent to kiss her exposed cleavage. Her nipples hardened with desire at the heat of his breath upon her and she pulled her chemise lower, offering to his devouring mouth all the fullness of her breasts. She held his head to her as he sucked first one nipple then the other, drawing them deep within his mouth.

Wanting to have all of her, unable to wait any longer, he released her momentarily. Quickly straightening the blanket, he pulled her down with him. Constance was no longer thinking, she could only feel. Helping him as much as she was able, she

272

shed her gown and underthings and lay before him.

"You are beautiful. I never dreamed you'd be so perfect," he told her before moving the rest of his clothes and coming to her.

"You are, too," she said, boldly caressing his manhood as he knelt over her. "Come to me, Rod, please."

Spreading her legs for him, he moved between them, lifting her hips and plunging deep within the womanly core of her body. He wanted to pause, to savor the sensuality of the moment but Constance was beyond control. Wrapping her legs around him, she bucked and writhed beneath him. Enslaving his desire, she wantonly teased him to the heights of passion. Straining together, they found the rapturous release they sought.

There, amidst the scattering of bright, fragrant flowers that disguised the ruins of the old life, Constance and Rod clung together, totally sensitive to one another. They rested, knowing that the bond just forged between them would keep them together throughout the difficult days ahead. They had come together in desire; they would stay together out of need.

As they lay in the sun-dappled clearing, Rod marvelled at the lush beauty of Constance's figure. She was firm, yet soft—her breasts deliciously full, her buttocks curved, yet tight. He ridiculed himself, now, for ever having been concerned with her age. They were perfect for each other.

Separating slightly, they moved apart to enjoy the gentle breeze that cooled their still-heated bodies. Constance glanced at Rod and was concerned by the frown on his handsome features. She wondered if he regretted their coupling. Her plans for the future included marriage to him and she hoped her uncontrolled need for him today hadn't put him off. She didn't realize that her uninhibited response to him had bound him to her more securely than chains ever could.

Hesitantly now, as the fear of losing him grew within her, Constance ran a caressing hand over his chest, pausing just below his waist. When he turned to her, she smiled lazily at him.

"We're good together," she said seductively and moved her hand lower.

Rod returned her smile, hardening at her gentle touch. "Very good."

He kissed her deeply, rolling on his side and bringing her with him. Constance continued to fondle him, her exploration creating the driving need within him to have her again. Still facing her, Rod guided her legs around his waist and entered her smoothly.

Constance gasped at his sudden possession and shivered with delight. "Oh, Rod. You feel so good to me. I've needed you for so long. I was so afraid . . ."

"Afraid of what?" he asked, holding her immobile against him.

"That you wouldn't want me," she confessed, frantic with the desire to be one with him again.

"Want you? Woman, you drive me wild," he murmured as his mouth explored her neck and shoulder.

Constance quivered as his kisses travelled lower and he lifted a heavy breast to his lips. Licking and biting, he teased the pink peak to erection before suckling it. Sensation exploded within her loins and she moved on his impalement, wanting satisfaction for the craving deep within her.

"Don't," he commanded, grasping her hips and

holding her motionless. "I'm not through with you yet."

Stilling her frenzied movements, she lay in his embrace as quietly as possible while he toyed with her other breast, stroking and kissing the silken orb until she cried out to him in her passion.

In one swift, powerful move, he clasped her more closely to him and they rocked together in the age-old rhythm of desire. His mouth sought hers in a plundering kiss as they moved together in an orgy of longing.

Shocking, pulsating waves of pleasure radiated from the center of her being as Rod took her to the heights with him again. Sated for the moment, they fell back on the blanket and rested.

"You're wonderful," he breathed, too exhausted to say more. "We should do well together."

"Yes."

"We'll marry soon."

"Yes."

He moved near her again, pressing a light kiss on her lips. "Between the two of us, we can rebuild the Landing."

"I know," she agreed, confidently. "But it won't be easy."

"As long as we're together, we'll be fine."

Now that her long-suppressed sexual desires were finally fulfilled, Constance felt at peace with herself. Pulling him down, she kissed him gently.

"I'll need you forever, Rod," she whispered. "You make me feel like a young girl again."

"And I need you, Constance, to help me become the man I once was."

Knowing that they were bound together now by their mutual desires, Constance and Rod embraced fiercely, confident that they would succeed in their ambition to rebuild Clarke's Landing.

Ellyn had just awakened and was standing at her bedroom window when her mother and Rod rode up the drive. Just by watching she could tell that something had changed between them. They seemed to share a certain closeness that hadn't existed before. Backing away, lest Constance see her, Ellyn sat down on the side of her bed, her shoulders slumped in defeat.

Last night, she'd hoped things would make more sense today, but everything seemed worse this morning. A depression settled over her as she realized that she was trapped this time in a situation of her own making. Her grandfather couldn't help her now. She had to face up to it. She was pregnant with the child of a man who didn't care about her. Price had promised to write, to send money even, so she could come to him, but she'd heard nothing. Probably, Ellyn decided, when he got home he'd forgotten all about her. She should have known better. She should have.

"Oh, what's the use!" she thought viciously. She wouldn't be able to hide her condition much longer. She might as well tell her grandfather before Constance did. Lord knows, Constance had probably told Rod already.

Getting up wearily, she went downstairs in search of Lawrence.

Lawrence was in the sitting room when Ellyn found him.

"Ellyn, darling, how are you feeling today? You don't look well at all," he remarked as she joined him.

"That's why I came to see you. I need to talk to you."

"Of course, sit down." He gave her his full attention.

"Grandfather, I—" But before she could tell him, Constance burst through the front door, humming merrily.

"Lawrence?" she called. "Oh, there you are! I've got—Ellyn!"

"Mother, I . . ."

"You slut! Have you told your grandfather about your 'delicate condition' yet?" Constance sneered, aware that Rod was right behind her.

"No, Mother. I didn't get . . ."

"Thought you could keep it a secret, did you?" Constance interrupted. "What did you plan to do? Marry Rod and pass your Yankee's brat off as his?"

"Constance! What are you talking about?" Lawrence demanded.

"Tell them, Ellyn. Let me hear you admit what I knew all along," Constance said arrogantly.

Ellyn flushed and stammered, "Grandfather, I . . . um . . ."

"She's pregnant, Lawrence, with the Yankee's baby," Constance finished for her.

Lawrence paled and Rod stood stock still.

"Ellyn, is this true?"

"You're pregnant? And you were engaged to me? You harlot!" Rod was livid and stalked toward her.

Frightened by him, Ellyn backed away, but Rod was too quick for her. Grabbing her by her upper arms, he yanked her to him.

"Are you?" He was seething.

"Yes, I . . ."

Rod slapped her as hard as she could. Her head rocked back by the force of the blow and her lip split, bleeding profusely. Ellyn tried to cower, but he didn't release his grip on her.

"You were my fiancée and you slept with another man! I should kill you." His tone was rigid and deadly as his fingers bit into her tender flesh.

Constance watched the scene in triumph, but Lawrence was alarmed.

"That's enough, Rod," he said, but Rod ignored him. "Let her go!" Lawrence ordered.

Rod looked up to see Lawrence advancing on him. He shoved Ellyn forcefully away from him, causing her to lose her balance and fall heavily against a small table.

"Ellyn, go to your room. I'll be up shortly," Lawrence directed and she pulled herself up and stumbled in blind terror from the room. "I want you two to stay away from her. Rod, I will demand satisfaction from you if you ever lay a hand on her again. She is my granddaughter and as such deserves all the respect due that position."

Rod couldn't hide the disgust he felt. "She's a whore."

Lawrence gave them a furious look and left the room to find Ellyn.

The soft knock at her door caused her to jump and she stood stiffly, holding a damp rag to her swollen mouth as the door opened.

"Ellyn, darling, why didn't you tell me sooner?" Lawrence said, closing the door behind him. He stood silent for a moment, his expression worried, and then opened his arms to her. With little hesitation, Ellyn flew to him, sobbing.

"Oh, Grandpa! I tried, but I was so afraid!"

He held her tenderly, patting her gently on the back until her wracking sobs quieted.

"What am I going to do, Grandpa?" she asked.

"I know it was wrong, but I loved him so much."

"And he loved you," Lawrence said.

"But I haven't heard from him in all these weeks. He couldn't care about me and desert me this way."

"Don't worry. We'll make the arrangements right away."

"What arrangements?"

"Why, for you to join him in Alton."

"No! I won't go! If he didn't want me as I was, I'm not going to force him to marry me because I'm pregnant!" Ellyn declared, not wanting to force Price into an awkward situation.

"Ellyn, I know the man still loves you and he deserves to know about his child."

"How do you know he still cares?" Ellyn asked suspiciously.

Lawrence cleared his throat, embarrassed by what he had to tell her. "I haven't been entirely honest with you lately, Ellyn."

"What do you mean?" She was totally confused.

"To put it bluntly, your mother and I thought it best to keep you and Richardson apart. So we've destroyed all your correspondence."

Ellyn looked at him, her eyes full of pain. "Price wrote to me and you took his letters?"

Lawrence nodded in shame. "I thought we were doing the right thing. I thought—"

"Did he get any of mine?"

"No."

Ellyn sank down on her bed, rubbing her forehead wearily. "How could you?"

Lawrence had no answer. "I'm sorry, Ellyn."

She sat solemnly, her expression bleak. As she started to speak there came another knock at the door and Darnelle came in.

"Ah heard what happened and Ah thought you

might want dis." She held out the partially burned pages to Ellyn. "Miz Constance tried to burn it, but I got it out in time."

"Oh, Darnelle!" Ellyn hugged her. "Oh, thank you. Thank you!"

Ellyn unfolded the scorched sheets and started to read them.

"Ellyn, I'll be back later," Lawrence told her and, with Darnelle, left the room.

Trembling, Ellyn's eyes skimmed over the fragile, charred pages.

June 10, 1865. . . . been worried that you . . . write. Please send . . . need . . . busy working and . . . office. The completed . . . by me. I want it all . . . you. . . . several balls since . . . thought them a bore . . . you. I can hardly stand . . . have you in my arms again. . . . hurry. Love, Price.

Tears fell unbidden and she choked back a sob. He did still love her! Even if she could read only half of his letter, she could tell that he did! Laughing and crying, she hugged the letter to her breast. She opened the door to go find her grandfather and stopped as she heard him arguing with her mother downstairs.

"I don't care what you say, Lawrence. I want her and the bastard that she's carrying out of his house today! What kind of an influence do you think she is on Charlotte? I don't care where you send her, but get her away from me!"

"It will be my pleasure. I wouldn't dream of leaving one so young and tender under the same roof with you."

"I think you are overly kind in your description of her, Lawrence," Rod said, his tone hard and unforgiving. "She was, after all, sleeping with another man while she was betrothed to me."

Lawrence gave Rod a deadly look. "And were you faithful to Ellyn for the past four years?"

Rod flushed. "My morals are not those in question."

"Thank God! Now, if you two will excuse me, I have arrangements to make." He turned on his heel and left the room.

Lawrence met Ellyn in the second-floor hall.

"You heard?"

She nodded her head, too numb to speak.

"I'll call Darnelle and we'll pack your things. I don't want you subjected to that kind of abuse ever again! If we leave in the next hour, I think we can book you passage north this afternoon." He paused. "It probably would be best if Darnelle went with you. Then, once you're settled in, she can return home."

"Oh, Grandpa!" Ellyn hugged him, starting to cry again.

"Wait a second, young lady! Are you crying because you're sad or happy?"

"Both." She sniffed and he smiled at her tenderly.

"Well, let's get you packed and ready to go. The sooner you're safely away, the better I'll feel."

"Fine." She managed a watery grin and returned to her room to begin collecting her things.

Chapter Eleven

As was normal for the end of the week at Alton Transshipping Company, things were a mass of confusion. Tim Radcliffe, the main clerk, had left early, ready to enjoy his first weekend off in months. Price had been gone since Wednesday on a business trip to St. Louis and St. Charles and was not due to return until the following Tuesday. Coop had been at work all day and had just driven off, heading for home, when the telegram was delivered to the office. It was marked "PERSONAL," Price Richardson, c/o A.T.C., Alton, Illinois. When the clerk in charge saw the "PERSONAL" notation he did not open it, but merely placed it on the desk in Price's office. Later that evening, as the invoices for the day's shipments came in, an office boy casually tossed them on the desk sending the fragile, important telegram floating to the floor, where it lay hidden from sight beneath a cabinet.

As dusk fell, Ellyn and Darnelle were closeted in their cabin, where they had been since coming aboard earlier that afternoon. Ellyn had managed to hide her bruised and swollen cheek beneath the broad brim of her bonnet when they'd boarded in Memphis, but there was little hope of disguising the temporarily disfiguring marks without the hat. And so they'd remained, hidden away from passengers and crew alike all afternoon. Ellyn considered it a blessing in a way, for the steamer was carrying a load of livestock to Cape Girardeau and she'd been quite nauseated by the smell. Darnelle had ordered their dinner to be served in the cabin and they waited patiently now for it. The day had been long and arduous and both women were anxious to retire early.

Darnelle had been watching Ellyn all day since Lawrence had told her about the letters. She had to admit that just that little bit of good news had changed Ellyn's whole demeanor. Where before she'd seemed to be wasting away, now she had regained some of her old enthusiasm and was almost radiant, despite the ugliness of the bruise that Rod Clarke's blow had caused.

"Does your face still hurt, Miz Ellyn?" Darnelle asked, protectively. "Ah can get you another cool cloth if you need it."

Ellyn, who was resting on the narrow bed holding a compress on her battered cheek, managed a painful, crooked half-smile. "No need. This one is still good."

"And you're feelin' all right?"

Ellyn's eyes sparkled as she responded, "I feel alive for the first time since that night!"

Darnelle rolled her eyes. "That was some terrible night. And poor Mr. Richardson, he's gonna be so happy to see you!"

"Do you really think so?" A small, nagging doubt still lingered and kept her a trifle on edge.

"I know so, Miz Ellyn. He was so upset that last day. He'd been up lookin' for you for hours. And then when your mama destroyed his note . . ." Darnelle shook her head in sympathy. "Well, he was fit to be tied. She's one evil woman, your mama."

"I know. For years, I thought it was all my fault that she didn't love me, but I know now that it wasn't. We're just too different. We've never agreed on anything."

"Well, doan' you worry none about her. You've got a whole new life jes' waitin' for you. Why, pretty soon, you'll have a husband and your baby."

Ellyn rested a hand briefly on her belly. "I hope he's pleased. We never talked about having a family. You don't think he'll be angry, do you?"

"Heavens, no! That man is jes' crazy about you. You'll see. By Monday night, you'll be Mrs. Price Richardson."

Ellyn sighed happily. "I sure hope so. I do love him, Darnelle."

"Ah know you do. So doan' you go gettin' all upset now. Everything will be jes' fine."

"I'm so glad you came with me."

"Ah am, too. For once, you needed help and Ah'm proud to be the one to do it." They smiled fondly at each other.

A steward brought their dinner then and they dined on the riverboat's delicious fare. Meal finished and cleared away, they went to bed. Ellyn, exhausted mentally and physically, immediately fell sound asleep. Darnelle was still a little excited by all that had happened that day and she lay awake for quite a while, praying that everything she'd told Ellyn was still the truth. She was worried that Price, after all this time of not hearing from Ellyn, might have turned his attentions elsewhere, for it had been over two weeks since Mr. Lawrence had received his last letter. Fighting down a moment of panic, she finally fell asleep, anxious for the upcoming reunion to be over.

Monday, the day of their scheduled arrival in Alton, was bright and clear with just a few puffy, white clouds dotting the azure sky. The cool breeze out of the northwest promised at least a few more days of sunshine and moderate temperatures before July arrived in all of her sweltering splendor. It was late that afternoon when Ellyn began to worry about her appearance.

"Well, what do you think?" Ellyn asked Darnelle, after applying a thick coat of powder to her discolored jaw.

"The swellin's down," Darnelle said, trying to think of a positive reply. And, in truth, the swelling had diminished, but the bruise was decidedly worse, Rod's handprint a vicious purple-yellow on her pale skin.

"I guess I'd better wear my bonnet again," she said, her spirits flagging.

"And Ah'll walk on that side and nobody will see."

"You think that'll work? Price will probably meet us."

"We'll worry about that when it happens." Darnelle wanted to distract Ellyn. "He's gonna see it no matter what, unless you want to hide out somewhere for a few weeks."

"You're right. I just wanted to look my best for him."

Ellyn was miserable. She'd alternated these past two days between euphoric happiness and depressing fear. How she loved Price! She could hardly wait to see him! But what if he didn't want her? What would she do? How would she care for her baby?

A whistle sounded above and Ellyn glanced nervously at Darnelle.

"We must be nearing Alton. Shall we go take a look?"

They left the cabin together for the first time since they'd come aboard at Memphis.

The scene coming upriver from St. Louis was picturesque as the little town stretched over the river bluffs high above the busy waterway.

"If it had a courthouse on one of the hills, it could pass for Vicksburg!" Ellyn remarked, pleasantly surprised by her first glimpse of Price's home. "Oh! Look, Darnelle!" Ellyn pointed to a wharf boat where a small steamer was tied up. A big "ATC" was painted on its side, leaving no doubt as to its ownership.

"Well, leastwise we know we're in the right place," Darnelle said, satisfied that the worst was now behind them. "Let's go get our things and be ready to get off once we dock."

"All right," Ellyn agreed, suddenly apprehensive at the prospect of seeing Price again.

It didn't take them long to gather the few belongings they had unpacked and soon they were back on deck waiting for the boat to tie up. Both women searched the crowd anxiously for Price and were disappointed to find he wasn't there. When it became obvious to them, after long minutes, that he was not going to meet their boat, they hired a carriage and instructed the driver to stop at the Alton Transshipping Company Office.

ATC's business office on Piasa Street was near the riverfront and Ellyn barely had time to get comfortable before they pulled to a stop before the wooden, two-story building. Too excited to wait for the driver, Ellyn climbed down unassisted and waited most impatiently as Darnelle got out. They bid the driver to wait for them and then hurried inside.

The office was deserted with the exception of a single clerk who was in the rear filing some papers.

"Can I help you?" he called, turning from his paperwork and striding to the front to greet them.

"Yes, please," Ellyn said excitedly. "We're here to see Mr. Richardson. Is he in?"

"No, ma'am. I'm sorry."

"Can we reach him at home then?" she asked eagerly.

"I'm afraid not," the young man continued. "He's out of town on business and we don't expect him back until sometime tomorrow afternoon."

"Oh." Ellyn was crushed and inadvertently turned her head, giving the man a view of her bruised cheek.

"Would you care to leave a message?" he questioned, his gaze probing her injury.

Suddenly conscious of his scrutiny, Ellyn became flustered. "No, we'll come back tomorrow, thanks."

They quickly exited the office and entered their conveyance. Directing the driver to the Lincoln Hotel on State Street, they registered and were shown to a tiny corner room.

"Not exactly Riverwood, is it?" Ellyn remarked, glancing about her.

"Doan' worry 'bout, that," Darnelle said easily. "This time tomorrow you'll probably be at Mr. Price's house."

"Do you really think so?" Ellyn asked wistfully. "It was quite a disappointment to find he wasn't there."

"Ah know, but Mr. Price'll be back soon and we'll get this all straightened out. He might not have gotten the telegram if he's been out of town."

"I didn't think of that." Ellyn sat down heavily on her small bed. "Oh, well, the worst is over and I'm exhausted."

"Me, too," Darnelle said, setting aside the case she was carrying and stretching wearily. "Ah'll order dinner for us in the room."

"That sounds great, Darnelle. Thanks." Ellyn kicked off her shoes and lay back on the bed. "What do you think we should do tomorrow? Just wait until the afternoon and then stop by his office again?"

"We'll have to. We probably should have left a message for him," Darnelle told her, unpacking some of their belongings.

"I got so upset when that man saw my face that all I could think of was getting away!" Ellyn touched her tender cheek hesitantly. "It still hurts pretty bad."

"It looks it, too. Ah'll put another compress on it after dinner, but for right now, you jes' take a nap. Ah'll wake you when they bring the food."

Ellyn nodded tiredly and closed her eyes, while Darnelle went to order their evening meal.

Ellyn and Darnelle slept so late on Tuesday that they missed breakfast entirely. They came awake slowly, feeling rested and fit for the first time in ages.

Ellyn sat up in her bed, rubbing her eyes sleepily. "Good morning!" She smiled, yawning.

"Ah should say so. Fact is, Ah bet it's near noon."

They grinned happily at the luxury of sleeping late.

"What time is it? Do you know?"

"11:15."

"Good heavens! We'd better hurry if we want to

eat before we go to his office." Jumping out of bed, she began dressing hurriedly.

Darnelle watched Ellyn in amusement and then joined in her enthusiasm. Today was to be one special day.

Time was running out for Mary Anne. She'd been trying for weeks now to arrange to meet Price alone, but so far she had been unsuccessful. She'd long since forgotten his bad temper on the night of the ball. All she thought of now when she thought of Price was his money. The taxes on her home were due next month, so she had to do something and fast. Alex had been pressuring her to marry and she'd avoided committing herself so far, but she couldn't delay too much longer.

Putting the finishing touches on her toilette, she checked the time. It was just past one o'clock and Price had been due in town around noon. Descending to the main hall, she let herself out, intent on her objective of Price alone.

Most of the ATC office staff were at lunch when she swept indoors, smiling warmly at the clerk sitting at the front desk.

"Has Price returned yet?" she asked.

"No, Miss Montague. He hasn't gotten back to the office yet."

"Oh." She pouted, a little disappointed, then brightened. "Well, I'll just wait in his office."

Brushing past the speechless young man, she entered Price's private office and sat in the wing chair that faced his desk. When she noticed the clerk standing nervously at the door, she smiled her most beguiling smile.

"Don't worry about me. I'll be just fine waiting right here. You go on with your work," she told him.

"Yes, ma'am, but . . ."

"Go on, now, and close the door as you leave," she spoke so imperiously that the clerk blindly obeyed.

Only a few minutes later, Price arrived, striding into the office confidently after a very prosperous trip.

"How did it go, Mr. Richardson?" the young clerk asked as his boss came in.

"Just fine, O'Riley. I drummed up a lot of new business for us."

"Great. Did Mr. Cooper meet you?"

"Yes, he did and then he went home for lunch. Mr. Cooper should return by three o'clock," Price said, moving easily toward the door of his workplace.

"Mr. Richardson . . ." he started, remembering that Miss Montague was waiting.

"Later, I've got to get to work on these contracts," Price called over his shoulder as he opened the door and went in, giving the door a slight push behind him.

Mary Anne had heard his entrance and had been waiting for him. This was it. Whatever was going to happen between them would happen now.

"I'm so glad you're back," she welcomed him warmly.

He stopped dead still, just inside the door. "Mary Anne? What are you doing here?"

"Why, waiting for you, of course," she said huskily.

"I don't know what for!" he said in disgust.

"For this," Mary Anne could wait no longer. She came to him and kissed him, catching him by surprise as she wrapped her arms around him and pressed herself to him. "Don't you know how I feel

290

about you? I've loved you forever!''

Ellyn entered the ATC office ahead of Darnelle in her eagerness to regain Price. Smiling at the young clerk, who recognized her immediately, she asked, "Did Mr. Richardson get back yet?"

"He sure did, just a few minutes ago, but . . ." Before he could get the words out, Ellyn had already started into his office, opening the door slightly.

The sight that greeted her was one she would have nightmares about for months to come. A woman was embracing Price, murmuring, "I've loved you forever!" Then they kissed deeply and passionately. Embarrassed, not making a sound, Ellyn backed out, pulling the door back with her.

"I'm sorry, ma'am. I tried to tell you about Miss Montague.

"Miss Montague?" Ellyn couldn't move or think, her whole being shattered by the scene she'd just witnessed.

"She comes in all the time to see him."

"Oh . . ."

Darnelle, concerned by Ellyn's sudden paleness, bustled up beside her. "What's the matter?"

"Nothing. Nothing. He's busy right now. We'll just come back later," Ellyn stated mechanically. "Thank you for your help."

"Yes, ma'am. Who shall I tell him came by?"

"We want to surprise him," Darnelle said, saving Ellyn the agony of answering. "We'll see him at home later."

Ushering Ellyn back outside, they returned to the hotel. Once safely in the privacy of their room, Darnelle began her interrogation.

"What happened at the office, Ellyn Douglass? You haven't said a word since we left there."

She looked up at Darnelle, her eyes bright with pain and filled with tears.

"He was there, but he was kissing a woman."

"Did he see you?"

"Oh, no! I would have just died if he had!" she sobbed, burying her face in her hands.

Darnelle tried to comfort her, but she pulled away, too miserable to tolerate another's touch. Collapsing on her bed, she cried brokenheartedly, grieving for the loss of her innocent love. A long time passed before she quieted and Darnelle sat the whole while by her bedside, neither speaking nor consoling. She waited silently for the storm to pass.

Darnelle was worried about what to do next for she knew that they were short on funds. Going home was out of the question, so their only real option was to notify Price of Ellyn's condition and hope that he would do the right thing by her, regardless of this other woman. When Ellyn finally had stopped crying, she turned to Darnelle.

"What am I going to do? He's found someone else." Her voice quivered with emotion.

"You doan' know that for sure."

"But I saw him kissing her!" Ellyn flared.

"I doan' doubt that you saw him kissing a woman, but you ain't for sure that he's forgotten you."

"What do you mean?" she sniffed, sitting up. "How could he kiss someone else if he loves me?"

Darnelle fought down a smile at Ellyn's naivete. "We'll jes' send him a note that we're here waiting for him and see what happens. All right?"

"I don't know. He probably doesn't even care anymore!"

"Where's your pride, Miz Ellyn?" Darnelle chided. "This Yankee needs to know 'bout his child and we're gonna tell him."

292

Ellyn stiffened as she realized how she'd been carrying on.

"I'm sorry, Darnelle. This won't happen again." She pulled herself together with an effort.

"That's all right. You feel better now?"

"Much. It was just such a shock and disappointment."

Darnelle nodded. "You jes' write that note and Ah'll see he gets it."

Ellyn drew a deep, shuddering breath and wrote the short, concise message.

When Mary Anne didn't end her clinging embrace right away, Price pried her loose and almost threw her from him.

"This is my business office. What in the hell do you think you're doing?" he demanded.

Mary Anne stood, backed up against his desk. In an attempt at coolness, she sat jauntily on the edge of it and smiled at him invitingly.

"You've been such a hermit these past weeks. I needed to see you."

"I can't imagine why."

"Don't you know I love being with you?" she purred.

"Mary Anne," he said, exasperated, "you haven't been with me in over four years."

"I know. But now that you're back . . ."

"What we had was over years ago!"

"It doesn't have to be." She moved sinuously off the desk and came toward him. "Does it?"

"What about your fiance?" he asked.

"I'm not here to talk about Alex."

"Obviously," he said coldly, making no effort to hide the contempt that he felt for her. He turned from her and moved to stand behind his desk.

"You still want me, I know you do!" She followed him and stood next to him, trying to take his arm.

"I think you're greatly mistaken." He looked her over with little interest. "What we had all those years ago was lust, not love. You destroyed everything I felt for you when I found you with Alex. Well, now that you've managed to get him to propose, why don't you go to him?"

"Because I love you! You're the one that I want!"

"I'm sorry, Mary Anne, but I don't want you." His tone was callous.

"I can change all that if you'll give me a chance!" she pleaded.

"It's over," he told her simply.

Mary Anne was furious and struck out at him viciously. "What's the matter, Price? Did all those years at war change you? Don't you like women anymore?"

He looked at her sharply, his gaze deadly. "I love women, Mary Anne. It's whores like you, I can't tolerate."

Mary Anne gasped, stunned by his comeback. "I was good enough for you before!"

"That was before you were so well used," he sneered. Then, dismissing her casually, he said, "Now, go on back to your destitute fiance. I've got work to do."

Mary Anne glared at him. "Alex is as well off as you are!"

Price just looked up at her, his expression one of pained boredom. "Hardly. I had to buy them off just so they'd have a roof over their heads."

"What are you saying?"

"Face it. The only reason Alex is willing to marry you is your money—and we both know what a joke that is."

294

"Why, you!"

"It's no secret that you owe everyone in town, Mary Anne."

She reddened at his disclosure. She had been so positive that nobody knew.

"Now, get out, before I tell Alex about your situation."

"You! You'll pay for this!"

"Spare me your threats. You don't scare me in the least." He stalked to the office door and pulled it open. "Goodbye, Mary Anne!"

As she moved haughtily into the outer office, Price spoke to the young clerk.

"O'Riley, no more interruptions, no matter what!"

"But, sir . . ." he said hastily.

"None, O'Riley. Understood?"

"Yes, sir," he acknowledged in defeat and returned to his work, forgetting all about the pretty Southern woman who'd been there earlier.

Chapter Twelve

Drawing a ragged breath, Price shifted uncomfortably in his chair and tried to force himself to concentrate on the papers spread out before him. Rubbing his forehead wearily, he finally gave up the attempt and threw down his pen in defeat.

"Damned Mary Anne!" he growled, standing up and stalking to the office window.

Her attack on his senses had brought home with a vengeance the fact of his long weeks of celibacy. During the war years there had been little time for any physical or emotional involvements. But now, back in civilization, Price was in daily contact with attractive women and he was very aware of his male desires.

Sighing, he ran a hand through his hair in a nervous gesture and turned back to his desk. He'd lasted this long and he could make it another fortnight until it was time for him to take his trip to Memphis to reclaim Ellyn. Trying to ignore the not-unpleasant ache in his loins, he sat down again and made a final attempt at his work.

It took awhile for him to realize that this paper work was not going to distract him from the feelings Mary Anne had stirred up in him this afternoon. Gathering the papers, he shoved them in a portfolio and left the room. Maybe once he was out of the confines of his office, he would be able to think more clearly.

O'Riley looked up in surprise at his unexpected appearance. "Yes, sir?"

"I'm leaving for the day. Tell Mr. Cooper when he comes in that I'm going to run some errands and then work on these at home," he said indicating the contracts.

"Anything else, sir?" the clerk asked a little nervously as he sensed his boss's strange mood.

"No, Kevin. I'll see you in the morning." Price half-smiled at the younger man. "Oh, and don't worry about Miss Montague. She won't be pestering you anymore."

"Yes, sir," Kevin O'Riley blushed as his employer left the office.

The young messenger boy entered the ATC office hesitantly about half an hour after Price had gone. He looked around questioningly before approaching Kevin.

"Excuse me, sir?"

"What is it?"

"I have a message here to deliver personally to Mr. Price Richardson." The youth showed him the perfumed note he carried.

"Mr. Richardson's out of the office and I don't expect him back until tomorrow morning."

"Oh." The boy seemed worried. "Well, the lady told me to make sure he got it personal-like." He paused. "Where's he live? I'll take it there."

"He's not home right now. He said he had other business to take care of first," Kevin explained. Then, sympathizing with the youth's dilemma, he offered. "I'll tell you what, were you supposed to wait for an answer?"

"No."

"Good. Then just give it to me and I'll drop it by his house on my way home."

"Would you really? Gee, thanks, mister!" Suddenly, though, he looked apprehensive. "But that lady said I was to give it to him personally."

"Believe me, kid, he'll have it in his hands by six o'clock tonight," Kevin reassured him.

"All right, thanks."

As the boy left the office, Kevin shook his head and smiled at his conscientiousness. Carefully folding the jasmine-scented letter, he put it safely in his vest pocket.

Price sat on the top of the high, limestone bluff watching the river drift by. He wondered, idly, if Ellyn was watching it, too. God, how he missed her. Her quick smile, her gentle voice. He was lonely and he didn't know how he'd ever lived alone before the war. The boring days stretched endlessly before him. The only thing that kept him going was the promise he'd made to himself about a trip to Memphis.

The renovation of the house was almost finished and he was proud of the job the workmen had done. It was more beautiful than ever and he hoped Ellyn would like it. This afternoon, though, he had had no inclination to stay home. His tense body and soul needed purging and the only respite he could give himself was through hard physical exercise. So, he'd saddled his favorite mount and rode out to the bluffs. The trek was a long, demanding one, but the view plus the brisk breeze and the warm sun had made it worthwhile.

Price wasn't a deeply religious man, not having attended any church services since his boyhood, but he did believe that everything in life happened for a definite reason. Even the horror of the *Sultana*'s explosion had resulted in good, for he'd met and fallen in love with Ellyn.

As Price relaxed in the bright sunshine, he somehow sensed that he would be with her soon. He knew it was a gut instinct, but he'd learned to recognize the validity of those feelings during the war when his intuition had guided him out of many a dangerous situation.

Feeling rested and calm, he headed back home, ready to bide his time once again.

Ellyn sat on the edge of her bed looking questioningly at Darnelle.

"Ah didn't see him anywhere downstairs, Miz Ellyn."

"Oh." She was disheartened.

What was happening? Ellyn felt as if she had no control over her destiny right now and it was driving her crazy. That, plus the fact that patience was not one of her strong points, had made the past three hours the longest in her life. They'd sent the note to him at his office around two p.m. and it was after five already. Surely, if he still cared for her, he would have come by now.

Blinking back hot, burning tears of disillusionment, Ellyn refused to cry anymore. She had spent the last few hours trying to decide what to do and she now knew.

Price evidently was in love with that other woman. What other possible explanation could there be for his not coming? So, if she hadn't heard from him one way or the other by tomorrow morning, she would arrange their passage back to Memphis. Hopefully, with her grandfather's help, she could find a nursing job until her pregnancy became too obvious. Life wouldn't be easy, but she could do it.

Squaring her shoulders, she lifted her chin and met Darnelle's eyes.

"Well, I'm getting hungry and I guess he's not coming by to take us to dinner. Please order us something to eat here in our room."

Darnelle had been watching Ellyn's reaction to the negative news and was proud of the way she was holding up. She was a fine, strong young woman. A lesser girl would have fallen completely apart by now, but not Ellyn. As she turned to go order their dinner, Ellyn called.

"Oh, and Darnelle?"

"Yes, Miz Ellyn?"

"Could you take another look for that messenger boy? Maybe there was a response for us."

"Ah sure will, honey." Darnelle couldn't hide the warmth and admiration she felt for Ellyn.

"Thanks." Ellyn gave her a weak, encouraging smile.

Kevin O'Riley got so bogged down in last-minute emergencies that it was close to seven before he got away from the office. Still a junior clerk and on limited funds, he began the long walk up to his boss's house.

Price prowled through the newly redecorated rooms on the main floor of his home. He had managed to buy back most of the family heirlooms that Rachel had sold off. And even though he'd been forced to pay some outrageous prices for them, he was glad to have them once again.

Stopping long enough in the dining room to pour himself a stiff drink, he wandered back down the hall to the study. Its renovation completed, it was his favorite room in the house. It was a man's room, with warm, dark wood paneling, a massive stone fireplace and floor-to-ceiling windows. The hardwood floor was highly polished and covered with an Aubusson carpet in rich, deep tones of orange and brown. Half-empty bookcases lined two walls and there was an ornate gun cabinet displaying all types of firearms near the hallway door. Collecting guns had been his father's hobby and Price was lucky to have gotten the collection back intact from the man Rachel had sold it to.

Settling in at the large oak desk, Price made yet another attempt at the work he had brought home with him. When the knock came at the door, long minutes later, he was still staring at the same sheet of paper. Glancing at his pocket watch, he was puzzled as to who it could be at this time of night. Fearing bad news, he hurried to answer it.

Brushing her hair in strong, vigorous strokes, Ellyn spoke, "The only thing we can do is return to Memphis. That way, you can get back to Franklin and I can get a job at the hospital."

"Have we got enough money left?" Darnelle asked. She felt defeated, too, as she noted the time once more: 7:30.

When she had gone down earlier to order their meal, she managed to locate the messenger and he'd assured her that he had hand-delivered the note hours before. Darnelle had hated to be the bearer of bad news, but Ellyn had accepted it in a mature, stoic manner.

"If we leave first thing tomorrow, we'll have enough."

"But what if you can't find work in Memphis?"

"Darnelle! Don't you see that I have to get away from here! I can't wait forever for Price to find the time to stop by. I won't live that way." Ellyn composed herself. "No. I have to face it. If he still felt the same as when he left me, then he'd have been here by now. I've been a fool. It's over!"

"It's not over! What about his baby?"

"My baby! I'll manage. I always have, haven't I?" Ellyn replied with more bravado than she felt and was pleased when Darnelle let it drop.

"Ah'll pack our things, then. And we'll leave nice and early," Darnelle told her, as she busied herself around the small room. It had been a wasted day and a wasted trip and Darnelle fervently hoped that Ellyn knew what she was doing.

"O'Riley! Is something wrong?" Price was surprised to find Kevin at his door.

"No, sir, Mr. Richardson. I just wanted to give you this letter. A boy dropped it by the office this afternoon right after you left." He handed Price the folded note.

"Thanks, I appreciate it," Price said, looking down at the envelope and not recognizing the feminine handwriting.

"See you in the morning." Kevin started off toward home.

"Good night," Price called distractedly as he closed the door.

Price caught scent of the perfume on those sheets and his heart lurched at the familiar scent. No . . . it couldn't be from Ellyn. She wouldn't have written a note, she would have come to him right away. She wouldn't have bothered with a letter.

Going back into the study, he sat at his desk and opened the letter, staring in breathless wonder at the signature. Ellyn!

His hands shook as he read and reread her note,

too excited to really understand anything in it except that she was there in Alton at the Lincoln Hotel. Stuffing the pages in his pocket, he rushed from the house to see her.

Tired beyond belief, Ellyn laid out her clothes for the morning's journey and got ready for bed. On the way to Alton, she had wanted time to fly so she could be with Price as soon as possible. Now she wanted time to fly again, so she could leave. Her dreams were shattered. Ellyn needed to retreat from this painful real world and get her life straightened out.

Clad only in her gown and wrapper, she jumped nervously when someone pounded on the door.

Darnelle was still dressed and she moved to answer it. "Who is it?"

"Darnelle? It's Price. Let me in!"

Ellyn stood up, shocked by the sound of his voice.

"I don't want to see him!" she declared in a heated whisper. "How dare he show up at this time of night!"

"Miz Ellyn!" Darnelle was surprised by her refusal, for once disagreeing with her young mistress. "You jes' talk with him for a minute."

"Darnelle! Hurry up!" Price knocked again, his eagerness to see them clearly evident in his voice.

"Yes, suh," Darnelle said and opened the door wide, defying Ellyn's wishes.

Price strode into the room, his spirits high.

"Darnelle, it's good to see you," he told her, but his eyes were on Ellyn.

The softness of the lamplight made Ellyn's beauty seem almost ethereal as she stood by the bed in her flowing negligee. At this first sight of her Price knew without a doubt that she was worth every minute of the long wait. With tender intent, Price started toward her, Darnelle forgotten, aching to feel the softness of her in his arms again.

"Ellyn," he breathed, the deep rich timbre of his voice was husky with emotion.

"Don't you come near me you despicable, false-hearted womanizer! How dare you come here at this hour of the night!"

"What are you talking about?" he asked, astounded by her savage attack.

"How ever did you manage to tear yourself away from your mistress?"

"Mistress? What mistress?" Price had no idea what Ellyn was referring to and took a step toward her. But the cutting look she gave him halted his approach.

"You are contemptible!" she cried, turning her back on him. "You disgust me. Why don't you just leave! I don't need you!"

All those nights she had lain awake, longing for him now seemed a hateful, vile joke. Why had she wasted her time? He wasn't worth it. For once maybe her mother had been right.

At her rejection of him, Price paled. Standing behind her, frozen in place, he couldn't begin to fathom her emotions. What in the world was she so upset about? A mistress? What was going on? Pulling himself together, he realized he needed some time alone with her.

"Darnelle, could you leave us for a few minutes?"

"Don't leave, Darnelle!" Ellyn ordered, but the older woman didn't look at her.

"Ah'll be in the hall."

"Thanks," Price said and she gave him a small acknowledging nod before closing the door behind her.

Ellyn turned to glare at her supposed friend as she left and, in her anger, inadvertently exposed her bruised jaw to Price's observant gaze.

"Ellyn! Your face! What's happened to you?" No longer put off by her belligerent attitude, he came to her, pulling away her hand as she quickly tried to cover her cheek.

Facing him fully, she knew it was useless to try to hide it any longer.

"Attractive, isn't it?" she remarked sarcastically. "It's just another memento reminding me of how stupidly naive I was."

"Memento? What are you talking about? Who did this to you?"

Ellyn looked up at Price miserably and was overwhelmed by the tenderness in his expression. Why had he shown up now? Just when she had convinced herself that she was strong enough to make it without him. It would have been so much easier for her to hate him if he had stayed away.

"Rod."

"He hit you? Your glorious Southern gentleman? Why?" Price touched her discolored cheek with gentle fingers.

Shaking from the conflicting emotions warring within her breast, Ellyn knew it was time for the truth.

"He hit me when he found out that I was carrying your child."

Price frowned, not quite believing what he had just heard. "You're pregnant?"

Her pride surging forth, her every word marked with determination, she answered him, "Yes, but you don't have to worry. If you've made other plans, I can manage."

"I can see that," he said sarcastically, pointedly looking at her injured face.

"No, I'm serious. I know you have someone else."

"Someone else? How can you even suggest that!"

"Because I saw you!" she fumed, amazed by his plea of innocence.

"Saw me do what? When?"

Ellyn hesitated and then plunged on, "Darnelle and I got into town yesterday."

"But I didn't even get back until today!" Price interrupted.

"I know. We stopped at your office yesterday but your clerk told us you wouldn't be back until today. So about one o'clock this afternoon, we went back." Ellyn waited, watching Price closely. "When I opened your office door, you were . . ."

"Kissing a black-haired woman, right?" he finished bitterly.

Her eyes misting with tears, Ellyn's chin tilted with prideful stubbornness as her lips trembled. "Yes."

"Ah, sweetheart," he agonized. "I'm so sorry. But it's not what you think."

Unable to restrain himself any longer, Price took her into his arms and held her close to his heart. Its heavy rhythmic beating seemed to soothe Ellyn for a moment, but then she struggled to push free of him.

"It's not what I think!? You were kissing her!"

"Ellyn," he said, his voice was low and seductive, "her name is Mary Anne Montague and she was kissing me."

She raised her eyes to his, wanting to believe him. "But why?"

Price sighed and sat down on the bed, pulling Ellyn down beside him.

"Years ago, Mary Anne and I . . . well, we . . ."

"Had an affair?"

"Yes." He paused, watching her reaction.

"Go on," Ellyn said, her expression unreadable.

"It ended before I left for the war."

"Then why was she kissing you this afternoon?"

"Mary Anne is deeply in debt and in desperate need of a rich husband."

"And you're rich?"

"We are," he told her proudly. "But as far as Mary Anne goes—if you hadn't rushed off you'd have seen her beat a very rapid retreat."

Ellyn's lips curved in a small smile. "Oh?"

"Yes, 'oh,' " Price grinned. "I threw her out."

Ellyn gave a small throaty laugh. "I'm glad."

"So am I." He gathered Ellyn to him. "After all we've gone through, there's no way I'd ever risk losing you."

"I love you, Price."

"And I love you," he told her before claiming her mouth in a heart-stopping kiss.

"You don't know how long I've waited for this moment."

"About as long as I have. Oh, Price, I was so hurt when you left. And then Darnelle didn't get to tell me the truth right away because Mother sent her into town." Ellyn clung to him.

"Sweetheart, it's all behind us now. We're together and nothing is ever going to change that." Tilting her face up to his, he kissed her again, parting her lips and tasting the sweetness of her mouth.

There was no denying the languorous, long-denied warmth that enveloped her at the touch of his lips. Ellyn's slumbering needs reawakened and she met his passion equally, knowing that they would never be parted again.

Price crushed her to him as his body flared with desire. Ellyn was his soul mate, his other half. Without her he'd been lost. She alone made his existence worthwhile.

As the kiss ended, they held each other tightly, overcome by their turbulent emotions.

"Did I ever tell you that I love babies?" he asked, pressing a soft kiss on her forehead.

"No, but I'm really glad you do." She smiled.

"You know that I want you and our child, don't you?" He held her away from him so he could see her face.

Ellyn searched his eyes for her answer. Seeing his true feelings reflected there, she looped her arms around his neck and kissed him.

"You'll make a wonderful father."

"Marry me?"

"Of course. Did you doubt it?"

"No." He hugged her to him, protecting her in the safe harbor of his arms.

The loud knock caused them to jump apart and they stood up, laughing, as Darnelle came back in.

"We're getting married!" Price told Darnelle happily.

"That's wonderful, Mr. Price. Everything will be jes' fine now."

"Listen, rather than stay here any longer, get your things together and you can move in with Coop and Betsey until we're married."

"Coop?" Ellyn asked, surprised.

"He's alive, Ellyn!" Price explained. "He got back home before I did."

"I'm so glad."

"Me, too." He smiled. "Finding out he was alive was the only good part of coming home."

Ellyn kissed him again. "Are you sure that they won't mind?"

"No, not at all. They're dying to meet you. How soon can you be ready?"

"Well, I've got to dress, but most everything is packed."

"All right, you get dressed and I'll get us a carriage." Price started for the door and then came back to her.

Pulling her into his arms, he kissed her passionately.

"That'll give you something to remember me by while I'm gone."

Ellyn bubbled with laughter at Darnelle's shocked expression. "Hurry up and get the carriage. I'll be right here waiting for you." '

"I'm going, I'm going," he mumbled and disappeared out into the hall.

After Darnelle shut and locked the door behind him, she turned to face Ellyn.

"Isn't he wonderful?" Ellyn asked, starry-eyed.

"Yes, Miz Ellyn," Darnelle agreed. "Now, aren't you glad I let him in?"

"Absolutely!" Ellyn smiled and hugged her friend. "Let's hurry. I want to be ready when he gets back!"

Mary Anne Montague, the source of Ellyn's needless worry, lay back in poised beauty against the bed pillow as Alex came back to her side with two glasses of sherry.

"What a wonderful idea this was," she purred, stretching sensuously. "Dinner out would have been so boring."

Alex, still nude himself, stood admiring the smooth unclad length of her before handing her the sherry.

"I'll never tire of looking at you," he told her, sitting on the edge of the bed, his gaze riveted on her small, pert breasts.

"And I love having you look," she said throatily, taking the proffered drink and sipping it.

Mary Anne was glad that Alex was easily entertained, for tonight her mind was crowded with vicious thoughts. Somehow, she would figure out a way to get even with Price—no matter how long it took.

After leaving Price's office, Mary Anne had checked on Alex and discovered, to her dismay, that everything Price had said about him was true. Except for the seventy-five-hundred-dollar pay-off, they were as broke as she was. She needed Price's money too, but until now, Alex hadn't confided any of their plans.

"I heard a very unsettling rumor today and someone told me that Price started it."

"Oh?" Alex caressed her slim thigh absently.

"According to what I heard, Price says that you are completely destitute except for his charity and that you're only marrying me for my money."

Alex looked up startled and Mary Anne knew that she had gotten his attention.

"I should call him out for that," Alex said viciously.

"Don't be stupid," Mary Anne said, having no patience with him. "Price is an excellent shot."

"That's true enough," Alex agreed thoughtfully, his eyes narrowing. "There are other, more promising ways of dealing with Price."

"Such as?"

"Never mind," he dismissed her inquiry.

"But, Alex, how do you think it makes me feel to know he's spreading such terrible lies about you? You're my fiance!"

"Well . . ."

"Tell me what you'd like to do and I'll help you all I can!" she offered eagerly, surprised at how easily manipulated he was.

"All right, but first we'll have to talk with Mother. She's been making the plans."

"Good," Mary Anne said softly. "Now, come here. I love it when you're so aggressive. It makes me want you!"

Setting aside their now empty glasses, Alex bent over her, his mouth claiming hers. Mary Anne pulled him down beside her and brazenly pressed herself to him. She enjoyed playing these seductive games with

Alex and she knew exactly how he would respond to all her initiative. Arching her back, she wrapped her legs tightly about his hips and moved teasingly against his arousal. But Alex was not ready to enter her and he lowered his head so he could caress her breasts, each breast in turn, with hungry kisses. She groaned with pleasure at the feel of his mouth sucking at her nipples and, encouraged, Alex slid lower, finding and exploring her center of feeling. Sliding his hands beneath her hips, he lifted her to him, ravishing her with his lips and tongue, tormenting her. Bringing her close to the peak of ecstasy time and again, he finally moved up over her, penetrating her depths. There, to seek and find his own release as she attained hers.

Mary Anne rested beneath him, sated. She was ready to be about her revenge. No one knew of Price's rejection of her, so if Price had a nasty accident, there would be no way that she would be suspect. As soon as she could, she would urge them on, for a successful plot against Price would mean money in her pocket. Smiling, she waited almost impatiently for Alex to stir. There was much to be done.

Chapter Thirteen

With the patched skirts of her travelling gown artfully arranged to cover her worn slippers, Ellyn sat sedately on the edge of the plush red velvet side chair sipping the cup of tea that Betsey had provided. Price and Darnelle had gone to help Coop bring in her things from the carriage and she was left alone with Betsey.

"I really appreciate your having me," Ellyn thanked her hostess.

"You're family, Ellyn. Why Price has talked about you so much, I feel as though I know you already." Betsey smiled warmly.

Betsey could easily understand why Price had fallen in love with Ellyn. The girl was a beauty. Her dark hair was long and thick, her green-brown eyes were bright with intelligence and humor. Yes, Betsey thought, Price had chosen wisely. But why had Ellyn not communicated with him in all these weeks. The poor man had been so worried.

"Your home is magnificent, Betsey. Have you lived here long?" Ellyn asked, admiring the black marble mantel and the warm, mellow wood tones of the walnut furnishings.

"Since we were married. I guess it's been five years now," Betsey said. "But it hasn't always looked like this. I've been doing just a little at a time, room by room."

"Well, you're doing a wonderful job."

"Thank you," Betsey accepted the compliment gracefully. "What was Riverwood like? Price tells us the house was huge."

"Mm-hmm," Ellyn agreed, taking a small drink, "it is big. We have sixteen rooms. It was quite a showplace before the war, but now . . ."

"Were things really that bad?"

"Worse," Ellyn said flatly. "I tried my best to keep it up."

"And you did a marvelous job," Price interrupted as he and Coop rejoined them.

Coop poured them both a tumbler of bourbon and Price sat in the chair nearest Ellyn's. Ellyn smiled at him in undisguised adoration.

"You mean you were running a plantation by yourself?" Betsey was amazed.

"Practically. You see the field hands ran off the first chance they got and, then, when my father and brother were killed there was nobody else. I had to do it."

"I'm so sorry about your father and brother. It must have been difficult for you."

"The hardest part was keeping food on the table. My grandfather helped as much as he could, but, being a doctor, he had to spend a lot of time in Memphis at the hospital."

"What about your mother?" Betsey asked. "Couldn't she help you?"

"My mother," Ellyn sighed giving Price a sidelong glance.

"You'd have to meet her to believe her," Price added.

"Why? What's she like?" Coop wanted to know.

"She's a very beautiful woman," Ellyn began and then stopped, not able to go on. Setting her teacup and saucer down on the small table next to her, she turned to Price. "Do you know what she did after you left?"

Price's eyes narrowed. "I wouldn't put anything past Constance. What did she do?"

"First, she sent Darnelle into town so I wouldn't find out the truth of what happened. And, then, she intercepted all of our letters. I didn't even know that you'd written to me until last week, after the big fight."

Price was surprised. "No wonder you had so many doubts about me." Taking Ellyn's hand, he squeezed it reassuringly. "Don't worry, we won't have to deal with her anymore."

"Whoa! Wait a minute! What's this all about?" Coop asked.

"I guess Price didn't tell you everything about what happened at Riverwood."

"No, I didn't, but go ahead if you want to talk about it."

Ellyn relaxed a little and sat back in her seat. "My mother absolutely hates Yankees. I mean, she wouldn't even let me bring Price in the big house when he was injured. I had to take him out to the old overseer's house."

"And you really dragged him out of the river?"

Ellyn nodded. "That was one wild day. Grandfather was gone and Mother was just in a fury when she found out you were a Union officer." Ellyn looked at him apologetically and then continued on with her story. "But with Franklin's help, he's Darnelle's husband, I managed to get you settled in."

"I'll forever be grateful," Price told her softly.

Ellyn blushed at his sentiment. "I'm glad I did it, too. Anyway, Mother gave me a hard time about nursing Price. She even threw me out of the house until Grandfather came home. But by then Price and I had fallen in love."

314

"You were engaged to somebody else though, weren't you?"

Ellyn nodded. "Rod Clarke. And when Mother found out how Price and I felt about each other, she did everything in her power to ruin things for us. And she nearly did."

"Thank God Darnelle told you what was really going on."

"Yes, once I found out, I wrote to you regularly, but Mother destroyed all my letters. You were probably angry, weren't you?"

"Not so much angry as worried," Price reassured her.

"So how did you manage to finally get away?" Betsey wanted to know.

"My fiance came home and I broke off with him. The only trouble was, since I hadn't heard from Price, I didn't know what to do." Ellyn paused, looking tenderly at Price. "Especially after I found out about the baby."

"You're pregnant?" Betsey was delighted. "How wonderful!"

Ellyn looked visibly relieved. "I was worried that you'd disapprove."

"Never." Betsey came to Ellyn and hugged her. "Price loves children. You should see him with our son, Jason. That's just marvelous. I'm so happy for you."

"Thank you. I am, too, now that we're together. But we almost didn't make it."

"Well, Ellyn's grandfather helped her book passage north and she arrived with Darnelle yesterday. Evidently Kevin just told her to come back today and didn't take a message," Price explained, smiling. "This afternoon, when I got back, guess who was waiting for me in my office?"

"Who?"

"Mary Anne."

"Mary Anne!" Coop and Betsey were surprised. "Oh, no!"

"Oh, no is right. Before I knew what she was up to, she kissed me."

Betsey groaned. "You didn't walk in on that?"

Ellyn nodded. "It was awful. Darnelle and I went back to the hotel and stayed there for hours trying to decide what to do. Finally, she convinced me to send him a note."

"But I didn't get it until almost eight o'clock tonight," Price said laughing. "By that time Ellyn was really angry!"

"So you really let Price have it, did you?" Coop laughed.

"She sure did." Price smiled at Ellyn proudly.

"I can see how Ellyn would get the wrong impression. We all know how brazen Mary Anne can be when she decides she wants something. She'll do anything to get it."

"Well, I don't think she harbors any love for me anymore," Price stated firmly.

"She better not," Ellyn teased.

"This has to have been one of the most memorable courtships on record." Coop laughed. "But you've got it all worked out now, right?"

"Absolutely."

"Good. So when is the wedding?"

"I'll check with the priest tomorrow and we'll do it as soon as possible. I've waited too long already," Price told them.

"Why don't we plan a party for you?" Betsey offered.

"That sounds fine. It would be a good chance for Ellyn to meet everyone," Price remarked. "When would be good?"

"How's Saturday? If you're married by then it can

be your reception and if you're not, it can be your engagement party.'' Betsey was excited by the idea.

"All right with you Ellyn?" Price asked as he noticed that she seemed less than enthusiastic.

"Of course, whatever you want is fine with me," Ellyn replied, trying to hide her embarrassment at not having a proper gown and no money to buy one.

Price was puzzled by her manner, but didn't press the issue.

"It's settled then, we'll have the party Saturday night regardless and you can get married just as soon as the priest can arrange it,'' Betsey concluded.

"Right," Price agreed. Then he realized how late it was getting. "I think we'd better call it a night. Tomorrow's going to be one busy day. Oh, Betsey?''

"What?"

"Would you have time to take Ellyn shopping in the morning?"

"Sure, that would be fun."

"Price, it's really not necessary," Ellyn protested.

"On the contrary, I want you to get everything you need," Price said warmly.

"I know, but . . ."

"What difference will a few days make? By this time next week you'll be my wife."

"All right," Ellyn relented. "Thank you."

"Good, we'll go first thing." Betsey was pleased.

"Ellyn, I'll walk you upstairs," Price offered.

As he stood, she came to his side, and they left the parlor together, their arms around each other's waist.

"Happy?" he asked as they started up the stairs.

Ellyn nodded and Price kissed her softly. When they reached the door to the guest bedroom, he pulled her into his arms and hugged her to him.

"I'll let you know what the priest says as soon as I find out."

"I can hardly wait."

317

"Me, too." He grinned, giving her a chaste kiss that greatly disappointed her. "You go on to bed and I'll see you in the morning."

"You will?"

"I'll stop by before I go to the office."

"I'll be waiting," she said huskily, as he started to leave. "Price?"

He turned back and Ellyn came into his arms.

"Goodnight," she murmured seductively, pulling his head down.

Her eagerly given kiss turned into a desperate, desire-laden embrace as Price briefly gave in to his need for her. Finally, tearing himself away, he smiled wryly.

"Good night, pretty lady," he said, his voice full of passion. "Very shortly, I won't have to leave you at all."

"I know," she responded, her eyes luminous with love.

When he'd gone, Ellyn entered her room, knowing that for the first time in months, she would sleep well.

Ellyn was surprised to find Darnelle waiting up to help her undress.

"How was your evenin'?" Darnelle asked as she unfastened Ellyn's gown.

"Wonderful," she answered. "Are you all settled in?"

Darnelle nodded as she hung Ellyn's dress in the wardrobe. "Ah even had time to unpack all your things. Rosalie, their maid, helped me."

"Where are you sleeping?"

"Miz Cooper arranged a room for me downstairs next to Rosalie's." Darnelle responded.

"Good," Ellyn smiled and then as her gaze took in her few worn gowns hanging in the wardrobe her expression saddened.

"What's troublin' you, Miz Ellyn?" Darnelle asked, sensing the change in her mood.

"They're giving a party for us Saturday." She paused. "Price has offered to buy me a new gown but . . ."

"You let 'im," Darnelle stated with conviction. "You wanna do him proud, don't you?"

"Of course!"

"Then, don't worry." She helped Ellyn don her nightdress. "Everything's gonna be all right."

Ellyn climbed into bed as Darnelle blew out the lamp and headed for the door.

"Goodnight, Miz Ellyn."

"Goodnight, Darnelle . . . and thanks."

The older woman didn't reply but smiled to herself in the darkness.

"Coop wants to talk to you for a minute. He's in the study," Betsey told Price as she met him on the stairs.

"Thanks Betsey," he replied, his mind still full of thoughts of Ellyn. "Oh, Betsey?"

"Yes, Price?"

"Encourage her to buy anything she wants. I think she's concerned about spending my money. But I want her to have everything she needs."

Don't worry, we'll have a good time." Betsey kissed him on the cheek and went on up to bed.

Coop smiled and leaned back in his wing chair stretching his long legs before him. Now that Ellyn was here, maybe things could get back to normal. As he heard Price coming back downstairs, he rose and refilled both their glasses, handing one to Price as he entered the study.

"That didn't take long," Coop commented, smiling in good humor.

"If I'd stayed with her any longer, I'd be spending the night." Price grinned in return.

"I wouldn't blame you. It's been quite awhile since you two have been alone."

Price took a drink of his brandy as he sat down in a chair facing Coop. "I hope we can arrange the wedding real soon, because I don't know how I'm going to keep my hands off her."

"Betsey will take care of that." Coop chuckled.

Coop had been charmed by Ellyn's soft-spoken manner and her openness. Her feelings for Price were unaffected and Coop was glad Price had been lucky enough to find her.

"What do you plan to do?" Coop questioned.

"I'll have the work on the house speeded up, so it's completed before Ellyn moves in," he said thoughtfully.

"That's good. What about Alex and Rachel? Have you drawn up a will yet?"

"No, not yet. I'll look into it tomorrow, too. Now that Ellyn's here, I can't afford to take any chances."

"That's for sure. Get it in writing. It's the only way that you can be safe."

Price agreed, "I'll see what I can work out with Mr. Barlow."

Finishing his drink, he rose. "I promised Ellyn that I'd stop by on my way to the office, so I'll see you first thing."

"Fine, see you then." Coop walked Price to the front door and bid him goodnight before starting upstairs to Betsey.

"We'll go to Hilda's first and if you don't see anything there you like, we can plan a trip to St. Louis later in the week," Betsey said happily.

"This is exciting." Ellyn finally was caught up by Betsey's cheerfulness. "I haven't had any new clothes since before the war."

"Well, I'm under strict orders to buy you everything you want. And you're not to worry about a thing."

"Isn't Price wonderful?" Ellyn sighed contentedly.

"I love Price. He is the nicest man I know, next to Coop, of course," Betsey said earnestly. "I'm glad you love him, Ellyn. I have to admit that I was worried about you for a while."

"Me? Why?"

"Price loves you so much. The whole time you were separated, he was just miserable." Betsey paused. "When he didn't hear from you in all that time, I thought you had just been using him. But now I understand."

Ellyn nodded. "It was a terrible time for both of us and I'm glad it's over."

Their carriage came to a halt in front of the small dressmaker's shop and they climbed down and went in.

"Good morning, Mrs. Cooper," Hilda Braun greeted Betsey. "What can I help you with today?"

"Hilda, this is my friend, Ellyn Douglass. She's just moved here from Memphis and she's in dire need of a new wardrobe. Do you have anything already made up that we can take with us today?"

"Miss Douglass, it's nice to meet you. Come in to the fitting room and we'll get your measurements."

Ellyn and Betsey followed the seamstress to the back of the shop and were shown into the dressing room.

Helping Ellyn out of her worn gown, Hilda took her measurements and went to see what she had available. Ellyn sat with Betsey in the crowded chamber, embarrassed by the threadbare condition of her chemise. But Betsey seemed to take no notice and spent the time showing her pictures from a new copy of Godey's Lady's Book.

Hilda returned with a pale blue daygown. "I think this might do. Shall we try it on?"

With their help, Ellyn slipped into the dress and stood quietly while the seamstress made note of the alterations.

"I should be able to have this ready for you by Friday."

"That would be wonderful." Ellyn's eyes were alight as she surveyed herself in the full-length mirror. "It's perfect."

"Now, we need a ballgown," Betsey advised.

And Hilda smiled. "I have something that might be perfect."

Dashing from the room, she was gone but a few moments before she returned carrying a delicate creation of white lace and pale green satin. "I hope this is what you had in mind."

"Oh," Ellyn and Betsey both gave a breathless whisper as Hilda held up the dress for their inspection.

"You like it?"

"I love it, but . . ." Ellyn began.

"Try it on, Ellyn," Betsey instructed.

Without another word, Ellyn complied. After Hilda took the daygown from her, she slipped into the party dress. Hilda carefully adjusted the bodice and straightened the full skirts for her.

"Oh, Ellyn, you have to have it."

Ellyn turned to the mirror and gasped at her reflection.

The bodice of the gown was of white lace and was low cut enough that it exposed her breasts to advantage. Its off-the-shoulder style emphasized their tempting fullness. It was fitted to the hips and had a large, white rosette set at the waist in the back. Matching rosettes adorned each scallop of the lace-trimmed overskirt. The pale green underskirt was softly pleated.

"You look exquisite, my dear," Hilda commented.

"And coming from Hilda, that's quite a compliment."

"It's lovely."

"We'll take it," Betsey said, not giving Ellyn a chance to worry about the cost.

Almost two hours passed before they were ready to leave, having ordered everything Ellyn would need for the coming months, including a sheer negligee for her wedding night.

"I'll have both these dresses ready for you on Friday," Hilda assured them.

"Thank you."

The door swung open just then and Mary Anne Montague swept into the room.

"Good morning, Hilda," she greeted the seamstress. "Betsey! It's so good to see you." Moving gracefully toward them, she asked politely, "How's Coop doing? And Jason?"

Ellyn recognized Mary Anne at first sight and stiffened. There was no doubt about it—Mary Anne was gorgeous.

"They're just fine, Mary Anne," Betsey replied, her eyes twinkling in mischief. "Mary Anne Montague, I'd like you to meet my friend Ellyn Douglass. She's just arrived in town from Memphis and she will be staying with us for the next few weeks."

"How nice. Are you related?"

"No. Betsey and I are just good friends." Ellyn smiled at Betsey.

"Well, enjoy your stay."

"Oh, I intend to."

"We've got to get going now, Mary Anne. You take care," Betsey told her as she and Ellyn headed out of the shop.

"It was nice meeting you," Ellyn spoke sincerely.

Then as they reached the door, Ellyn asked Betsey, "How soon do you think we can arrange the wedding?"

"Coop and Price are going to meet with the priest this afternoon."

"Good," Ellyn said with determination as the door closed behind them.

Mary Anne stood frozen in the middle of the shop. Coop and Price to see a priest about a wedding? Panic almost seized her. Was Price to be married? To Ellyn Douglass? If so, it would put a whole new light on the situation.

She had just spent the morning with Rachel and Alex discussing her plans. But if Price was getting married soon, they would have to do something right away. They couldn't wait a month or even a week! Pulling herself together, she joined Hilda, anxious to find out from the seamstress what was going on.

Less than an hour later, she left the shop and rushed to Rachel's new home. It was all true! Price and this Ellyn person were to be married as soon as it could be arranged. If they were going to make an attempt on Price's life they would have to do it soon . . . before he had a wife who could inherit all his money.

Ellyn could hardly wait to get into the carriage with Betsey.

"Did you see the look on Mary Anne's face after I asked you about the wedding?"

"Did I ever! She almost went through the floor!" Betsey laughed.

"Do you think I was too obvious?"

"No, not at all. I'm sure she had no idea that you knew who she was."

Ellyn paused. "Do you think she still cares for Price?"

"Not after what Price told us last night. Knowing Mary Anne, her feelings may be hurt, but she'll get over it. The important thing is that you and Price are together and there is nothing she can do about it."

"Thank goodness," Ellyn said, "I don't ever want to be separated from him again."

* * *

"I want to make sure that Ellyn Douglass, soon to be Ellyn Richardson, is my primary beneficiary along with any children of our marriage."

"Fine. And is there anyone else, just in case you are not survived by any offspring?"

"Yes, if there's no one living, then I would like it to go into a trust fund for Jason Cooper, to be his when he reaches his majority."

Mr. Barlow studied his notes carefully for a minute and then handed them to Price who went over them, too.

"It looks like you've got it all down."

"Good. It will take a week to ten days to draw it up. I'll notify you when I am ready for you to come back in and sign it."

"Thanks. I appreciate your seeing me on such short notice." Price shook hands with the older man as they stood.

"I'll be in touch with you."

Price left the lawyer's office then, bidding the clerk at the front desk goodbye. As he exited and headed back to ATC, Alex caught sight of him.

Why was Price meeting with Barlow? Alex hoped it was ATC business, but one could never be sure. Checking the time, he noted that it was near noon. In a few minutes, the office would close for lunch and it would give Alex the opportunity he needed to find out exactly what was going on.

Within a half hour, the shades were drawn and both Barlow and his clerk left to eat their midday meal. Without drawing suspicion to himself, Alex made his way to the alley behind Barlow's office. When he was certain that no one was watching, he pried open the back door and went in undetected.

It was a simple matter to locate the papers on Price and Alex read and reread Barlow's notes. It was all that he had feared and he slammed the papers back down on the desk.

"Damn!" he muttered to himself and then hurried from the office, taking care not to be seen. He had to let Rachel know at once.

Rachel looked at Mary Anne in consternation. "He's what?"

"I overheard Betsey Cooper and this Douglass woman talking at the dressmaker's. Then, to make sure, I stayed to visit with Hilda. According to her, Price and Ellyn Douglass will probably be married within the next few weeks."

Cold fury shone in Rachel's eyes. "Then we'll just have to speed up our plans."

There was a stony silence as Rachel began to plot. She glanced up nervously as Alex came into the house, slamming the front door behind him.

"Bad news!" he exclaimed as he entered the small parlor. "Price has been to a lawyer and he's having a will drawn up leaving everything to somebody named Douglass."

"He's been very busy. Mary Anne just found out that he's getting married," Rachel explained as Alex moved to the liquor cabinet and poured himself a bourbon straight.

"What are we going to do? We can't put it off any longer," Mary Anne asked excitedly.

"Has Price been working late at the ATC office?"

"Whenever he's in town," Alex confirmed.

"Good. We'll arrange a surprise for him." Rachel grinned evilly. "Tonight, if we're lucky."

Glancing at his pocket watch, Price smiled ruefully, indicating the stack of papers before him. "I've got to finish these. I put it off last night, but I can't delay any longer."

"I'll explain," Coop said with a laugh, "and I just hope they don't get mad at me."

"Tell Ellyn everything we found out from Father Simmons today. And then I'll come by as soon as I finish. It shouldn't be too late."

"Fine. We'll be looking for you." Coop left the office on his way home.

It had been a long day filled with irksome little problems and Coop was glad it was drawing to a close. And so he started off, leaving Price alone at the office to labor over his much-avoided paper work.

As the sun went down and his office darkened, Price paused to take a break. Stretching tiredly, he flexed his broad shoulders, easing the stiffness of his back and neck. Usually, Price enjoyed this part of his job, but tonight he could hardly wait to finish. Ellyn was waiting for him and though he was sure Coop had explained to her his reasons for working late, Price was still anxious to be done.

Rising, intent upon locating a lamp, Price went into the outer office. With all the shades drawn, the room was very dark, but he managed to find a lamp without too much trouble. Just as he lit it, he heard a muffled sound coming from the second-floor storage area. Not quite sure what the noise was, he decided to check it out. Taking the lamp with him, he opened the door to the second floor and started up the steep stairs.

It never occurred to him that it might be dangerous. And he was so preoccupied with thoughts of Ellyn that he ignored his instincts. As he reached the top of the darkened stairway and moved into the room he saw no sign of anything out of order. Crates and boxes were piled high, blocking the few windows and forming long, darkly shadowed aisles.

Price felt no fear as he moved easily down the narrow passages, truly believing that the culprit was nothing

327

more than a small animal or rodent. When he could find no trace of any disturbance, he shrugged easily and started back to work. Ellyn was waiting.

The moment Price's guard was completely relaxed, Alex struck. He had been hidden away in a protected place that afforded a good view of the main aisle and when he saw Price preparing to leave, he'd seized his opportunity. Hitting him solidly from behind, Price had no chance to defend himself and he fell, unconscious, to the dirty, rough-hewn wood flooring. The coal lamp flew from his grip and shattered against the far wall. The oil spread menacingly across the floor as the flames blazed to life.

Glad for this unexpected help in getting rid of Price, Alex stood mesmerized, watching the fire grow. Then, as he realized that the flames were getting out of control, he quickly emptied Price's wallet and cast it aside. Hurrying down the stairs, he left his cousin lying lifelessly among the boxes. Shutting the door to the stairway, Alex left the ATC building, undiscovered in the darkness of the night.

Coop, Betsey and Ellyn were relaxing in the front parlor after a delicious evening meal.

"So what did you find out from Father Simmons?" Betsey asked Coop, eager to find out when they could plan the wedding.

"He told us either Monday or Tuesday morning next week. And Price said you should choose."

"The sooner, the better," she replied happily. "Let's make it Monday."

"Good," Coop and Betsey agreed.

"Do you think he'll be much longer?" Ellyn questioned. "It's already after eight."

"I don't know, Ellyn. Price had a lot he wanted to do tonight."

"Coop, will you drive me over to the office?"

"Why?"

"He's got to be hungry. I thought I could take him something to eat."

"That's a wonderful idea," Betsey agreed enthusiastically. "We'll all go."

As Rosalie and Darnelle quickly put together a meal for Ellyn to take along, the stableboy brought the carriage around.

The evening was pleasant, cooled by a damp, chilly breeze that blew in off the river. Though the sun was gone, light lingered, as if the day had left behind a part of itself as a gift. A memory to be treasured. Streaks of pink and gold pointed the path that gilded orb had taken. But a sliver of the moon, shining almost prematurely, seemed to indicate that as always the darkness would win.

In a jovial mood, they left on the short drive to ATC, eager to tear Price away from his industrious endeavors. The streets were nearly empty as they made their way through town and drew up in front of the office. Coop jumped down and then assisted each lady before moving to unlock the front door of the seemingly deserted building.

Ellyn went in first and knew immediately that something was wrong.

"Coop? Do you smell smoke?" Dropping her basket of food, she raced through the semidarkness to Price's deserted office.

Coop was right behind her. "He must be upstairs!" Running to the second-floor door, he grabbed the knob to throw it open.

"This door is warm. Betsey! Go for help!" he ordered tersely, wondering how a fire could have started upstairs.

Not waiting another second, Coop threw the door

open and staggered back as smoke and heat belched forth.

"Price!" he called at the top of his voice, somehow knowing that his friend was trapped upstairs. "Price!"

"I've got to see if he's up there, Ellyn. You stay down here, no matter what," Coop insisted as he took off his jacket and threw it protectively over his head.

"Can't I help?"

"No. It's too dangerous!" With a last long look at Ellyn's pale, stricken face, he rushed headlong into the smoke.

Choking on the fumes, Coop battled upward, until halfway to the top blistering heat forced him back. Pausing, drawing another deep breath, he fought his way up the narrow passage again, but to no avail. Flames had completely engulfed the top of the steps, barring entrance. Defeated, but only momentarily, he stumbled back out into the main office gasping for fresh air.

"Let's get out of here, Ellyn. You watch for Betsey. I'm going to try the back window." He threw off the jacket and carried it with him as he ran outside and around to the back of the building.

Ellyn followed him outside, wanting to help but realizing that she should stay out of Coop's way. Seeing Betsey running toward her, Ellyn waited for her.

"Coop's going to try to get in through the back window! Come on!"

They raced after him, hoping to aid him in some way.

Coop climbed onto the side rails of the small back porch, grasped the roof and hauled himself over the edge. Wrapping his coat about his arm, he smashed the glass in the window farthest from the stairs and pushed with all his panic-induced strength at the crates that blocked it from the inside. His fury aiding him, he managed to shove them over on the second try. Smoke poured forth and he was driven back.

Coop took a deep breath as the smoke cleared and climbed through the window. "Price!"

Braving the heat, Coop searched the abandoned aisles. To the front, the fire was uncontrolled now, a beast devouring all in its path. A flashback of the *Sultana* immobilized Cooper, but he shook it off and continued his quest to find his friend.

A low, muffled groan came from somewhere closer to the fire and Coop forged forward knowing that every second counted. He was so blinded by the smoke he almost stumbled over Price. Coop rolled him over and shook him, but couldn't rouse him completely. Grasping both his arms, he dragged Price away from the searing heat. It seemed an eternity before he found the open window again and with the last of his strength he pushed his barely conscious friend out onto the porch roof.

Betsey and Ellyn had watched in terrified helplessness as Coop disappeared into the burning building. As the minutes dragged by and Coop didn't reappear, Betsey grew frantic.

"My God! Ellyn, where is he? Was he sure Price was even up there?" Betsey was near hysteria. "Where's the fire department? Why don't they get here? What's taking them so long?" she cried, looking around anxiously.

A crowd gathered to watch the excitement as the fire department finally arrived and set to work.

"Betsey! Look!" Ellyn shouted joyously as Coop helped Price through the back window and then climbed out himself.

"Thank God." Betsey went limp with relief. Then she shouted to the men standing about. "Somebody get up there and help them!"

Her words spurred the bystanders to action and they rushed to Coop's aid, helping him and Price down from the roof.

Ellyn and Betsey were waiting and trailed nervously behind as Price was carried some distance away from the danger.

Price lay still, attempting to focus on his surroundings. Not only was his head pounding and his vision blurred, his lungs felt as if they were on fire. He coughed deeply, hoping to ease the ache, but the pain stayed with him.

"Coop?" he croaked, his throat parched from the acrid smoke.

"I'm right here," he answered, kneeling at Price's side.

"Thanks," Price told him as he finally focused on his friend.

"You're welcome. You gonna live?"

" 'Fraid so," he said, his voice cracking.

"What happened in there? If we'd been five minutes later, you'd be dead," Coop inquired gravely.

"I'll tell you later," Price spoke hoarsely and struggled to sit up as Ellyn came to him. "Ellyn."

"Price, I was so worried." She hugged him.

"I'm fine," he lied, grimacing as he touched the back of his head. There was a good-sized lump from the blow he had taken.

With Coop and Ellyn's help, Price dragged himself upright and stood on uncertain legs. When he swayed noticeably, Ellyn put her arm about his waist to steady him.

As Coop stood alone, Betsey could no longer contain herself and flew into his arms, crying.

"You weren't hurt?"

Coop nodded tiredly and hugged her to him, not wanting to think of how close to death he and Price had just come.

As both couples stood embracing, Tim Radcliffe and Kevin O'Riley came running around the corner of the building.

"Are you both all right?" they asked worriedly, taking in the condition of their bosses.

"We'll be fine in the morning, Tim," Coop told him wearily. "Will you two keep watch here?"

"Sure thing," they agreed.

"Good. Stop by later and let us know how bad it is," he instructed.

"Will do, Coop," Tim replied.

Thanking them, Coop and Price turned away from the destructive scene before them.

"Now, tell me what really happened," Coop asked Price pointedly, hours later, after Betsey and Ellyn had gone to bed. They were alone in the parlor, their throats sore, their bodies aching.

"I'm not sure. I heard a noise upstairs and I went up to take a look around."

"Somebody hit you?"

"From behind," Price replied nodding. "Took my wallet, too." Coop frowned, shaking his head in frustrated anger. "Why would anybody be up there that late?"

"I wish I knew. But I doubt we'll ever find out now. I'm sure the upstairs was gutted. I must have dropped the lamp when I fell," Price concluded, rubbing his aching forehead. "Listen, I've got to get some rest."

"Spend the night here. As badly as you feel, there's no point in going home to any empty house."

"You convinced me. But where do I sleep? Ellyn's in my usual bed." His eyes almost twinkled at the possibilities, but the throbbing pain in his head dulled all his amorous desires.

"I'll have Rosalie fix up the sofa in the study for you. Good enough?"

"Right now, anyplace halfway soft will be

333

heaven," he said gratefully as Coop left the room to find the maid.

Price longed to be with Ellyn right now. He needed her gentleness and her soft manner, just as he had that first day after she'd pulled him from the river. But this was not Riverwood. He would have to wait.

When he hard Coop and Rosalie in the study, he made his way there slowly, relieved to find his bed ready. Thanking Rosalie for her help, he lay down, closing his eyes against the pounding agony.

"You feeling any better?"

"No," he responded, not opening his eyes. "But I should be by tomorrow."

"Well, get some rest. I'm going to wait up for Tim and Kevin."

"I'll be right here if you need me."

"I'll be sure to wake you." Coop gave a chuckle and closed the study door behind him.

The hours passed slowly as Ellyn lay in her bed, tense and upset. Unable to sleep, she had tossed and turned ever since coming upstairs. Price could have been killed! The horror of losing him forever tore at her heart.

The urge to see Price one more time this night drove Ellyn from her bed. Drawing on her wrapper, she started downstairs wanting to tell him of her love. She couldn't bear to be without him.

Tiptoeing quietly down the staircase, she paused at the open parlor door. A lamp, burning low, cast heavy shadows about the room. Peeking in, she caught sight of Coop. He had fallen asleep in a wing chair, no doubt as he waited to hear from Mr. Radcliffe. Coop looked tired and drawn, even as he slept, and Ellyn knew the terrible excitement of this night would not soon be forgotten.

Price was not in the parlor and for a moment Ellyn worried that he'd gone home. But glancing toward the study, the closed door beckoned her on. Ellyn approached and opened it, silently entering and shutting it behind her.

She recognized his long form at once as he lay resting on the sofa. Moving slowly nearer, she stood looking down at him. Price, too, appeared exhausted, his features almost haggard in the dim light. The temptation to touch him was overpowering and she knelt beside him, caressing his arm gently.

"Price?" her voice was a soft murmur.

He stirred and looked at her. "Ellyn."

She leaned toward him, meeting him in a kiss of mutual need. When they broke off, Ellyn rested her head on his shoulder, not wanting to separate from him.

"I was afraid you'd gone. I needed to see you, to be with you."

"Coop convinced me to stay," he told her, holding her protectively.

"I'm glad," she sighed.

Price twisted on his side and pulled her up next to him, so they lay together in intimate contact.

"Sleep with me for a while," he invited.

Ellyn nodded and Price held her tightly, kissing her tenderly. Then, closing his eyes again, he relaxed. With Ellyn in his arms, rest came easily.

Ellyn savored the closeness of their embrace. In Price's arms, she was whole again.

"I love you," she whispered, but Price was already asleep.

As the dawn's first weak light filtered through the drapes and brightened the room, Price and Ellyn awoke. Ellyn smiled sleepily up at Price, having enjoyed the closeness of the last few hours.

"Good morning."

"Good morning," he answered, kissing her softly. "How do you feel?"

"I don't know yet." He gave her a smile as he touched the back of his head experimentally.

Ellyn murmured sympathetically, "Maybe you should see a doctor?"

"No, I'll be fine."

She moved from him. "I'd best get back to my room."

"I know, but first . . ." Price pulled her back down to him and kissed her again. "I'll see you at breakfast."

"That was nice," she said softly as he released her and she hurried upstairs to dress.

After Ellyn had gone, Price sat up slowly and waited for his aching head to clear. When the throbbing had finally quieted, he rose and went in search of Coop.

Coop was drinking a cup of hot, black coffee at the dining room table.

"Did you just get up?" Price asked, pouring himself a cup.

"No, I never made it to bed. Tim and Kevin didn't get here until after three."

"What's the news?"

"The second floor is a total loss." He paused. "What the fire didn't destroy, the smoke and water did."

"What about the files?"

"Tim did manage to get them out. They're wet, but we should be able to use them."

"We were lucky on that one." Price breathed a little easier.

"So, how's your head?"

"It hurts like hell right now."

"I wouldn't doubt it. That was some lump you

had." Coop grinned. "It's a good thing they didn't hit you where it might have done some damage."

Price grimaced at Coop's attempt at humor. "What time are you going down?"

"I'm going to leave as soon as I finish this, but there's no need for you to come. Stay here and rest."

"No, I'll go. I'll probably feel better if I get out for a while."

They were just finishing their coffee when Ellyn and Betsey joined them.

"Good morning, you two," Betsey greeted them cheerfully, giving Coop a kiss on his cheek.

"Good morning, ladies," they responded.

Feeling bold this morning, Ellyn kissed Price.

"How do you feel?"

Price smiled at her question. "Much better now that you're here."

Ellyn returned his smile and sat next to him.

"Did you get a chance to tell them what Father Simmons said?" Price asked Coop.

"He sure did. How's Monday morning sound?"

"It sounds fine." Price was pleased. "Coop and I are really going to be tied up getting the mess at the office straightened out, so you go ahead and plan whatever you want."

"All right."

"Do you still want to have the party?" Betsey worried.

"Sure. Why not?" Coop answered. "By Saturday night we're going to need a little fun."

"Good," Betsey said, relieved. "Well, you be careful today."

"Don't worry, Betsey. After last night we're going to be extra cautious," Price told her as they stood up to leave.

Kissing their women goodbye, they started off to

survey the damage to their business.

"What do you mean, it didn't work?" Rachel demanded fiercely.

"I don't know how, but he got out of it," Alex said with disgust. "I was talking to Tim Radcliffe and he said Price had been trapped in the fire but Coop had managed to rescue him."

"Damn! Now what? That was the perfect setup." Rachel glared at her son. "It would have been a hell of a lot less complicated to just shoot him!"

"Don't worry. There's no way they'll suspect us. It looked like a robbery, pure and simple."

Rachel grunted in disbelief. "Well, if we're off the hook for this one, what are we going to do next?"

"Let me talk to Mary Anne. Maybe she'll have an idea."

"Oh, all right, but don't take too long. That will should be ready by next weekend. Whatever we do, we'll have to do it before then."

Chapter Fourteen

This moment was making all the sorrow and heartbreak of the past week worthwhile, Lawrence Douglass thought as he listened to the lawyer explain the documents spread before him.

"Then it is legal?" Lawrence asked.

"Absolutely," Melvin Whitmore stated.

"That's all I wanted to know." Lawrence rose and stepped out into the hall. "Let me call Constance and Charlotte down."

Standing at the foot of the staircase he yelled, "Constance! Charlotte! Come down here, please."

Constance Royale Douglass Clarke appeared at the top of the steps, her expression disdainful.

"What is it, Lawrence?" Constance asked, irritated by his interruption. Since the confrontation with Ellyn, she considered him a crazy, old fool and fervently wished there was some way to get rid of his obnoxious presence. Anyone who would side with that slut of a daughter of hers . . .

"Melvin Whitmore is here and he has some news for us," Lawrence said obliquely.

"Mr. Whitmore, the attorney?" Constance asked as Charlotte joined her.

"Yes," he replied impatiently. "Now, if you'll both please come down."

Charlotte gave her mother a questioning look and with a slight shrug Constance led the way.

"Shall I send for Rod?" she asked, thinking that her new husband should be included.

"No, it's not necessary. This does not concern him directly."

Constance gave Lawrence a haughty look. "He is my husband."

"Constance, it could take hours to locate Rod and Mr. Whitmore doesn't have the time. Please, let's go in the study and sit down. He's waiting," Lawrence spoke firmly.

With a swish of her skirts, she swept past Lawrence and entered the room.

"Good afternoon, Mr. Whitmore. It's nice to see you."

Melvin Whitmore rose as Constance and her daughter came in. "Ladies, you're looking as lovely as ever."

"Thank you."

"Won't you sit down? We have a few matters here that have to be cleared up."

Charlotte sat on the sofa, but Constance took a chair right in front of the desk. Lawrence came in, closing the door behind him.

"I believe we're ready when you are," he told the lawyer.

"And Ellyn is no longer living here, is that correct?"

"Yes. She has gone north to be married." Lawrence explained.

"Fine. Let us begin." Mr. Whitmore cleared his throat and put on his wire-rimmed glasses. Shuffling through the papers before him, he pulled out an official-looking document. "Madam, what I have here is your husband's—Thomas Douglass's—will. It is dated February 23, 1861."

"Will? Thomas had a will?" Constance was aghast. "He never made mention . . ."

"I found it yesterday, Constance. Thomas had hidden it away in the attic with the rest of his personal papers."

Constance nodded numbly. "Please, continue."

"The easiest way to handle this, I'm sure, is to just read it. It's quite brief and to the point." Melvin Whitmore looked up at Lawrence for his approval. At Lawrence's nod, he read aloud.

"I, Thomas Clayton Douglass, being of sound mind and body do hereby draw up this will to provide for my family in the event of my death.

"To my wife, Constance—I bequeath one half of Riverwood Plantation and all its holdings, plus one half of all my Confederate war bonds.

"To my only son, Thomas—I bequeath the other half of Riverwood and its holdings, plus one fourth of my Confederate war bonds.

"With the stipulation that should either Constance or Thomas die, their inheritance reverts to the other so that Riverwood remains forever intact.

"To my youngest daughter, Charlotte—I bequeath the remaining fourth of my Confederate war bonds to provide a proper dowry for her.

"To my eldest daughter, Ellyn—I bequeath the remainder of my investments to be used in whatever manner she deems necessary.

"To my father, Lawrence Douglass—Should he survive me, he shall be guaranteed a home at Riverwood for life and, to supplement his income, all monies derived from crops grown on the five hundred acres bordering Clarke's Landing shall be his."

Whitmore concluded, "It is signed and dated. And I have already verified its legality."

Constance sighed. "I knew Thomas would leave me well provided for. What are the bonds worth?" She knew they had invested a fortune in them at the start of the war.

"That's the only bad news I have, Mrs. Douglass . . . er, uh, Mrs. Clarke."

"Why?"

"With the war lost, the bonds are virtually worthless."

"You can't be serious." Constance was horrified.

"I'm afraid so."

She was suddenly furious. "That's ridiculous. We had thousands of dollars tied up in those bonds!"

"I know. And I'm sorry." Mr. Whitmore was apologetic. "So many families lost everything. At least, you've still got the land . . . and his other investments were successful."

"Other investments?"

"Those that he left to your daughter, Ellyn."

"They were?"

"Very." He sorted through some more papers. "I have the exact amount here somewhere. Ah, yes, here it is." He held up a sheet with long columns of figures. "A very wise man, your husband. He put modest amounts into three speculative ventures and they've all paid off handsomely, especially the mining venture. Let's see, Ellyn's total inheritance comes to approximately fifty-seven thousand dollars, should she choose to sell at this time."

"Fifty-seven thousand dollars? And I get nothing?"

Mr. Whitmore was stunned by Constance's venomous tone. "My dear woman, you've just gotten clear title to one of the most productive plantations in the state."

"Fifty-seven thousand dollars!" Constance was outraged. "What were the bonds worth originally?"

"Mr. Douglass invested over one hundred and fifty thousand dollars in the bonds. But they're worthless now," he informed her..

Lawrence sat back in his chair, trying not to show his true feelings. He was happy that Ellyn had inherited so much. After the misery she'd been through, he knew she deserved it.

"How do you plan to notify Ellyn?" Lawrence asked.

"I suppose I could hire a courier."

"I have a better suggestion. I'll take a few days off from the hospital and take it up to her. If that meets with your approval?"

"That sounds fine. Can you leave tomorrow?"

"I should be able to. I'll stop by your office in the morning."

"Good." Gathering his things together, he gave Constance a quick, nervous glance and followed Lawrence from the room.

"Don't worry about Constance," Lawrence chuckled when they were out of earshot. "She'll calm down. It just irritates her that she didn't get everything."

"I can appreciate her sentiments about the bonds though. I lost quite a bit myself."

"I'll see you first thing tomorrow," Lawrence said as he assisted the lawyer into his waiting carriage.

"Goodbye, Mr. Douglass. And I do appreciate your help in this matter."

Lawrence watched until Melvin Whitmore's carriage had turned onto the road and then went back to face the storm of Constance's fury.

Constance was coming down the hall with Charlotte when he entered

343

"I've got to find Rod right away," she was saying.

"But, Mother, Ellyn deserves her share," Charlotte protested.

"Ellyn forfeited any claim to this family when she became involved with that Yankee!" Constance snarled.

"I'm afraid you're wrong there, Constance," Lawrence said with great authority.

She looked up in surprise, not aware that he had come back in.

"I heard every word, my dear," he told her. "Ellyn is legally entitled to that money and I am personally going to see that she gets it."

Constance knew when she was cornered and she walked past him without speaking, her manner one of barely contained anger.

Charlotte remained behind, looking confusedly after her mother. "Ellyn will get her money, won't she?"

Lawrence gave his granddaughter a small hug. "I'll make sure of it, Charlotte. Don't worry."

Constance left the house in an unladylike fury. It was totally unacceptable to her that Ellyn should get anything. Everything that Thomas had should have passed to her. Rod needed that money to get Riverwood and the Landing operating again, and here every cent had gone to Ellyn!

Lifting her skirts, she trudged down the overgrown path toward the stable hoping to find her new husband there. Rod would know what to do and she trusted his judgment.

Rod had just returned from working at the Landing and was turning his horse out into the small paddock when he saw Constance coming down the walk. It was unusual for her to come down to the stables and he wondered at her purpose.

344

"Rod! Oh, Rod, I'm so glad that I found you," she called to him, picking up her pace.

"Constance? What's wrong?" He was concerned by her tone.

"It's Lawrence! He's found Thomas's will," she told him, almost collapsing in his arms.

Rod's brows drew together and he embraced her. "Will? I thought he hadn't left one."

"Well, he did. Lawrence found it hidden away somewhere up in the attic."

"What does it say? He did leave you Riverwood, didn't he?" Rod questioned, wondering what could be so terrible.

"Of course." She pulled away from him slightly. "But Ellyn got *all* the money!"

"Money? What money? I thought he'd invested everything in war bonds."

"So did I. But it turns out that he made a few investments that were very profitable."

"And those are what he left to Ellyn?"

"Yes. Fifty-seven thousand dollars worth, while our bonds are worth nothing," she complained.

Rod pulled her back against him, calming her, as his mind flew. Maybe he should have married Ellyn. Fifty-seven thousand dollars would more than restore the Landing. Then the possibility of Ellyn as his wife stopped his musings. The thought of being shackled to her for the rest of his life unnerved him. Ellyn was a cold woman and he had no desire to spend his nights with an unresponsive mate. No, Constance was the woman for him. They were ideally suited and any money problems they had, they would handle on their own. It would not be easy, but he knew that a life with Constance was infinitely preferable to any kind of existence with Ellyn.

"I know it's hard to accept," he said, trying to

345

soothe her. "But think of it this way: when Ellyn gets this money, there will be no reason for her to ever return. Even if the Yankee rejects her, she'll have the funds to provide for herself. You wouldn't want her to come back, would you?"

"No! She has shamed me for the last time," Constance declared vehemently.

"I feel the same way. So we'll talk of this no more." Rod lifted her chin and kissed her. "Agreed?"

"Agreed," she murmured against his lips. Then, kissing him fervently, she hugged him tightly. "I'm so glad I have you."

Rod didn't speak as the kiss ended, but led her into the cool, deserted stable. The darkness of the old building momentarily blinded Constance and she blinked confusedly, waiting for her eyes to adjust.

"Rod?" She looked around for him, wondering where he'd gone.

"Over here," he called and she followed the sound of his voice to a concealed spot at the back of a clean stall.

Constance's eyes narrowed with quick, flaming desire as she watched Rod spread a blanket over a pile of hay.

"We're very alone," he told her invitingly.

She smiled easily and walked slowly toward him. "Undress me?"

"With pleasure." Rod came to her, loosening the buttons at her bodice.

Her dress was discarded, following by her underthings, and soon she lay nude on the blanket eagerly awaiting his coming. Rod stripped quickly and joined her on the sweet-smelling hay.

Constance's craving for him grew as she enjoyed the sight of his firmly muscled body and she reached out for him, caressing the hard length of his desire.

Rod hungered for her, too. So far, their brief

marriage had been a journey through desire for them, for they had spent every possible moment exploring their mutual wants and needs.

The soft prickles of the hay through the blanket added to the sensuousness of their coupling as the heat of him burned deep within her. The power of his passionate penetration left her mindless as she surged against him, arching to receive even more of him.

Wanting to please her, Rod moved in a slow, steady rhythm. Relishing the hardness of his body against the softness of her own, Constance writhed and bucked beneath him. She delighted in his possession and craved the exciting, exhausting release only he could give her. Avidly meeting his every thrust, she clung to his broad shoulders, urging him on.

The hot, pulsing waves of her climax stunned her with their intensity and Constance collapsed against Rod as he, too, reached the pinnacle of his desire. Wrapped in each other's arms, they were lost in a sea of bliss, where their problems did not exist.

It was only much later, when awareness came to them, that they rolled apart and began to dress.

"Will you come up to the house with me now?"

"Of course. We'll face this together," he reassured her.

Finally, presentably dressed, they returned to Riverwood House to speak with Lawrence.

Lawrence tucked the small packet of papers protectively under his arm as he left Whitmore's office the following morning on his way to the riverfront. He was happy and relieved that things had gone so smoothly at Riverwood the day before. Constance had been more agreeable than he'd ever thought possible and Lawrence attributed that to Rod Clarke's influence.

Lawrence knew Rod had not been overjoyed at the

prospect of Ellyn getting the money, but there was nothing anyone could do. Ellyn deserved every cent, and if it made her more secure in her relationship with Richardson, then he was all for it.

He waited on deck to watch as the steamer backed out into the river and headed north. If things went smoothly, he would arrive in Alton sometime Saturday. And it would please him greatly to give Ellyn her totally unexpected inheritance. Leaving his place at the rail of the promenade deck, Lawrence went to locate his cabin and settle in for a relaxing journey upriver.

Chapter Fifteen

Thursday and Friday passed in a flurry of activity for Ellyn and Betsey as they busily made all the arrangements for the party. Musicians were engaged, invitations sent out, refreshments planned and the trip made to Hilda's shop for the final fitting of Ellyn's gown.

Price and Coop had been working long hours since the fire relocating. The damage to the ATC office had been so extensive that they had been forced to rent another building while the repairs were being made. Now, as Saturday was nearing, they both knew they would enjoy an evening off.

Saturday morning arrived—a bleary, blustery dawn that resembled late October more than late June. The dreariness of the day encouraged little activity and Ellyn and Betsey both stayed abed later than usual. Jason, who could be distracted by Rosalie no longer, finally burst into his mother's bedroom and pounced on her with uncontrolled glee. Hugging his small, wiggling warmth to her, Betsey laughed at Rosalie's despair.

"I'm sorry, Mrs. Cooper."

"Don't worry," she told her. "It's time I got up."

"Jason's been up since six. He even had breakfast with Mr. Cooper this morning."

"Has my husband already left for the office?"

"Yes, ma'am. He said to tell you that he should be home by five."

"Good. Thanks." Betsey was pleased that Coop would be home in plenty of time for the party. "Is Miss Douglass up yet?"

"Yes, ma'am. She was just going downstairs when we came in."

Turning her attention to Jason, Betsey spoke, "Why don't you go with Rosalie and see if you can find any of those chocolate cookies you like so well?"

Grinning happily, he gave his mother a wet kiss and toddled to Rosalie, his eyes alight at the prospect of such a wonderful treat.

"Tell Miss Douglass that I'll be right down."

"Yes, ma'am."

As the door closed, Betsey rose, eager to begin a most exciting day.

The morning slipped by as Betsey and Ellyn opened the sliding doors between the two front parlors and rearranged the furniture to make room for dancing.

"What do you think?" Betsey questioned, her hands resting on her hips.

"It looks great. I had no idea it was so big," Ellyn said, looking about her in satisfaction.

"I guess we'll fit everybody in. Usually all the men stay in the study or the card room anyway."

Ellyn laughed a little nervously. "Betsey, I haven't been to a party in years."

"Don't worry about a thing. Everybody is going to love you," she replied sincerely. "And frankly, I can't wait to see Price's face when you come downstairs in your new dress."

"It is beautiful."

"And you're beautiful in it." Betsey broke off at the

sound of a carriage in the drive. "Who could that be?" Parting the drapes they looked out.

"It's Price and Coop and they've brought someone with them. Let's go see."

The front door opened and Price came in first.

"I'm glad you're here Ellyn. We've got a surprise for you."

Ellyn looked at him questioningly and then saw Lawrence entering behind him.

"Grandfather!" She flew into his arms. "I'm so glad you're here! Did Price tell you we're to be married?"

"I just found out." He kissed her soundly. "Congratulations!"

"Thank you." She hugged him tightly. "Betsey and Coop are even having a party for us—tonight. Oh! You haven't met Betsey yet. Betsey Cooper, this is my grandfather, Lawrence Douglass. Grandfather, this is my friend Betsey."

"A pleasure, my dear," Lawrence greeted her warmly.

"Please, come on in," Betsey directed as Coop closed the door. "We'll sit in the study."

As they settled in, Betsey ordered a light lunch for them.

"Ellyn, darling, your grandfather has some very good news for you," Price ventured as he sat next to her on the sofa.

"Good news? What's happened?" She was caught totally off guard.

"It seems your father did leave a will after all."

"He did?"

"I found it just a few days after you'd gone—and Mr. Whitmore has verified that it was legal."

"What did it say?"

"As expected, your mother and Tommy were to share Riverwood, but since Tommy's dead, Constance

351

inherited all of it plus most of the Confederate bonds. Charlotte got a share of the bonds, too. But you . . . well, he left you the proceeds from some modest investments he'd made."

"He did?"

Lawrence nodded, immensely happy with the news he was about to impart. Handing her the packet he'd safeguarded since leaving Memphis, he smiled. "Fifty-seven thousand dollars worth."

Ellyn's eyes opened wide. "Fifty-seven thousand dollars?"

"Yes, dear."

"Price?" His arm came around her as she opened it and looked at the papers. "Oh, Grampa! How wonderful! Thank you!" Crying and laughing at the same time, she went to her grandfather and hugged him. "I never dreamed . . ."

"I know. That's what makes this so special. I hope it helps you."

"You'll never know," she murmured to him, her pride in herself returning as she no longer felt totally dependent on others.

"Will you stay with us, Mr. Douglass?" Coop offered.

"Please call me Lawrence. And thank you for the invitation, but I've already taken a room at the Lincoln Hotel," he answered. "When is the wedding?"

"Monday morning at the cathedral," Ellyn told him eagerly. "You'll stay, won't you?"

"I wouldn't miss it." He patted her hand.

Her serenity restored, she smiled brightly up at him. "And you'll dance with me tonight?"

"I'd love to. You know, it's been years since I've been to a party." His voice trailed off as he remembered different times.

"Lunch is ready, Mrs. Cooper," Rosalie announced

and they all went into the dining room to enjoy the light repast.

It was after four o'clock when Ellyn and Betsey made their way upstairs to rest. Coop and Price had had to return to work right after lunch, but Lawrence had stayed on for a long time visiting with Ellyn.

"Judging from what you'd told me before about your mother, I'm really surprised that she didn't make trouble about your getting all the money," Betsey said as they climbed the stairs.

"I am, too," she told Betsey truthfully. "But maybe it's like Grandfather says. Now that she's married to Rod, she's changed."

"I hope so." Betsey smiled. "I'm so happy for you and Price. Things are going so well for you."

"I'll tell you, this money makes all the difference in our relationship. I'm not completely dependent on him now and he wouldn't have to marry me just because he felt sorry for me."

"But he doesn't!" she protested.

"I know. And now, I'm sure of it."

"Good," she said as they came to her bedroom door. "Let's get a couple hours of rest. It's going to be one late night."

"I can hardly wait!" Ellyn hurried on to her room, eagerly anticipating the coming evening.

It was almost dark when Price got home and he knew he had to hurry if he was to arrive at Coop's on time. His housekeeper, Mrs. Edwards, prepared a bath for him and he rushed through it, taking no time to relax.

His hours with Ellyn had been few and far between since the fire and he was looking forward to tonight's party. Perhaps they could even find a few minutes alone together. Shaking away the distracting daydreams, Price shaved and dressed. Putting on his best evening clothes, he combed his hair and stood back to survey the results of his efforts. Passing his own curt inspection, he left for Coop's, anxious to be with Ellyn.

Mary Anne Montague smiled at herself in the vanity mirror. She looked her best and she knew it. Her dark hair was pulled up and away from her face, emphasizing the perfection of her features; the unadorned aqua gown she wore was stunning on her petite figure.

She was sure Alex would be pleased with her appearance for tonight was very important. They had to convince everyone that they were glad about Price's upcoming nuptials.

Mary Anne sneered, unconsciously, at the thought of another woman getting what she felt should be hers. It was going to take all of her acting ability to carry this off successfully. The only thing that made the evening tolerable for her was the thought that very soon she and Alex would have it all. Price was a fool if he had dismissed her threats so easily.

Catching sight of her reflection, she quickly smiled, hiding her disapproving look behind a mask of cool politeness. Leaving the dressing table, she moved regally from her room to await Alex's and Rachel's arrival downstairs.

Darnelle straightened Ellyn's skirts for the final time.

"There. Ah'm done," she said stepping back to look at Ellyn. Her gaze went over her critically from head to toe.

"Well?" Ellyn asked nervously, knowing Darnelle to be her most honest critic.

"Miz Ellyn, tonight you even outshine your mama," Darnelle said seriously.

"Really?" Ellyn asked breathlessly and then hurried to look at her reflection in the full-length mirror. Her eyes widened at what she saw. "Oh!"

Ellyn couldn't believe she was looking at herself. Darnelle had artfully done her hair, pinning it back and letting it fall in a cascade of glossy curls. Her eyes sparkled more green than brown tonight and her cheeks were rosy with excitement. The gown was exquisitely elegant and for the first time ever, as she gazed at her image, Ellyn considered herself a woman full grown. The white lace gave her an innocent-fragile air; the low-cut bodice was most revealing. Her breasts swelled daringly against the soft material and Ellyn felt a surge of female pride at their alluring fullness. She twirled once, enjoying the feel of the skirts as they swayed about her.

"Oh, Darnelle, I feel so pretty."

"Pretty? No, you're not pretty. You are beautiful."

Ellyn hugged her impulsively just as Betsey knocked and entered the room.

"Ellyn! You look gorgeous!"

"Thank you. So do you," Ellyn told her friend as she admired Betsey's modestly cut, pink gown.

"Thanks. You know—" she walked a full circle around Ellyn—"Price is going to love this dress."

"You really think so?" Ellyn worried needlessly.

"I really think so," Betsey teased and then, grabbing Ellyn's arm, she urged her toward the door. "Come on, he just got here a few minutes ago. I think he's having a drink with Coop in the study."

"He's here?"

"Yes, come on!"

With a quick backward glance at Darnelle, who was smiling broadly, Ellyn was hustled out of the room and down the hall.

* * *

Price took a drink of the bourbon Coop had just given him and then walked slowly to the window.

"What time is Lawrence coming?"

"I sent the carriage for him about half an hour ago, so he should be here at any time."

"Good. I'm really glad he's here. I know Ellyn was overjoyed to see him."

"He's a very nice man and his timing was perfect." Coop smiled.

Price grinned. "That's for sure." Then he said, more seriously, "The only thing bothering me is Mary Anne."

"Mary Anne? Why?"

"I haven't spoken to her since that miserable day in my office and, frankly, when she left, she wasn't happy with me."

"So?"

"I just don't want her making any trouble for Ellyn, that's all."

"I wouldn't worry. Alex and Rachel have their reputation to uphold. They aren't about to let her make a scene while she's engaged to Alex."

"That's true enough," Price acknowledged, draining his drink and setting the glass aside. Turning toward Coop, he asked, "When's Ellyn coming down?"

"Betsey went up to get her. They should be right down."

"Good. I've been looking forward to tonight. I haven't had much time alone with her these past two days."

"Well, don't expect much time tonight! You know everybody wants to meet her."

Price sighed heavily.

"It's only one more day until the wedding. You'll make it," Coop said, laughing.

Looking mildly irritated, he growled. "I don't know how long I'll be able to put up with all this nonsense. All I really want to do is take her for a walk in Betsey's garden. It isn't raining again, is it?"

"No. I think it's clearing up."

Price smiled, his eyes twinkling devilishly. "Good."

At the sound of footsteps, he moved to the study door, catching sight of Ellyn on the staircase.

She was a vision of loveliness as she seemed to float down the steps and Price stood mesmerized by her beauty. Smiling at him invitingly, she descended and came to stand before him.

"Good evening, Price," she cooed, her voice was softly seductive.

"You look wonderful," he said, kissing her tenderly. His gaze took in all of her, lingering on the pale fullness of her bosom, so enticingly displayed.

"Thank you." Her confidence grew as she felt his eyes upon her.

"Betsey, you look lovely, too," he added gallantly as Betsey and Coop joined them.

"Thank you." She smiled sweetly. "Oh, Coop?"

"Yes, dear?"

"Come with me for a minute, will you? I need your help."

"With what?" he asked obtusely.

Betsey flashed an exasperated look at him. "I thought they might want to be alone."

"Oh," Coop drawled. "Well, I suppose we could leave them unchaperoned for a little while."

Grinning, he took Betsey's arm and moved off down the hall to the front parlor.

"Alone at last!" Price whispered loudly to Ellyn as he led her into the study and closed the door.

Turning to him, Ellyn took in every detail of his

357

appearance. She had never seen him in evening clothes before and he looked devastatingly handsome. The jacket fit his broad shoulders perfectly and the trousers hugged his lean hips. The thought that this man loved her left her a bit breathless and she watched his gentle approach with eager eyes.

"I love you," he said quietly, taking her in his arms and kissing her. He broke the kiss off quickly. "If I start that, we'll never make the party."

Ellyn's eyes twinkled. "I know. I feel the same way."

He held her close for a second longer and then regretfully let her go. "I have something for you." Reaching into his coat pocket, he pulled out a ring box. "I hope you like it."

Ellyn took the proffered box and opened it, gasping at the diamond engagement ring it contained. "Oh, Price . . . it's gorgeous."

Price took the ring from the box and slipped it on her finger. "I love you, Ellyn."

"And I love you," Ellyn replied, her eyes shining.

Then with infinite tenderness, he pulled her to him again, kissing her deeply this time. Despite all of his good intentions, he crushed her to him, dipping a hand into her bodice to caress that silken flesh. Ellyn shivered as his fingers found the sensitive peak of her breast and teased it to hardness.

"Oh, Price," she moaned as his mouth left hers to seek the softness of her throat.

"You smell so sweet," he murmured, inhaling the erotic, delicate scent she wore.

Ellyn was lost as the heat of his lips sent tingles down her spine. Her body reacted automatically, arching to him, as he sought and found the exposed tops of her breasts.

Suddenly, Price stopped his seduction, holding her

a bit away from him. Ellyn looked up at him quickly, wondering at his withdrawal from her.

"Price?"

"Oh, pretty lady," he spoke hoarsely, "you are such a temptation."

Ellyn felt him shudder as he regained the control he'd almost lost. Her whole being still throbbed with desire for him, too, and she stayed in his arms wanting more but knowing it was not to be.

"Shall we go find Betsey and Coop?"

"That sounds nice and safe." She smiled as he opened the door for her and they went to find their friends.

Brightly gowned ladies in the arms of their partners danced gaily about the room to the schottische the musicians were playing. The party had been in full swing for three or four hours now and everyone seemed to be having a good time.

Betsey stood by the refreshment table watching Coop and Ellyn as they danced by. Sipping at her cup of champagne punch, she glanced about the room, catching sight of Mary Anne heading in her direction.

"Betsey, darling, your party is going so well," Mary Anne said in greeting.

"Thank you," she returned, wondering what was on her mind. Mary Anne never did anything without a reason.

"Price's engagement was certainly a surprise. Why he never mentioned her to me at all," Mary Anne stated.

"We kept it quiet. He wasn't sure how long it would be before Ellyn could join him here, so he decided not to make mention of their engagement until she arrived."

"Well, Ellyn is certainly one lucky girl," Mary

Anne said, her tone giving away none of her inner hatred. "How long have they known each other?"

"He stayed with Ellyn's family while he was recuperating from his injuries."

"Oh," she replied and wondered why Betsey hadn't given her a more definite answer. "Is Mr. Douglass the only family she has?"

"Her father and brother were both killed in the war. Her mother and sister weren't able to travel, so Lawrence made the trip."

Mary Anne nodded and went silent, fuming to herself. She was livid that Ellyn had won the only man she had ever loved. Money and all! How could Price have preferred Ellyn to her own petite beauty? Her eyes roved over Price's tall figure as he stood in the hall talking to some business acquaintances. She still found him to be the most attractive man she'd ever met. And love and hate being but a whit apart, she allowed herself to remember the nights when she'd wrapped her legs about his slim, driving hips and held him while he had given her his passion.

She cursed herself under her breath for having thrown his love away all those years ago and then cursed him for not wanting her now. God! How she longed to have him just once more! Fury at his snide rejection welled up inside her, killing all the desire she felt for him. She would enjoy seeing him suffer, she decided with finality.

"I'll talk to you later, Betsey," she said smoothly and moved off to find Alex.

Mary Anne took the cup of champagne punch from Alex and sipped it appreciatively. "How soon can we leave?"

"As soon as we find out where they're going on their honeymoon. Have you heard anything?"

"Not a word."

"Me, either."

"Maybe your mother is having more success than we are."

"I hope so."

"Where is she?" They both looked around the crowded room, trying to locate Rachel.

"There she is, talking to Agnes Jones."

"Terrific. If Agnes doesn't know, no one does," Mary Anne commented sourly as she watched Rachel deep in conversation with Alton's most prominent busybody.

"Having a good time?" Betsey asked when Coop and Ellyn joined her after their dance ended.

"It's absolutely perfect!" Ellyn was breathless. "Have you see my grandfather lately?"

"He was in the hall with Price a little while ago," Betsey replied.

"I think I'll go claim him for a dance. I'll be right back." Ellyn left the room in search of Lawrence.

The hall was deserted, but she could hear the deep voices of the men coming from the study and the card room.

"Ellyn!" Price's tone was warm and loving as he saw her walk past the study door. "Come join us!"

She went to his side willingly.

"Darling, this is Ralph Jones and Phineas Crowell. Gentlemen, this is Ellyn, my fiancee." Price made the introductions proudly, his arm about her waist possessively.

"It's a pleasure to meet you, young lady," they said, almost in unison.

"It's nice to meet you, too," she returned. "Price, I was looking for my grandfather."

"Ellyn," Lawrence greeted, joining them. "I've been searching for you, too. Are you ready for another dance?"

"Absolutely," Ellyn agreed taking his arm. "Gentlemen, if you'll excuse me?"

"Have fun," Price told her as she left the room with Lawrence.

The musicians were playing a waltz when they entered the ballroom. Sweeping out onto the floor, Ellyn laughed delightedly.

"Grandfather, you are a wonderful dancer."

"Thank you, my dear, but I am slowing down a bit." He smiled. "Are you happy, Ellyn?"

"Ecstatic," she said honestly. "Price is everything I've ever wanted or needed."

"Then you're not upset about Rod and your mother?"

"No. I never was. I've loved Price almost from the moment I pulled him out of the river."

"And he loves you. Never doubt that."

"I know. I don't."

"Good. If I know you're happy and well cared for, then I can go home with no regrets."

"Have none, Grandfather. I love him."

As their dance came to an end, Price was at her side.

"The next one's mine," he whispered in her ear. "I ordered another waltz."

Her eyes sparkled as she glanced up at him. "Another one?"

"Just for us." His tone was seductive. "Shall we get some punch?"

"Fine," she agreed and they went to the refreshment table.

The heady punch was cool and refreshing and Ellyn had long ago lost count of how many glasses she'd had.

When the soft, lilting music began again, they set their glasses aside and Price whirled her away amid the crowd of dancers. Time was suspended for them as they glided about the floor, lost in the wonder of each other.

Ellyn gazed up at him admiring the strong line of his jaw and the sensuous set of his mouth. As if feeling her eyes upon him, Price looked down, his firm lips curving in a tender smile.

"I feel the same way," he murmured, correctly interpreting the desire in her eyes.

"I wish this was Monday night instead of Saturday," she told him, her voice husky with emotion.

Holding her more tightly, he bit back a groan as the burning need to have her flamed through him.

"Shall we walk in the garden? I've wanted to be alone with you all night."

"Please," she urged as the music ended.

Taking her hand, he led her outside, across the terrace and down the stone steps into Betsey's flower garden.

The scent of roses and late-blooming iris hung heavily in the humid night air, as the lovers followed the winding path to the secluded center of the garden. Surrounded by low-hanging ornamental trees, it was a most romantic spot.

"It's a beautiful night," Ellyn remarked softly as they sat close together on a small, wrought-iron bench.

"It's been perfect. And being out here alone with you only makes it better." Lifting her chin, he kissed her.

As their mouths clung, their bodies strained toward each other. In a simple, easy motion, Price freed her breasts from the confining, flimsy material and caressed them to hard peaks.

"You are so beautiful," he told her as he looked down at her in the softness of the moon's glow. "Your breasts seem fuller."

"They are," she said and he crushed her to him,

wanting the feel of her against him.

Price kissed her deeply, a sensual, promising kiss that stirred them both.

"Oh, Price. It's been so long." Her words of longing urged him on and he bent to kiss each breast, enjoying the feel of each taut peak against his lips.

Her head thrown back in passionate surrender, Ellyn savored the hot, pulsing pleasure that the touch of his mouth on her breast created. She knew the need once again to be one with this man and she tightened her arms around him to encourage him.

"Ellyn, Monday seems so far away," Price groaned, resting his head against her silken skin and listening to the rapid beat of her heart.

"We can go upstairs."

"No," he stated firmly, pulling away from her and covering her once more. "We can wait one more day."

"But I want you."

"And I want you. But not here, like this. I want you as my wife."

Sighing, she knew he was right, and dejectedly finished arranging her bodice as he stood. When she rose, he tilted her chin up to him.

"Pretty lady, don't you know I hurt just like you do?"

She nodded, unable to speak.

"Smile for me," he asked and she gave him a tremulous half smile. "That's better."

Taking her hand, they started back through the garden to rejoin the party, their bodies still aching with aroused awareness of each other.

Chapter Sixteen

In contrast to the dull, sleepy morning of the day before, Sunday arrived in a dazzlingly brilliant burst of sunbeams guaranteed to send many a party-goer back under the covers.

Betsey lay quietly beside her still-sleeping husband reviewing the excitement of the night before. It had been a fun evening and she was reasonably sure that everyone had had a good time. Ellyn had looked beautiful and had charmed everyone she'd met, even the most vocal of the Rebel-haters. All had agreed that Price was a lucky man and they had easily understood his eagerness to marry.

Letting her mind wander, Betsey reminisced about the days before her wedding. The tension and excitement leading up to it had been almost unbearable, but the results had made it worthwhile. It had been a wonderful beginning to a happy life together. And, oh! their wedding night. Betsey stifled a giggle. *That* had been a revelation! She had been a virgin and totally unprepared for the actual consummation of their vows. Thank heaven Coop had been a patient, gentle lover. He had taught her love's joys slowly and with infinite care, so that when the moment had come, she had been more than ready for him.

Turning carefully in the bed, she gazed at her slumbering spouse, her eyes full of love and devotion. Asleep, he still looked like the young man she'd married—vulnerable and idealistic—and she smiled tenderly. The war years had been difficult for them, but they'd survived. They knew now what a precious gift their love was and they were going to spend the rest of their lives nurturing it.

Reaching out gently, she brushed an errant lock of hair from Coop's forehead and his eyes opened at the unexpected caress.

"Good morning," she said, smiling warmly.

"What time is it?" he questioned, rolling onto his back.

"It's early."

"What woke you?" he asked, throwing a forearm over his eyes to ward off the attacking sunshine. Groaning almost painfully, he spoke. "That was quite a party."

Unable to stifle the laughter that welled up inside her, Betsey giggled. "Yes, I'd say you had a pretty good time. Does it hurt much?"

"Only when I answer ridiculous questions," he teased.

"Ah," she replied knowingly. "It's that bad, is it?"

"Yes, but last night was worth it," he commented. "Ellyn and Price seemed to have a good time, too."

"I'm glad. We've waited so long for him to settle down. I'm just relieved that it's Ellyn. For a long time there, he had me worried."

"Not me," Coop said. "He was just looking for somebody as lovely as you."

Betsey curled against his side. "Thank you."

"Just the truth, darling." He gathered her to him. "You know before you woke up, I was thinking about our wedding . . . and our honeymoon."

"You were?" His eyes darkened as he, too, remembered.

She nodded, running a hand over his chest.

"That was a very special night for me. You were so sweet and giving."

"It was special for me, too." She rose above him and kissed him. "I loved every minute of it, although I have to admit I was afraid."

"Of me?" Coop was surprised.

"Not so much you as of the unknown."

"That didn't last long." He grinned.

"I know." She pressed against him intimately. "You were such a good teacher, I just couldn't wait to learn more."

"I taught you well." He grasped her hips and rolled over, pinning her beneath him.

Looping her arms about his neck, she pulled him down for a passionate kiss. "Do you want to go over everything I've learned?"

"Everything," he breathed as his lips met hers.

They melded together in blissful rapture, thinking only of each other and the joy of their union.

Ellyn came awake slowly, fighting it, not wanting her dream to end. But the brightness of the new day forced its way into her room and her mind. Blinking against the light that she found exceedingly harsh this morning, Ellyn quickly sat up and immediately regretted her action. Her stomach churned at the motion and she sat perfectly still, breathing deeply, in hopes that the unexpected nausea would pass.

Finally, feeling confident that her stomach was settled, she lay back slowly on the bed, wondering how she could have forgotten her vow never to drink to excess again. Closing her eyes, she rested, blocking out the pounding that had started in her head.

The knock at her door made her jump.

"Who is it?"

"It's me, Ellyn," Betsey responded. "Price and your grandfather just got here."

"Oh, no," she groaned. "Tell them I'll be down in a few minutes."

Struggling upright again, she made her way to the washstand, wondering how long it would take to make herself presentable.

Price was enjoying his second cup of coffee when Ellyn finally made her way downstairs. He met her at the foot of the staircase, kissing her warmly.

"You look a little pale this morning. Do you feel all right?"

"I will in a little while."

"Oh," he said grinning, "maybe some coffee will help."

Leading her into the dining room, he held her chair while she sat down and then resumed his place across from her.

"Good morning, Grandfather," Ellyn greeted.

"Ellyn, darling, are you feeling well?"

"I'll be fine shortly. I just had too much champagne punch last night."

"A common affliction, I assure you," Lawrence told her.

"I imagine most of Alton is moving slowly this morning," Betsey quipped.

"That's for sure," Coop added, looking none too bright himself.

Betsey laughed. "Well, what are we going to do today? And don't say, 'Take a nap.' " She gave Coop a good-natured look of warning.

"But that was the best idea I had," Coop said, grinning.

Rosalie came bustling in then with platters of ham and eggs and hot coffee. Betsey, Price and Lawrence ate a robust breakfast, but Coop and Ellyn ventured nothing more than the strong, steamy brew.

"What do you think?" Betsey asked again, wanting to plan her day.

"First, I think we'd better get most of Ellyn's things moved over to the house, so we don't have to worry about that tomorrow."

"Are the workmen finished?"

"Yes, they put the final touches on everything yesterday afternoon."

"Then we'll all go. I'm anxious to see what changes you've made," Betsey said enthusiastically.

So within the hour, Darnelle had packed Ellyn's clothes and they were off to Richardson House.

"Well?" Price asked after they had toured all the rooms.

"Price, it's beautiful," Ellyn said sincerely as they stood once again in the main-floor hallway.

"You've done a marvelous job. Was it really all that bad when Rachel moved out?" Betsey asked.

"It was a mess. She'd sold off just about all the downstairs furniture and the house hadn't been painted in years."

"As much as Rachel prided herself on appearances, I'm surprised that she didn't take better care of it," Betsey remarked.

"She had better things to do with 'her' money," he explained, his tone brittle.

"Well, that's all over now." Ellyn took his arm.

"Yes, it is." He smiled down at her.

"Is that all you could find out?" Alex asked his mother as he paced the small parlor.

"Agnes wasn't too helpful. All she knew was that the wedding was to be at ten tomorrow morning and that for a honeymoon they are going down to St. Louis for a few days."

"But you don't know where they're staying or when they'll be back?"

"No. And I asked everyone I could." Rachel was disgusted.

"Do you really think shooting him will be the easiest?"

"If you don't miss," she sneered, still irritated by Alex's first failure. "But you have to make it look like a robbery attempt. And you can't be seen."

"All right, all right." He was tired of her continual harping. "I'll see what I can do in the morning, before the ceremony. But it may have to wait if I don't get a clean shot at him."

"Just make sure that he's dead before he gets a chance to sign that will!" Rachel ordered with finality.

"Tomorrow's our big day." Price kissed Ellyn gently as they sat alone in the front parlor at Coop and Betsey's later that night.

"Are you coming by here in the morning?" she asked, resting against his shoulder.

"No. I'll meet you at the church."

"All right." She drew a long, sighing breath. "Just think, this time tomorrow night we'll be married."

"I know. I can hardly wait." He bent to kiss her again. "Betsey's planned a big luncheon for us and I've booked us passage on a steamer leaving for St. Louis at three."

"You've taken care of everything, haven't you?" she said smiling.

"I even ordered sunshine." He grinned back. "It's our day and it's going to be as perfect as I can make it."

"It will be." She kissed him hungrily, breaking off as they heard Betsey and Coop returning.

"Is everything set?"

"I'll meet you at the church about a quarter to ten," Price said. "Lawrence is riding with you, right?"

"Yes, I'm sending the carriage for him at nine," Coop explained.

"I guess we're ready, then." Price stood, drawing Ellyn up with him. "I'm going to go now, but I'll see you first thing in the morning."

"Goodnight, Price," Coop and Betsey told him. Then Betsey added, "This is your last night as a bachelor. Maybe we should keep an eye on you!"

Price laughed at her observation. "Thank heaven. I don't think I can stand being foot-loose and fancy-free too much longer. Goodnight."

Ellyn walked him to the front door, not wanting to be parted from him.

"I don't want you to go," she protested softly.

"I don't want to leave either, but this is the last night ever." He pulled her to him. "Goodnight, pretty lady. Sweet dreams."

His mouth claimed her in a searing, poignant kiss.

"Tomorrow . . ." he muttered, pulling reluctantly away from her.

"Tomorrow . . ." Ellyn promised and she watched until he'd ridden off into the darkness.

The sun was shining brightly Monday morning as the carriage pulled up in front of the house. Lawrence climbed down, his step sprightly, as he went up the porch steps and inside to see his granddaughter on her wedding day.

371

Ellyn was already dressed and downstairs awaiting him. "Grandfather!"

"Ellyn, you look just beautiful," he told her, taking in every detail of the sedate, pale blue dress she wore.

"Thank you." Her voice broke and she rushed into his arms. "I'm so glad you're here. It means so much to me."

He held her quietly for a long time. "Your father would be so proud if he could see you today."

"Do you really think so?" she sniffed.

Lawrence nodded. "He would have liked Price. Price is a strong man and he loves you very much." He caressed her cheek. "Now, stop your crying. This is your wedding day and I've brought you a present."

Ellyn wiped her eyes dutifully with the handkerchief he gave her. "You did?"

Lawrence took a small, gaily wrapped box from his pocket. "I want you to have this."

Ellyn unwrapped it eagerly. "Oh!" She was stunned by the gift. "It's Grandmother's brooch."

"I'm sure she would want you to have it."

"Thank you! Please pin it on for me."

And he pinned the small cameo brooch to her bodice. "Now you're perfect. I think Coop and Betsey are waiting . . . if you're ready."

"I'm ready," she told him, smiling brightly, and they went into the hall to meet them.

Alex was cursing his own stupidity as Price disappeared into the church. He should have done it last night. He should have broken in the house and killed him while he was asleep. But instead, he'd waited until this morning, hoping to get a good shot at him on his way to the cathedral. The way his luck had been running, Alex knew he shouldn't have expected it to be easy. Turning his horse away from the vantage point, he rode toward Mary Anne's, not wanting to face his mother just yet.

With her grandfather's help, Ellyn alighted from the carriage and, led by Betsey and Coop, they entered the church. It was dark and cool inside and smelled a little of incense, and Ellyn shivered in anticipation. Lawrence smiled down at her as he felt her nervousness.

"Don't worry. As best I can recall, getting married is totally painless," he whispered.

Ellyn flashed him a quick smile as they followed Betsey and Coop to the small chapel, where Price and the priest awaited them.

As his friends entered the chapel, Price looked up from his quiet conversation with Father Simmons.

"Father, I'd like you to met my fiancee, Ellyn Douglass, and her grandfather, Lawrence Douglass," Price introduced them as they joined him. "You already know Mr. and Mrs. Cooper."

"Of course. Coop, Betsey, how are you? Miss Douglass, Mr. Douglass, it's nice to meet you on such a joyous occasion," the priest greeted them.

"Good morning, Father," they responded.

"Is everyone here now."

"Yes, Father."

"Good. Price, Ellyn, if you two will stand here before me. The rest of you may be seated. We'll begin."

As his words encircled them and bound them together, Ellyn and Price spoke their vows in hushed tones, aware of the deep, abiding commitment they were making. Ellyn lifted her hand to receive his ring, dwelling on the priest's words: "The ring is a circle, a symbol of your unceasing love. It has no beginning and no end." Looking up at Price as he slipped the simple gold band on her finger, her gaze locked with his and they seemed suspended in time, only conscious of each other.

Ellyn studied his expression as he spoke softly, "With this ring, I thee wed." She memorized the emotions there, the tenderness and devotion, and her heart swelled with love for him.

"I now pronounce you man and wife. What God has joined together, let no man put asunder." Father Simmons paused, smiling warmly. "You may kiss your bride, Mr. Richardson."

Price paused, savoring the sweetness of the moment and then kissed her gently.

"Best wishes, Mrs. Richardson," Father Simmons told her cheerfully as the kiss ended and Ellyn beamed up at him.

"Thank you," she managed before being swept into Coop's arms for a big hug.

Betsey was kissing Price and Lawrence was thanking Father Simmons as Ellyn smiled up at Coop.

"Mrs. Richardson. I like that."

"So do I." Price slipped an arm possessively around her waist and drew her to his side as he accepted congratulations from Lawrence and the priest.

"Let's get back to the house, shall we?" Betsey encouraged. "Darnelle and Rosalie should have everything ready by now."

"Father, will you join us?"

"Thank you for the invitation, but I won't be able to. You go on and have a good time. Price and Ellyn, have a wonderful life together."

"Thank you, Father. We will."

"What do you mean, you didn't get the chance?"

Mary Anne demanded. Then, glancing at the mantel clock, she sneered, "Well, it's too late now. He's married."

"I know," Alex said somberly, pouring himself a drink at her small liquor cabinet.

"Do you realize how this complicates things?" she continued, aggravated at his bungling. "Now we'll have to get rid of both of them."

"So?" Alex shrugged. "I'll just catch them alone somewhere and make it look like a robbery. Nobody will ever suspect us."

Mary Anne snorted in disgust. "Just make sure it's before he signs that will."

"Don't worry, Mary Anne. I'll handle it."

And Mary Anne knew that that was what she was concerned about.

"The luncheon was lovely, Betsey. Thanks." Ellyn hugged her friend.

"You're welcome." Betsey hugged her back. "You have a good time, all right?"

"We will," Ellyn told her as she finished packing her last few things.

Ellyn picked up the small valise and went downstairs where Price and Coop were waiting in the hall.

"All set?"

"I'm ready," Ellyn said, smiling.

Darnelle came down the hall just then to see her off. "Miz Ellyn, you have a wonderful time."

"Thank you, Darnelle. Are you going back with Grandfather?"

"Yes, ma'am. We're leaving first thing tomorrow morning."

"Tell Franklin and Glory hello for me." Ellyn hugged the older woman.

"Ah will."

Turning next to Coop, she hugged and kissed him. "We'll see you when we get back."

"Have fun."

"Grandfather . . ." She went to him and embraced him. "Take care."

"Don't worry about me." He kissed her cheek. "I'll be back for a visit as soon as the baby's born."

"You will?"

He nodded. "Now, you'd better get going or you'll miss your boat."

They all went outside to the carriage.

"I'll drive you down," Coop offered, and with Lawrence's help, Ellyn climbed in as Price loaded the luggage.

"See you Thursday," the newlyweds called to Betsey as they waved one last time and then settled back to begin their honeymoon.

As the steamer backed out into midstream, Ellyn stood close by her new husband's side. She was glad for the opportunity to enjoy the sights on their way to St. Louis for she had missed them on her trip north.

"I love the river," Price told her, pulling her arm through his. "It's always changing."

"I know. It was the same way at home. Is it a long trip to St. Louis?"

"No, just a few hours. We'll be there well before dark."

"Good." She smiled archly at him.

Price gave her a quick leering grin in expectation of the night to come and then, to distract both Ellyn and himself, he led her about the promenade deck pointing out to her all the notable sights.

It was after six o'clock when they finally arrived at the St. Louis riverfront. A horse bus from the hotel picked them up and soon they were checked in and following a servant upstairs to their rooms. Price swung Ellyn up into his arms and carried her across the threshold, much to her delight. Setting her gently on her feet in the middle of the room, Price saw the servant to the door and locked it behind him.

Without a word, he moved back to Ellyn and took her in his arms.

"Do you know how much I've looked forward to this moment, pretty lady?" he asked her solemnly.

"I hope as much as I have."

"Shall we forget about supper tonight?"

"My thoughts exactly." She pulled his tie loose and began unbuttoning his shirt.

"In a hurry, are you?" He grinned.

She gave him her best lecherous look. "Am I ever."

Laughing heartily, he hugged her close. "I love you."

Wiggling free of his embrace, Ellyn stood up and began unbuttoning the back of her dress. Inspired by her endearing eagerness, Price rose and helped her with the more difficult buttons. Slipping the new gown from her shoulders, Ellyn stepped free of the billowing skirts and petticoats. Bending over, she picked up the dress and spread it over a chair. Price stood back, admiring her trim figure so alluringly displayed in her new, sheer chemise.

"How many gowns did you and Betsey order?"

"Ten. Why?" Ellyn was surprised by his question.

"Maybe we should cancel your order. I like you better without clothes," he teased.

"Oh, you . . ." She advanced on him in mock anger, but her eyes, darkened with passionate intent, gave her away.

He chuckled and took her in his arms. "Have I ever told you that you're beautiful when you're angry?"

"I don't think so. Am I?" she asked.

"Positively stunning," he replied, kissing her deeply.

Ellyn's lips parted under the gentle persuasion of his as he explored fully the sweetness of her mouth. Without ending the kiss, Price pushed the chemise from her shoulders. Pulling her tightly to him, he delighted in the feel of her soft, bare bosom against his naked chest.

Ellyn's hands slipped beneath his parted shirt and caressed the hard-muscled length of his back. Then, sliding around to the front, she unfastened his belt and pants.

Aroused by Ellyn's aggressiveness, Price released her momentarily while he shed his clothing. Turning back to her, Price marvelled at the erotic picture she made as she stood half-nude in the fading light of the evening. Her chemise was caught at her waist by the gentle swell of her hips revealing to him all the glory of her heavy, pink-tipped breasts. The dark mass of her hair was loosened and falling about her shoulders in wild disarray. At just the sight of her, he felt himself harden and he went to her then, his body openly revealing her effect upon him.

Ellyn smiled bewitchingly and pushed the chemise down as Price came to embrace her. The heat of his body was a brand against hers and her knees weakened as his arms came around her protectively.

They stood unmoving, relishing the intimacy as their bodies met in unhindered contact. Without speaking, Price picked her up and lay her on the bed, then quickly stretched out beside her.

Facing him, Ellyn smiled dreamily and traced the hard masculine angles of his face with a gentle touch. Capturing her hand, he pressed a heated kiss on her palm.

"Shall I save it?"

"No need. I'll always be here with you now." His lips curved in a slight smile that softened his features. "Whenever you want a kiss, you just ask."

Wrapping her arms about his neck, Ellyn moved closer to him and lifted her lips to his. "I want one."

And he obliged as desire surged through him. It had been so long! Clasping her closer, his mouth claimed hers in a searing kiss and they strained together, wanting to be even nearer . . . to be one.

Ellyn welcomed his long-denied passions. She could hardly believe that they were finally man and wife. Instinctively, she tightened her hold on him. Those endless days of despair were still very real to her and the security of his embrace was her haven.

Responding to her sudden tenseness, he drew a little away. "Ellyn?" he coaxed and she opened her eyes to look at him.

"Oh, Price," she sighed. "Being with you means everything to me. I was just remembering."

His voice deepened as he spoke, "Darling, we've got only our future to think about." His big hand rested on her slightly rounded stomach. "And our child."

Ellyn looked up at him with trusting eyes. "You are so special. You're my whole world."

"I'm just lucky to have you. So many things could have kept us apart, but you trusted me. We'll always believe in each other—it's so important."

Where before his desire had been a raging, lusting fire, now Price felt only the need to please her, to give to her all of his love, tonight and all their nights together. Ellyn had risked her life for him. She had given up everything that she had held dear to be with him and he was overwhelmed by her sacrifice. She was his friend, his lover, and now, most importantly, his wife. And he would spend the rest of his life loving her.

He drew her back into the circle of his arms, their mouths meeting in a breathless, promising kiss. Ellyn reached out for him, pulling his lean hips closer and pressing wantonly against him. Offering herself to Price in total surrender, she was stunned as waves of pleasure pulsed through her.

Enraptured by her response, Price sought the center of her womanly softness and, as Ellyn wrapped her legs about his waist, he moved to slide deep within her. He shook with emotion as she opened beneath him. Her velvety depths softly enveloping his maleness created such a torrent of feeling within him that her name was a hoarse cry from his lips.

Cleaving to him, Ellyn, too, was overcome by his possession. As she sobbed her need, he began to move, each rhythmic thrust driving them on to the ultimate completion. As the explosion of ecstasy claimed them both, they clung together, their bodies shuddering with the passion of their mating. At peace, content, Price rolled to his back, bringing Ellyn atop him and they rested, heart to heart.

The hours blended in soft, sensuous splendor as they made up for all the long, lonely nights that they'd spent apart. Time and again, Price reached out for Ellyn, needing the reassurance that she was truly there beside him. And each time, as she came to him, her need was as fervent as his. They loved their way through the darkness of the moonless star-dusted night and did not sleep until the first light of dawn brightened the eastern horizon.

As the sun burned its way higher in the pale, cloudless sky, the confining heat of their room finally roused them.

"Good morning," Ellyn greeted him sleepily.

"I'm not so sure it is morning!" he teased as he gave her a quick kiss before rolling from the bed.

Stretching contentedly, Ellyn watched in fascination the play of muscles across his back and shoulders as he moved to look out the window. Her eyes dropped to his naked buttocks and long, straight legs and she smiled appreciatively to herself. He was one attractive man.

"What are we going to do today?" she asked innocently.

"I had quite a few good ideas originally, but none of them are as appealing as staying here, alone with you," he told her as his warming gaze swept over her bare form.

Ellyn was quite an enticement, lying nude amid the rumpled sheets, and he came back to her, wanting once more to hold her close. Ellyn rested her head on Price's shoulder and teasingly caressed his hair-matted chest with one slim hand.

His reaction to her touch was immediate and Ellyn gave a small, throaty laugh as she realized again the power she had over him. With lips and tongue, she explored his male essence, bringing him to new heights of desire. When he could bear it no longer, Price drew her up to him and kissed her deeply, parting her thighs and driving into her welcoming wetness. They rocked together in love's timeless motion, aware only of one another and the mindless ecstasy of their embrace.

It was hours later when they finally left their room for dinner and an outing. They ate in the hotel dining room, passing up such delicacies as buffalo tongue and broiled grouse for a far more ordinary fare. Then, their meal finished, they toured the renowned St. Louis Museum, enjoying the unusual exhibits on display in the upper hall.

As the evening shadows lengthened, they returned to their hotel and ordered a meal brought to their rooms. After supping on wild duck stuffed with rice and all the trimmings, they relaxed, enjoying the sweet serenity of being together.

"What would you like to do tomorrow?" Price asked from the small sitting room of their suite.

"I don't know, I've never been here before. What do you suggest?" Ellyn's voice came to him from their bedroom.

"We'll sleep late, go shopping in the afternoon and then attend the threater in the evening. Sound good?"

"Mm-hmm," she assented. "I especially like the part about sleeping late."

"You do?"

"Of course. That means we'll be up late tonight!" she came into the doorway between the rooms and posed for him in her carefully selected, sheer, white negligee. "Do you like it?"

His eyes widened in surprise as he took in her scantily clad figure.

"I do." Price let his gaze sweep over her, lingering on her full bosom where the diaphanous gown served to enhance the feminine loveliness of her.

As she walked toward him, it shimmered about her, clinging with each step and seeming to reveal all, yet revealing nothing. The power of suggestion was great, though, and by the time Ellyn reached his side, he was ready to tear the tantalizing garment from her slim body and take her in a frenzy of lust. Instead, fighting down his maddening desire to hurriedly slake his almost overpowering need for her, Price took her hand and pulled her down next to him on the sofa.

Pushing her hair gently back, he framed her face with his hands and kissed her softly. Parting her lips, their tongues met in a tentative, exploring caress that sent chills down her spine. Her nipples hardened, seemingly of their own volition, and the constant silken contact with the flimsy material of her gown only heightened Ellyn's awareness of them. She ached to feel his lips upon her, and moaned deeply when his mouth left hers to press hot kisses down her throat and over her partially concealed breasts. As his lips touched one erect peak through the gown, shock waves radiated through her. Ellyn arched to him, wanting the erotic weight of Price's hard male body on top of her.

Her arms around his neck, she reclined on the narrow sofa and took him with her, spreading her legs so he could fit himself more intimately to her. Ellyn moved seductively against the throbbing hardness of him, her actions encouraging him to do more, much more.

Unable to refrain any longer from the love treasure she offered, he freed himself from his pants and, brushing aside the gown, penetrated her. The sensation that overcame him was one of wondrous torment as he tried to steady his thrusts. But the need for consummation was too great and he tensed above her as the spasms of desire overwhelmed him. Passion spent, he rested against her, murmuring to Ellyn of his love. Moving to the bed some time later, they passed the night totally enraptured with each other.

It was midmorning before Ellyn and Price ventured forth to explore the shops on Veranda Row. Price enjoyed spoiling her and his purchases were many as they went from store to store admiring the merchandise on display.

Hunger finally forced their return to the hotel, and after taking their meal in the dining room, they spent the afternoon reviewing their purchases and resting up for their excursion to the theater that night.

They attended an eight o'clock performance of *Richard III* at the People's Theater, enjoying it tremendously, and then headed back to the hotel in a hired carriage. Relaxing, Ellyn leaned contentedly on Price's shoulder and fell deeply asleep as the excitement of the past few days caught up with her.

She stirred and blinked as Price kissed her awake. "We're here."

Straightening up rather stiffly, she gave him an impish grin. "I'm afraid you've worn me out."

He returned her smile and drew her close for a warm kiss. "Tired?"

"Exhausted," she told him as they climbed out of the carriage.

"I guess it's a good thing we're going home tomorrow so we can get some rest," he spoke softly, for her ears only, and Ellyn blushed.

Guiding her across the lobby and up the stairs, they entered their rooms.

"What time do we leave tomorrow? In the morning?"

"No, not until 1:30."

"Good." Her eyes twinkled.

"Good? But I thought you were tired."

"We can't waste the last night of our honeymoon sleeping," she said in mock indignation and moved into his arms. "Can we?"

It was well past sunup when Price opened his eyes, and he was surprised to find that Ellyn was already up. A noise in the sitting room drew his attention and he pulled on his trousers and went to investigate.

"Good morning," she greeted him. "Did you sleep well?"

"Well enough that I didn't even know you'd gone. What are you doing up so early?"

"I haven't been up that long. Just long enough to order us both a bath and breakfast in our room."

"How long will it take to get here?"

"The maid said about ten minutes on the bath and half an hour for the food." A knock interrupted her and Ellyn opened the door to admit the maid carrying the hot water.

Price stepped discreetly back into the bedroom as the young servant filled the tub in the bathing chamber. When she had gone, Price came out again.

"Do you want to go first?" Ellyn offered.

"Since time is of the essence, why don't we bathe together?"

Ellyn was shocked by his suggestion, but he loosened her dressing gown and lifted her into the steamy, soothing water. Shedding his pants, he climbed in with her, holding her comfortably on his lap.

"Well?" He grinned and Ellyn blushed. "Give me the soap and I'll wash you."

Handing him the bar, she was tense and nervous as he slowly began to soap her neck and shoulders.

"Better?" he asked as he felt her begin to relax under his massaging hands.

"Much." Ellyn leaned back against his chest as his arms came around her to lather her breasts and stomach.

Despite her best efforts, her nipples hardened as Price sensuously soaped each rounded breast.

"My turn!" Ellyn interrupted as he ventured lower and, taking the soap, she turned to face him.

Scrubbing vigorously, she washed his shoulders and

chest, stopping teasingly at his waist. His body responded involuntarily to her touch and he ran an idle finger down the slope of her breast to encircle the taut, pink peak. Ellyn's breath caught in her throat.

"Oh, Price." Ellyn leaned toward him, her breasts grazing his slippery chest.

"God, woman, do you see what you do to me?"

Guiding her forward until she straddled him, Price pulled her down upon his rigid maleness and they rocked together to completion, caressed by the warmth of the water.

The knock of the servant bringing breakfast startled Ellyn from her sated haven in Price's arms and she jumped nervously from the tub, sloshing water all over the floor.

"Be careful. You'll slip," he ordered as she hurried to pull on her dressing gown.

"Shush! They might hear you!" she hissed at him, but he just gave her a lopsided grin.

"What's wrong? Don't you want them to know I took a bath?" he teased and Ellyn rushed from the small room, closing the door behind her to shut out Price's laughter.

They ate their breakfast leisurely, enjoying the peace and contentment of the morning, before the trip home. A servant came to help them pack and by 12:30 they were ready to leave for the levee. After their bags had been taken down to the waiting carriage, Price took Ellyn in his arms one last time.

"These few days have been the best in my life," he told her solemnly and her eyes misted at his sentiment.

"Mine, too." She raised on tiptoe to kiss him. "I love you."

"And I love you."

Chapter Seventeen

"Did Coop know when we were coming back?" Ellyn asked as Alton came into view.

"I told him we'd be back sometime this afternoon," Price explained. "If there's no one from the office to meet us, we'll just hire a carriage."

Ellyn nodded and turned back to admire the scenic panorama of the city on the bluffs.

"There's O'Riley." Price pointed out the young man waiting in a buggy.

"Oh, good."

Kevin O'Riley pulled up closer to the wharfboat when he caught sight of Price coming down the gangplank with his new bride.

"Welcome back, sir," he greeted him.

"Thank you, O'Riley. Have you met Mrs. Richardson yet?"

"Briefly at the fire last week. It's good to see you again, ma'am."

"Thank you."

"How are things going at the new office?" Price asked as he and Kevin started loading their luggage.

"We're doing pretty well. Mr. Cooper's been working on the files all week, but they're still not in order."

"It's going to take awhile," Price said as he

handed Ellyn into the buggy and got in himself.

"To your house, sir?" Kevin asked, climbing in and taking up the reins.

"Please." They drove off unmindful of Alex's watchful eyes upon them.

Kevin took them home and, after bringing in their bags, he headed back to ATC to let Coop know that they had returned and were expecting Betsey and him for a visit that evening.

"So they're back?" Rachel stated.

"I just saw them," Alex said.

"This is it, then," Mary Anne remarked. "What did you find out about the will?"

"It's ready. Barlow has just been waiting for Price to get back so he can sign it."

"There's no time to lose. You'll have to do it before he meets with Barlow."

"I know, but . . ."

"No exceptions! Do it!" Rachel commanded and Alex knew the time had come.

"Come in! Come in!" Ellyn told Betsey and Coop happily as she greeted them at the door later that evening.

"How was your trip?" Betsey inquired, hugging Ellyn.

"Just wonderful. Let's go in the parlor. Price will be right down."

"So what did you do? Did you go to the theater? I see he took you shopping. I love your dress. Veranda Row?" Betsey chattered.

"We were so busy." Ellyn said with a laugh. "Tuesday, we toured the St. Louis Museum—it was really interesting. Then yesterday, we shopped all day and went to the People's Theater at night."

"What did you see?"

"*Richard III* and it was excellent. This morning, we just took it easy. And here we are . . ." She ended breathlessly just as Price entered the room.

Ellyn let her gaze follow her husband as he went to kiss Betsey's cheek and then shake hands with Coop. Just the sight of his tall, lean body quickened her pulse and their eyes met across the room. The white shirt he wore was fitted to his broad, powerful shoulders and his dark pants hugged his slim hips. Ellyn's eyes smoldered with the now-familiar emotions that he roused in her and Price, recognizing her reaction, gave her a secret, tender smile. He, too, appreciated her loveliness and felt the first stirrings of desire as he regarded her from Coop's side.

"So, you two had a good time?" Coop was asking, smiling wryly as he observed Price's preoccupation with Ellyn.

"It was most enjoyable." Price forced his attention back to his friend and partner. "Did you get much work done this week?"

"Business has been good. We haven't lost out on anything. But I really need your help getting all the invoices and contracts straightened out."

"We'll start in earnest on Monday. I think we both deserve the weekend off."

"That's not a bad idea. Oh, by the way, Barlow sent word that your papers are ready to be signed."

"Good. I'll do that tomorrow afternoon."

"What have you got planned for the morning?"

"I thought Ellyn and I could just ride out to the River Road. I'd like to show her the cliffs and the Piasa Bird. Want to go with us? We could pack a lunch."

"I can't tomorrow. I've got meetings all morning," Coop declined. "Why don't we plan on going in the fall?"

"Sounds good. We'll plan on it. It'll be beautiful after the first frost."

"Plan on what?" Betsey asked, coming in on the end of their conversation.

"Riding up to see the Piasa Bird. He and Ellyn are going tomorrow, but I can't get away," Coop explained.

"The what?" Ellyn asked. "Where are we going tomorrow?"

"Up the River Road to see the Piasa Bird."

"Piasa Bird?" Ellyn looked questioningly at Betsey.

"It's an old Illini Indian legend. Piasa means 'bird that devours men,' " Betsey began.

"A man-eating bird?"

"It was a birdlike creature with horns, red eyes, a scaled body, wings and a long tail that hunted the area in search of human prey. The Illini were terrified of it and they tried to kill it for years before one brave chief—Ouatoga—finally devised a plan. Using himself as bait, Ouatoga lured the Piasa down and his warriors shot it with poisoned arrows. Luckily, they succeeded and the chief lived. The mysterious Piasa was killed and the Indians engraved its image on the bluff. For years, every time an Indian passed by they fired arrows at the hideous beast."

"And you can still see it on the cliff?"

"Yes. We'll ride up in the morning. It's a beautiful drive."

Plans made, the conversation drifted on as the evening sped by. It was after eleven before Betsey took note of the time.

"We have to get going," Betsey said. "Coop has to be at the office early."

"Well, I'm just glad you came over," Ellyn told

390

them as they walked to the door. "Why don't we have dinner over the weekend?"

"Fine. Let's plan for Saturday night at our house," Betsey offered. "All right?"

"Good. Ellyn, we'll see you Saturday. Price, if you get time after seeing Barlow tomorrow afternoon, stop in at the office for a while," Coop said.

"Right. I'll see you tomorrow. Goodnight," Price called as Betsey and Coop waved and drove off toward home.

Closing the door and locking it, Price took Ellyn in his arms and gave her an affectionate kiss.

"Shall we call it a night?"

"I think so, it's been a long day." They walked, arms around each other's waist, up the stairs.

He held the door to the bedroom for her and admired her trim figure as she moved ahead of him into the room.

"Will you help me with my dress?"

"You had to ask?" he said chuckling, his eyes alight with passion's glow.

Ellyn smiled at him archly and presented her back to him. Easily unbuttoning the new gown, Price slipped it from her and, brushing her long hair aside, kissed the back of her neck. The warm caress of his mouth sent shivers down her spine. She leaned back against his chest, pulling his hands up to cup her breasts. Price pressed his hips to her buttocks and Ellyn could feel his arousal, hard and throbbing, against her.

Twisting to face him, she pulled his head down for a long, lingering kiss that further inflamed him. Parting only briefly, they finished undressing, carelessly tossing aside the rest of their garments in their rush to be together. Finally, unencumbered by clothing, they melded, searching for and finding the perfect completion together. Falling asleep in each other's arms, they passed the night in blissful rapture.

Hugging every curve of the winding river's path, the River Road north of Alton skirted the edges of the mighty Mississippi, providing a breath-taking view for all who chose to travel it. River traffic was slow this mild, midsummer morning and the undisturbed surface of the wide river glistened sedately as it reflected the brightness of the day.

Ellyn was enjoying the cool river breeze against her face as they rode along in the small open carriage. She loved being outdoors and hadn't realized how much she missed it until now. Breathing the sun-dappled fresh air, she relaxed, savoring the sweetness of her life.

Everything had turned out so well for her. Price loved her and she was carrying his baby. That, alone, gave her a secret thrill. How she longed to hold their child. She had already decided that the baby was a boy and that he would be a miniature replica of his handsome father—minus the mustache, of course. And she giggled aloud at the thought.

Cocking an eyebrow, Price gave Ellyn a sidelong glance but she just smiled serenely at him.

"What a glorious morning! I'm glad you suggested this. I really needed to be outside."

"It is relaxing."

"Do we have much farther to go?"

"No," he told her as he expertly maneuvered the buggy along the bumpy road.

Ellyn looked out across the wide Mississippi to the greenery of the Missouri countryside. The flat, fertile flood plain over there was quite a contrast to the magnificent bluffs of the Illinois side.

As Price slowed the carriage, he pointed high up the face of the cliff. "There it is."

Ellyn stared a long minute at the likeness of the strange creature whose stony-eyed gaze glared threateningly out over the waters.

"I wonder if Chief Ouatoga was terrified when he faced it down?"

"No, I doubt it. According to the legend, he was a very brave chief." Price grinned.

They lingered on, imagining the final confrontation between man and the beast.

Then as Ellyn surveyed the rocky landscape, she asked, "Are we going to have our lunch here?"

"No, there's a much better place a little ways back downstream."

"Good, because I'm getting hungry."

They headed back then and a short time later turned off onto a side road that led to a partially secluded clearing. After unloading the few things they'd brought along, Ellyn unfolded a blanket and spread it out on the grass, eager to begin their picnic.

Alex had trailed them from town, keeping far enough back that he wouldn't be seen. There could be no error on his part this time.

Circling above them as they drove into the woods for their picnic, Alex tried to find a vantage point from which he could get a clear shot, but it was too thickly wooded. Forced to wait, he rode back toward town, trying to locate a good place for an ambush. At last, he found a spot that afforded an unobstructed view of the road and he settled in to wait.

"I guess we had better head back home," Price said sleepily as he lay with his head on Ellyn's lap.

"Why so soon?" They had only just finished eating a few minutes before and she was enjoying the serenity of their hideaway.

"Coop said that Barlow—my attorney—had some papers ready for me to sign, so I thought I'd better do that this afternoon."

"Oh." Ellyn sounded disappointed.

"We'll come back with Betsey and Coop in the fall and make a day of it. Once it frosts and the trees start to turn, the scenery is magnificent."

Ellyn looked up at the high, jutting bluffs that nature had crowned with dark green foliage and she could easily imagine the beauty of it when winter's threat turned the trees and bushes to all shades of gold and crimson.

"That sounds like fun."

Price stood and offered her a hand up, giving her a lingering kiss.

"Thanks for being my pillow."

"Any time." Ellyn smiled, and after gathering their blanket and picnic basket, they headed back toward town.

Alex was tired of waiting and more than a little irritated by the way things were going. He was sick of following Price all over creation and he was hungry and the damn insects were eating him alive. Swatting miserably at another voracious mosquito, he checked his rifle again to make sure it was ready and sat back against the tree trunk once more.

When Alex finally heard the returning horses, he ran to the small outcropping of rocks and ducked behind them. Before him, the road stretched for a good half mile without any obstructions. Sighting down the barrel of his rifle, he waited for the perfect moment to fire.

Mary Anne paced restlessly about her bedroom. All morning she'd been troubled as doubts of Alex's ability assailed her. Was he man enough to carry this off? She hoped he was. The possibility of what would happen to them if he failed today was unnerving.

Sighing nervously, she left her room and went downstairs in search of a drink. It was going to be a long day.

Rachel sipped her tea and listened politely to her hostess, Agnes Jones, chatter on.

"How's your wonderful nephew, Price, doing now that he's a married man?"

Rachel smiled, the actress in her coming into play. "He's doing fine, Agnes. He and Ellyn just returned from their honeymoon late yesterday."

"That's wonderful. It was high time that boy married and settled down," Agnes said in matronly approval.

"We were wondering . . ." Rachel let the sentence trail off.

"Well, what about your boy? When are Mary Anne and Alex going to tie the knot?"

"They haven't set a date yet, but I'm sure it will be sometime this fall."

"Good. And a big wedding, I hope?"

"Of course," Rachel remarked almost condescendingly and Agnes changed the subject.

Glancing up at the mantel clock, Rachel paused to wonder where Alex was. It was high noon. Surely he had done it by now. Agnes Jones's pointed question brought her attention back to the conversation and she was forced to abandon her thoughts of Alex for the moment.

The sound of the rifle shot and the shock of Price suddenly slumping beside her, blood streaming from his head, stunned Ellyn. Looking wildly about, she caught sight of the rifle as the sun glinted off the polished barrel and she threw herself in front of Price as another crack of gun fire split the silence of the noonday countryside. Her body jerked violently as pain exploded in her back and she fell unconscious atop him.

The horses, no longer controlled by Price's firm hand, panicked at the shots and rushed crazily ahead. The buggy, not built to withstand such abuse, broke loose, careened off the road and crashed into a grove of trees.

Alex stood up to get a better view of the havoc he'd wrought and then smiled to himself in great satisfaction. Rachel and Mary Anne would be proud of him. He had never killed anyone before and it gave him an overwhelming feeling of power. As he stood there staring at the now-deserted road, Alex visualized over and over in his mind the sight of Price as the bullet had hit him—jerking slightly and then collapsing.

Alex's eyes glazed as he felt for the first time in his life invincible. A surge of wild, painful excitement burned through him. He had done it! Untying his horse, he slid the rifle into its case and mounted, riding slowly toward the carriage that had come to rest at a precarious angle amidst the trees.

He tethered his horse some distance away and approached on foot, in case someone else happened by. Silence reigned as Alex quietly neared the buggy; only the occasional call of the birds broke through the deadly stillness.

Drawing his handgun, Alex circled the wreckage until he could see them both, sprawled brokenly beneath the tilted vehicle. He smiled and holstered his gun. Price was lying face down, his head bleeding profusely, his blood pooling darkly in the dust. A clean head shot, Alex lauded himself, trying not to look too closely at the carnage he'd caused. Ellyn lay on her side, partially beneath Price, the back of her gown soaked with blood.

Alex took what money there was from Price's pockets and moved quickly away, not wanting to touch him any longer than he had to. The act of killing had thrilled Alex, but he found viewing the gory aftermath nauseating.

Climbing on his horse, he spurred it to a gallop, anxious to get away from the bloody scene.

Emily Edwards heard the sound of the horses and was surprised that Mr. and Mrs. Richardson had returned so early. Opening the front door to greet them, her surprise turned to horror at the sight of the team standing by the stable, lathered and quivering with exhaustion.

Racing down the porch steps, she called for help from the stableboy, Johnny, and they took control of the animals. When the horses were safely in their stalls, she turned worriedly to the young man.

"You say the harness was broken? Oh, dear, come up to the house just as soon as you're finished here."

"What do you think happened?"

"I don't know, but we've got to let Mr. Cooper know right away."

"Yes, ma'am."

The housekeeper hurried back inside and wrote a note to Coop.

"You make sure Mr. Cooper gets this immediately."

"Yes, ma'am!"

Coop was in the middle of an important business meeting when Kevin knocked on his office door, interrupting him.

"What is it, O'Riley?" Coop called out in irritation.

Kevin opened the door. "It's important, sir. Mr. Richardson's stableboy, Johnny, is out here and he insists he must see you right away. He claims it's an emergency."

Coop frowned and then stood up. "Mr. Martin, if you'll excuse me for one minute." Stepping into the outer office, he spoke to the boy, "What's wrong?"

"It's Mr. Richardson, sir. His horses . . ." Johnny was breathless from his run to the office.

"Slow down," Coop ordered. "Now, what's happened to Mr. Richardson?"

"We don't know, sir. The horses came back without them. The harness was broken." He gulped. "Mrs. Edwards told me to come tell you!" Johnny handed Coop the note.

He read it quickly, then asked, "What time did they leave this morning?"

"It was right about nine o'clock, sir," he responded.

"What condition were the horses in when you found them?"

"They'd been runnin' real hard, sir."

"Thanks, Johnny." Coop's expression was worried as he dismissed the boy. When Johnny had gone, Coop turned to Kevin, "O'Riley, bring the wagon around. Tim!"

"Yes, Coop?" the main clerk asked.

"Tell Mr. Martin that I was called away on an emergency and that you are taking over in my absence."

"Sure. But what's wrong?"

"It looks like there's been an accident." Coop was heading out the door. "I'll be back as soon as I can."

* * *

398

As soon as the sound of the single rider's hoof-beats faded away, Price rolled to his side with a groan, hatred coursing through his body. He'd seen him! It had been Alex! With a muttered curse, he wiped the blood from his eyes and struggled to sit up, looking around for Ellyn.

"Ellyn!" Her name was a horrified whisper as he turned to her.

She lay pale and still, the back of her dress soaked with blood. The precarious position of the carriage forced Price to crawl as he moved to free her from the wreckage. Though his head was pounding and he felt dizzy and weak, he concentrated only on pulling her from beneath the ruined vehicle.

When he could stand, he carried her to a patch of cool, soft grass a short distance away and lay her down. On unsteady legs, he ran back to the buggy to get the blanket and a canteen.

Kneeling beside her, he ripped the blood-soaked dress from her injured shoulder. The gunshot wound was relatively clean, the bullet having passed completely through, but it was bleeding heavily. Tearing off two pieces of the blanket, he pressed them to the wound front and back hoping to staunch the flow of blood. The force he applied, helped and he took a minute to look around for something he could use to bind it. Remembering the table cloth they'd used at lunch, Price rushed to find their picnic basket. Sorting through the jumbled contents, he found the cloth and brought it back to Ellyn. Wrapping the length of it about her shoulder, he tied it tightly to keep pressure on the raw injury. Laying her gently back down, he covered her with the blanket as she moaned softly. Ellyn's eyes fluttered open and she frowned at the sight of him, covered with blood.

"Price?" His name was a whisper.

"I'm right here, my love." He smoothed her hair back from her forehead.

"You're hurt?" she asked weakly.

"Just a scratch." Amazed at her concern for him, he could barely speak.

Her eyes closed as she lost consciousness again and Price knew a moment of total panic. He had to get her back to town, but how? There had been no traffic on the road all morning and it would be hours before they were missed. Price wasn't sure that he could carry her the whole distance, but he knew that he had to try or take the risk of her dying here.

Searching through the basket once again, he pulled out the half-finished bottle of wine from their lunch. Tilting the bottle to his lips, he let the liquid burn down his throat and fortify him. Opening the canteen, he poured the rest of the wine in with the water for later. Then, slinging it over his shoulder, he went back to Ellyn.

Coop and Kevin rode anxiously along the River Road in search of Price and Ellyn, stopping to check anything that looked the least bit unusual. They had been out nearly an hour when Kevin shouted.

"Look!"

Ahead in the dust of the road a solitary man trudged forward, staggering under the weight of his burden.

"Thank, God!" Slapping the reins to the horses' backs, Coop urged them on.

Price knew he would have to rest soon. He'd been walking for what seemed an eternity and Ellyn's slight weight seemed to grow heavier with each step he took.

He looked down at her pale face resting against his

shoulder. She hadn't made a sound in all this time. A new determination surged through him and he pushed aside all thoughts of stopping. There would be no rest! Not until Ellyn was safe. Not until he had dealt with Alex. Putting one foot in front of the other he kept going, concentrating only on moving continuously closer to town.

The sound of his name being called jerked Price's head up and he focused with some difficulty on the vehicle coming toward him.

"Price!" It was Coop's voice.

Relief flooded through him and he swayed, dropping painfully to his knees, as the wagon came to a stop beside him. Coop and Kevin jumped down and ran to him.

"Let me take her," Coop offered and Price relinquished his hold on his cherished burden.

"Be careful. She's been shot," Price managed and then stood again with O'Riley's help.

"We'll get you right back to town," Coop said, laying Ellyn gently in the back of the wagon.

"Thanks," Price croaked, his throat tight with relief.

"Price and I will sit with her back here. You drive," he directed.

"Yes, sir," Kevin responded.

Coop gave Price a hand up as Kevin took the reins.

"I'll hold her," Price insisted and he took Ellyn across his lap in order to help absorb the bumps for her.

Kevin turned the wagon and they started back as quickly as the road would permit.

"How bad is she?" Coop asked.

"Shoulder wound, but the bullet went straight through. She's lost a lot of blood though."

"What happened? Who did it?"

Price looked up at his trusted friend, his expression guarded. "We were ambushed, and robbed. Whoever did it thought we were dead."

Coop nodded, sensing Price's reluctance to discuss it. "How's your head?"

"It looks worse than it is," he said, dismissing his friend's concern. Ellyn was all that mattered to him right now.

Alex pounded on Mary Anne's front door, eager to see her. As the maid opened it, he brushed past her.

"Where is Miss Montague?"

"Upstairs in her room, sir."

He started up the steps. "We are not to be disturbed."

"Yes, sir."

Alex didn't bother to knock on Mary Anne's bedroom door. Opening it without ceremony, he strolled in and found her sitting at her vanity, clad only in her dressing gown.

"Alex! You're back! What happened!"

He slanted a cocky smile at her. "Of course I'm back. I hope you weren't too concerned about me."

"How did it go?" Her eyes were feverishly bright, waiting for his news.

"There were a few tense moments, but it's over." He sat negligently on her bed.

"They're dead?" Mary Anne was astounded. Her color faded as she pictured Price—brutally slain—but then she brightened again as the thought of all his money excited her. "You really did it."

"Yes, I really did it," Alex mocked. "Come here and reward me."

Mary Anne got up and came to stand before him. And Alex, feeling dominant and masterful, ripped

402

the silken garment from her body and pulled her down on the bed. Rolling on top of her, he kissed her. Mary Anne sensed a viciousness in Alex that hadn't been there before as he claimed her body with hard, devouring kisses.

"You think I don't know how you felt?" he demanded, squeezing her breast painfully. "Ha! I've known all along that you expected me to fail. But I won this time! I did it! And you'll never have the opportunity to doubt me again! You or my mother!"

The feeling of power he'd experienced earlier returned, rushing through his body like a potent aphrodisiac. And he tore at his clothes, needing to be free to take her as his will dictated. Naked against her unresisting flesh, he wasted no time on Mary Anne's pleasure. This was his moment. *He* was successful.

Parting her legs, he forced his entry and was even more excited to find her wet and ready for him. Driving deep inside her, he climaxed almost immediately, his desire slaked for the moment.

Pushing away from her, he lay on his back, arms folded beneath his head.

"I'm hungry. Get me something to eat," he ordered and Mary Anne obeyed, wondering how to deal with this new Alex.

The ride seemed endless to Price as he cradled Ellyn close to him. There had been no change in her condition even as they reached the outskirts of town.

"Kevin, take us to my house," Price ordered. "Then get the doctor."

"Yes, sir," Kevin answered, glancing quickly at Coop who nodded in agreement.

As they pulled to a halt in front of Price's house, Coop jumped out first to help Price down.

"Get going, Kevin," Coop ordered as soon as Price had climbed down with Ellyn in his arms.

Kevin whipped his horses to a gallop and raced off in search of Dr. Webster.

Coop ran to open the front door for Price. Mrs. Edwards heard the commotion and came into the hall to see what was going on.

"Mr. Richardson, what's happened?" She was stricken by the sight of him carrying his unconscious wife.

"Mrs. Richardson's been injured. We've sent for the doctor," Coop explained as Price headed mutely up the steps with Ellyn in his arms.

"I'll turn the bed back," Mrs. Edwards announced and rushed ahead of Price to prepare the bedroom.

Price entered the room and gently laid Ellyn upon the bed. He stood looking down on her without speaking. His eyes burned with emotion and he shook as he fought to control the savage rage within him. Taking deep breaths to steady himself, he took charge.

"I'll undress her," he said. "Mrs. Edwards, we'll need clean sheets, bandages and hot water. Coop?"

"Yes, Price?"

"Could you send for Betsey?"

"Right away."

Mrs. Edwards and Coop left the room, closing the door behind them and Price calmly began to remove her clothing. When Mrs. Edwards returned with the sheets and soft bandages, Ellyn was already undressed and covered with a warm blanket.

"I'll stay here with her if you'd like to bathe, Mr. Richardson," Emily Edwards offered.

"No!" Price responded curtly. "I'm not leaving her. Where the hell is the doctor?"

404

"I'll wait for him downstairs. If you need anything . . ." Mrs. Edwards said nervously.

"Yes, yes, I'll call you." Price paced the room like a caged animal, walking from the bedside to the front window. After Coop knocked and entered, Price paused before him.

"I just sent Johnny to bring Betsey back."

"Good. But where's the damn doctor?" His voice was strangled. "Coop, if she dies . . ."

"Don't even think it!" Coop said tersely and Price moved away from him to stand by the bed.

"Here, sit down." Coop pulled up a chair for him. "Are you sure you don't want to get washed up? You look terrible."

"I don't want to leave her!"

"Then wash in here. If she wakes up and sees you all covered with blood, it might upset her."

Price considered this and relented. "You're right. Have Mrs. Edwards bring up some hot water."

"Sure." Coop left to tell the housekeeper.

A small movement drew his attention back to the bed and he hurried to Ellyn's side just as she opened her eyes.

"Oh, Ellyn." He dropped down on his knees beside her. "Sweetheart."

She reached up weakly to touch his temple. "Your head . . ."

"I'm fine." He took her hand and kissed it. "How do you feel?"

"Awful," she spoke in a whisper.

There was a knock at the door and Dr. Webster entered followed by Coop and Mrs. Edwards.

"Dr. Webster, thank God you're here." Price stood up and shook hands with the older man.

The doctor took off his jacket and rolled up his sleeves. Washing his hands in the water that Mrs.

405

Edwards had brought for Price, he moved to examine Ellyn.

"Would you please leave the room?" he asked.

Coop and Mrs. Edwards complied, but Price refused.

"I'm staying."

"All right, but keep out of my way," the doctor ordered.

Price moved away from the bed as Dr. Webster set to work. Ellyn drifted in and out of consciousness as the physician's hands probed, then cleaned the wound. As he was bandaging her shoulder, Price spoke.

"How bad is it?"

"The wound itself is not fatal, but she's lost a lot of blood." Dr. Webster looked down to find Ellyn's eyes upon him. "Hello, young lady. Feeling better?"

Ellyn started to speak, but her eyes suddenly filled with fear as a pain seized her and she clutched at her abdomen. "My baby!"

"She's pregnant?"

"Yes, but . . ."

"How far along?"

"Just a few months." Price was worried.

Dr. Webster strode to the door, opened it, and called for Coop.

"Mr. Cooper, please take Mr. Richardson downstairs and fix him a drink. Have Mrs. Edwards come up. I may need her help."

"Let me help," Price insisted.

"Get him out of here," the older man spoke sternly.

Coop took Price almost forcefully out into the hall as the doctor closed and locked the door behind him.

Alex finished eating the huge meal Mary Anne had

served him in bed and put the dishes on the night stand.

"That was delicious," he told her, belching loudly. "What time is it?"

"Almost four."

"Is that all? Come here then, but take off that gown first."

Mary Anne stripped off the gown and sat beside him on the bed.

"Proud of me?"

"Of course."

"And well you should be," he told her as he idly toyed with her breasts. "Things will be different now."

"Oh?" Mary Anne was curious.

"You'll see." And he pushed her back on the bed giving her no time to take control of the situation.

Rachel walked to the front parlor window for the third time in the past five minutes. Where was he? It was 4:30 and she hadn't heard a word from him all day. Angrily stalking back to the sofa, she sat down and picked up the book she'd been reading. He had to show up soon. And if he didn't, well, she wouldn't think about that right now.

Price strode impatiently about the study. What was going on up there? Why had the doctor thrown him out? Was Ellyn losing the baby?

"Here." Coop handed him a double bourbon straight.

"Thanks." He drank it silently, then walked to the study door to look up the stairs.

"Betsey should be here soon," Coop commented, hoping to distract Price. But Price wasn't listening to him.

"You don't think Ellyn's dying, do you?" Price asked, imagining the worst.

"No!"

Price looked up at Coop's forceful answer, his face reflecting his torment. "Why else would he send me out?"

"I think with the shooting and all . . . well, she may be losing the baby."

Price turned away from his friend. Coop's thoughts had only confirmed his own.

The front door opened and Betsey rushed in unannounced. Coop heard her and moved to the doorway to beckon her in.

"What's happened, Coop?" She looked worriedly up at her husband.

"There's been a shooting. The doctor's with Ellyn now."

"What?" she was horrified. "Where's Price?"

"In here," Coop began and Betsey entered the study to see him standing by the window, his clothes blood-stained, his manner tense.

She went straight to him, putting a gentle hand on his arm. "Price."

"Oh, Betsey." His voice was full of anguish.

"Are you well?" She stared up at his haggard features.

"I guess," he answered numbly.

"Sit down, I want to look at your head," she instructed and he obeyed.

"Coop, get me some water in a bowl and a washrag, please." Then, turning her attention back to Price, she ordered, "Price, take off that shirt."

Mechanically, he unbuttoned it and Betsey took it from him.

"How did this happen? I want to know everything," she said firmly, sitting down next to him.

"We were coming back on the River Road—right about noon—and we were ambushed. I don't remember much of anything. I guess I was hit first." He shuddered as he recalled the sudden, shattering pain. "When I came to someone was going through my pockets, so I pretended to be dead until I heard them ride away."

"You didn't get a look at them?"

"No," he lied.

"Do you have any idea how many there were?"

"No," he lied again.

"And Ellyn, she was shot too?"

"In the shoulder. She's lost a lot of blood."

"He was carrying her when I found them," Coop added as he came back in with the water, towels and washcloths.

"There was no other way. I didn't think we'd be missed until tonight."

"What happened to your horses?"

"They broke free and our buggy ran off the road." Price looked up at Betsey, his dark eyes filled with pain. "I didn't know Coop was coming. I had to try. She would have bled to death if I'd just stayed there waiting."

"I know." Betsey put her arms around him. "She'll be fine. I'm certain of it."

Price hugged her tightly as he attempted to master all of his conflicting emotions again. Under control once more, he released her and sat back.

"Hold still while I wash this blood off." She wet the cloth in the basin of warm water and laid it on the dried blood on his forehead. "Coop, can you go find him a clean shirt?"

"In the dressing room," Price directed.

Coop left the room while his wife examined Price's injury.

409

"It looks worse than it is," she told him, rinsing the cloth and wiping at the blood again.

"I know."

"Do you want to finish? I've cleaned the wound and it's stopped bleeding," she asked, knowing he didn't like being fussed over.

"Yes. Thanks, Betsey."

"Go over by the mirror so you can see what you're doing," she instructed.

Price hadn't looked at himself before now, and he finally understood why Coop had insisted he get cleaned up. He looked positively ghoulish. Scrubbing vigorously, he washed off all traces of blood. As Coop came back in, he handed Price a clean shirt.

"Did you hear anything?"

"No," Coop told him. "The bedroom door was still shut."

"Oh." He pulled on the shirt.

"You look much better now."

"Thanks." Fastening his buttons, he moved wearily to the doorway, looking up the stairs anxiously once again.

Coop gave Betsey a concerned look and she took the hint.

"Come sit down. Coop will get you another drink." She took his arm and led him over to the sofa again. "Do you want me to put a bandage on that?"

"No," he said absently as he sat down next to her and took another bourbon. "Damn!" he exploded. "Why don't they come down and tell me something!"

Mary Anne lay beside Alex, amazed and pleased by the changes in him. Their lovemaking had been fierce and passionate. Alex had been in total control

410

for the first time and she'd found it a novel experience. She had never expected him to become so aggressive, but the results were very satisfying.

He moved away from her and sat up on the side of the bed.

"You're leaving?"

"I haven't told Mother the good news yet."

"I'll come with you."

"All right. That's a good idea. We can celebrate."

"I'll send your husband right up," Dr. Webster offered, looking down with concern at Ellyn's pale, strained features.

"Please," she murmured.

When he'd gone, Ellyn turned her head away from Mrs. Edwards's sympathetic gaze. "I'd like to be alone for a few minutes."

"Of course. Can I bring you anything?" She wanted to help Ellyn, but she wasn't sure how.

"No. Thank you," Ellyn replied faintly.

Mrs. Edwards left the room as quietly as possible.

When the door closed and she was alone at last, her composure broke. A sad, frightened cry of misery escaped her and she sobbed wildly, mourning the loss of her unborn child, the baby she had delighted in, the baby she would never hold in her arms. When she finally quieted, she felt drained and lifeless. Where was Price? She needed his comforting presence and the warmth of his love. Sighing heavily, she stared listlessly about the bedroom, trying to ignore the pain in her shoulder and in her heart.

At the sound of firm footfalls on the stairs, Price ran into the hall.

"Dr. Webster, how is she?"

"Is there somewhere we can go to talk?" the

411

physician asked solemnly.

"Why?" he worried. "She's not dead?"

"No, no, but I do need to speak with you privately." His tone was grim.

Price breathed a deep sigh of relief. "We can go in the parlor."

"Please."

Price led the way and the older man followed, pausing only to put his bag on the hall table.

"Would you like me to look at your wound?"

"No," he answered curtly. "I'm fine. Or at least I will be once you tell me how Ellyn is."

"She's very weak right now, but I have every hope that she'll make a full recovery," he said seriously. "I do have some bad news for you."

Price looked up sharply, his relief short-lived. "What?"

"She's lost the baby. The trauma of the gunshot wound and the loss of blood were just too much for her."

"Oh, no," he protested, his voice hoarse with emotion.

"I'm sorry. There were no complications, though. So there's no reason you can't have other children," he explained gently, trying to somehow soften this painful blow.

"And Ellyn, how is she taking it?" Price jaw was tight as he struggled for control.

"She's very ill, and this has upset her tremendously." Dr. Webster paused studying Price. "She'll need you to be strong."

Price nodded and turned away. He couldn't respond, not yet. The doctor, in understanding, left the room, closing the door behind him.

Finally alone, Price leaned against the mantel sobbing quietly to himself. He couldn't break down.

Not now. He had to help Ellyn, to support her. He took several deep breaths and, bracing himself for the scene to come, left the room.

Betsey and Coop had been waiting to talk to the doctor and they met him on his way out of the parlor.

"Dr. Webster? Can you tell us how Ellyn is?" Coop asked, grief and worry showing plainly in his and Betsey's faces.

"She's out of immediate danger, but still very weak. She lost so much blood."

"What about the child?"

"I'm sorry, there was nothing I could do."

Coop put his arms around Betsey as she swayed faintly.

"Oh, Coop. They so wanted that baby," she cried tearfully as she clung to him.

"She'll be all right, though?"

"Yes. There were no complications."

"Thank God."

"I've left some laudanum with Mrs. Edwards in case Mrs. Richardson is in any pain."

"Dr. Webster, we can't thank you enough." Coop shook his hand.

"No thanks are needed. But tell me, how did this happen?"

"They were ambushed and robbed on the River Road. And whoever did it left them for dead."

The doctor was concerned. "Have you gone to the sheriff yet?"

"No. Price has been too upset to leave her. I'm sure he'll go as soon as he's sure Ellyn's going to be all right."

"Good. Something this vicious needs to be reported. See that he does it," he said earnestly. "I'll

413

be by again tomorrow to check on her."

"Thank you, Dr. Webster." They saw him to the door.

Rachel saw Mary Anne's carriage arrive and hurried to open the door.

"You're here! At last! I've been desperate for news. What happened?" she asked hurrying them inside into the sitting room.

"It took longer than I anticipated, but it's done."

"They're dead? Both of them?" Rachel's eyes widened in excitement.

Alex nodded proudly. "I knew you would be pleased. Mary Anne certainly was." He smiled slyly at his fiancee.

"Tell me about it. I want to know everything," she demanded eagerly.

"Well," Alex began, pouring himself a stiff drink and going to sit next to Mary Anne on the sofa, "I trailed them all morning but I didn't get a chance to shoot until they were on their way back."

"Where did you do it?" Rachel wanted all the details.

"This side of the Piasa—about half an hour out, I guess." He took a deep drink. "It was perfect. Two shots. The first got Price in the head. The second got her in the back."

"And you're sure they are dead?" Rachel insisted.

"I even got his money." He nodded and tossed the wad of bills with Price's money clip on the table. "Their horses panicked and ran and broke free of the harness. Then the buggy ran off the road and crashed into some trees. It was all quite bloody."

"I wonder how long it will take for his estate to be settled," Rachel voiced her greedy thoughts aloud.

"Not too long, I hope." Alex smiled confidently

at them. "I have plans."

Long minutes after the doctor had gone, Price came out of the parlor, his expression bleak. Somehow, he had managed to pull himself together and now he had to help Ellyn. Pushing aside his own grief, he headed toward the stairs.

Betsey and Coop had been listening for him. When she heard him in the hall, she rushed out to him while Coop hung back, lingering in the study doorway.

"Price?"

"Did you speak with the doctor?"

Betsey nodded sadly. "Yes, we did."

"Then you know . . . everything." Price's voice was strained.

"What can we do to help you?"

"Betsey, I don't know," he groaned, glancing up the stairs as Mrs. Edwards came out of the bedroom. "I've got to go to her. Will you stay? She may need you."

"We'll stay," she promised.

Price hugged her quickly and then hurried on upstairs.

"She wants to see you," the housekeeper told him as he reached the top of the stairs.

"Thank you. Would you see to it that Mr. and Mrs. Cooper have everything they need?"

"Yes, sir," she replied and continued on down to look after the guests.

Price stopped in front of the door and took a deep breath before entering.

Ellyn sighed as she stared unseeingly about the room. She was worried about Price. Where was he? Why didn't he come? Had his injuries been more serious than they had originally thought? She looked up anxiously as the bedroom door opened.

Price stood hesitantly, his hand still resting on the doorknob. He was, for the first time in their relationship, at a loss. What should he say? Do? His nerves were stretched taut as he looked at her. His heart ached as he noted the pallor of her complexion. She looked so fragile and delicate and trusting. All he wanted to do was to protect her from more hurt.

"Price!" she cried his name urgently, needing his arms around her.

Her call spurred him to action and he came to her side after shutting the door behind him.

"Darling." He stood there rather helplessly, wondering what to say until she took his hand. "How do you feel?"

"Tired." She tried to smile. "Sit by me."

He started to get a chair, but she stopped him.

"Here." She shifted on the bed and made room for him next to her.

Price sat down slowly, not wanting to disturb her.

"How's your head?" she questioned.

He lifted a hand experimentally to the slight wound at his temple. "All right, I guess. I haven't had much time to think about it."

"You got cleaned up." She knew that she was babbling, but she found it difficult to broach what was most important between them.

"I looked pretty bad and Betsey insisted." His mouth twisted as he tried to smile.

"Betsey's here?" Ellyn brightened.

"She's waiting downstairs with Coop."

"They are such good friends." She blinked back tears. Finally the words came out in a whispered rush. "Did you talk with Dr. Webster?"

"Yes . . . Ellyn . . ." His voice cracked as his

416

carefully controlled emotions flooded through him. "Ellyn, I'm so sorry! I know how much this baby meant to you."

"Oh, Price!" she was crying. "I wanted your baby so much!"

He held her then, tenderly. Taking care not to jar her heavily bandaged shoulder. He was surprised when Ellyn clung to him with all her strength and he relished the feel of her so warm and alive in his arms.

Ellyn held fast to him, never wanting to let him go. Tears fell unheeded as she pressed against his strong chest. It was a time of mutual need, each drawing on the other's strength and love to help them through the ordeal.

He rocked her gently, soothing her, trying to convince her that everything would be all right—and in the process convince himself.

When she finally relaxed against him, he kissed her forehead and lay her back down on the pillows with infinite care.

"You'd better rest now. We don't want your shoulder to open up again."

Ellyn nodded wearily, but managed a loving smile. "I love you. God, when you were shot and I thought you were dying—it was terrible."

He lifted her hand and kissed her palm, curling her fingers closed over it.

"I know. When I came to and you were bleeding so heavily, I was desperate."

"How did we get back?"

"The horses ran back here and Mrs. Edwards sent word to Coop. Coop and Kevin came looking for us."

Ellyn nodded. "Do you think I could see them for a few minutes?"

"Sure. They're anxious to see you, too." He bent

to kiss her softly. "I'll go get them."

Ellyn smiled as he rose and left the room. Moments later, Betsey peeked in.

"Are you sure you feel up to this?" she questioned.

"Absolutely. Come on in. Is Coop coming up?"

"In a minute. I think they wanted to give us a little time alone," Betsey confided. "Are you in any pain?"

"My shoulder still hurts, but the doctor gave me some laudanum just before he left. I guess that's why I'm so sleepy."

Betsey pulled up a chair to the bedside.

"Do you know about the baby?" Ellyn asked.

"Yes, the doctor told us. I'm sorry."

"So am I. But Dr. Webster said there was no reason why I couldn't have others." Her words were full of hope.

"Good." Betsey laid a hand on her arm. "Can I do anything for you? Is there anything you need?"

"No. I just need to rest. But tell me, how is Price really?"

"He's all right now, but he was very upset earlier. The doctor didn't tell him anything, he just threw him out of the room when you started to miscarry."

"Oh, no." Ellyn's heart swelled with love for him.

"He was afraid you were dying. Coop managed to keep him halfway calm."

Ellyn nodded her understanding. "It's a good thing Coop came after us, or we might both be dead."

They fell silent for a time, thinking of the horror of the day just passed.

"When are you going to the sheriff?"

"Maybe tomorrow," Price replied evasively as he

418

and Coop shared another bourbon.

"Why wait? I'll go with you now if you want."

In a rare display of temper, Price flared at his friend, "Don't push me! I'll go when I'm damn good and ready!"

Coop was totally stunned and unable to understand Price's reaction. Surely he wanted to see the gunman caught? Coop watched him through narrowed eyes, trying to figure his reasoning.

Price stood at the window, staring out at the river. In contrast to its deceptively placid appearance this morning, the Mississippi was showing its true colors this afternoon. The water was brown and ugly as it surged roughly by on its never-ending race to the sea.

"True colors," Price thought, applied to more than just the river. But how was he going to handle this? He understood everything now. Even the fire at ATC. It all fit together. The motive was money and Alex was the conniving bastard who'd planned it all. Who else would be cowardly enough to ambush him or hit him from behind?

Feeling Coop's eyes upon him, Price forced an apologetic smile.

"I didn't mean to fly at you like that. It's just that I don't want to leave Ellyn yet." He searched for something more convincing. "Besides, whoever did it is long gone by now."

Coop shrugged. "Don't worry about it."

He sensed something was troubling Price but as touchy as he was, Coop let it go.

"Why don't we go on up?" Price suggested

Coop's probing look had made him nervous and he had to be careful. He didn't want Coop involved in any of this.

"How are you feeling?" Price asked, coming to

419

Ellyn's side.

"A little better since I got to talk with Betsey. Hi, Coop." She gave them a weak smile.

Coop came to her and kissed her cheek. "I'm glad you're going to be all right."

Betsey, knowing how tired Ellyn was, stood up. "We're going to go, but I'll check on you later. And Price, if there's anything you need, just let us know."

Price hugged her. "I will, Betsey. Thank you."

"Thanks for everything," Ellyn said sincerely.

Price saw Coop and Betsey out and then returned to Ellyn. She appeared to be sleeping, but when he came closer to the bed, she looked up at him.

"I'm not asleep, I was just resting."

"Go ahead and sleep. I was just checking to see if you wanted anything."

"Only your love," she whispered.

"You've got it." He kissed her, fighting down the desire to hold her tightly to him and never let her go. "I'll be right downstairs if you need me."

She smiled at him tenderly. "I'll always need you, you know."

"I know." He took her hand and squeezed it reassuringly. "Rest well."

Ellyn closed her eyes and sighed as Price left the room.

Chapter Eighteen

The late-afternoon sun slanted through the study windows as Price sat grimly at his desk. Indecision had immobilized him. He had been struggling with his situation for over an hour and still had no solution. All he knew was that he had to act and act fast.

Roughly pushing away from the desk, he stood and strode from the room.

"I'm going out for a while. I won't be long," he told Mrs. Edwards when he located her in the kitchen.

"Any message for Mrs. Richardson if she should call for you?"

"No. Just tell her I'll be back within the hour."

"Yes, sir."

Saddling his own mount, he rode into town to Barlow's office. Though the shades were drawn, the clerk recognized him and let him in.

"I'm running late today, but I appreciate your seeing me," he greeted Barlow.

They shook hands. "Please have a seat while I find your file."

Price sat uncomfortably in the chair, too tense to

remain still for long.

"Here it is. All ready for your signature." The attorney presented him with a sheaf of papers. "If you'll sign where I've X-ed on each page, we'll have George, here, witness them and everything will be completed."

Price hurriedly scribbled his name on each copy of the will.

"I'm finished." He handed the papers to the office clerk, who also signed them.

Barlow looked them over carefully and then gave Price his copy.

"It's legal and binding as of now?"

"Right."

"That's what I wanted to be sure of," he remarked cryptically. "Thanks for everything, Mr. Barlow."

"You're more than welcome." He walked Price to the door. "By the way, congratulations on your marriage."

"Thank you, sir. I'll be seeing you later." Price left the office feeling that he'd wasted too much time. He had to hurry. It would be dark soon.

It was almost dusk when he returned to the house. Going straight to his desk, he put the will in a big envelope and marked, "ELLYN" on the outside and then left it in his top drawer. Just in case . . .

Price climbed the stairs quietly, not wanting to disturb her if she was sleeping. Entering the bedroom silently he found the drapes drawn and he had to move closer to the bed to make out Ellyn's sleeping form. He stood over her in the semidarkness, staring at her, memorizing everything about her—the darkness of her hair spread out on the pillow, the curve of her lips softly parted in sleep.

When his gaze fell to the awkward dressing on her shoulder, the loving tenderness he'd been feeling froze. From the depths of his soul, his long-contained rage was loosed, burning away all of his gentler emotions and driving him on in his desire for revenge. His expression hardened with intent. She was safe and she would recover. Now, he would finish what Alex had started. Turning abruptly, he quit the room.

He made his way, without conscious thought, back to the study and got his gun from the gun case. He sat at the desk and cleaned it thoroughly, checking and rechecking every part. Then, as he finished, he loaded it, sliding the bullets smoothly into their chambers.

Mrs. Edwards gave a brief knock at the door and, at his call to enter, came into the room bearing his dinner on a tray.

"I've brought you something to eat, Mr. Richardson."

Price looked up from his work on the revolver. "Just set it over by the liquor cabinet."

"Yes, sir. Did you want anything else?"

"No," he said abruptly.

"Yes, sir." She was puzzled by the change in him. Since the Coopers had left, he'd been silent and reclusive—a far cry from his normal behavior. Not wanting to disturb him any further, she quietly backed out of the room and shut the door.

Mrs. Edwards was almost back to the kitchen when she heard someone at the front door. Answering it, she admitted Coop and Betsey.

"He's in the study. I'm sure it'll be fine if you go right on in."

"Thanks, Mrs. Edwards." They casually walked in on Price.

"Alex, you bastard," Price muttered, sighting down the barrel of his rifle as the door opened unexpectedly. "What the hell?"

"We're back." Betsey smiled, but stopped short as she found him sighting down the barrel of a rifle.

"Oh, Betsey." Quickly covering his resentment with a smile, he put the rifle down. "That was fast."

"It's been four hours. We were worried and we just wanted to make sure that you two were all right."

"As you can see, I'm fine." He sounded almost sarcastic and Coop looked at him questioningly.

Price fended off Coop's searching eyes with another easy smile. "Mrs. Edwards just brought dinner; you want to join me?"

"No, thanks. We've eaten already," Betsey answered. "You go ahead, though. Don't let us stop you."

Betsey, too, sensed something was wrong but she couldn't decide what.

"Is Ellyn still sleeping?" Coop asked.

"Yes, I just checked on her. She fell asleep right after you left. I guess the medicine the doctor gave her is working."

"Well, sleep is the best thing for her right now." Price nodded, trying to be pleasant, but desperately wishing they'd leave. His thoughts were full of Alex—and hate. He wanted to concentrate on what he had to do and not sit here making small talk.

"Are you feeling all right?" Betsey asked, wondering if his wound was beginning to bother him.

"I'm fine," he emphasized the words. "Don't I look well?"

"You seem tense tonight," Betsey ventured, trying to draw him out, but he refused her overtures.

"I'm just tired," he said flatly.

"We'll go then," Coop stated firmly, stopping Betsey's efforts to find out what was troubling him. "If you need us, just send word."

"Right." He followed them to the door, barely returning their goodbyes, and shut it firmly the minute they were outside.

Betsey looked up at Coop more than a little perturbed. "What was wrong with him?"

"I don't know," Coop answered thoughtfully. "But something is very wrong."

Coop had known Price since childhood and in all those years, he'd never seen him like this. Not even during the war.

"What can we do?"

"Nothing. He has to work whatever it is out on his own. When he wants us to know, he'll tell us."

Betsey knew Coop was right, but it didn't stop her worrying. She had seen the look on his face when he'd been sighting that rifle. Coop hadn't.

Price closeted himself in the study once more, laying out his side arm and the rifle he planned to take. It was dark now, he noted with satisfaction. It was time. He started to strap on his gunbelt and then stopped. He wanted to see Ellyn one more time before he went after Alex.

Exiting the study, he went upstairs and entered their bedroom, leaving the hall door open so he could see.

"Price?" she spoke softly.

"Let me light a lamp for you." He made his way to the mantel and, striking a match, lit the lamp. "That's better."

He brought it to her bedside and put it on the small table nearby.

425

"Are you feeling any better?" he asked as he sat next to her on the bed.

"I feel a little stronger, but my shoulder really hurts."

"Do you want some of the medicine that the doctor left for you?" he questioned again, his concern obvious.

"Maybe later. Right now, I just want to talk to you for a while."

Price leaned over her and kissed her welcoming lips. They parted for him softly, but he drew away.

"This is an awful way for our honeymoon to end," Ellyn complained, knowing that it was the injury that caused his reluctance.

"Our honeymoon is far from over, pretty lady. It's just been postponed for a while."

"Good." She was pleased by his statement. "That gives me something to look forward to."

The night was dark and the summer-sweet breeze was cooling as it stirred the bedroom drapes. The flickering of the mellow lamplight softened all harshness as Price knew a moment of pure, unselfish love so profound that it overwhelmed him. Reaching out with a shaking hand, he touched her cheek.

"I love you so much."

Her eyes widened with emotion as she read his expression accurately. "And I love you."

As if in slow motion, he bent to her again, their mouths joining in a searing caress that shattered their composure.

"Oh, Price," Ellyn breathed, "I wouldn't want to go on without you."

She was crying as she kissed him again, her response to him surprising him. Price drew away once more.

"You're too much of a temptation." He smiled at

her and she was glad that his mood was lighter. He'd seemed so solemn when he'd first come in to see her.

"Will you sleep with me tonight?"

"I think it best if I wait a day or two to make sure you're healing properly," he explained.

"Do you really think it's necessary?"

"Yes, I do. I want you well again as soon as possible."

"All right, but I'm not going to like it."

"Just a few nights, Ellyn. Then we'll have a lifetime."

She raised luminous, love-filled eyes to his. "Kiss me."

And he did, but only a chaste one, before standing to leave.

"I have to meet Coop over at the office tonight, so I'll be gone for a few hours," he lied.

"This late?"

"I insisted, because I wanted to see you again before I went. I didn't want you to wake up and find me gone."

"Oh. Well, please hurry back."

"I will. You know it's important, or I'd never leave you."

"I know."

He kissed her fleetingly and headed for the door. "I'll send Mrs. Edwards up with your medication—and I'll be back before you know it."

"All right. I love you."

"I love you."

And he was gone.

Rachel sat back comfortably and observed Alex and Mary Anne as they sat on the sofa. She'd noticed a definite change in Mary Anne's attitude toward her son this afternoon—as if he had finally earned her respect.

"Dinner was marvelous, Mother," Alex complimented her.

"Thank you, dear. It was special. Just as this day has been special."

"It's been a wonderful day," Mary Anne agreed, giving Alex a smoldering look.

"I'm glad you both enjoyed it. Now, if you'll excuse me, I'm going upstairs for a few minutes."

"Of course." Alex rose as Rachel left the room, giving him time alone with Mary Anne.

Alex sat back down and pulled her against him, slipping a hand into the bodice of her dress.

"I've been wanting to do this for hours." He pushed the offensive material aside and sucked hungrily at one exposed breast while his hand fondled the other.

Mary Anne took the opportunity to daydream about the riches to come. Her fantasies and her body's delights blended together in her mind. When Alex slid his hand up under her skirts, she arched in invitation.

"How long will she be gone?" Mary Anne asked excitedly.

"Long enough," he spoke gruffly as he freed himself from his pants and, bunching her skirts about her waist, thrust avidly inside her.

The illicitness of the act, so openly performed, excited Mary Anne and she responded wantonly, climaxing almost immediately beneath his driving, determined body. Alex, too, reached satisfaction quickly and moved away, taking no time to linger on her slim, pliant body. Rachel would be returning shortly.

Mary Anne straightened her skirts and bodice,

looking cool and composed once again. Alex had made himself presentable and had gone to the liquor cabinet for a drink when he heard his mother's footsteps in the hall.

"Now that was what I call a celebration," Mary Anne whispered to Alex.

Alex smiled wickedly at her as he turned to greet his mother.

"Coop, something is not right! I can feel it," Betsey declared as they entered their own house. "Couldn't you just go back and talk to Price. Maybe he'd tell you what was troubling him?"

"No, Betsey. I'm not going to interfere."

She gave him a frustrated look and stalked away, leaving him standing in the hall.

Price strapped on his gun belt, picked up his rifle, and left the house for the stables. He had already told Mrs. Edwards about his meeting with Coop and sent her on up to Ellyn with the laudanum that the doctor had prescribed, so he knew there was no one to see him go.

He saddled his horse efficiently, his mind focused only on his upcoming confrontation with Alex. Riding as quietly as possible from the house, he rode to Rachel's by way of the dark back streets. He tied up the horse and went to the lighted parlor window and looked in. The sight that greeted him, first stunned him and then nauseated him.

Mary Anne lay sprawled beneath Alex on the sofa, her clothes in disarray, as he thrust rhythmically into her. When Alex had finished and moved away, Mary Anne spoke.

"That's what I call a celebration."

Her words burned into his mind as he saw his

money clip lying on the table. They were celebrating! Celebrating his death!

With fury in every movement, he searched for and found an open window and climbed in unobserved.

"Betsey, you shouldn't be so worried. Price is only trying to adjust to everything that happened today," Coop tried to explain. "I'm sure he didn't mean to be sharp with you."

"Coop!" she said in exasperation, "it has nothing to do with that."

"Well, what is it then?"

"Didn't you see him when we first went into the study?"

"No, why?"

"He was sighting down a rifle and mumbling something about Alex. And, Coop, he had the most vicious look on his face."

"Alex?" Coop was confused. "Why would Price even be thinking of him?" Slowly, a dawning took place, and he looked worriedly at Betsey. "I'll be back as soon as I can!"

Coop raced from the house, hoping he was wrong but knowing in his heart that he was right. Alex had done it all. No wonder Price had refused to go to the sheriff. It had been his own cousin trying to kill him and he wanted to settle it by himself. Coop jumped in the carriage and raced off for Price's house. He had to stop him before he did anything foolish.

Pounding on the door, Mrs. Edwards opened it quickly.

"Mr. Cooper, what is it? I thought Mr. Richardson was supposed to meet you at the office."

"He what?"

"He just told Mrs. Richardson and myself that

430

you were meeting him at the ATC office and that he'd be back in a few hours."

"How long ago did he leave?"

"It's only been about ten minutes or so."

"Thanks, Mrs. Edwards," Coop called as he hurried back to the buggy.

Travelling as fast as he could, Coop raced toward Rachel's house.

Price entered through the dining room and made his way cautiously to the hall door. He had just heard Rachel returning to the parlor and knew that it was the perfect time to join their little celebration. Knowing Alex to be unarmed, Price didn't bother to draw his gun, but walked stealthily down the hall. Then in one motion, he stepped into the doorway, leaned negligently against the jamb and folded his arms easily across his chest.

"So this is a family celebration, of sorts, and I wasn't invited?" His low voice cut through the trivialities they'd been discussing and brought a stunned silence to the room.

"Oh, my God!" Mary Anne whispered and fell back in a dead faint.

"She never was big on surprises," Price mocked, his eyes piercing Alex. "Do you always celebrate so vigorously, *cousin?*"

Alex paled at Price's words. "What are you doing here?"

"I suppose you would wonder about that." He glanced at Rachel who stood open-mouthed by the mantel. "Since you never expected to see me *alive* again, I emphasize alive for I'm sure you would have dutifully come to my funeral and mourned with the best of them . . ."

"I don't know what you are talking about," Alex

denied nervously.

"Would you like me to refresh your memory?" Price tensed, his hand resting on his revolver, as Alex shifted his position to help Mary Anne, who was stirring. "Don't move too quickly. It won't pain me in the least to shoot you right now."

Alex gulped.

"By the way, why don't you toss my money clip over here. Your lies might have been believable if I hadn't seen it earlier, through the window."

Alex moved smoothly and threw it at Price's feet. In one easy motion, Price picked it up and put it in his pocket.

"I thought you were dead," Alex snarled, feeling humiliated now that Mary Anne was conscious again.

"Obviously, and not from a lack of trying on your part. But, Alex, you always were a fool. Even as children, you never did anything right," Price sneered.

"Why you!" Alex flew at him, hoping to redeem himself in Mary Anne's and Rachel's eyes.

Price met him, blow for punishing blow. His lean build gave him the advantage over Alex's slower, fatter bulk. There was no real contest as they grappled, Price easily knocking Alex to the floor. Tired of the game he'd been playing, he drew his gun.

Eyes narrowed in hate, he clicked the hammer, letting his fury feed his desire to kill.

"You not only tried to destroy my business, you injured my wife and murdered my unborn child," he ground out savagely.

Only the sudden commotion in the hall stopped Price from pulling the trigger. He glanced up to see Coop in the doorway.

"What the hell are you doing here?" he snarled.

"Put the gun down, Price. We'll take him to the sheriff."

"Get out of here and let me shoot him. I should have done it years ago."

"Coop, do something!" Rachel and Mary Anne cried.

"Shut up!" Price took careful aim at Alex's cowering form.

"Price! You are not thinking straight." Coop tried to reason with him. "If you shoot him in cold blood, you'll be the one to pay—no matter what he's done. Think! Ellyn needs you!"

Price finally began to hear the logic in Coop's words and wavered. "I want him dead!"

"Let the sheriff have him. He'll see justice done," Coop said, keeping his voice calm.

Logic replacing primitive instincts, he holstered his gun and turned toward Coop. In that instant Rachel moved, tossing Alex the small derringer she kept hidden on the mantel. In that split second, catching Alex's furtive movements out of the corner of their vision, Price and Coop both ducked. Price drew and fired automatically as Alex's bullets splintered the woodwork where their heads had been moments before. The force of Price's shots slammed Alex to the floor, leaving a gaping bloody hole in his chest.

"Alex!" Rachel knelt by her fatally injured son, all her hopes and dreams dying with him.

Coop and Price looked at each dazedly and slowly stood back up. It had all happened so fast.

Mary Anne sat sobbing on the sofa, her face buried in her hands, as Rachel's servant rushed to the room.

"Send for the sheriff. Now!" Coop ordered tersely and the maid ran from the house.

* * *

It was late, well past midnight, as Price and Coop sat in the study, doing justice to a bottle of aged bourbon.

"I'm glad it's over," Price stated flatly.

"Once Rachel and Mary Anne clear out . . ." Coop let the sentence drop. Price had given them one week to get out of town or else he would turn them over to the sheriff as Alex's accomplices.

"They'll go. There's nothing left for them here."

"Will you tell Ellyn?"

"I'll have to."

Coop nodded. "Betsey's probably in hysterics by now. I rushed out of the house like a madman."

"Coop, I appreciate what you did tonight."

Coop shrugged it off, smiling. "We've got a business to run. I couldn't afford to lose my partner."

Price smiled crookedly. "Thanks. How did you figure out where I was?"

"It was all Betsey."

"Betsey?"

"She started on me the minute we left your house, wanting to know what was wrong. She practically begged me to go back and talk to you, but I put her off. I didn't want to pester you, because I knew when you were ready, you would tell me." He stopped to take a drink. "So, I ignored her until she mentioned your mumbling Alex's name as we walked in on you. It all came together then."

"She knows me too well." Price grinned.

"She loves you and she was worried." Coop drained his drink. "I guess I'd better head home and let her know you're all right."

Price stood as Coop rose to leave and they walked into the hall together.

"I'll be by sometime tomorrow. And I'm sure

Betsey will want to visit with Ellyn."

"Any time is fine."

"Goodnight."

Betsey was in bed but wide awake when she heard her husband's return. Jumping up, she met him at the top of the staircase.

"Where have you been? I've been so worried that I almost came looking for you! Is Price all right?"

"Everything is fine." Coop took her in his arms and hugged her.

"You're sure?"

"Positive. You were right, you know."

"What do you mean?"

"Alex was the one who ambushed Price and Ellyn."

"Oh, my God!" She was stunned. "Alex?"

"Yes. He's the one who was hiding upstairs at the office, too."

"And Price knew?"

"Not until today. After Alex shot them, he came down to steal Price's money and make it look like a robbery. That's when Price got a look at him."

"So he'd known all day that it was Alex. And he was just waiting for the chance to go after him?" Betsey shivered. "No wonder he was like a stranger to me. What happened? Did you catch up with him?"

"Over at Rachel's. He was about to shoot Alex when I got there and I managed to talk him out of it. It was pretty tense for a while. And Rachel was so stupid. She threw Alex a gun. Price shot him in self-defense."

Betsey listened in amazement. "But why? For money?"

"Yes. They wanted it all. Even Mary Anne was in

on it." Coop started to undress as they entered their bedroom.

"Mary Anne?" Betsey was shocked. "I knew she was jealous of Ellyn, but . . ."

"Price told Rachel and Mary Anne, both, that they had a week to get out of town or he was going to turn them in to the sheriff."

Betsey was completely surprised. "What about Alex? Is he dead?"

Coop nodded as he blew out the lamp and came to her in the darkness of the night.

"Next time I don't listen to you, remind me of tonight. All right?" He pulled her into his warm embrace.

"Yes, dear," she answered and kissed him deeply. "I love reminding you of the times when I'm right."

Coop growled teasingly and pressed closer to her, needing the sweetness of Betsey's love after the bitterness of the past few hours.

Price mounted the steps slowly. He was exhausted, mentally and physically. Opening the bedroom door, he went in to check on Ellyn. The lamp he'd placed beside the bed was burning low, but he made no move to put it out. He simply stood, looking down at her.

The desire to hold her close was powerful, but Price knew that Ellyn needed rest more than anything else. Mrs. Edwards had prepared the guest bedroom for him but he had no wish to be separated from his wife. Instead, he sat on the straight-backed chair that had been pulled up next to the bed. Stretching his long legs out before him, he sought what little comfort he could find in that unyielding seat. When the lamp sputtered and finally went out, Price had long since fallen asleep.

* * *

Ellyn came awake slowly, her mind still cluttered with remnants of the terrifying dreams she'd suffered all night. Dreams first of her mother screaming and hating her, then of Price leaving her for Mary Anne and then the nightmare of the ambush and seeing Price shot. A shudder ran through her as she fought off the effects of her mind's imaginings. Trying to change positions, she accidentally moved her injured shoulder and gasped at the sharp pain that tore through her. Panting, not so eager to move anymore, she looked around the room that was now brightening with dawn's first light.

The sight of her handsome husband, asleep in the chair by the bed, touched her heart. He looked so tired, even as he slept, that Ellyn resisted the temptation to wake him. Instead, she lay still, cherishing the knowledge that he'd wanted to be as close to her as possible.

When Mrs. Edwards came up an hour or so later with Ellyn's medication, Ellyn beckoned her into the room, silently.

"Could you bring Mr. Richardson's breakfast up with mine?" Ellyn whispered.

"Of course," she spoke softly, and after making sure Ellyn took her medicine, she went down to the kitchen to prepare their morning meal.

When Mrs. Edwards returned, Price still had not stirred. Ellyn waited until the housekeeper had gone before waking him.

"Price?"

His eyes opened and he regarded her warmly. "Good morning, sweetheart." Shifting stiffly, he gave her a quick kiss. "How do you feel? Any better?"

"A little, I guess." She smiled at his concern. "Mrs. Edwards brought our breakfast up."

"Oh, good," He noticed the trays. "I'm starved. Let me help you sit up," he offered.

He instructed her to put her good arm about his neck and pull herself upright. This done, it was a simple matter to pile the pillows up behind her for support.

"Thank you." She smiled, enjoying having him near.

Price brought her her breakfast tray and resumed his seat, pouring them both a cup of hot, steamy coffee. They ate in peaceful contentment, appreciating the joy of being together.

"How did your meeting with Coop go last night?" Ellyn asked innocently as she finished eating.

Price had dreaded this moment, but knew that he had to tell her. He cleared his throat. "There's something I have to tell you about last night."

"What?" She looked worried.

"I didn't have a meeting with Coop," he told her honestly.

"But you said it was important. Where did you go?"

"I went after the man who shot us."

"You knew who it was?"

"Yes."

"Why didn't you just tell the sheriff?"

"Because the man was Alex!"

Ellyn was stunned. "But why would . . ."

"Money," he said in disgust. "I had no idea that they could be so vicious."

"They?"

"I found out last night that Mary Anne and Rachel were in on it, too."

"What happened?"

"I cornered him at Rachel's. Luckily, Coop tracked me down and stopped me from doing anything foolish.''

"Are they in jail?''

"No. Alex tried to shoot us with a pistol that Rachel slipped him and I fired back. He's dead, Ellyn. I killed him.'' Price was worried that Ellyn would be upset by this disclosure, but she surprised him.

"I'm glad,'' she stated vehemently. "He tried to murder you. Do you think he was behind the fire, too?''

"I'm sure of it.''

Ellyn's expression turned fierce. "What are you going to do about your aunt and Mary Anne?''

"I gave them a week to leave town. If they don't go, I told them I'd turn them in to the sheriff for helping Alex.''

"They'll go.'' Ellyn leaned to him and kissed him. Price nodded but didn't speak.

"It's over now,'' she said, drawing him down next to her on the bed. "All that matters now is that we're together.''

He kissed her fervently. "I need you, Ellyn. Yesterday was hell for me.''

"For both of us,'' she told him, their mouths meeting again in a desperate union of longing.

When the kiss ended, he held her close knowing that he'd found his heaven in her arms.

Chapter Nineteen

The month of July passed in sunny, sweltering splendor. Ellyn loved hot weather and she bloomed under Price's tender care. During the first days of her convalescence, Price was never far from her side. He catered to her every whim, and for the first time ever, she felt completely loved. Ellyn had not thought it possible, but her love for Price had grown. He was everything she needed in her life to be happy and she could hardly wait for the time when she could show him once again how much she loved him.

Dr. Webster had insisted on at least three weeks of bed rest and Ellyn had been greatly relieved to finally be up and about. Her own weakness surprised her, though, and she'd been forced to take it very easy her first week back up.

Betsey and Coop had been Ellyn's most frequent visitors, delighting her on occasion by bringing Jason along to liven up her day. It was on one of these numerous visits, while Betsey had been out of the room, that Coop confided his plans to give his wife a surprise party on her birthday, August third. Ellyn had been thrilled for she was due to see Dr. Webster that day for her final checkup and hoped to have two reasons to celebrate: Betsey's birthday and her own full recovery.

Now, as Ellyn sat on her bed, awaiting his final decision, she was a bit nervous. He had made his examination without comment and then asked her numerous questions about the state of her general health before falling silent. She watched him expectantly as he put his things back into his bag.

"How am I, Dr. Webster?" she finally asked, too anxious to wait any longer.

"Just fine, Mrs. Richardson. I believe you are fully recovered."

"Oh, good," She was ecstatic. At last, she could be with Price again. These long, torturous nights of sleeping in each other's arms, yet not making love, had left them both frustrated with longing. Tonight was the night. "Thank you, Dr. Webster."

"I'll see you later, Mrs. Richardson. You take care," he told her as he showed himself out.

Ellyn jumped up excitedly as soon as he had gone and raced into the dressing room. Though it was just past two and they weren't due at Coop's until six, she set about getting ready. Ellyn wanted to be her absolute best for Price tonight. Tonight, they would begin, again, their honeymoon.

Price grumbled and glanced at his timepiece. It was almost five and he was still at the office, bogged down with last-minute emergencies. He was frustrated with all the problems, but knew there was no one else who could deal with them.

Coop had gone home early to take Betsey out to dinner and he and Ellyn were supposed to be at their house at six to greet the other guests. But from the way things were going, Price knew he would be late. As the hour struck, he called Kevin O'Riley into his office.

441

"O'Riley, I need you to deliver this note to my wife," Price instructed. "And then drive her to the Cooper's house when she's ready."

"Yes, sir. Anything else?"

"No. Just tell her it was unavoidable and that I'll meet her there as soon as I can get away."

"Yes, sir." Kevin took the note and left the office as Price turned back to his work.

Ellyn heard the carriage and hurried downstairs to greet her husband. But her delight at thinking him finally home faded as she found it only to be O'Riley with a note.

The housekeeper had admitted Kevin who watched Ellyn's descent slack-jawed. He knew Mrs. Richardson was pretty but he had had no idea that she looked that good.

Her dark hair was done up in soft curls on top of her head giving her a sophisticated elegant look. The soft pink gown she wore was full-skirted with a very-low-cut bodice causing O'Riley to swallow nervously at the sight of her deep cleavage.

"Good evening, Mr. O'Riley," she greeted him, well aware of her effect on him.

"Good evening, Mrs. Richardson. I have a note for you, ma'am, from Mr. Richardson." He handed her the letter as she led him into the parlor.

"Thank you. Please sit down while I read this." Ellyn directed him to a seat.

Kevin sat down unable to take his eyes from the enchanting, sensual picture she made and he knew, now, why this woman above all others had managed to win his boss's heart. She was lovely!

Ellyn was thoroughly disappointed that Price wouldn't get home before the party, for she had daydreamed all afternoon of a few precious moments in his arms before they had to leave. Now, gritting her teeth against the heated yearnings of her long-denied body, she gave Kevin a bright smile.

"We may as well go on. He's going to meet me at the Coopers'."

"Yes, ma'am."

"I'll get my wrap."

It was going on seven before Price finished up at the office and he rushed home to bathe and change into his dress clothes before going to Coop's. Finally, at quarter to eight he arrived, tired but happy.

"Did you get finished?" Coop greeted him at the door.

"All of it." Price smiled as he entered. "Where is Betsey?"

"I have no idea." Coop grinned. "I haven't seen her since we came through the door together an hour ago."

"I'd better find her. And Ellyn?"

"She was by the refreshment table last time I saw her."

"Thanks." Price made his way slowly down the hall toward the open parlor doors, stopping every few feet to greet business acquaintances and friends.

He saw Betsey first, surrounded by a group of well-wishers and then searched the crowd again looking for Ellyn. When their eyes met across the width of the room, his breath caught in his throat. She was beautiful. The new hairstyle exposed the long, graceful line of her neck; the low-cut bodice revealed just enough to lure a man; and her lips, full and curving, smiled a secret invitation only for him.

All thoughts of Betsey and her birthday were driven from his mind as he strode to lay claim to the magnificent woman who was his wife.

"Good evening, Price," she said breathlessly, trying to control her raging desires.

The sight of him, so tall and handsome in his dark suit and white shirt and cravat set her heart to pounding. He was a virile, attractive man and Ellyn wondered now how she had slept in his arms all those nights and not made love to him.

"Ellyn," he murmured, "you are stunning this evening."

"Thank you." She smiled up at him, letting him read the need in her eyes.

Price stiffened and had to restrain himself from sweeping her into his arms, "Don't look at me like that, pretty lady, or I'll be hard put to control myself."

Her soft laughter reached him like an invitation. "I didn't know you had to restrain yourself on a honeymoon." Ellyn heard his sharp intake of breath and gave him a smoldering look. "You'd better greet Betsey, don't you think?"

"Vixen!" he muttered under his breath as his hand found her waist and he guided her toward Betsey. "The doctor said you're recovered?"

"Completely," she said, wetting her lips as she gave him a sidelong glance.

Heat rushed through his body as he gave her a gentle squeeze.

Betsey looked up and saw their approach. "So you finally got here!" Hugging him, she gave him a big kiss. "Everything is so wonderful."

"It's a lovely party, Betsey," Ellyn told her as the musicians began to play a polka.

"All right if I claim him, Ellyn?" Betsey took Price's arm. "You haven't danced with me in ages."

"He's all yours, for a while." Ellyn laughed as

444

Price swept Betsey out onto the floor.

Her eyes followed his progress as he and Betsey danced about the crowded floor, and she couldn't wait until she was the one being held in his arms. It was long minutes before the dance ended and Price escorted Betsey back to Ellyn.

"Thank you, sir. You were marvelous as usual," she said, smiling.

"You're most welcome." Price kissed her cheek, then added, "And you don't look a day over thirty!"

"Oh, you!" She laughed. "I'll have you know I'm only twenty-two! Well, I'd better find Coop. I haven't seen him since we got here. I'll see you later."

Betsey glided gracefully off in search of her husband as a waltz began and Ellyn looked up at Price.

"My turn?" Her voice was husky.

Without a word, he pulled her close and they spun out onto the dance floor totally enamored with each other.

"I'm sorry I was so late."

"I missed you," she said, her hand straying sensuously across his broad shoulder. "But you're here now."

His eyes glowed with feverish desire. "How soon can we leave?" He had only one thing on his mind.

"Not until after Betsey cuts the cake," Ellyn whispered regretfully.

"I hope I can last that long."

"Shall we go for a walk in the garden?" she asked as they danced near the doors.

"That's a very good idea," he said eagerly and he led her out of the house.

The moon was a bright, silver disk in the star-

445

spangled summer sky. Its beams created magical shadows that danced and swayed with each passing breeze. It was a lover's night.

Alone in the shadow of a big shade tree, Price pulled Ellyn into his arms, kissing her with unrestrained passion. All those restless nights of tossing and turning were at an end. Tonight she would be his again and he would lose himself in the glory of her body. He hardened at the scent and taste of her and he fought himself not to hide away somewhere on the lush lawn and take her now.

"I love you, darling," he groaned, kissing her throat.

"Oh, Price, I want you so badly. I thought about you all day. I wanted you to come home." Her hands were frantic as they explored him and he held her tightly to him wanting more, so much more.

"Ellyn, it's been so long." He freed her straining breasts from the low bodice and explored them with heated kisses until she was moaning her desire.

Afire with the need for her, he suddenly stopped as he realized exactly where they were and what they were about to do. He pulled slightly away, and stood quietly as his throbbing body slowly cooled down.

"Sweetheart, you are one sexy lady," he murmured in her ear and she shivered, leaning weakly against him. "But we waited this long, we can wait just a few hours more," he said, trying to get control of the situation.

"I know," she sighed, longing to hold him and touch him once more.

"Just until she cuts the cake—all right?" he asked, his eyes twinkling.

"All right," she said in frustration. "The cake."

Reentering the house, they spent the next few hours circulating together, making pleasant conversation and trying to keep their hands off each other. Each glance, each casual touch sparked flames of desire.

Coop called to Price to join in a discussion for a minute and Ellyn went to find Betsey.

"How are you feeling? Didn't you see the doctor today?"

"This afternoon and he says I'm completely recovered."

"That's wonderful! Have you had a chance to tell Price yet?" Betsey asked mischievously.

"As soon as I saw him."

"Good," Betsey said laughing lightly. "I'll bet he can't wait for me to cut the cake."

"Neither can I!" Ellyn smiled warmly at her dear friend.

"Let me see what I can do," she told her, heading off toward Coop.

Within minutes, the cake had been brought out and all the candles lighted. After a rousing rendition of "Happy Birthday," Betsey made a valiant attempt to blow out all the candles, but failed miserably. Laughing delightedly, she cut the cake served Ellyn and Price very generous portions.

When they had eaten their cake, they found Coop and Betsey and made their excuses.

"You get a lot of rest tonight," Betsey said in mock seriousness to Ellyn.

The carriage ride home seemed far too long and when they finally entered the house, Price swept her into his arms and carried her up to bed.

The night was still young as they met in a love-starved, passionate embrace. Ellyn slid Price's jacket from his wide shoulders and untied his cravat as Price freed her breasts from her gown, exposing them to his heated caresses. Unfastening the back of her gown, it fell about her feet and he lifted her free and carried her to the bed. He laid her down and then stepped away to shed the rest of his clothing.

"Hurry," she urged as she wriggled free of her chemise.

Price moved over her, the heat of his body an erotic brand on hers. They came together in a rush of desire wanting only to be joined as one—to feel the total ecstasy of their love. Ellyn's hands searched and found the essence of him. She caressed him sensuously, teasing him to the heights with her bold, daring lovemaking. Price kissed her deeply as he fondled her breasts, tantalizing the pink peaks to hardness. Lowering his head, he kissed each breast until Ellyn moaned in desire. Kneeling above her, he lifted her hips and slid deeply into the hot, pulsing center of her body. Rocking together, they strained closer and closer to that ultimate joy, giving and taking until it burst upon them in a fiery, throbbing climax of desire.

They lay together, replete, savoring the closeness of the moment.

"How long do honeymoons last?" Ellyn murmured sleepily against Price's shoulder.

"How long do you want it to last?" he asked, pressing a soft kiss to her temple.

"Forever," she smiled softly.

"I'll do my best," he grinned.

And his mouth claimed hers in a kiss of enduring promise as they clung together once more, eager again to share in love's delight.